ONLY Oona

ONLY *Oona*

TAMATHA CAIN

Maitland, Florida

Orange Blossom Publishing
Maitland, Florida
www.orangeblossombooks.com
info@orangeblossombooks.com

First Edition: January 2023

Library of Congress Control Number: 2022919900

Edited by: Arielle Haughee
Formatted by: Autumn Skye
Cover design: Sanja Mosic

Print ISBN: 978-1-949935-58-5
eBook ISBN: 978-1-949935-59-2

This novel is a work of fiction based on an intriguing true-life story.

Printed in the U.S.A.

"Time is the best author.
It writes the perfect ending."
- "Cordero" (Charlie Chaplin), *Limelight*

Table of Contents

Prologue

Bermuda, April 28, 1927

*O*n the day Eugene O'Neill consented to pose for a family photo with his wife Agnes and their two young children, a tempest was brewing. Forecast winds blew ahead to buffet the sun-darkened cheeks of Bermuda, where the O'Neills lived in a storied old home called Spithead, precariously perched at the water's edge. An expectant horizon promised a full moon, but the golden hour now offered a wash of idyllic perfection. For now, the surface was calm, and the naïve shoreline below the home of the family O'Neill shrugged off the harbinger waves tapping blatant warnings on its golden back.

No storm could ever reach them here.

The playwright looked most distinguished in the new clothes he'd brought back from his latest trip to Manhattan. He settled on a bench at the bottom of the lawn, crossed his wiry legs, and watched as his wife Agnes made her way downhill along the path. His eyes narrowed, and his lips pursed. He could really use a cigarette.

Agnes paused. After nearly a decade of marriage, that look of his was still a mystery, the line between discernment and condescension being a fine one, like a delicate thread of spider silk.

She wondered when her husband found the time to shop for new clothes—a natty blazer and fine linen trousers. The style was so different from the casual bohemian chic they'd shared since their Greenwich Village days. Not that she minded the new look. It perfectly suited the idea she had in mind for their family photos—which was to show friends and family that the O'Neills were moving up in the world, chugging up the social register on their own steam.

Agnes held the hand of their young son Shane, adorable in his crisp new short pants and handsome cardigan. The boy was the image of his father, the same hang-dog expression around the mouth, the same woeful eyes, capped with a mop of sun-bleached hair. Eugene's chest swelled involuntarily, though his face remained unmoved. Emotions rarely rose as far as his face. They got sidetracked before they ever got that far, transmuted somewhere around the solar plexus—where his own childhood pulsed incessantly— and stewed for a while before being shunted to his hands and onto the pages of his plays.

Mrs. Clark, the perpetually cross-faced but doting nanny, whom the children called "Gaga," ambled behind the mother and son, keeping an eye on their backs rather than on the small figure toddling deter- minedly beside her. The child clutched the nanny's finger as she knew was the rule and stomped along the gravel path in her white Mary Janes. Eugene cocked his head to one side, then the other, to see around his wife and son.

Oona.

On those occasions when Eugene was obliged to take notice of his daughter, he sometimes remembered with some amusement his reaction at learning Agnes was once again, most unfortunately, pregnant.

"I think I may be expecting again," Agnes had said, placing a protective hand on her lower belly.

He had lowered his head, defeated.

"All right then," he'd muttered. "But I hope if another must come, at least let it be a girl."

These children. They struck a chord in him that refused to resolve. Like the discordant buzz of a blue note on one of his favorite jazz records, so was the confounding state of fatherhood. What was he meant to do with all these children? He who never wanted children in the first place, but feared tempting God by wishing them away once they existed.

Before all this—this marriage, the overwhelming success of his plays, these children, this house—he and Agnes had each left the relative financial stability of their childhoods for la vie Boheme, eschewing comfort for the virtue of scratchy hand-woven fabrics and a cold-water walkup flat, favoring the underbelly of society and nights in a bar called The Hell Hole over the conventional lives they found insufferably dull. The squalor had fed their imaginations. They'd trusted the self-imposed struggle would help them both to become great writers.

Agnes hadn't minded, not really, setting aside her literary dreams. She'd written countless pulpy stories for a lurid magazine in order to support Eugene's dream—to make the American theater a new and glorious creation.

The perverse thing was that they'd worked their way back up, to the conventional level, even surpassed it at times, depending on how Eugene's writing was going. While Agnes was expecting for the second time, the couple hung their chance at future happiness on the child being a girl. In an act of positive thinking, Agnes had written to fellow writers, Mary Colum, the wife of Irish poet Padraic Colum, to ask if they might suggest the perfect Irish name for an O'Neill daughter, and they replied with "Oona," the Irish version of "Agnes," though Eugene argued it was James Stephens who convinced him of the name. Even in naming a child he did not want, he had to have the last word.

Oona.

Standing beside his chair, Agnes had watched the news of another pregnancy hit him, watched him uncross his lanky legs and lean forward, resting his elbows on his knees without dropping a single ash from the end of his cigarette. His back hunched in his particular brand of scrawny elegance, and Agnes had heard his mumbled imperative prayed to the universe: At least let it be a girl. From her vantage point above him, she could not see his eyes, but she knew they would be half-closed. This was how he shut out unpleasant topics, those unwanted distractions he simply could not, or would not, be prevailed upon to face. At the news of another child, he had assumed the position which had become so familiar in their nine years of marriage. He did not want any children, let alone more children. Agnes knew this. But hadn't he wooed her years ago by declaring he wanted to spend every night of his life with her? Surely he'd imagined she might have children somewhere within that life, despite their vow against it. When she'd broken the news, he'd taken it at first with the sad resolve of a malnourished ox, about to buckle under the yoke across his shoulders. But then all at once, the bright spot had occurred to him.

At least let it be a girl.

At least.

The child hadn't asked to be here at all. Perhaps he had somehow willed this daughter into existence despite himself, like some hapless Greek god. He'd known deep down he shouldn't be a father. And yet he'd married two women now who, despite their early promises to the contrary, had both proven themselves treacherous and fertile as the Amazon.

He bowed his head and thought of Carlotta. If not for all this—this wife, this home, these blasted lovely children—he would be with her now. She wanted him, had left her husband, waited for him, free and willing and unbelievably beautiful, back in New York. Suddenly he longed to leave this Bermudan paradise and inhale the poisonous Manhattan air once more. This had all been one long mistake.

"Careful you don't tramp that rain puddle there now, child," Mrs. Clark snapped. "Those socks don't stay white by magic."

Little Oona's brows drew together under her fringe of sunny brown hair with a seriousness beyond her not-quite-two years. "Gaga!" she said, and let go of the nanny's hand. She stopped just short of the puddle and Gaga was forced to stop, too, as Oona straightened her arms and legs, splaying her chubby hands for balance.

Agnes noticed Eugene's face stiffen, and she stopped and turned. Oona had dug in her heels at the edge of the sparkling puddle, and now jigged from one foot to the other, straining her pillowy knees to avoid stepping forward into the water. Her head tilted down and her eyes closed half-way, just like her Daddy, as if shielding herself from the impending catastrophe of ruining her socks and new shoes while also looking just enough to find her footing.

All the while, her sweet smile remained serene and unbothered.

"Extraordinary," Eugene thought. A near-miss like that would surely draw peals of petulant squawking from an average little girl. The sound of screeching children was entirely intolerable, but he'd braced himself for an outburst unnecessarily. His hopes for this one's future raised just slightly.

With the crisis averted, Oona bent over as she caught her own reflection in the puddle and, the downhill path being rather steep, she tipped forward. The adults gasped.

"Mrs. Clark!" Eugene shouted. "Catch her!"

The nanny frowned and reached out, but Oona pressed her arms to her side, hiding them against the soft fabric of her romper. She smiled sweetly at her own reflection as Gaga's hand found her shoulder. Oona waved to her own ripply, grinning visage.

Gaga made a clicking sound with her tongue, and she didn't need to say anything more. Oona straightened her sturdy legs, looked up at Gaga's stern face, and once again took hold of the nanny's finger as she gingerly stepped away from the puddle.

She looked further down the path and saw for the first time that her father was there, waiting on the garden bench with his hand resting on the ponderous head of his favorite dog, Finn MacCool, the Irish wolfhound. A grin spread wide across her pretty round face. She pulled on Gaga's arm, wanting to go faster, but old Gaga would only ever go at her own pace, and the child didn't want to disobey again, not with Daddy watching. As she walked toward him, the natural grin that dimpled her cheeks began to change, taking on the expression, sweet and composed, that had on several other occasions coaxed a sincere smile to her father's usually morose face.

Agnes hung great importance on her husband's declaration that Oona had been the only little baby "whose appearance he ever liked," and Oona's emerging idea of herself absorbed the message, forming and conforming to the approving nods of neighbors on the lawn, townspeople at the market, strangers on the beach, even Gaga who had heard Agnes tell the story a thousand times. Eavesdropping on her mother's conversations, Oona heard the tale told and retold, felt it hover over her head till the words floated down and settled on the deepest parts of her mind, the furthest corners of her heart, like dandelion seeds finding fertile soil. The idea that her father thought she was 'beautiful,' the same word he might call a flower in the garden or a colorful sunset, somehow made a deeper impression overheard than it might have if Mother told her directly. It was all right if Daddy was always too busy to play with her. She was his little girl, his only daughter. She had at least this one thing no one else could have.

Later on, when she was bigger, she might add fine feminine qualities—read the big books he admired, learn to play all the sports he enjoyed, speak like a fancy lady. But for now, though she hadn't yet the understanding to ponder it so deeply as all that, she knew this simple fact with a clarity beyond anything any child psychologist could put into words. If it was important to Daddy that she be pretty, then something inside her began to believe it must be the most important thing about her.

Even in play, the child was self-conscious, careful to preserve the smooth sheen of her hair and the fresh swing of her dresses. She loved to run and dance, but she learned to stop at the precise moment when her cheeks glowed pink like her baby dolls, just before breaking into a sweat.

More and more lately, Mother and Daddy spent their days in different parts of the house. Both children learned to do everything quietly, with an economy of motion and no ruckus at all. If they did make a sound, then Agnes tracked them down. "Your father is working! He needs complete silence. Do you understand? Keep. Quiet!"

Now, Oona dropped Gaga's hand and rushed straight to her Daddy, stopping herself when she reached him with her palms against his angular knees. He took her hands gingerly by the wrists and lifted them away. Oona's open smile melted down her face.

"Agnes, can't you control the children, please?" he said. "I'll have to have another pair of trousers pressed if these get mussed."

Mother and Shane reached the bench together, and Agnes took the direction of the photographer, sitting down and turning her lithe body precisely as he directed.

"I want to stand beside Daddy, please," Shane said softly, but Mother clenched her teeth and made him stand beside her. Gaga lifted Oona and placed her on her mistress's lap. The photographer stood behind his tripod and looked through the viewfinder, squaring the shot. He started to direct them to smile, as he'd heard was the new fashion in some circles, but seeing the family so grim and stiff, he thought better of it. Hunkering behind the camera, he shrugged at the tense image they presented through the lens—the famous playwright and his privileged family posing all together at their beachside Bermuda estate, and not a smile in sight.

PART
One

Chapter 1

ONLY FOURTEEN

Manhattan, Upper East Side
Late Summer 1939

Oona had read somewhere that the places you remember from childhood might seem smaller and much less imposing as you grow up. Instead, on this visit back to the city, she could swear Manhattan's buildings had sprouted taller, their shadows longer, making the bewildering map of boulevards and avenues feel less like progress and more like great mountain passes. Central Park was much better where that was concerned, but she avoided that area whenever she could. One bad childhood memory was all it had taken to ruin the place for her, for good. Even now, at fourteen years old, she shuddered when she thought about that awful incident.

She double-checked the address on the card Mother had left among the various scarves and dark glasses on the foyer table of their hotel room. On the back, Mother had jotted in her nearly illegible hand: "Class at 4:30 PM." Oona checked her watch, 4:15, then opened the door with a gloved hand.

The lobby was narrow and echoey, with gilded moldings around doorways leading to halls on both sides and a stairwell straight ahead. She wiped her feet on the mat before stepping onto the green marble floor, checked the building directory, climbed two flights of stairs, and then searched down a long gray-painted hallway dotted with bright brass door-knobs till she found the right door. Black painted lettering on the glass read "Park Avenue School of Dance."

A leotard-clad girl at the front desk checked off her name and pointed a laconic finger toward the studio. Oona hesitated at the doorway, pulling her coat around her waist. She raised her chin. No need to be nervous. It was just a silly dance class.

She chose a spot at the far end of a wooden bench that ran along the side wall, hung her satchel on a brass hook, and crossed her arms across her waist. She stared at the wall, avoiding eye contact with the other students. Their appraising glances tingled on her back.

Hand-drawn posters hung between the hooks, announcing the details of upcoming junior proms and theme dances, the testing grounds of this social dancing class, the sole purpose of which was to teach the next generation of fashionable society how to properly mix and mingle. The grayish-gold light of a Manhattan mid-afternoon filtered through sheer white curtains on a wall of floor-to-ceiling windows and reflected off the mirrored wall opposite. A single wooden stool stood at one end of the room as if purposely placed in a beam of sunlight.

The room smelled of antiseptic and adolescence.

Oona looked around for a friendly face. It seemed her fate to be forever the new girl. Unsure of class procedures, she had just taken a seat on the bench and begun a serious study of the linoleum floor when a pair of pink dancing shoes stepped into view.

"Hello, darling. My name is Carol," a voice above her said. Oona looked up, following stockinged legs to a fluttery skirt, past a tiny waist and enviable chest, to the smiling face of a character straight out of a fairytale. "Carol *Marcus*," the girl said. She held out a pale, doll-like hand, palm down, and Oona wondered if she was meant to kiss it. She squeezed it lightly instead.

"I'm Oona," she said. She wrapped a chiffon scarf around her ponytail, wondering whether she should have included her own last name, and with equal emphasis. Being the daughter of a renowned play-wright did seem to impress people in this city. All the more reason to leave it out.

Carol adjusted the elastic waist of her skirt, then separated her own ponytail in halves and pulled it tight. "I wonder which of these truly dire prospects I'll be paired with today," she said, looking from one group of boys to another. "That one there nearly put me on crutches last week." She took the narrow space on the bench beside Oona.

Oona stole glances around the dance studio while she untied the laces of her saddle shoes. Groups of girls of various heights hung together in the middle of the room, twirling their hair or swirling their skirts. The boys were mostly shorter than the girls, or else gangly and out of sync with their newly large feet. They sported irregular patches of sprouting facial hair and voices of widely varying pitch. They jabbed and joshed each other in the corners. The girls murmured and giggled, broke out in attempts at womanly laughter, shushed each other, and looked at the boys with sidelong glances. Oona shook her head.

"You're Oona O'Neill."

This Carol girl spoke with a very practiced Park Avenue accent, and Oona found it rather adorable coming from such babyish lips. Really, her mouth looked as if she'd only just given up her pacifier. Oona smiled and nodded, slipping her feet into her dancing shoes.

"You're new," Carol said. She pointed toward the front desk. "I was eavesdropping."

"That's all right with me," Oona said, her smile growing wider. "Eavesdropping is one of my favorite hobbies, too." She finished tying the ribbons on her shoes and stood. "We're moving here soon, before tenth year. My mother wants me to go to Brearley."

"That's a *fine* school. Oh, but I'm at *Dal*ton!" She pursed her lips and pouted prettily, as if this news meant she would be tragically separated from her dearest friend.

"Are you going to any of these dances?" Oona asked, nodding at the wall of posters.

"My mother has already signed me up for all of them, including the sub-deb ones." Carol clasped her hands behind her back, thrusting forward a bosom truly beyond her years, and swung her ponytail over the back of her downy neck. Oona inhaled and stood up straighter.

Standing beside this delightful, droll girl who behaved as if they'd known each other all their lives, she thought how opposite they were—Oona with her thick dark hair, piercing dark eyes, and naturally sanguine lips (she'd heard her mother call them that), and Carol impossibly blonde with soft doe eyes and a blooming pink mouth like a cherry blossom.

"No one ever wants to dance with me," Carol sighed.

"You *must* be joking," Oona said. If that were true, what chance did any girl have of ever dancing again?

"I'm perfectly serious," Carol said. "Except my friend Truman, but he doesn't *really* count."

Carol chattered on as Oona surveyed the class again. More young male specimens skulked through the door, some obviously against their will. She lowered her head to roll her eyes. These poor boys wouldn't know what to do with themselves at the dances back home in Bermuda.

An older woman strode into the middle of the room and tap-tap-tapped the dance floor with a long stick. She wore a long-sleeved leotard that clung to her wiry muscles and a black skirt wrapped neatly around her waist. Her hair was pulled back into a severe low bun. "Five minutes, everyone!"

"Ooh, I'd better run to the latrine," Oona said.

Carol laughed, a little snorting sound. "Run to the what now, darling?"

"The *latrine*," Oona said more slowly. "The water closet? The...well...you know!"

Carol stepped closer and affected a serious, conspiratorial air. She shook her head and clucked her tongue. "Darling Oona." A funny glint came into her eye and she leaned closer, "On Park Avenue, it's called a 'loo.'" She whispered the last word, as if passing a vital bit of intelligence to a fellow spy.

"Oh, how silly of me!" Oona replied, playing along. She lowered her voice to match Carol's. "Tell me, Agent Marcus, when did the borough of Manhattan fall back into the hands of the British?" She leaned her head closer. "And more importantly, where might I find the royal 'loo'?"

Carol cupped her hand beside her face and pointed toward the back of the studio with small secret jabs of her finger and mouthed, "Over there." Oona raised her chin to indicate the message was received, and they both looked around as if to confirm it had not been intercepted.

The instructor tapped the floor again. "Four minutes, ladies and gentlemen!"

"Go!" Carol urged, scanning the room. "Go now! The coast is clear."

Oona put on a nonchalant expression and sauntered away, looking right, then left, then right again. Carol burst out laughing.

Tap-tap-tap! The dance instructor raised her eyebrows.

"Sorry, miss!" Carol said, pressing a contrite finger to her lips. Oona looked back, pointing a finger and a teasing grin at her as she slipped through the door.

Maybe moving to New York City wouldn't be so bad after all. Washing her hands in the porcelain sink,

Oona gazed out the high transom window, found a patch of blue sky through the comforting wavy glass, and thought the city might feel smaller already.

Chapter 2

ONLY FIFTEEN

Manhattan, 1940

Oona's mother had taken up an apartment in Greenwich Village, her old haunt from her bohemian Provincetown Player days. Agnes threw herself back into the community of artists, the place where her dreams had come true once before. She'd met Eugene there. He'd loved her there. Her new apartment felt like a fresh beginning for her, full of hope and promise. She started writing again in earnest. But for Oona, staying there would have meant a daily bus ride to and from the opposite end of Manhattan, only to sleep most nights in an empty apartment.

Instead, since the beginning of fall semester, she slept over at Carol's Park Avenue apartment. Oona's bed in Carol's room became a permanent fixture. Agnes spent most nights out and was rarely at home anyway, and when she was at home, she wasn't alone, so the arrangement was really very convenient all around. She'd grown so comfortable there, she'd step out of her shoes the moment she arrived and pad around barefoot like a member of the family. Oona's new school, the tony all-girls Brearley, was on East 83rd Street, and Carol's, the even more exclusive Dalton, was on East 89th. Every day after school, they each braved the cold winds rushing up and down the avenues to meet half-way between the two. They'd embrace, both for greeting and for warmth, and then decide what part of the city to explore.

Oona introduced her hothouse friend to the wonders of the city public transportation system, and the freedom it afforded girls like her who didn't have chauffeured cars at their disposal. Carol found buses curiously fascinating. The rubber floors covered in gray slush and the cold vinyl seats added an extra thrill to the whole adventure. It was all so *real*. Almost theatrical, the little human dramas that unfolded unexpectedly on a city bus. They'd choose an interesting street and wander up and down, looking in the shop windows before stopping for pre-supper burgers and fries. Then they hopped back on the bus uptown, back to Carol's world.

Agnes was all too happy to allow Oona to stay over at Carol's as often as she liked, and Oona put on her best behavior for Carol's beautiful mother Rosheen. She used her finest manners, and flashed her widest smile tempered with just a touch of demure deference before saying, "Thank you, Mrs. Marcus," or "Good evening, Mrs. Marcus." Rosheen was enchanted, and Oona's famous surname only added to the effect. A friendship between the playwright's daughter and her own was highly favorable,

and she not-so-secretly loved the idea of this dazzling young lady practically living in her own home.

"Do you want to know how we came to be here?"
Carol said one evening.

"On the planet Earth?" Oona said, straight-faced.

"Oh, you are the most clever girl I think I've ever
met!" Carol tried for a sarcastic expression, squinting
and pinching her lips together. Instead she managed
to look even more like a beautiful cherry blossom.

To be able to entertain a witty, clever girl like
Carol gave Oona endless pleasure, and to get a rise
out of her was perhaps small confirmation of her
own cleverness. She smiled to herself, but Carol's
eyes flashed, and she instantly shook the tart expression from her own face. It didn't suit her, and as she
always said, a girl could get wrinkles making silly
faces like that. "I *meant* how we came to live in this
ridiculously divine apartment," she said.

Carol was at her best when she had a story to tell,
because it wasn't enough just to tell it. She had to act
it all out. All the world was Carol's stage, and all the
men and women players in her tales. She trod the
boards of her bedroom, throwing her voice to the
back of the audience, all the while frequently looking
off to the left, as if thinking of what line comes next.

Tonight's play was the story of how a very young,
poor, but improbably lovely woman named Rosheen
had found herself with two small children and no
man, no good men anyway, so she'd put her children
into foster care while she tried to make a better life
working in a hat factory. And make a better life she
did, for she was set up on a blind date with a man

who turned out to be a millionaire aviation executive, and how overnight Rosheen found herself living on Fifth Avenue, in a fabulous duplex with a ridiculous number of rooms and servants and clothes and jewelry and everything a princess could ever dream of. Later, they had moved here, to this preposterously luxurious haven on Park Avenue, further from Central Park but closer, in Carol's opinion, to the fun.

By now, Oona could tell when Carol's stories veered off into make-believe, but this story appeared to be real, whatever 'real' was to Carol. It would seem Rosheen was a real-life Cinderella.

One evening, after eating supper on trays on Carol's bed, Oona read while Carol lightened her hair, carefully brushing peroxide onto her roots.

"Listen to this," she said. "It's Willa Cather's *O Pioneers*." She read a passage about a man who has to accept that his daughter is more like him than his sons are. When she finished, she clutched the open book, splaying it across her chest. Tears came to her eyes, and so Carol got misty, too. Oona held the book close, as if it were alive and could hug her back, and Carol moved to put her arms around her. But Oona quickly recovered herself and changed the subject.

"How long is that stuff supposed to stay on your head?" she asked. "It smells like something's burning."

෴

They were spending entirely too much time at Hamburg Heaven. The place truly smelled like heaven, if heaven had a grill and fryer. While they waited for their food, they blotted their red lipstick in preparation for the wonderful greasiness ahead.

"This is better than a hand up my shirt," Carol said through an unladylike mouthful of hamburger. She swallowed. "Or up my skirt."

"What does that say about the choices *you've* been making?" Oona said, pointing a hot French fry at Carol and then dipping it in her milkshake.

She indicated to the red logo on her plate and read it out loud: "'Only the Best Steers May Enter.'"

"Ooh...that's terrible!" Oona said, swallowing the fry. Her eyebrows drew together. "True though."

They ate in silence, relishing every bite, then Carol got out her giant compact.

"Truman thinks you are absolutely divine," Carol said, wiping a drop of ketchup from her chin.

"He's a doll, and I rather love him, too," Oona said. "Where is he tonight?"

"Who knows? That boy somehow always finds the fun."

"Maybe he *brings* the fun," Oona said. She dabbed her fingers on a napkin and picked up another fry.

Truman Capote was an enigmatic type of friend. Somehow, he made her feel both free and cautious at the same time. It was probably all the questions about Daddy. It wasn't his fault. It was never any of her friends' faults. They asked questions any girl with a father should be able to answer, even if Truman's questions did go beyond the normal getting-to-know-you kind.

When she'd attended Warrenton School, the school before Brearley, her best friends had been a pair of sisters, the daughters of one of her mother's writer friends, a fellow divorcé. It seemed so long ago already! The mother and daughters spent part of the summer as Agnes's guests in Bermuda, and Mother got an earful about how unimpressive Warrenton School was. The girls were learning to speak French entirely wrong, plus the students were expected to serve as hostesses for the school's big annual hunting event, which meant they couldn't go home for Thanksgiving. The mother planned to transfer her girls to Brearley in Manhattan, so Agnes followed suit. And now here Oona was, sitting at Hamburg Heaven with Carol Marcus. Carol socialized with society people. Gloria Vanderbilt, the girl whose face was in the papers practically every other week, was just another one of Carol's friends. Life was so funny sometimes, how it wound around itself and dropped you places you never knew existed, at least not for girls like her.

Sometimes, in her mind, she was still on a boat in the middle of the pond, at Warrenton. She and the two sisters had rowed out on an early autumn day and let the boat drift around as they took turns reading passages from plays to each other. And then, of course, the topic turned to Oona's playwright father.

So many questions. She tried steering the answers back to what little she really knew of him, but when the other girls became confused at how long it had been since she'd seen her father, she'd shut down. They must have thought she was being cagey—he was awfully famous after all—while the truth was she had no answers for them besides the ones she made up for herself, the ones that came from the life she lived with him in her imagination. But the older she got, the less charming those cute stories were, to her or anyone else.

"Oh!" Oona sputtered, dropping a half-eaten fry. She looked at her watch. "Have I missed the last train? I don't want to walk again." She swiped her mouth with a napkin. To keep up the pretense that she didn't actually *live* at Carol's house, Oona's unspoken, self-imposed rule was that she would go "home" to Mother's apartment on Friday nights.

"I think you'll make it if we leave now," Carol said, slurping the last of her milkshake.

"I don't think Mother will be home when I get there anyway."

"Why don't you just stay with me tonight? We'll send a messenger boy over to leave word for your mother."

"All right."

It was really a formality at this point. Mother would most likely be out till the early morning hours. By the time she got the message, Oona and Carol would be drooling on their pillows.

Before they left, Oona scurried back to the counter and grabbed two matchbooks. Smiling at the man running the grill, she tucked them in her pocket and then straightened her hat.

"See you next time, Arnold!"

"Bye now!" The fry cook grinned back. He wiped his hands on his apron then used it to wipe his forehead. "You little ladies take care out there now."

"We will," Oona said. She practiced her Park Avenue accent on everyone these days, and she was getting the knack of mixing precise pronunciation with a languorous drawl and dropping her *R*s in all the right places. It was turning out to be a valuable skill; people treated you differently. Not Arnold, though. He thought her new airs were funny. So she said it again. "We will."

Outside, Carol chastised her. "Honestly, Oona, you will talk to just about *any*body."

Oona shrugged it off. "Everybody is somebody, Carol," Oona said. "And what's more," she gave Carol a pointed look, "you never know who knows who."

Chapter 3

NEW IMAGE

Winter, 1940

The girls spent all of their after-school time together in Carol's bedroom, picking each other's brains about life and art and books, forming what they saw as their own private literary salon. Carol mooned romantically over *Wuthering Heights* day and night, but she tried any book Oona suggested. Her father was the playwright, after all. When Carol considered writing an essay on T. S. Elliot, Oona warned her off of him with the gravity of a wizened socially conscious literary critic: "He is an anti-semite."

But whatever the high-brow topic of conversation, it invariably came back around to boys. Comparing their lives at fifteen and sixteen years old to those of the heroines in the novels they read, their lack of romance was the most terrible burden. They each possessed bits of knowledge that seemed to fit together somehow, but hardly any complete stories about anything. Oona knew more about the basic mechanics of what went on 'in the bedroom,' having spent some time around animals in Bermuda and Point Pleasant, and she figured it couldn't be that different, mechanically. Carol knew more about how the females got the males to want to do whatever it was they did with them, which couldn't possibly be exactly the way the animals did it, unless... maybe it was?

The world of dating was a mysterious and unknown, tempting wonderland that seemed to beckon them with catcalls and whistles and hand gestures simulating mysterious and somewhat fascinating acts, but it was too vast and uncharted to take on alone. They pledged to share with each other everything they knew and everything they might learn in the hopes of putting it all together eventually into one coherent primer, like a field guild or an instruction manual. Then maybe they could both step into the grown-up world without falling on their faces, either pregnant or with something called a 'clap,' or both.

They went to the awful school dances and stood on the sidelines, watching everyone pair off to practice manners and movie romance on each other. At one late fall social, the girls finally resorted to dancing together, drank too much sugary punch, and then left early to commiserate and debrief over plates of comfort food at Hamburg Heaven. That place was better than psychotherapy.

"All right, enough is enough," Oona had said. She kicked off her shoes the second she slid into the booth and her toes wriggled with relief under the table.

"I'm not done feeling sorry for us yet," Carol said. She tucked a paper napkin into her lace collar in anticipation of the burger she planned to inhale.

"Do you know what? I think the boys are simply scared of us," Oona said.

"Scared of us?" Carol said. "Why would *they* be scared of *us*?"

"I don't know. I do know I'm tired of trying to squeeze myself into these silly little girl dresses and wearing matching ribbons in my hair," Oona said. She dipped a fry in ketchup and shoved it in her mouth. The magazines said this stuff was terrible for the complexion, but it hadn't hurt hers so far. She chewed thoughtfully, her brows furrowed and her eyes half-closed. "That's it," she said, suddenly wide-eyed and clapping the salt off her hands. "We need a change. Look at us!" She waved a hand between them. "Do these figures belong in these ridiculous dresses?"

Carol looked down. "I love this dress."

A waitress with ketchup stains on her apron and dark circles under her eyes came to take their order.

"Two cheeseburgers with fries, please. And two chocolate milk shakes," Oona said.

"Extra cheese, please," Carol said. "It's been a rough night."

"Carol, how many boys asked you to dance tonight?"

"Zero," Carol said. "Precisely zero boys asked me to dance."

When she'd been at Warrenton School, Oona had gotten a reputation as the girl who knew how to dress. Though she'd only been there long enough to make a few friends, they seemed to think she knew what she was talking about when she told them, "Get your hems above your knees, girls." Maybe it was time to reinvent themselves.

"We're not getting anywhere sitting around your room talking about books and dreaming about *Wuthering Heights* and Heathcliff coming over the moors," Oona said. "We have to do something."

"Okay, but how about let's start tomorrow? I'm absolutely shattered," Carol said, slumping against the booth.

"Tomorrow it is," Oona said. "Our new lives start tomorrow."

ℭℬℰ

"We'd like to try some perfumes, please," Oona said. She and Carol put their new handbags on the shining glass counter and began removing their gloves. The women behind the Bergdorf's cosmetics counter shared a knowing glance.

They tried on scents until they ran out of spots to spray themselves. Then Carol chose a huge bottle of Chanel No. 5 *eau de perfum* and charged it to her mother's account. Oona picked a small bottle of Emeraude, which the saleswoman said was made for brunettes, and she paid with cash she was meant to use for a new gym kit and trainers.

"Our other purchases are being sent to my building," Carol said. "Would you be so kind as to add these to the delivery?" She smiled sweetly and batted her eyelashes. Oona elbowed her and caught her eye, shaking her head slightly. If they were going to be sophisticated, Carol would have to tone down the baby doll act.

Carol nodded at Oona and did her best Marlene Dietrich glower. Oona snorted to hold back the laughter, but recovered quickly and gave the saleswoman an apologetic smile.

As they traipsed to the store's giant front doors, the girls started putting their gloves on, but then Oona stopped.

"Why do we even wear these things?" she said. "It's so passé. I mean, what's the point of painting our nails if we just cover them up all the time?"

"You're right," Carol said, "as usual." She held up two shopping bags full of all the little things they'd simply loved too much to leave behind for delivery—delicate stockings, small jars of face lotion, smooth satin sleeping masks, pieces of lingerie so light and flimsy they might float away. The bags were just full enough to swing gleefully around as they made their way home, just large enough to let other people know they'd been shopping. Carol handed one to Oona.

They removed their gloves and ceremoniously dropped them into their bags and swept out the doors into the brisk December air, laughing at the ridiculous freedom of walking around with bare hands exposed for all to see. Moments later, their laughter was replaced with the chattering of their teeth. Like two bag ladies, they hunched over and rifled through to retrieve the gloves.

Step one of their big transformation was complete, but they weren't done yet.

The next day after school, they met up outside Carol's apartment building and walked to the bus stop together. It was time to go dress shopping. Oona had raided the last of the emergency spending money from the box Agnes kept in the apartment. Her mother hadn't dropped by there for a while, so it was running low. $20. That should get her something decent at a discount place like S. Klein, and Carol thought the idea of slumming it sounded like a novel adventure.

"Now remember, Carol, the dresses here won't be the newest designs, but that's not what matters," Oona explained on the bus to Union Square. "What matters is they suit us and flatter us, so we know we look our best."

Carol nodded earnestly. All Oona's ideas had been winners so far, like the way she'd done Carol's hair the night before with a deep side part and sleek wave over one eye. Just like that new actress Veronica Lake. Then she'd done hers the same, only parted on the opposite side. (She had some kind of vision in mind for the two of them, but she wouldn't divulge it yet.) And then they'd practiced flirting with each other over their shoulders in the mirror. Oona lowered her head and looked up from under her long, dark lashes. Carol made her eyes wide and licked her lips, parting them just slightly. They practiced until they were satisfied they could do it all without looking in the mirror, and then they smiled at each other.

"I'd fall in love with you," Carol had said.

"And I with you," Oona said. Then they washed off their makeup, slathered their faces with night cream, and put on their new sateen sleeping masks.

They were determined that this time would be different. This time, they would *not* come home from the dance and cry and make themselves sick on Rosheen's secret chocolates.

Inside S. Klein, Oona perused the racks with a discerning eye while Carol wandered around holding pretty clothes up to herself in mirrors and having pretend conversations with her own reflection.

"Oh, this old dress? Why, Errol Flynn, it's just something I had in my closet. What's that? You like it *that* well? Oh, you like it on *me*..."

Oona rolled her eyes, but Carol waved her over and they stood side-by-side, holding up Oona's finds.

"Are these the ones?" Carol said.

"Definitely." Oona's eyes sparkled. She nodded confidently. "These are the ones."

❧

When Oona and Carol arrived at The Plaza Hotel Christmas Dance, the entire ballroom seemed to come to a standstill. The girls stood at the top of the dance floor and watched as all eyes turned to them.

In a moment, they were surrounded by eager boys, offering them punch and asking for a spot on their dance cards. With every swirl around the dance floor, Oona caught Carol's eye, and they giggled at their secret victory. They didn't miss one dance unless it was to catch their breath.

Girls from their set who had never paid them much attention in the past now sidled up, striking up chirpy conversations. They wanted to know how they'd done their hair, their makeup, their everything. Oona danced with every boy and a few of the girls, and then she took Carol's hand and led her out of the ballroom slightly early, so as to cause a wave of bereavement in their wake. She retrieved their coats from the coat check, and their laughter exploded onto Fifth Avenue as they burst through the hotel's front doors into the cold December night.

"Just think of all the time we've wasted being sad and pathetic!" Carol said as they swayed triumphantly arm in arm down the icy sidewalk. "Who would have thought we were so beautiful!"

All evening, Oona had tried to start sparkling conversations on intelligent topics with boys who brought her offerings of punch and cookies and crumbly bits of Christmas cake, but her carefully curated conversation starters were met with blank stares. So she'd gone back to eyelash batting and soft giggling, and all was well again.

"Is it possible that being beautiful is more important than being brilliant?" Carol said, swinging her sparkly clutch around and around her wrist.

It was one of those rhetorical questions Carol asked just to get Oona thinking. When Oona was busy pondering, Carol could daydream and make up fantastical versions of things that had happened to her. It worked. Though Oona was fully aware of Carol's clever tactics, she couldn't resist following the question down a complicated rabbit hole maze.

Was it possible she'd been spending her energy in the wrong places? How outstandingly brilliant would a woman have to be to succeed in the literary world, like her father had done? Or the engineering world, like Carol's stepfather? Aunt Gertrude had been a wonderful artist, but she'd had to pretend to be a man in order to be admitted to places where her work belonged. Mother was a talented writer, but she couldn't seem to make any real headway in her career. She wasn't taken seriously at all. The older she got, the more true it seemed that the most valuable thing a woman could hope to be was a beauty.

Who was a better example than Carol's own mother?

Rosheen had changed her whole life with just her looks and her charm. She was as sharp and capable a woman as Oona had ever met, but without her beauty she'd still be making hats in the garment district instead of living the high life on the Upper East Side.

Beauty was a commodity Oona hadn't considered, not in this way, until she realized she'd somehow managed to possess it. Did the women up on the silver screen know it? Had they known it all along, before they went to Hollywood and someone told them so? While the Great Depression could get any one of them at any moment, beautiful people created their own destinies based solely on the angles of their faces and the shapes of their bodies. Like goddesses, women like Veronica Lake glided around as if their beauty brought their surroundings into being. Maybe that's what Mother had been trying to get through to her. Maybe that's what she and Carol should be telling each other.

ରୟ୫ର

After the triumph of the Christmas dance, they went on a spree in earnest, trying on yet more perfume samples in the drugstore to see which ones suited their individual chemistries, like the magazines suggested, and matching their skin tones to just the right shades of lipstick.

"It might be boring, but I absolutely adore lipstick, don't you?" Oona said, spinning a golden tube between her fingers. There was something irresistible about the way the color rose smoothly from within, starting with that perfect point and growing as she twisted it up to its full height. She would watch them spin up, then down, up then down, click the lids on and off, on and off. The saleswomen at all the beauty counters in town frowned when they saw her coming. She wished to have every shade of red lipstick ever made, while Carol searched for the perfect face powder.

"White and pearly, like a courtesan. That's for me." Carol had gotten it in her head that glamour meant skin as white as she could get it, whiter than white—Victorian white, snow white, white like an ethereal, arsenical ghost.

They window shopped at Bergdorf's and Bloomingdale's and Macy's and Saks, then shopped at S. Klein. One day, they passed a storefront on Seventh Avenue just as a woman was dressing a mannequin in a fine mink coat, draping the shoulders just so and smoothing the sleek lapels. The girls stopped to stare at it, licking ice cream cones though the weather was cold and gray.

"I wonder if I'll ever wear a fur," Oona said, then instantly felt bad for saying it. Her own coat was new and perfectly stylish in its own way. She'd been thrilled when she found it, and on a very good sale. People were worried about whether we would join the war, and here she was lusting after a fur coat.

Carol looked at her, then back at the mannequin. She had several fur coats hanging in her closet at home, and she likely didn't think twice about them. But her mother would probably kill her, several times over, if she even thought about giving one away.

"You can borrow one of mine, if you want," Carol said, licking her cone and missing the point entirely.

Oona shook her head. "That's awfully nice of you, Carol," she said.

But it wasn't only about wearing a fur coat, or even about owning one. It was about having someone who loved you enough to want to give you one of your own, someone who thought you were so wonderful that you deserved the best of everything. A fur coat meant you had one person, just one person, who thought you were the most lovable girl in the world. It meant you had someone who would wrap you up in their love and hold you tight, never letting you go.

Bermuda, 1928

*M*other's plate of food remained untouched, but she had emptied and refilled her glass. After a particularly tense family dinner, Mother and Daddy refilled their drinks and sat on opposite sides of the living room.

"What business does Carlotta have giving my husband an expensive fur coat?" she said.

Eugene looked away, gazing out the window.

Powerful waves crashed on the beach below and sharp salt air hung in the space between them. Shane had disappeared the moment he was excused, but Oona crept to the corner and sat on a cushion, brushing her doll's hair. Mother's quiet anger had a presence of its own.

"Do you remember what you said to me on the night we met?" Agnes said. Eugene didn't reply, but his raised brows encouraged her to go on. "You said, 'I want to spend every night of my life from now on with you.' I didn't believe you, of course. But you said, 'I mean it. Every night of my life.'" Her voice broke on the last words, but she pushed them out as a shout, trying to stifle the coming tears. Eugene bowed his head, half closed his eyes.

"I knew you had a secret sorrow, and it did not scare me away. I lived with you when we had nothing. Encouraged you. Supported you."

Oona's brush snagged on a knot in the doll's hair. She held its body between her knees and tugged harder.

"But not now!" Eugene said. "Not any more. You have no time for me. Carlotta says—"

"Carlotta! Don't say that name in my house."

"Aggie—"

"Don't call me 'Aggie.'"

Mother and Daddy's voices were hard. Oona brushed harder.

"Does she know you said you didn't find her attractive in the least?" Agnes hissed. "Shall I tell her?"

"This is madness."

"If it is, it's because you've driven me mad!"

Oona stood up, and her doll fell to the ground. Its ceramic face clattered against the tile. "This is madness!" she said, her childish mouth combusting the fiery words to heartbreaking embers.

"Oh, son of a bitch," Eugene mumbled.

The nanny bustled in. "I'm sorry, sir. Come along, Oona."

"Oona, go back to bed, darling," Agnes said absently, hardly completing the sentence before parting her lips for another sip of her glimmering drink. The ice clinked around the glass like sharp hail against a window. The golden twilight hit her parents' highball glasses and dazzled Oona's eyes through her tears as Gaga led her from the room by her shoulders. Agnes took up where she had left off.

"I knew you then, and I know you now," she warned. "You will regret what you are doing."

◌⃝◌

There were different rules for inside the house and outside the house.

Grown-up matters were discreetly conducted and discussed in hushed tones when in public. The only place they were aired without restriction was at home, in front of one's own children. Oona heard everything, her mother's side of conversations shouted into the phone. She ached with the loss of her father but held on to hope, to the belief that they would see each other soon, and when they did, she must be the most perfect girl he could imagine. The hopeful image she held in her mind, in her heart, of their perfect, joyful reunion sustained her and fed her drive to be always ready, always at her best, since who knew when the day might come that Daddy would walk through the front door, his arms wide open to her?

Shane believed it, too. "Father promised he'd be back, then he promised he'd write. I believed him," he said to Gaga, but not to Mother, though she was right there in the room. Mother hadn't seemed to be listening, distracted as always by her papers and her drinks and her cigarettes, but she spoke up now: "I believed him when he said he wasn't attracted to Carlotta." She laughed bitterly.

Oona didn't want to hear any more. Mother shouted her rage into the phone, and Oona imagined Daddy on the other end, making that chewing motion with his jaw, the one that came before he exploded.

Listening at the sitting room door, she heard everything. Mother gave him every decibel of her wrath.

"I know what I said! We both said if one of us ever
wanted to go, the other would step aside," she said
in a maddeningly slow and methodical shout. "That
was before I spent ten years supporting you before
anyone wanted to read you! Before anyone cared who
you were!" She stopped. and when she spoke again
her pitch went up half an octave. "I'm sure she does!
Because you're a hot property now, aren't you? And
what? She's the new improved version? It wasn't long
ago you said you couldn't stand her!"

She paused, breathing hard, and Oona imagined
her mother listening. While she waited, she wondered
what the things Mother said might mean. What was a
'new improved model'? She peeked around the corner.
Mother had the phone to her ear and her face turned
up, pressing two fingers at the inner corners of her
eyes. Oona's stomach was hot and churning, like when
she drank her milk too fast and then ran in the hot
sun. She stood just behind the doorway and wondered
what to do to make Mother happy again.

"She feeds your ego. Bows your genius, is that
it? Tell me, Eugene, is it really genius if one cannot
manage to access it sober?" She laughed bitterly. "We
all have brilliant thoughts when we're high. Only
others who've been as high as you will understand
you. The rest pretend to understand, and prove themselves to be the dullest of the lot."

Without understanding exactly what she was
doing or why, Oona raised her small hands and placed
them on her cheeks, feeling them rise as she formed a

desperate smile, then she clasped her hands together and tiptoed into the room.

Agnes began shouting again. "I will not. NO. Not until I've spoken to a lawyer. Because I can't trust you, that's why. The children need to be cared for. I need security, don't I?" A pause. "I should take your word for it?"

Oona crept closer. Her cheeks burned from holding the smile. Her eyes burned from holding back tears. The only thing that mattered was getting to Mother, to help her.

"You are making a fool of yourself. How unoriginal of you. How expected. How typical. How—"

"Mother?" Oona said through her determined smile. Her bottom lip quivered, but she pressed it with a finger until it stopped.

Agnes waved a hand in her direction and continued shouting. "I don't care about that. That is not my problem. You are the one at fault, Eugene." She raised a glass of the amber liquid she liked to drink when she was upset. The ice cubes clinked as she tipped the glass, tinkled as she lowered it down.

"Mother..."

"My god. What is it, Oona!" Agnes covered the mouthpiece and shouted toward the hall. "Gaga! Come and get this child!"

Oona's smile, the only thing she had to offer, dissolved into tears.

The next morning, Agnes was somewhat contrite. "Now, Oona, darling," she said, setting down her coffee cup. She glanced up at Gaga who stood with her arms crossed over her bosom. Agnes rolled her eyes and looked back to Oona. "I'm sorry you saw Mother so upset," Agnes said. "But little girls should not eavesdrop on adult conversations." She dabbed her breakfast napkin on Oona's dry cheek. Gaga dropped her hands to her apron and turned away, exasperated.

"I want Daddy," Oona said.

"I'm afraid that's not possible right now," Agnes said, then under her breath, "he's been quite busy."

"But I want Daddy. I love Daddy," Oona's chin quivered slightly and she sucked her bottom lip. She didn't have the words to ask the question deepest in her heart: Does he still love me?

Chapter 4

ONLY 15—AND A HALF

1940

"This article says it's normal to lose up to one hundred hairs per day," Oona said. She sat against the headboard of her twin bed in Carol's room. Only the top of her dark head was visible behind a giant *Mademoiselle* magazine.

"What if I lose one hundred and one?" Carol said.

"Then you're doomed to live a lonely and childless life in your parents' attic."

"I don't know if we have an attic," Carol looked wonderingly at the ceiling.

"Ooh, then I don't know what would happen to you. Maybe it's best not to count the hairs."

"But I have to, now that you've said it."

"Sorry." Oona put down the magazine and picked up the new *Harper's Bazaar.* She flipped through, purposely avoiding the horoscopes. Those she saved for the end of the month. It was a fun game to see how accurate they'd been. Suddenly she stopped flipping pages and laid the magazine flat on the bed. "Gads," she coughed. "It's Gloria!"

Carol dropped her brush and jumped on Oona's bed. "It IS!"

"You didn't know about this? I thought you were such bosom friends?"

"She probably wanted me to see it like this, a surprise," Carol said, though she looked doubtful herself. She held the magazine closer to her face, turned the pages slowly, inspecting every detail. "Wow, she looks divine."

Carol peered at the photo and tilted her head as if to catch a whispered secret. "I can't look at this genteel photo without thinking of her in real life. All I can see are those dark eyes flashing and those pouty lips curling just at the edges, the way they did when she spilled all the details of her 'grand passion' with her boarding-school girlfriend." Oona put her hand to heart and feigned utter shock, but only momentarily before lifting the magazine again.

"Does she draw on those eyebrows?"

"I don't think so."

They paused and locked eyes, then they scrambled off the bed and rushed to the vanity table. They dug through Carol's makeup drawer, pushing aside lipsticks and curlers and powder compacts. "Here!" Carol said, pulling out a thin black pencil.

Oona sat in the vanity chair first, placing Gloria's picture against the mirror for reference. "I wish I had a magnifying glass," she mumbled. Carol watched as she put the pencil to her eyebrows and began drawing. They both watched Oona in the mirror, and when she drew her hand away, her brows were a perfect copy of Gloria's.

"Gorgeous," Carol said. "Now do me." They switched places and Oona drew the same brows on Carol. She stepped back to look at her work. "A little dark?" The ebony arches were a stark contrast to Carol's white-blonde hair.

"No," Carol said. "It's perfect. It'll make people wonder..." As she spoke, she waggled her new black brows, admiring the effect.

Oona held Gloria's magazine photo beside her own face, posing in the same way, pushing out her lips in the same alluring pout. They could have been sisters. Carol's composed expression fell.

"You should meet her," Carol blurted, then repeated with a confirming nod, "I want you to meet her."

"Meet who?" Oona put the pencil down.

"Gloria." Carol pushed her lashes up with two fingers, obscuring her face.

Oona looked from her own reflection to Carol's and caught a flash of something—a twinge of doubt, or insecurity—in Carol's expression. She leaned closer, gently bumping Carol's shoulder with her own. "You're the best friend I ever had, Carol."

Carol smiled and inhaled hard, lifting her chin. "Yes, I am." She wrapped an arm around Oona's shoulder. The gold shade on the vanity lamp gave their faces both a golden glow, and they fell in love with the perfectly-browed girls in the mirror just a little bit. "Want to practice making eyes at dance partners?"

"Always," Oona said.

❧

Dear Mother,

Carol and I are going to Long Island for the weekend. We are going to stay with her friend Gloria Vanderbilt (yes, those Vanderbilts) who I guess is getting up a weekend party. She lives with her Aunt Gertrude Whitney, but I'm sure you know that.

I hope you have a nice time with the new fellow. I've stopped memorizing their names. You'll have to marry one if you want me to remember what he's called.

Will let you know when we're back in town. If I happen to get a letter back from Daddy (don't scoff, it could happen) would you telephone Carol's house and leave a message? Or ask the doorman to do it? When Carol calls home on Sunday, she'll get the message.

I signed up for the drama club so now you can stop asking. Some boy gave me chocolates, and I left half the box for you on the foyer table.

Love,
Oona

P.S. Don't give the chocolates to the new fellow.

Chapter 5

GLORIA'S HOUSE PARTY

Long Island, 1940

Gloria lived with her Aunt Gertrude in the Wheatley Estate in Old Westbury, Long Island. Oona wished she'd started counting at the beginning of their journey, because Carol must have called Wheatley a 'mansion' no less than twenty times on the train ride from Manhattan. By the end of the ride, Oona's mental image of the home to which they were headed for Gloria's weekend party had grown into one of a royal castle with ivy-wrapped flagged turrets, probably surrounded by a mote, and maybe guarded by a golden dragon.

"They call it 'The Manse,'" Carol said. "It's breathtaking. It is unlike anything you've ever seen."

"I *have* seen nice houses before, Carol," Oona said. Spithead wasn't exactly a Bermuda beach shack.

Once in the car Gloria sent for them, driven by a dapper man named Freddy who recognized Carol from previous visits, Carol became uncharacteristically reverent, describing the Manse's sunken pools and luxurious baths in hushed, almost warning tones, until finally she simply grew quiet as they reached their destination, the place Gloria Vanderbilt called home.

The car slowed as Oona's pulse quickened, and they turned onto a private lane lined with evergreen trees. Multicolored paper lanterns hung from boughs that seemed to bow in welcome as they drove up the graceful path. The car wound past a stand of climbing rose bushes and into a clearing, and the road widened to a view of a pasture dotted with fruit trees and a picturesque brick windmill. Flowers of every shade danced in the breeze like a riotous dream of an impressionist painting.

Then the house came into view, and Oona's eyes went wide, as if unable to take it all in at once. No matter how much Carol went on about it, she could never have imagined a house like this. Like a page from a beautiful old storybook, the view unfolded, then waited to be discovered.

A butler met them at the door.

"Welcome, Miss Carol," he said with a small bow.

"Hello, William. This is my friend Oona," Carol said, pulling off her gloves and handing them to the lady's maid as if it were the most natural thing in the world. "Oona *O'Neill.*"

Oona winced at the emphasis on her surname, then reached out to shake his hand, noting the flash of recognition as he hesitated before reciprocating, giving the tips of her fingers a polite squeeze. Carol elbowed her and shook her head. The butler nodded to a house boy who jogged to the car for their small pieces of luggage.

"Thank you, William," Carol said pointedly.

"Oh, yes," Oona said, "thank you…sir."

Inside the house, the wide foyer had the hushed effect of a fine museum. The girls followed William through, but Oona stopped for a moment at a doorway, her mouth in open awe of the glowing drawing room beyond, filled to every sumptuous corner with gleaming wooden furnishings and fine upholstery, enormous portraits and landscapes in gilded frames, and carpets so richly woven and intricately beautiful she couldn't imagine they were actually made to be walked upon.

Gloria's Aunt Gertrude was an well-known artist, a renowned sculptor, and her work was on display around the world. She'd often been forced to use a pseudonym to avoid the difficulties of both her sex and her name. William relayed all of these details in a proud tone, befitting his position as top man of the estate, as he led them through to a sweeping staircase. Oona gazed toward the top as if it must certainly lead to heaven.

"Thank you, William," Carol said. Her voice had taken on a snipped, haughty pitch. "We'll find our way from here. Is Gloria in her room?"

"Yes, miss. She is preparing for the party. Please, inform me or one of the housemaids should you require anything during your stay." He walked away, his heels clicking precisely on the marble floor, and Oona followed Carol up the winding staircase.

Carol had been to Gloria's home before, and she made a production of showing Oona around, playing the expert docent as they strolled past room after gorgeous room. "I'm taking the long way," she whispered as they entered a long hall.

She stopped in front of a painting of a man with rather wild hair and an imposing set of mutton chops. "That's Gloria's great-great-grandfather Cornelius Vanderbilt," Carol said importantly. "They called him—"

"The Commodore," Oona said. She peered at the pale skin—so lifelike, yet waxy and strangely smooth—the regal nose, the creamy points of light that had been painted into his dark eyes. She looked for traces of Gloria. This man's grandson was Gloria's father. The man who died young when she was small, almost the same age Oona had been when her father left her, leaving Gloria to be fought over in a court battle between her mother and her paternal aunt. Everyone in the country knew the sad story of the "poor little rich girl." But for Gloria, Oona already knew from the newspapers, the worst part had been when her mother, Big Gloria, dismissed the nanny she had loved like a mother, the one person who had cared for her since she was a baby. The story always reminded her of Gaga. Mother had explained the dismissal away with a flick of her hand: Gaga told Daddy something she shouldn't have.

Oona already felt an uncanny affinity with Gloria, and they hadn't even met yet. Was it because of their childhoods? Though her own father was alive, he'd been a phantom since he left her, left all of them, in Bermuda. She'd never forget those months spent alone at Spithead with Shane and a housekeeper whose job title did not include coddling children.

She remembered the waiting, the confusion, of the echoing limbo while Mother went after him determined to get him back. And she remembered the dark days when Mother returned, defeated and bewildered.

She and Gloria had both been hurt by short-sighted, self-centered parents. But if the quotes in the newspapers and magazines were true, then Gloria, like her, was determined to make something of her life. Like herself, Gloria had also been born with a name that was as much a burden as a blessing.

"Carol!" Gloria's voice echoed down the hall. Oona recognized it from half-hearing it so many times over the phone in Carol's room. Carol ran to meet Gloria and they hugged and kissed each other as if it had been years. Then Gloria pulled away, dejected. "Oh but, darling Carol, I've just had the most terrible and wonderful news."

"What is it, darling?" Carol said, smoothing Gloria's hair on her shoulder.

Oona's stomach tensed with an unexpected pang. She'd never cared before when Carol called everyone she met 'darling,' but somehow she hadn't realized Carol called other friends by the same term of endearment. A shuddery feeling, like the floor had turned to water, shivered up her legs. She shook it off, forcing her face to form appropriate expressions as Carol and Gloria huddled closer to each other.

"Aunt Gertrude says this house is going to be demolished and rebuilt, and so..." Gloria said, squeezing Carol's hands, "...we're moving to the Washington Square house, in the city."

"That *is* terrible and wonderful," Carol said. "This beautiful house? It should stand forever! But to have you right there in Manhattan? How marvelous!"

They hugged, and then they both looked at Oona. "Yes!" Oona said, summoning her brightest smile. "How marvelous!"

"Gloria, darling, this is the girl I wrote you about," Carol said, pressing a cool hand to Oona's arm. "This is Oona O'Neill. Isn't she fantastic?"

"Lovely to meet you, Oona darling," Gloria said. "Thank you for coming to my party."

"Thank you for having me," Oona said. "You're home is wonderfu—"

"Of course, I'm devastated," Gloria said, turning back to Carol. Her eyes narrowed. "This has been my home since I was a *child*. Well, my main home anyway. To think of it simply gone…" Gloria touched the corners of eyes, though no tears had appeared. She sniffed.

"But on the other hand, think of all the fun we'll get up to," Carol said, "the three of us."

Gloria took each of their hands and they stood in a triangle in the hall for a moment.

"Shall I show you my room?" Gloria said, clapping her hands. "Of course you'll both bunk with me this weekend. Is that all right? I'm really hoping for a true sleepover."

She led them down halls and up and down stairs. The place was an unbelievable maze of sumptuous velvet and intricate brocade, deep leather and inlaid wood. Oona lost track of how many rooms they had passed. On the way, Gloria showed them the hall to an attached cottage where the party would be held in a few hours. Finally, Gloria stopped.

"Ah, here we are at last!" Carol said, like a weary traveler finally returning to a familiar place. Gloria opened the door, and Carol followed.

Oona stepped in last, and tried hard to hide her surprise. Had they entered the wrong room? They seemed to be in a man's bedroom, with dark, heavy drapes and deep brown carpet accented with some sort of animal hide throw rug. Oona couldn't tell what kind of animal it might have been in its previous life, though it was shaped exactly like the splayed body of whatever creature it used to cover. There was an oxblood leather wing chair and footrest, a sturdy wooden bureau, and impressive equine portraits over the bed. They were entirely surrounded by walls of dark mahogany.

The air smelled of all these masculine things, subtly mingled with the perfumes and powders of a teenage girl. The only decorations that showed a young lady lived there were a floral pillow sham on the bed and a desk near the window, the surface of which was entirely covered in a jumble of cosmetics and scarves and jewelry.

"I've got to run to the loo," Carol said, and disappeared through a door across the room.

Their bags had already been delivered to the room and placed at the foot of twin cots which had been set up for their visit, each with fluffy pillows and blue satin duvets. On the wall over the cots was a portrait of a regal man with a fine horse.

"That's my Uncle Henry Payne Whitney," Gloria said. She came to stand beside Oona, looking up. "And his champion filly Regret. This was Uncle Henry's room. He was married to my Aunt Gertrude, but he died." She pouted, her full lips pressing out for a moment then snapping right back. "When she got custody of me, she brought me here, and gave me this room."

"He liked horses," Oona offered.

"He was a great horseman," Gloria said, then she remembered her manners. "Do you ride?" There were remnant traces of a childhood lisp when Gloria spoke more softly.

"I had a pony when I was small," Oona said. "In Bermuda, where we lived, the children have ponies to ride to school or to town, or to a friend's house. I would ride all by myself and then tie him up and give him his water, some oats, or a lump of sugar. He was lovely, with big brown eyes and those soft lips that felt like little velvety kisses when he ate from my hand." She paused and bit her own lower lip, shook her head. "Anyway, my mother got him for me after my father left, and I loved him so much. I was terribly sad when I had to leave him behind."

"A pony can be a good friend," Gloria said. "Sometimes the very best friend."

The girls stood there another moment, side by side, looking up at the magnificent horse in the painting. Then Oona felt Gloria's eyes on her.

"You must tell me what shade of lipstick that is, darling," Gloria said.

"Of course. You can try it if you want."

"Could I? Tonight, do you think?"

"I don't mind."

"You're a doll." Her deep, narrow eyes seemed to scrutinize every detail of Oona's face. "I'm glad you could come to my party," she said.

"So am I," said Oona.

Gloria gave Oona's hand a gentle squeeze. Oona looked over at her, and then squeezed hers in return. They both smiled, a fundamental sort of understanding passing between them.

08 80

By the time they had all bathed, dressed, fixed their faces, and re-curled their hair, early guests had started arriving. The house staff had instructions to gather everyone in the foyer until Gloria came down.

She had a clever plan to kick off the party: Oona and Carol would go down the winding stairs to the foyer first. They'd pause and wait until people noticed their arrival (which shouldn't take long), then they would turn and face the top of the stairs where Gloria would appear and make her entrance. That was the whole theatrical plan, since the fun of watching the boys get all excited would take care of the rest. They giggled with nervous anticipation.

Oona carefully blotted her rosy lipstick and fluffed her hair. Carol added another layer of white face powder. Gloria pulled the front of her bodice down enough to expose the top of her cleavage. They checked the mirror one last time, then Gloria led the way with her little entourage close behind.

It all went exactly to plan, with Oona and Carol descending the stairs and standing to either side like a pair of wedding cake bridesmaids. The guests joined them at the foot of the stairs, milling closer and closer. The foyer was soon filled with Gloria's young guests, each dressed more stylishly than the next, and an anticipatory din arose as everyone wondered when Gloria might appear. Just as Oona was about to abandon her post, Gloria materialized on top step, one hand resting on the banister and the other on her waist.

A young man leaned closer to Oona. "It's amazing," he said, a bit too close. "You two could be sisters." Oona rubbed her ear, but smiled as Gloria quit the pose and glided down the stairs.

With its dark wood and gleaming brass, the grand living room was better suited for cigars and brandy snifters, but helium balloons in deep pink, burgundy, and gold in every corner brightened it up to receive Gloria's young guests. Heavy floor-to-ceiling velvet drapes were pushed aside to allow starlight to serve as a backdrop for the festivities, and the full moon might have been hung like a glowing ornament especially for the occasion.

As the room filled with the bustle of young people eager to mingle, Gloria's Aunt Gertrude arrived with several friends, all walking together in a close, brisk huddle, deep in discussion about a news report they'd just heard on the car radio. She paused to hand over her fur coat to the maid who met her at the door with a silk lounging robe, but her wide-brimmed hat remained in place. She gave instructions to William regarding the car, took a surveilling glance over the party proceedings, and then moved on, her guests in tow.

Oona hung around the doorway to watch Aunt Gertrude. She was a handsome woman with a strong nose and a soft, slightly droll mouth drawn down by the beginnings of distinguished jowls. Her striking profile added to her intriguing presence as she passed. Her hat was perched at a precisely perfect angle, a luminescent rope of pearls hung around her neck below a peacock-green chiffon scarf, and on her feet were a pair of matching green shoes. The formidable heiress's quiet arrival somehow made the house complete.

After a short welcome reception, Gloria led her guests down long halls, this way and that, passed portraits of dead Vanderbilts and Whitneys and magnificent, glossy horses, until they reached another large space Gloria called "The Cottage." On the way, she explained that her Aunt Gertrude had recently granted her free rein to decorate the living room in this space however she liked.

"My mother wants me to come to California next summer, but Aunt Gertrude and my grandmother want me to think it's more fun here," Gloria explained matter-of-factly.

Her inspiration was obvious the moment they saw it. Gloria had chosen to make the room look as if Egypt exploded all over it. Gloria's idea of Egypt, anyway.

While Carol effused over the completed effect, Oona smiled graciously. She would have chosen good Irish lace and subtle antiques, but then there was enough of that in this house already. In fact, this house was as near to perfect as Oona could imagine. But the Egypt Room, as Gloria blithely called it, did make a funny sort of sense: Gloria had taken her first chance to express herself and had gone entirely to the other side of the world.

Butler William led in a couple of latecomers, and while Gloria saw to them, Oona followed Carol's lead and went to look at the food.

A feast awaited them. Entering into the fabulous parlour, guests were fairly bowled over by a wave of singular sights and enticing aromas. A long, narrow buffet table covered in peony pink silk was artfully strewn with an overwhelming offering of sweets, nuts, and hors d'oeuvres. An enormous tiered pink cake decorated with rose petals and sprigs of fresh, fragrant greenery rose from the center of the eye-popping spread, like a hothouse specimen in full bloom. On one end of the table was a sparkling cut glass punch bowl surrounded by dozens of delicate, matching cups.

Carol led Oona through the crowd to the front of the line. A small, dark-eyed man in striped trousers and suspenders served them each a cup of the punch, then winked. The girls sniffed the cups and Oona coughed, but recovered quickly, her eyes darting around to make sure no one had seen. The first sip burned going down, but after that it was just sweet and warm and relaxing, and gone before she knew it.

They made room for others at the punch bowl, but each of them kept one eye on the abundant food platters. The other eye they kept on the intense, lanky fellow talking to Gloria.

"That's her beau," Carol said. "And the boys with him, well, I kissed a lot of them at the last party..." She popped a delicate choux puff into her mouth and handed one to Oona. "Eat this if you're going to drink any more of that," she said, then she pulled her giant compact from her wrist bag and inspected her face. She pointed the mirror at Oona, and Oona checked her lipstick, her teeth, then nodded, and Carol snapped the compact closed with a loud 'click' and dropped it back in her bag.

As if on cue, a group of boys came towards them, exclaiming.

"Aww gee, it's Baby!"

"Baby brought a friend!"

"That's awfully terrific of you, Baby. What's her name?"

The boys began circling around them, taking them in from every angle. Carol straightened her back and dialed up the girlish charm, clearly in her element.

Oona had a strange and sudden urge to run.

"Hi, Joe. Hello, Biff. What's the word, Smitty?" Carol said, making each boy light up at her remembering their names. "This is my darling friend Oona. Isn't she divine?"

Oona wondered which of these winners Carol had kissed. Maybe all of them. None of them looked like anyone Oona would have liked to kiss, except maybe the one with the mop of curly black hair, and even he was a maybe. But he looked like he could dance and really that was what mattered.

Someone had brought a stack of jazz records for Gloria's victrola, and Duke Ellington's "Cottontail" brought everyone cheering to the middle of the room. At first, they danced separately, but as soon as Gloria had been asked to dance, the boys began asking other girls. Oona found herself surrounded by eager faces, and she counted them off, numbering them to assign their turns. She danced straight through as one tune went into another, song after song. Whatever was in the punch kicked in and her head spun. The music took over her body, flowing from a rhumba, to a cha cha, to another rhumba. She lost track, declaring each song her new favorite.

One boy, a stocky fellow with a muscular build and the cauliflower ear of a letterman wrestler, kept finding his way to Oona in the crowd of dancers, grabbing her hand and spinning her toward him out of turn. He wore a linen blazer over a polo shirt and navy pants, a look she supposed was meant to show the other guests how and where he fit into this crowd, and why any girl should be thrilled to dance with him. He might have been handsome, with thick sandy hair that had come free of its pomade and flopped over one side of his forehead, but his face was pinched with a menacing look around the eyes that seemed to become more intense with each pass around the dance floor. After several times, Oona tried to keep her distance without seeming rude. He was one of Gloria's guests, after all.

He brought her a cup of punch, and she politely took it, but she didn't take a sip. These boys thought they were so clever, spiking drinks with sleeping pills swiped from their mother's bedside tables. She'd heard all about it, eavesdropping on a group of older girls at Brearley. The punch at this party was strong enough as it was, lurid red and sweet, with a vapor that had gone to Oona's head before she'd had the first sip. She didn't need whatever Master Cauliflower Ear might have added.

Familiar laughter rose above the unfamiliar voices, and Oona turned to see Carol and Gloria giggling in the center of the room. Her heart fell, landing with a dull thud in her chest. Someone grabbed for her hand, but she waved them off with the most good-natured smile she could muster.

Oona had chosen one of her favorite party outfits—a white eyelet blouse and a navy print skirt with ruffled hem, just at the knees. Her shoes were a bargain find from S. Klein and a half size too small, but she'd been sure they'd stretch out and bought them anyway. They already pinched, the pain pulsing into her toes with her racing heartbeat.

Someone stopped the gramophone mid-tune to change the disc, and the crowd let out a collective groan. Oona took her chance to slip out of the crowd to find a seat, but there were none available, so she found a spot against the wall and leaned back on her heels. Her head spun. The room had become round and soft around the edges, and the floor was almost certainly wobbling. To one side, a flash of peacock green caught her eye and she turned to see Gloria's

Aunt Gertrude passing outside the wide doorway which led to the hall. The room turned again as she craned her neck to see the last of the scarf flutter by.

Doesn't she have the most amazing style?

On the dance floor, the boy-to-girl ratio weighed heavily in the girls' favor. Allowing for cutting-in between verses, each song involved three or four different partners. Carol taught Gloria the fox-trot, gliding around the dance floor to Artie Shaw's "Frenesi," and their smiles beamed like beacons flashing a secret signal with every turn, even when the boys clomped and cursed their own two left feet. Carol employed all the flirting techniques and dance moves they had practiced together in her room, every girlish eyelash flutter and coquettish smile which had taken them from tearful wallflowers not so long ago to the most popular girls in their set. Boys kept asking Oona back onto the dance floor, but she begged off on account of her feet.

"Aww come on, sugar, don't break my heart," pleaded a fraternity boy with a persistent cowlick punctuated by an unfortunate pimple.

"Just kick your shoes off!" said another boy, his face florid and shining and keen.

"I've got something that will make your feet numb," said another, raising his eyebrows suggestively and reaching for her hand. She pulled it back.

"I'll just go change my shoes," Oona said. Her collection of admirers protested, and she conjured a good-natured smile while backing toward the door.

"Come back soon, won't you?"

"She's dancing with me first when she gets back."

"Fat chance!"

Oona smiled and slipped by them, but not before the boy who had been monopolizing her on the dance floor caught her eye. She looked away quickly and exhaled only after she was safely out of the room. She leaned against the wall and gingerly pulled off her shoes, spread her toes and sucked in a breath at the painful relief of freedom.

The strains of Artie Shaw's "Begin the Beguine" grew softer as she climbed the stairs toward the hall to Gloria's room. It was a song she and Carol had danced to that first day they met in dance class. They'd bought the record so they could practice before that big dance. Oona remembered her black dress and Carol's white, how they'd been like negatives of each other, each of them emphasizing the other's extremes. They would always have the memory of that great night, no matter what else happened or who might come between them.

She pressed a hand to her forehead as she opened the door to Gloria's room, shutting her eyes tight. A vice clamped the back of her head and a wave of nausea threatened. As she paused near the door, trying to remember where she'd put her other dress shoes, there was suddenly someone right beside her.

She looked up and there he was, the pushy boy from the dance floor, the one with the cauliflower ear, smiling as he looked at her from head to toe, licking his lips. The fuzz on his chin was like dandelion fluff ready to blow away. She almost started to laugh at his ridiculous confidence, coming toward her like that, but his eyes changed in an instant, glazing over, looking through her. His jaw clenched and his smile dropped, becoming a hungry, lascivious leer.

He used his whole body to push her into the room, then quietly closed the door behind him before she could know what was happening. She realized no one would probably hear her now and wished she had thought to shout in the hall. She tried to call out anyway, but it came out like dry gravel against glass. He wrapped his arms around hers and pushed her up against the door.

She tried to shout again and he leaned harder, covering her mouth with one hand while he yanked at her skirt with the other, then pulled at her garter until it snapped away. She twisted, but her hip was pinned by his and when she struggled, he pushed harder until she thought her hipbone might snap. He shoved his hand to the top of her leg and pressed hard when his rough fingers found flesh.

She inhaled hard through her nose and screamed under his hand, and when he only held her tighter, she thought quickly. She forced her tongue past her teeth and through her lips, which seemed to surprise him. The pressure on her face eased and she took the chance to bite down, catching the fleshy part of his palm, right below his thumb.

He squealed and pulled back, then raised the hand above her head, ready to bring it down across her face. She winced and tried to twist away, and as she did someone pounded on the door, the percussion pounding through her head and into her back like the beat of a war drum reverberating through her body.

"Open this door!" A woman's voice. *Thank God.* The boy stumbled back and looked around for another way out, and Oona threw open the door.

Chapter 6

PIECES

Aunt Gertrude. Her face was stone as she looked Oona up and down, understanding the situation immediately. She tightened the sash of her cocoon robe as she flew by Oona, cornering the cowering boy in the corner.

"What is your name, boy?" she said, her voice a slap in his face. He didn't reply, but tried to step around her. She moved to the side and blocked him. He looked down, refusing to speak. She leaned closer. "That's fine, you little pissant. I'll find out, don't you worry." Her words were a spitting fire. "You are pathetic, and I won't waste another moment on you. Now get out of my house, and don't ever dare come back."

He ducked around her and she let him pass, pushing him with her eyes as he skittered away and hunched out the door. Oona had been holding the door frame, but as he approached, she let go and stood up tall, trying to match Gertrude's power with her own, though her insides were a landslide. Once he was out of the room and out of sight, she crumbled against the wall.

Gertrude put her arm around Oona's shoulders and stood with her, silent but solid, until Oona's breathing calmed. She stayed in the room, sitting on the edge of Gloria's bed, while Oona washed and changed clothes. When she came out in her night-gown, a tray was waiting, and Gertrude sat with her quietly while she nibbled a bit of toast and sipped a mug of tea. Afterward, Gertrude brought some bicarbonate and water and again sat wordlessly while Oona drank it.

Only after Oona was cared for did she speak.

"My room is next door, and at first I didn't know what I was hearing or I would have come sooner," Gertrude said.

"Thank you, Mrs. Whitney," Oona said. She felt ashamed, hoping the woman didn't think she had invited the boy up there, but somehow she felt it wouldn't make any difference to Aunt Gertrude. What he'd done was abominable either way.

Oona inhaled the woman's warm, floral scent and suddenly wished she would put her arms around her again, let her lay her head on her velvet-draped shoulder. She began to come back to herself, her thoughts forming more clearly as the alcohol and the adrenalin burned away. Gertrude placed her hand on Oona's knee, her strong artist's fingers and sensitive touch infusing a measure of her womanly strength.

"I am so glad you were there," Oona said. It occurred to her that she hadn't introduced her-self. Gertrude hadn't asked her name, yet there was already a familiarity between them.

Gertrude spoke, as if she'd read her mind. "You're Agnes Boulton's daughter Oona, isn't that right?" she said.

Oona nodded, confused. No one ever asked if she was Agnes's daughter. People only ever mentioned her father. *Daughter of Eugene O'Neill.* Gertrude smiled. "I know your family. Your mother's aunt Margery Williams Bianco and her daughter Pamela? I'm a patron of the arts, and when I saw Pamela's work in London, I knew she must come here, to Greenwich Village. I brought them over from London and set them up at the MacDougal Alley studios so Pamela could work and produce pieces for an exhibition. She was a smashing success." Her eyes twinkled with the memory.

Oona stared in wonder. That was it. Aunt Gertrude had known her family before she was born.

"Have you inherited any artistic talent then?"

Oona's stomach froze. "Well, I don't know. It is one of my best subjects at Brearley..." She tried to picture her cousin's lovely work, mentally comparing her own sketches and paintings, which her teacher had called 'promising.'

"I also attended Brearley," Gertrude said.

"Yes, ma'am."

"But we can't all be prodigies, you know," Gertrude said. "I certainly wasn't. I had the privilege of training with masters, honing my skills at their feet, so to speak. Even so, I often submitted my work for shows under a male pseudonym. Can you believe that? I had both my name and my gender against me." She gave Oona an appraising look. "I suppose you can understand that, can't you?"

Oona didn't know where to look. Aunt Gertrude's gaze went deep, as if penetrating her skin, truly seeing her.

"Yes, ma'am, I suppose I can." She studied her fingernails. She bit her lip, then winced. It was tender from the grip of the nameless boy's damp, salty hand.

"Do you also write?" Gertrude asked. "It's certainly in your blood. Not only are both your parents writers, but Margery's *Velveteen Rabbit* was quite the smash, wasn't it?"

"Yes, ma'am."

She was going to slap herself if she said "yes, ma'am" one more time. But what could she say that might begin to impress this woman? Suddenly filled with a longing to distinguish herself somehow, she cast about the room for inspiration, but her eyes fell on her makeup and perfume bottles still sitting on the bureau, her prissy coat hanging beside Carol's, her silly, too-small shoes that had made her come up here alone to begin with.

"I read a great deal," she said.

"Good things, I hope."

"Yes, Ma'am." She flinched. "Willa Cather is a favorite—"

"Oh, indeed?" Gertrude's brows rose, and Oona wondered if it meant she was impressed. Or was it the look of an adult who knew something but was reluctant to say? She knew Cather had lived in Greenwich Village at the same time as Daddy and Mother, and she loved imagining them passing on the street, eating in the same diners, attending the same stage shows. Perhaps they had even known each other? Before she could work out how to ask, Gertrude spoke again. "Well, my dear, if you choose an artistic path, do be sure to keep me informed."

"I will," Oona said. Gertrude stood. For the first time, Oona noticed the slightest artist's hunch to Gertrude's back before she straightened and strode to the door. She paused with her hand on the gleaming brass doorknob. Her pearls swung with her as she turned back toward Oona.

"Oona, my dear, there will always be people who think they have a right to a piece of you," Gertrude said. "They are mistaken."

⚭

Gloria and Carol burst into the room soon after, laughing, it seemed, about nothing at all. It made Oona laugh, too, and soon they were all trying to out-laugh each other. Oona tried to put the events of earlier out of her mind, and smile.

Carol's lips were swollen from too much kissing, and Gloria walked a bit awkwardly. Every so often, the two of them looked at each other and locked eyes before breaking into fresh peals of laughter.

In that moment, Oona knew she wouldn't tell them what happened. She couldn't do it. She'd only just met Gloria, and now she was supposed to tell her she'd been mauled in her bedroom? Both Gloria and Carol were so tipsy and caught up in their own stories that neither of them seemed to notice she had already washed and changed clothes anyway. If she did say something, and if Gloria was upset about it, Carol would wish she had never brought her here. Instead, she listened to them whisper about their little trysts, and the stories of tonight spilled into those of the recent past, some of which Carol hadn't mentioned to her before, at least not in such graphic detail. Oona held her pillow to her stomach and listened to them, pulling her brush through her hair for something to do and giggling when it seemed appropriate.

Was she the odd one? She dated as much as Carol did. Every Friday and Saturday night was booked weeks in advance. It made her head turn in circles, juggling hopeful young men from 'good' families, the type Mother wanted her to date, while giving them a lot of nothing. All the while, Carol had been giving more than she let on, and Gloria seemed completely obsessed. Seriously, did that girl think about anything but sex?

Maybe she should be doing more by now, too. It certainly would be easier, a relief even, not to have to wonder anymore how it would happen and with whom. But how did a girl know which boys were all right and which were like that nameless boy? They all looked so innocuous, so cute and obliging and desperate, with their wide eyes and goofy grins. Was that supposed to be sexy? Was she supposed to have been flattered that Cauliflower Ear chose to follow her up to this room tonight?

One thing she knew for sure was that she would not do anything with someone who was doing anything with someone else. And everyone was apparently doing something with someone. It seemed that in this world, the thing was to have a reputation. Good or bad, a person *must* have one in order for people to find you interesting.

What would Mother think about that? She probably had no idea what she had gotten her daughter into, wanting her to mix with high society, with these glorious, dazzling girls who thought it was *que sophistique* to constantly dwell on what it was like to 'fock,' as they inexplicably put it.

Oona waited for the smallest opening in the charged conversation, and then interjected a new topic.

"What shall we wear to the Christmas dance?"

Gloria and Carol looked at her as if they'd forgotten she was there, then Carol seemed to forget the previous conversation entirely. "Something lacy and frothy and very, very low cut," she said.

Gloria nodded enthusiastically. "I'm dying for a black gown! But I don't know if I can get a low-cut dress past Aunt Ger. Oh! Maybe a bolero to cover up until we get there!"

Oona's shoulders relaxed a bit and she smiled, relieved to be back in comfortable territory.

She'd brought along a copy of *Lucy Gayheart*, but once the other girls had washed and changed, it became clear there'd be no time for reading tonight. Gloria was ready for the sleepover portion of her big weekend.

They sat in a circle on Gloria's enormous bed, and their general twittering turned serious as the topic of discussion changed to the filling of their dance cards for the next sub-deb ball, and then progressed to the planning of a secret evening out at the night-clubs once Gloria was settled in the city.

They huddled, their pretty heads close together, as if planning an attack. They were on the brink of what they'd been raised for, Carol said. Gloria and Carol plotted and planned the perfect night out on the town, and Oona got a notebook and pencil and wrote it all down, fine-tuning the itinerary. She was one of them now, but only to a point. Gloria and Carol's friendship was their own separate entity.

Now that she'd observed them together, Oona saw herself differently all at once. They were two of a kind. Maybe she'd been wrong to think she could belong in their world. A famous name only got you so far, and a plus-one invitation to a Vanderbilt house party didn't make her one of them.

"Now that we're all almost grown up, let's all three of us make a pact," Gloria said. "We can have all the affairs we'd like, but we will find real, true, certified geniuses to *marry*."

"Let's do it!" Carol said, looking at Oona.

Oona hesitated, and her doubtful expression made both the other girls' shoulders droop dramatically, as if she were the world's biggest party pooper.

They didn't know what they were saying. Of the three of them, Oona was the one whose father was considered a 'certified genius.' She wasn't actually sure she wanted a man like that for a husband. Then again, she had spent most of her life trying to win his love and attention. Maybe a genius husband was exactly right, exactly what she should hold out for.

"All right," she finally said, and the other girls cheered and clapped. "But—they have to love us, too. I mean really, *really* love us!"

Gloria and Carol looked at each other and tried not to giggle.

"Oh, of course!" Gloria said.

"How could they not?" Carol added.

"Now we have to spit on our hands and shake on it," Gloria said, depositing a small dollop of saliva on her own palm. Carol instantly followed suit, then Oona. They gave each other one businesslike shake each before racing off to the loo, squealing, to wash them off.

Later, as they each slid between their cool, satiny sheets, Oona looked around the luxurious room and wondered at how she'd gotten there. Would she ever have a home like this? A home of her own? She stared at the fine painting that hung over Gloria's bed, the trays of sweets and sandwiches they had picked through and forgotten, the closet stuffed full of custom-made dresses.

Had her new friend ever seen how regular people lived?

Point Pleasant

NEW JERSEY 1929

*T*he morning newspapers strewn on Mother's library floor had huge black letters on the front, and the topic of adult conversation began to revolve around 'markets' and how they were crashing. Oona's stomach turned over at the thought of the markets where she used to walk with Gaga, and the ones on the Main Street here in Point Pleasant where Gaga bought her favorite sweets on Saturday mornings. Were the people still inside the markets when they crashed?

She dreamt that night of Maria who sat on a low stool beside her fruit stand and Mr. Edward who rode up and down the road on his too-small bicycle calling every woman he saw "my dear lady." Had the market fallen on them? When she tried to ask after them, Mother had stared at her for a moment with a deep, glassy gaze and then broken into the most terrible fit of laughter, and so she hadn't asked again. When Shane tried to explain, in his forthright and unvarnished way, he'd started to say it meant people were going to become poor now, and lose their homes and *starve to death—including babies—and Mother had shushed him and Shane had run away to the beach, or somewhere.*

So it was many days before she could find out whether Maria and Mr. Edward were all right and if the market stalls and shops back in Bermuda were still standing.

One day mother had some of their things packed, and Oona felt she'd fallen asleep in Point Pleasant and woken up in Bermuda, on the road up to Spithead. Days and nights blended, like when she swirled all the colors in her paint box until everything turned a murky brown. Nothing was like it used to be.

What did it all mean? Until that moment, Oona hadn't ever thought, in all her four years, about what money was or how one went about getting it. The markets hadn't crashed until Daddy went away, as if her family's break apart truly was the end of the world.

What did it mean to be 'poor'? There were differences between people they passed on the street. Some wore beautiful clothes and shining shoes, the ladies with feathers in their hats and lipstick. But some ladies had no lipstick and their hats were not so fine. They looked as if they hadn't slept for a long time. They shouted in their doorways for children who ran in the streets with no shoes at all. Was that what it meant to be poor?

Oona didn't know what it really meant to live like that, but some of those women and children still had their husbands and fathers, and that must make them richer than she was. Fathers with rough working hands shared sandwiches with their little ones at the beach. They had something important she did not. Daddy had a new wife he liked better than Mother. He was tired of them, of their noise and mess and having to dole out pin money to Mother all the time.

Mother started reading the society pages before the headlines, saw writers and actors and politicians going about life as if unaffected by the bad news, this thing they were calling 'The Great Depression.' She read aloud articles about her own former husband, upset that he was written about now in the same pages as royalty and movie stars, while she was nowhere to be seen, a nobody. Maybe it was some kind of divine punishment, Oona overheard her say, like something Eugene wrote about in his plays, but nothing about it felt divine at all.

Oona pored over the pages mother left on the parlor floor. She clipped every mention of her father and pasted them carefully in an album. She strained her new reading skills to pick out words. Somewhere there were people who still had money. They were the glittery ones—the actors, the musicians, and the writers—the ones everyone loved to read about. Maybe people liked to read about them just to see it was still possible for things to get better for them, too.

Sometimes the society pages even made the front page. Mother read about the Vanderbilts' newest scandal with great interest. Now two of them were fighting over a little girl, a girl named Gloria who was close to Oona's age. Even those lucky ones had their problems.

People in the streets and all around read the papers and talked and talked about what they read, *but they were never so animated as when they talked about celebrities and their comfortable lives. There was a better life out there, and you could have it too, only you would do it better. If we had their money, boy, we wouldn't fritter it away on petty things like these people did. But when things got better, sure, you could just save up enough money to take a trip to the city and sit right where they were, in one of those swanky booths at one of those exclusive nightclubs.*

Mother seethed openly at the unfairness of all she'd lost. It should be illegal to steal another woman's husband. She should be able to press charges for loss of fortune, loss of status. Loss of life.

Oona kept her sadness to herself. Mother had enough of her own; she didn't need to hear hers. She tried to stop crying for her father when she saw one of his photos, at least not in front of Mother. She continued cutting his pictures from the papers and pasting them into her scrapbook. She wanted it complete for when she showed it to him, when she saw him again. Surely that would be soon.

But the Bermuda days that were supposed to last forever, the days of Daddy, Mother, Shane, and Oona together on the sand in the bright sunlight, were gone forever. She felt a bit guilty for the way her family's breakup had hurt the world. It truly was a Great Depression.

Chapter 7

TALL TALES OF MOONBEAMS

1940

Of all the amusements the city could offer, none was more fun for Oona than taking in a one-woman show put on by Carol in her own bedroom. She fluffed a cumulus of pillows and wriggled into the featherbed, ready to be entertained: Carol was feeling theatrical.

"You know how I love my bath, right?" Carol said. And she was off. As she began the story, she crawled up from the bottom of the bed like a cat, chose a suitable spot, then leaned on her elbow and curled her legs behind her.

"Wait," Oona said. "Should I get some popcorn, or...?"

"I can call for some." If Carol got Oona's sarcasm, she hid it well behind her dumb blonde act.

"Never mind, go on."

"So I came home from school one day, and I heard Elinor in the front room, talking and laughing—so irritating," she rolled her eyes. "So I passed on by and came in here for my long afternoon bath."

"As one does," Oona said.

"Exactly," Carol said.

Oona shook her head. This girl was too much. And she loved her dearly, more than she'd ever intended. She loved people who could make her laugh, and Carol made her laugh more than anyone she'd ever met. Tonight she had promised to tell the story of how she met her friend Truman Capote.

Oona had come to understand that Carol's florid stories simply had to be taken with several grains of salt. She didn't mind. Carol was honest when it mattered. She didn't flirt with Oona's beaus (well, not too much) or cheat at school. She simply insisted that life be as big and wonderful and fabulous as it was in her own mind, and sometimes that meant taking a bit of literary license with her own life stories.

"Well, I came home from school, and I heard Elinor with some friends, but I ignored them and came here for my bath. When I got out, I walked over here," she patted the end of the bed, "sat down to apply my moisturizer, all over." She waved her hands over her body to demonstrate.

Oona nodded. "Mmhmm, all over, got it," she said.

"So I'm naked..."

"Ri-i-ight."

"And I'm rubbing cream all over on my legs, and I look up to that transom right there," she pointed above the door, "and there in the window is a pale little wide-eyed face topped with yellow-hair, looking at me!"

"No!"

"Yes!" Carol stood now, then strode across the room, hitting her marks. "I screamed! Ahhh! Like that. And I go to grab my towel, my robe, a pillow, anything. Even my own mother hadn't seen me naked since I got these!" she said, gripping her chest protectively with both hands.

Oona gasped sarcastically and made her eyes wide, then narrow. "But why would you stand there, where he could see you?"

Carol ignored her and went on. Oona closed her mouth and gave a deferential nod, remembering proper theater etiquette.

"And he taps on the transom window, and he says, 'Oh please, please don't ever wear clothes again!' in this little voice like a woodland fairy or something. 'You came straight from the moon. You're made of moonbeams. You should never wear clothes again, that's how divine you are...' He went on like this until I opened the door. When I realized he didn't mean to ravish me—me or any girl—I let him in, and we had the loveliest talk." She traipsed across the room as if from stage right to stage left. The only thing missing was a spotlight. Then she turned and lowered herself into an armchair, resting her chin on her hand. "We talked and talked, about books and writers and who we were, where we came from, what sorts of people we each knew. He seemed impressed by the family names of some of my friends—Vanderbilt, Whitney, Rockefeller. He started hanging around me instead of Elinor, which I don't think my sister minded too terribly much since it was really his friend she was interested in to begin with. And so," she said, concluding the scene, "we've been friends ever since."

She gave Oona an expectant look.

"What?" Oona said, in a near whisper.

Carol raised her eyebrows and pursed her lips.

"Oh, I'm sorry," Oona said. "I was waiting for you to take your bow."

Missing the tease entirely, Carol hopped to her feet and raised both arms, then dropped them and gave a deep prima donna curtsey.

Oona clapped enthusiastically, raising her arms above her head. "Brava!" she said. She wiped a fake tear from her eye and threw invisible roses at Carol's feet. "Brava!"

They collapsed across Carol's bed, rolling with laughter.

ᘓᘔᘒᘌ

1940

Oona's quirky group of friends had become a kind of little family, if a slightly dysfunctional one. They played at family like a game, directing all the related emotions at each other with the intensity of siblings. Affection morphed into exasperation, and then to jealousy, then bitterness, and back again to affection, sometimes all within a single day. They formed a pack, a tribe of untethered youngsters, no longer children and not quite adults, from completely different backgrounds but with eerily similar stories. Perhaps they understood each other in a way no one else could, sometimes better than they understood themselves. With a shared experience of coming last in a parent's life, they fell without pretense into parenting each other, driving one another to reach for something better. How exactly that 'better' life might manifest was still a mystery, but it was essential the adult life that loomed in the near distance be different from the loneliness they'd inherited.

They devoured books and plays and poetry, and they cried at the tenderness and redemption of deep, pure love. They believed in possibilities beyond what they were given, and the belief nurtured a hope that if they were good, whatever 'good' was, then perhaps they could believe in the possibility that good things in turn were around the next corner.

Carol's father was a mystery. Gloria's father was dead. Truman's father was gone (and so, often, was Truman).

Oona's father was a myth.

All of them motherless, they mothered each other. Each of them fatherless, they sought security in romance. Until they found it, they had each other.

Gloria, Carol, and Oona. A unit. A trio. Three girls with beauty, brains, and just enough money between them to get into trouble. Their personalities jived: Gloria bold and self-possessed, Carol deceptively feminine, and Oona reserved and mysterious. They obsessed over movies and movie stars. They'd taken to wearing their hair long, bobbed and swooping, like Veronica Lake. As much as the boys didn't notice them a few years ago, now they would not leave them alone.

Still, Oona felt the important difference between herself and her friends: Oona's father was alive. He wasn't lost, nor was he hiding. Her father, the world-renowned Nobel laureate, simply didn't want her. Her beautiful, sparkling, fatherless friends could never understand what it was to know their father simply didn't care to be part of their lives.

Perhaps it would have hurt less if he had been honest from the beginning. If he had made a clean break, told her the truth. *I did not want children. I never did. You should move on and forget about me.* But just when she would begin to accept the idea that Daddy had probably forgotten about her (given the fact he hadn't replied to her letters for months upon months, or that if a reply did come it was written by Carlotta), a guilt-laced little note would arrive, peppered with a few generic parental trivialities and superficial questions, and signed off with a heart-stabbing "Don't forget your Daddy!"

All she could glean from the sparse letters and the handful of hours spent with him over the years since he left was that he wished for her to be self-sufficient as soon as possible, to be off his dime by the time she was eighteen. Guilt hung above her head like a thundercloud when he (or Carlotta) complained, via their lawyer, about the expensive boarding schools her mother chose and for which he was compelled to pay. Her stilted and choppy education before Brearley was the cause of particular irritation to him, but one in which she had little say, so that at least wasn't her fault.

What was it he wanted from her?

If only she could see him, alone and without Carlotta looming. Then maybe she could figure out who he really wanted her to be. Only now it might be getting too late to change who she was. She couldn't pretend her childhood wasn't over, there was no way to fix it now. It was done, for better or worse. She hadn't felt childlike for a very long time, and as the weight of her own ambitions and desires steadily grew, and she wondered when it would outweigh the need to mold to her father's indecipherable expectations.

∞

Truman's parents had split up when he was very small. His father was in the wind, and his mother had left him behind with a relation in Alabama when he was four years old in order to pursue her own dreams, which could not come true with a precocious little boy in tow. Eventually, she'd sent for him to join her and her new husband, a successful Cuban businessman, in New York.

Oona recognized a familiar, searching look in his eyes. It was the same look she saw in the mirror in her most unguarded moments, the look ingrained in the tiny muscles and still-tender cheeks of those who shared a very particular experience—that of a child left behind.

But there was a sort of bottomless need in his interest that kept her constantly and ever-so-slightly on guard. Whether sitting across a candlelit table at the glamorous Stork Club or beside him in the back of a taxicab full of the day's blown smoke, his hunger was palpable. Was it only their shared understanding of the painful longing for an absent parent, one who lived on the edge of a child's imagination, that drove his near-constant interrogation? Or did he long to hear her most personal stories in order to possess them in some intimate way?

Whether natural or cultivated, he possessed an impeccable talent for drawing people out, offering up a little portion of his pain in exchange for a larger portion of theirs. He possessed the writer's way of absorbing the experiences of others—encouraging, but almost invasive in its closeness. To be listened to the way he listened, as if she made him so happy just by being herself, was intoxicating. But when he reciprocated by sharing the private stories of others, a cold dread filled the pit of her stomach.

Still, he could be so dear, a precious little collector of people, so interested in their stories, as changeable and malleable as fresh clay in his hands.

Romantically, he was safe, a boy who didn't want anything from them except to be with them, to bask in their light, in what it meant to be a beautiful young woman in Manhattan. Once, he looked at them and said it was like they didn't know they were girls at all. They told him they were trying. That it took a bit of figuring out.

His interest was not physical, but his intense care and attention felt nearly paternal.

At least, that was how it felt to Oona.

Manhattan with Truman was the New York of the movies, heightened and sparkling and glamorous.

When summer break came, they roamed the streets, imagining themselves at the center of all.

"Look at it, my lovely sisters!" Truman exclaimed one afternoon as they tumbled out of bar that didn't care about your age as long as you had cash. He waved an arm toward gothic building façades covered in mysterious windows towering overhead. "New York City is a long way from Alabama!"

"New York City is a long way from Bermuda, too," Oona said.

"Hell," Carol quipped, "New York City is a long way from itself." Oona and Truman giggled.

"What does that mean?" Gloria said, her mouth going slack, and they all laughed and patted her on the back. Gloria had only ever seen the New York City that took place in parkside mansions and penthouse suites with heavy, silk drapes.

That summer, even the steaming manhole covers and dark, dank alleys smelling of urine and sweat and base human acts of all kinds became part of the story. Their story.

They wandered the city together in various configurations of their little clique: sometimes all four of them, sometimes Truman and one, two, or three of them, and sometimes just the trio of girls in those inexplicable times when Truman simply disappeared for a while, leaving the girls to miss him good and well enough that when he returned he was sure to showered with their bountiful love and attention, their darling little boy. They would smooth his hair and press his cheeks. "Where have you been? We've been so lost without our Truman," they would say, escalating in proportion to his response. The stories of his adventures grew wilder with each return, and although Oona saw through them, she encouraged him. Here was another born writer with an artist's soul, and these rare creatures must have complete freedom in order to survive.

When she got a chance to see Daddy again, she'd show him she understood that now.

Truman returned one day with a plan to meet at Carol's and go on to lunch at El Morocco. They hadn't seen him in several weeks.

"Darlings, I've just come from—well, never mind where I've come from just now, it's not the point. What *is* the point is that I come bearing momentous, life-changing information." He unwrapped his scarf as he did his swaying walk around Carol's bedroom.

"Here it is, girls," he said, and stopped in the middle of the room, arms out, ready to make his earth-shattering announcement. "*All* of these white light bulbs *have* to go." He turned his face from the garish light as if it caused him physical pain. "They aren't flattering, not one bit. The thing now is to use pink bulbs. I went to Gloria's, to tell her, and she already knew! Her room is lousy with pink bulbs! They make her look like a damn Botticelli angel. She said she'll only be photographed with them now." As he spoke, he began to unwind a bulb from the lamp. "Of course, her silver-leafed walls don't hurt either."

All other amusements were forgotten in light of Truman's report. If Gloria was doing it, and Truman admired it, then Carol would do it.

Gloria was beautiful and clever, and though they were all aware of a sadness that lived in the deepest parts of her, she was determined to do more, see more, be more. She could have become dark and bitter over what had become of her childhood, but she had a hopefulness that drove her past all of that, a sort of indomitable anticipation of good things coming.

Oona loved when people mistook her and Gloria for sisters. Her own half-sister Barbara, Agnes's older daughter, was one of the mysteries of Oona's childhood. She had drifted in and out of their lives, but by the time Oona was old enough to wonder much about her, Barbara had been sent from living with their grandparents in Point Pleasant to boarding school, and that was that. She saw her in Point Pleasant, but it was always like reuniting with one of the cousins. A sister sounded like a wonderful thing—a built-in friend you could never lose.

When Gloria said she admired Oona's "personal style," Oona had tried to dismiss a pang of dread that Aunt Gertrude may have told Gloria what happened with that boy in her room, and that had compelled Gloria to say something nice to her. Her words had repeated in Oona's mind, replaying just exactly *how* she said it, how reassuring and direct her voice been, leaving her with the grounded sensation of solid stone under her feet. Not mere flattery, but as if maybe she really meant it, and it left Oona wanting more.

"What am I supposed to do until I get new bulbs?" Carol said, quite sincerely alarmed.

"Just drape your lamps with sheer scarves," Oona said distractedly, as if stating the obvious.

Carol instantly jumped up and ran to her closet, emerging with an armful of chiffon. She dumped the whole lot on the bed and let Oona choose the right shades.

"You have the best eye for these things," she said as Oona plucked rosy tones, pinks and corals.

"Try these," Oona said.

Carol held individual colors up to the light and settled on the barest pinks while Truman twisted a finger through his hair behind one ear and Oona sat back to watch the transformation.

Once Carol had covered each lamp in the room, she looked around to assess the effect. When she beheld her friends' glowing faces, her eyes grew wide.

"We're gorgeous!" she said.

Oona posed with her hand under her chin and turned her face this way and that, like the models in the magazines, as Carol drew closer.

"I can't believe the difference! Do other people know about this? Can we just put a big pink scarf over the sun?"

"The effect is positively romantic! If I didn't know better, I'd think I want to give each of you glorious creatures a passionate kiss," Truman said.

Oona looked at Carol, and Carol raised her eyebrows, and they both pounced at Truman.

"Oh, *do* kiss me!" Oona said.

"No, kiss *me*!" Carol pleaded.

Alarmed, Truman shook them off, jumped off the settee, and ran to the window, clutching at his shirt collar.

"Why Truman, you said if you didn't know better, you'd want to kiss us!"

"Passionately!" Carol said. "Didn't he say 'passionately,' Oona?"

"He did, Carol," Oona said, "but I suppose he was just teasing us." The back of her hand went to her forehead. "How cruel!"

"How inhumane!" Carol said.

"Girls, girls! Get ahold of yourselves!" Truman said, fanning himself with his hand. "Unfortunately for the both of you, I *do* know better."

◌৪৯

1941

The three girls dove headlong into café society, often with Truman as their jaunty escort. Evenings were filled with dates with eligible matches—often more than one date per night. Sometimes the dates were set up by the boys' mothers. It just showed what those mothers knew, setting up their dopey sons with girls who could already chew them up and spit them out in between bites of hamburgers and fries. Even when they did have other dates, the evenings usually ended up with the four of them—or two or three, whomever was free. No one waited up for any of them, except perhaps Gloria's Aunt Gertrude when she was in the city, so they swayed arm-in-arm down the boulevards looking for the next adventure.

Each day when they got together, on the weekends or holidays (or bunking off from school), the
first order of business was whether to have lunch at
El Morocco or The Stork Club, but usually the Stork
won out since they started offering them free lunch
after realizing the advertising value of their names
in the paper:

**Subdeb Oona O'Neill, Daughter of Eugene,
Lunches at The Stork:
Stunner says it's right back to her studies
after one of
Billingsley's famous steaks!**

They shared every little thing that happened to
them in case the others might somehow make use
of the information. Truman made a lot of lewd jokes
about his dates, outrageous enough for them to
think he was simply trying to shock them and wasn't
above extreme exaggeration—a theory which was
often confirmed when they compared notes on what
he'd told them. His stories grew with each retelling,
unlike Carol's, which started out exaggerated and
simply changed crucial details over time. All they
knew was it was a good thing, and also not fair, that
boys couldn't get pregnant.

Gloria lived in the city full-time, at her Aunt
Gertrude's house on Washington Mews. She and
Oona enjoyed going to lunch at a tea room and whispering conspicuously, dropping the rumor that Oona
was Gloria's long-lost sister. They'd keep up the cha-
rade until someone in the place inevitably knew one

or both of their parents and ruined the whole game. Carol always managed to rearrange her schedule and turn up any time Oona and Gloria made plans together, though she often canceled on Oona if a fellow she liked called for a date.

"It's only that I get so anxious if I think you two are having some great fun without me," Carol would say, letting her voice break just a little. "It must be because of how I was left in a foster home all those years."

How could they fault her for a thing like that? Oona's heart would immediately soften for her fragile little fairy friend.

Though she was the youngest of the group, Oona found her place as the practical and level-headed one, the integral but put-upon member of any group of friends. She played mother hen of a raucous brood, but they often conspired, as children do, to persuade Mama to cut loose. Ice cream for dinner wouldn't kill them, bed times were for humbugs. But when the piano player at their favorite bar got fed up with Carol's constant requests for Cole Porter tunes, Oona was the one to settle things down and herd the whole troupe out into the waning sunlight. She knew just how to distract Truman with a question about the latest story in *The New Yorker* at the precise moment the people at the next table were about to reach their limit with his wicked mouth and get them all tossed before the food even arrived. And it was Oona's frank assessments of Gloria's beaus that only made her more determined to see them.

Carol had a way of forgetting what had happened just the day before, starting over each day as if the previous day were simply a page in a book. If she didn't like how it went, she could just tear it out. Strangely, Oona soon realized, Gloria also shared this ability. Like an overwhelmed young mother, sometimes all Oona could do was watch and pray they didn't hurt themselves, all the time wondering who had learned the behavior from whom, always ready to kiss their skinned knees when they fell down.

It was an ability Oona did not share, this convenient situational amnesia, though she did try for a while to cultivate it. It seemed necessary in order to take part in the group's hijinks the way the others did, without a single care to the consequences. Wouldn't it be lovely to kiss a boy, if that were really all the others were doing—besides Truman, who boldly claimed to do everything everywhere with everyone—and feel no regret when you wipe your smeared lipstick on a lace handkerchief and move on to the next? Or to accept the free drinks the bar owners offered in exchange for telling their older friends, and to not feel instantly guilty about it?

She couldn't fathom how they did it, this continuous washing clean of their mental blackboards, starting over day by day, sometimes hour by hour, with fresh white chalk. It would make sense if it were a product of being their parents' children. But if that was the explanation, shouldn't it come just as naturally to her?

It made her think of her big brother. Her days floated above a near-constant undercurrent of concern for him. If it was possible, Shane was even less capable of casual self-preservation than she was. His soft heart never fully healed from an injury, and it had already taken more than its share of blows.

Bermuda, 1928

*O*nly Oona noticed when Shane slipped out of the house. He had taken to walking right out the front door on his own, wandering the beach and walking around the marketplace in town. When it got too hot, he would duck behind a building to dip from its barrel great ladles of rainwater sweetened by the purifying journey over the bright white steps of a limestone roof. He looked up at the pretty women, practicing a charming blink of the eyes and a forlorn expression to appeal to their feminine sides. He walked beside them, imagining they were his girlfriends. When he first began taking his solo sojourns, eight-year-old Shane would return furtively, closing the door carefully behind him to keep it from slamming and alerting Gaga he'd been gone. But he soon learned he need not be so careful. When he came back after hours of tromping from one end of town to the other, up and down the beach, through the market stalls and to the docks where the fisherman worked and cursed and smoked and drank, it was as if no one realized he'd been gone. Even Gaga, his darling, didn't mind his disappearances. She let him do whatever he wished. Boys wanted their freedom. At least with Gaga, he could do no wrong.

Oona however, could do plenty wrong, though she tried to be on her best behavior always. At two and a half, she constantly modified herself to fit the small quiet places between her parents' moods. She listened and observed, absorbing every emotion that hung in the charged atmosphere of her home.

Agnes sat on the edge of the bed and watched as Eugene lifted the contents of his bureau drawers one by one into a large steamer trunk.

"I'll let you know when I might be able to come back, Aggie," he said, rubbing his chin. "I'll make it quick. A few weeks at most." He turned and headed for the wardrobe to hide the falseness on his face.

Not one, but two of his plays, Marco Millions and Strange Interlude, were in rehearsals in New York. "They need me to oversee the productions. You must understand that!" He pulled out two linen shirts and frowned at the rumpled state of the collars.

Mother pulled at a loose thread in the quilt, her face mimicking the puckering of the fabric. She tried to smooth both out, but neither cooperated. She swiped at the offending snag and stood up.

"I do not understand, actually," she snapped. "You're already finished overseeing staging, and you told me weeks ago the backers were lined up straight, but now you have to go back? Why do they need you to come back again just now?"

That was a good question. However, Eugene didn't appreciate being questioned, nor blatantly called out. "I have asked you to come with me. Do you want me to ask again?" He tossed a stack of undershirts in the trunk. "All right, I will. Please, Agnes, would you come to New York?"

"To do what?" Agnes said. "To keep the children quiet so you can work? To play secretary?" She scoffed. "I don't think so. No, thank you."

Eugene raised his hands. "Then I don't know what you want me to tell you." He turned back to the wardrobe, pulling ties from their clips and imagining beautiful Carlotta waiting to put all his things in order for him when he got back to the city.

Agnes watched him dart around the room, pulling items from the drawer, from the wardrobe, from under the bed. His tongue clicked with dissatisfaction when he found his shoes there, and he looked pointedly at the sand on their heels, as if someone else had left them that way, then brushed them off with a careless swipe of his hand before tossing them in the trunk.

He was usually so fastidious about his packing. Something was wrong.

"Someone has to oversee the renovations here," she said. "There are workers in and out all day whether you're here or not, you know. And the children will get ill if they go from this weather to a New York winter." Her mind raced around all the possible arguments, while at the same time, another part of her wondered, *What exactly am I arguing for? There was another, excitement-loving side of her that understood if it hadn't been Eugene's idea to shift to New York, she might have suggested it herself. A visit to Point Pleasant and her family and friends could be lovely.*

Nevertheless, she held up her end of the argument, waved it ahead of herself like a bright red muleta.

Agnes saw their future moving into the rarified stratus they'd once roundly rejected. Eugene already moved in those circles, but without her, and with a practiced, performative disdain. Their lives were not the least bit affected by prohibition or any Great Depression besides the ones in Eugene's troubled mind.

❧

Oona lay in her bed listening for sounds from corners of the house. She heard glass shattering, paper tearing, Mother talking. Mother crying.

Gaga had bathed her and helped her pull on her soft nightgown, then tucked her in with an extra pat on her head.

"Now don't you bother about your mommy and daddy, Oona," Gaga said. She closed the curtains then turned and crossed her arms. She'd cared for many children in her time, but this one was different. Finely tuned to the adults, not so interested in other children. She watched her parents and their friends, mimicked their behavior—from the formal literary salon manners of the afternoons to the absurd tipsiness of the evenings, Oona had already, at two years old, learned how to please the adults with a tilt of her head, the widening of her eyes, and most effective of all, the composure of her smile. She wouldn't call her precocious. That was too common a term for this little one. Gaga had met many little girls whose feminine wiles appeared early and who practiced those skills

exclusively for their own purposes—to manipulate, to get what they wanted.

But Oona was different. Her social skills, so important to cultivate in female children, were certainly on par with those other little girls, but Oona's unique disposition was unselfish. Undoubtedly, she charmed adults, but she seemed more interested in their happiness than her own. Her sole purpose with each new day was to seek out the parent who seemed most distracted and cross and to simply be with them, adding her sweet company to the room whether noticed or not. She brought an atmosphere of calm energy when she quietly played in a corner or gently stroked a stray island cat. In everything she did was that same innocent charm. When the adults were happy; she was happy. So really one might argue hers was as selfish a personality as that of most any four-year-old children. The difference in this girl, Gaga had come to think, was that Oona seemed only to see herself exclusively through the eyes of others, more so than any other little girl she had cared for. It was as if she didn't exist without the approving glance of her parents, especially her father. Oona tended to hold her natural emotions inside when other children might devolve into tantrums. It made her job much easier, but Gaga wondered how this personality would serve Oona when she wasn't so little any more.

Gaga sat on the edge of the child's bed. "Do you promise to go to sleep, Oona?" she said.

Oona tucked her chin below the blanket and half-closed her dark eyes. The blanket smelled like lavender and ocean.

"Oona-a-a..." Gaga said. She lifted the child's chin with one finger. "Do you promise?"

"Yes, Gaga," Oona said, and offered her sweetest smile. But inside, she worried that if she kept her promise and went to sleep, she would miss something important. The nanny finally left, closing the door with a soft click.

Oona held her body stiff and straight, straining to hear what was happening outside her room. After a while, she made out the sound of footsteps—Mother paced the hall, up and down, back and forth. On one pass, the footsteps stopped and started, first outside her door, then outside Shane's. Finally, Mother's bedroom door creaked, then clicked shut.

Her toes wriggled against the soft sheets. She closed her eyes, sighed, then opened her eyes again. She blinked and remembered her promise, then closed her eyes again with purpose. After listening so intently, the quiet now was too quiet.

She slipped out of bed and crossed to Shane's door, dragging her blanket behind her. She pushed open his door and blinked into the darkness until she could see the edge of his bed.

"Shane?" she whispered. There was no answer. "Shane?" She stepped into the room and crossed toward her brother's bed. When her feet left the hardwood floor and found the rough bedside rug where her brother kept his slippers, she realized she'd forgotten to put hers on.

"Shane, I sleep here please?" she whispered. She pulled her blanket closer. "Shane?" Her eyes adjusted to the darkness and a look of confusion and fear crossed her face.

The blanket was rumpled and thrown back, but Shane wasn't there.

☙❧

When he got home from his wandering, Shane found Oona sleeping in his bed.

"What are you doing here?"

Her brother's whisper easily roused Oona from a fitful sleep, but he poked her in the shoulder for good measure.

"I was looking for you." Oona murmured, rubbing her eyes. Moonlight streamed from the window. "Where were you?

"I was outside. Just walking," he said. "It was too loud around here."

Oona lay still, hoping he wouldn't tell her to go back to her own bed. In the shadows, he took off his clothes. The briny scent of the sea wafted as he pulled off his shirt off, and she listened as clumps of sand sprinkled to the floor from the damp cuffs of his jeans.

"Scoot over," he said, and Oona obeyed. He slid into bed beside her, crossing his arms behind his head for a pillow so she could have his. He was quiet for a few moments, his breathing reassuring and steady in the dark, and Oona began to drift to sleep. But then he spoke again, into the darkness.

"I don't want things to change," he said. "I don't know why they can't be happy. Why can't it be like before, forever?"

He sniffled, and Oona's heart broke. She didn't know what to say. Shane's voice held a sadness deeper than her young mind could fathom, different from the young boy's voice she knew as his. He sounded like someone else, though she couldn't make it out at first. Then she knew all at once. He sounded just like Daddy.

Her heart pressed against her chest with the need to help him, to make him feel happy again. What could she do? She was powerless, like when she dropped her porcelain baby doll on the tile floor and its face cracked right across the middle. She could try smiling at him, but it was too dark, and anyway that never really worked with Shane. He probably didn't even know she was awake any more. And if he did, and if he knew she'd heard him, he might send her back to her own room. She pulled her blanket to her lips, and stayed quiet. Maybe if they could fall asleep at the same time, they could both have the same dream and be happy together again for a little while.

Key West, 1931

*O*ona woke up to a thump when the small plane landed, twisting slightly to slow itself as the engine juddered. The smell of tires on hot asphalt filled the cabin, reminding her of the bicycle she'd left behind in Point Pleasant.

"Are we there, Nanny?" She yawned and rubbed her eyes.

"Yes, dear," the nanny said. Since Gaga, there had been a few new women brought in to help care for Oona, and she'd taken to calling them all 'Nanny' when she spoke to them. In her head, they were "New Nanny" until they'd been around a little while. They always looked so put out when she mistakenly called them 'Gaga,' and it was easier to call them 'Nanny' than to learn and unlearn new nicknames all the time. New Nanny rifled through her purse for a tissue, spat a piece of chewing gum into it, dropped the tissue in the purse, and clicked it shut with a metallic snap. Oona rubbed her eyes again.

"Don't do that, dear. You'll pull your skin and get wrinkles some day."

"Is that what happened to your eyes, Nanny?"

The woman pulled her sunglasses down and stuck out her tongue. Oona giggled.

"So this is Key West?" Oona looked out the window. "The sun is very bright here. It's like Bermuda."

Nanny nodded, a sort of sideways nod.

The palm trees along the edge of the runway passed by her window, casting shadows in the plane like the flicker of a movie (dark, light, dark, light). Just last week, she'd seen one of those little films when she went with New Nanny to the market. They'd been walking by a theater and the sound of a lively piano drifted from inside, calling to them.

"Listen, Oona," New Nanny had said. She had a very thick Boston accent and Oona's ear hadn't quite adjusted to it just yet. "We'll stawp at the nickelodeon first, but don't tell anyone, ya r'understand?" She took Oona's quizzical eyebrows to mean she might not grasp the finer points of subterfuge. "Oh, nevah mind then..."

"No, no!" Oona countered. "I won't tell anyone."

At first Nanny wasn't sure, having had experience with little girls with powers of manipulation beyond their years. Those little heathens would work a poor nanny for treats before bedtime or a skipped bath only to sell them out with a shameless show of tears when the mister and missus caught on. This little girl's smile seemed genuine, though, with her big dark eyes and mournful mouth, so she had trusted her after all, and they'd enjoyed a silly movie about a man with a bowler top hat and cane who waddled around making delightful faces at pretty ladies. The man had a comical brush mustache and he wore shoes that were too big and on the wrong feet, and he would fall down and get right back up as if nothing had happened. Oona laughed until tears came to her eyes. She hadn't wanted it to end.

As the plane lurched to a stop, Oona thought back to her mother's words when she'd said good-bye. Oona knew she was being sent off to boarding school now that her parents' divorce was settled, and Daddy agreed to pay for "decent schools." Mother may not have known she listened at doors, but she didn't try very hard to keep the children from hearing when she talked about their father.

"So now, darling," Agnes said, "you're becoming a big girl, and it's most important for you to be educated. Do you understand?"

Oona nodded, though she knew she shouldn't have since it wasn't really true. She didn't understand why she couldn't stay home and read books to be educated. After all, what more was there to learn than what could be found in a room full of books?

The Mother Superior of the Key West convent school had personally called Agnes on the convent's new telephone line immediately upon receipt of Agnes's telegram inquiry, a note of excitement in her voice when she confirmed Oona's surname.

"Yes, Mother Superior, that Eugene O'Neill. The Nobel Prize winner, yes. Indeed." Mother had rolled her eyes, holding the collar of her blouse up to her chin to imitate a wimple, as Oona giggled. The Mother Superior's thrilled response filled the room, as if she felt it necessary to project her voice in order to *reach the whimsically named, faraway town of Point Pleasant, New Jersey.*

"Who would have thought the Sisters of the Southernmost Point—or whatever they're called—were such fans of the great and powerful Eugene O'Neill?" Agnes said as she hung up the phone.

The convent school building was three stories tall with a verandah along the entire bottom level and a balcony stretching above for the second floor. Great arched windows marched along the windblown façade. Oona held New Nanny's hand and climbed a two-story staircase, winding toward a gabled central rotunda topped with an open cupola which, under less intimidated circumstances, might make the perfect setting for a swashbuckling sword fight or a beautiful damsel's captivity. To their left, the face of the building was softened by a curved corner feature offering a covered balcony space to each floor. A wide, cone-shaped spire guarded by a metal cross seemed to bend toward them. Oona leaned back, holding on to her hat, trying to see to the top, but the white sun in a piercing blue sky shot dark streaks through her vision.

"Come along, Oona," New Nanny said. "What's the matter with you?"

"Nothing," Oona said, blinking. She didn't want to say she was dizzy with the Mother Superior standing just there.

By noon, Oona had been introduced to the Head Mistress and marched around the entire campus. New Nanny saw her to her room and took her leave, promising to come by the next day before she flew home, but when she leaned close to give Oona a parting hug,

Oona caught sight of a bathing suit strap under the woman's prim cotton shift. Devoted as she was to her young charges, the nursemaid was not one to waste a free trip to paradise.

Only one day ago, Oona had felt the cold wind on her face at The Old House in Point Pleasant. Now it seemed a world away. Her new room was sparse and humid, with thick ivory walls that appeared to move closer every time Oona closed and opened her eyes. She sat on the edge of her strange new bed and tried to recall every corridor and door they had passed through on their way into the dormitory.

She went to sleep that night determined to figure the fastest way out as soon as possible.

The fastest way out came sooner than she'd expected. First thing the next morning, she lined up with the other girls and filed into the chapel for morning vespers, silent and barely breathing. An organ droned chords with no discernible melody as the girls arranged themselves in the pews, and little boys in white frocks lit candles below a huge bronze crucifix. Soon everyone rose from their seats, so Oona did the same, and a man in robes walked down the center aisle carrying a pole from which he waved something that looked like an oversized tea ball. It appeared to be on fire because puffs of white smoke streamed from each of the precise little holes that covered its surface. As the man passed, she realized he must be the priest, and therefore the man in charge. A strong aroma wafted through the air as he passed and Oona held her breath. The fire ball must contain some sort of oil. The priest waved the ball slowly from side to side, and Oona shuffled back, alarmed, holding her breath even harder.

The chapel grew dim, and she thought someone must have turned off the lights. Sparkly stars appeared, and before she knew what had happened, her eyes opened to a view of the chapel ceiling, vaulted and spinning, and then the face of the Mother Superior peering down at her from inside the frame of her wimple. It all struck Oona as ridiculously funny, and she laughed, quietly at first, and then more loudly, until Oona's headmistress scooped her up and carried her down the aisle, out of the chapel, and directly to the infirmary. Oona again held her breath, only this time to keep herself from laughing any more.

Telegrams flew between Agnes and the Mother Superior, and Oona soon found herself waiting on the school's verandah, her bags packed, watching wild Key West chickens peck the gravel. They reminded her of home.

She missed Bermuda.

Point Pleasant

AND MANHATTAN, 1931

*E*verywhere *they went in Point Pleasant, in the shops with their empty shelves and in the few cafés and diners still open, people in ragged clothes and tattered shoes huddled together, murmuring about something called "the depression."*

Depression, depression, depression.

In Oona's mind, the Depression took on the form of a dark cloud hanging low, making people look tired and thin, or like they had seen a ghost. After the daunting experience of her convent school, Oona's pale countenance and drawn, worried expression fit right in with those of the downtrodden residents aimlessly walking up and down the main street of West Point Pleasant.

Oona yearned to go to the water. The rushing waves of Jenkinson's Beach reminded her of happy times in Bermuda, when every corner of her life was completely furnished with the faces she loved. Her parents might have been busy, leaving her to Gaga's care more often than her infant heart wanted, but

she could always look for them and find them somewhere. Even when Daddy was away for one of his plays,
she could find his picture in every room. Now Mother
didn't even like the scrapbook in the house. She turned
the page with a terrible crumple when she saw him in
the newspaper. Oona dug the pages out of the trash
and smoothed them out with the big girl hands that
had replaced the chubby baby ones she used to have
in Bermuda.

She begged for a beach day with all the family,
especially her favorite girl cousin Dallas, but to no
avail. Mother had been working hard on a book about
a road trip through Florida ever since visiting Shane's
military school down there, and she also needed time
to investigate new boarding schools for both of her
younger children, all while planning a solo writing
retreat to Spithead.

There simply was no time for a beach day. There
was no time for anything exciting at all.

But then out of the blue, a miracle! Oona and Shane
had been invited to their father's Manhattan apartment for lunch. Before Agnes could finish reading the
invitation aloud in clipped, sarcastic tones, Oona was
flying around the house, pulling her best dress from
the closet and tracking down her good Mary Janes.
They would need to be polished. Was there enough
time? And where were Shane's good shoes?

She and Shane were both just back from failed
attempts at boarding, with Shane having left his latest
military school in St. Petersburg and Oona swooning
her way out of the convent in Key West. Shane banked
on his father's ignorance of his behavior at school,

having heard his father had told the headmaster not to contact him regarding Shane's exploits any more. Had he heard about her embarrassing fainting episode? Oona was determined to make the most of the visit, to make a good impression on her handsome, intelligent daddy, the man from her scrapbook, but she worried that Shane would misbehave. Then they'd never be invited back to their father's house. She hardly breathed until the next day, her stomach in knots until she was standing in the dining room of Daddy's beautiful new apartment.

Carlotta had decided on a dish of kidneys for this lunch with Eugene's children. The table was set with flowers and cloth napkins, and the silverware glittered with a Park Avenue shine. As they crossed the fine rug to take their seats, Oona's stomach tightened again. How long would Shane be able to keep up his best behavior? He made a face at her across the gleaming table, and Oona warned him with a pleading stare.

"What's all this they say about you fainting at school, Oona?" Eugene said by way of a conversation opener. He spread a napkin across his narrow lap and tucked into his plate.

Shane looked surprised, then relieved, then perversely disappointed. He sank in his chair. Oona smoothed her own napkin and cleared her throat. She tried to remember the last time she'd seen her father. What was it she used to do that always made him smile? She stared at her plate. A single purplish-brown kidney lay in the center of it.

"Yes, Daddy," she said feebly. "I fainted from the smell of the smoke."

"You mean the 'incense,'" Eugene said, glancing up from his own plate.

"Yes, sir," Oona said. "I mean 'yes, Daddy.'" Carlotta watched her with a subtle, piercing gaze, so Oona picked up her fork and knife and changed the subject. "Where do kidneys come from?"

Carlotta made a snorting sound. "Don't tell me you've never heard of kidneys?" She took a small, mincing bite from the tip of her fork.

Eugene stopped chewing. "Why, they come from pigs, cows, pretty much all animals, really. They clean bad things out of the blood." He patted his own flanks.

Oona half-closed her eyes. "Oh."

"Yeah," Shane said, "and then the bad stuff comes out when you—" He pointed to his lap.

"Shane," Eugene warned.

"What?" Shane sank in his chair again, then added under his breath. "That's what happens."

Shane's self-control was starting to fade. Carlotta shook her head just slightly. Oona swallowed slowly. "Oh, yes. I see." Just as she'd feared, she would have to be extra good, for the both of them. She looked at Carlotta and smiled, then took another tentative bite.

Could it be they were teasing her, all in on it together? If it had only been Shane, she might have believed she'd been tricked, but Daddy and Carlotta seemed quite serious. Daddy even described what it was that kidneys did for the body. Oona's back began to ache thinking about it, tender little red organs filtering all the bad things out of her blood, making the yellow water that filled her bladder with the same liquid that made the alleys smell dirty and sour. Why would anyone eat those? But Carlotta seemed to find them delightful. They must be a very fancy food indeed. Shane gobbled them up, but Oona couldn't tell if he actually liked them or wanted to be rid of them as quickly as he could. As the table conversation went on around her, she focused on the perfect floral centerpieces and shining candlesticks and took bite after bite until her plate was clean. Carlotta noticed and, to Oona's horror, told the server to give her another serving.

After the meal, Carlotta called for Eugene's chauffeur to take them all out for a ride in Daddy's new Cadillac for a drive through Central Park. All the while, the image of those two kidneys danced around in Oona's head. She felt every cobble stone in the road and struggled to control her throat. Down, down, stay down. She distracted herself by thinking of other things, such as how this new car must be why Daddy didn't like to pay Mother her alimony. He must have been trying to save up all along for the Cadillac, and of course a chauffeur to drive it properly.

Distraction wasn't working. She could not stop thinking about kidneys. She tried lying to herself.

Surely, they had been teasing her.

"Oh, driver, do avoid the area where the Blacks congregate, won't you?" Carlotta said blithely, patting the dark curls which snaked around her ear.

The words caused a wave of disgust to rise in Oona's throat. Beads of sweat formed on her forehead.

The thought of being sick in front of her father—

As the thought entered her mind, she could not control it any more. Her lunch came up, projecting *all over the back of the car, over Carlotta's fur blanket, onto Daddy's shoes. Carlotta shouted in her melodramatic manner, "GOOD GOD, CHILD! Why didn't you SAY SOMETHING? We could have stopped the car. You must have KNOWN you felt sick!" She gaped at the damage Oona had done to Eugene's NEW CAR. Eugene let out an awful, low groan, and Carlotta gathered herself somewhat, eyeing Eugene as she softened her voice. "It's not her fault," she said. "She felt sick, but why didn't she SAY SOMETHING?"*

Oona pulled a handkerchief from her coat pocket and wiped her mouth, wishing she could escape the wretched closeness of Daddy's ruined Cadillac and let Central Park swallow her whole.

Chapter 8

ONLY SIXTEEN

Late Summer, 1941

The taxi pulled to the curb and Oona grinned out the window. She flung open the door, jumped out, suitcase and travel case in hand, and hurried through the doors of Grand Central Station.

The big day was here. Her calendar was full of thick black *X*s leading up to today's date, the box she'd filled with exclamation points after reading her father's letter way back in spring. She could hardly believe it. She was on the way to her father's house—in California! The pocket calendar was extra, a talisman she could pull out of her handbag and check whenever she doubted this day would come. She certainly didn't need the extra help keeping track of the days since Daddy's letter arrived—*Daddy's* letter, not one of Carlotta's snippy missives that always started with a sour "Dear Child"—bringing the news that her father wanted to see her. Finally!

It had been a year of confounding near misses and confusing correspondences with "Tao House," the name Daddy and Carlotta had given their home in Danville. A full year ago, Carlotta had replied to one of Oona's letters to her father, stating in secretarial terms that her father would be writing soon to confirm plans for her summer visit. Oona could hardly believe it. She waited for that letter, checking the mail after school every day for six months, sometimes making the trip to Mother's apartment, which stood largely empty, in case his reply had come there. One day in March, a short note finally arrived. Daddy said he and Carlotta expected visitors to stay at Tao House that summer, but she could come for a visit after they all left—at the end of summer.

Oona replayed the words of that letter in her mind several times a day: "...I will pay your fare, and you can stay for a week, perhaps ten days," and "... very happy with your fine school work this year..." and "It has been too long since the last time..."

She calculated how long it had actually been from the running tally etched in the back of her mind. Eight years. It had been more than eight years since she'd seen her father. How many letters had she written and sent over those years, asking to visit them? She'd lost count. When they lived in Sea Island, on the Georgia coast, after building their palatial, twenty-two-room house, she'd written regularly. Carlotta inevitably replied that it was 'not a good time.' Reading her letters, Oona cringed at herself, at her own desperation. Still she persisted. Over and over the same requests and the same responses. Daddy *had* replied himself once, but it was only to offer an explanation that made no sense at all: "It is all right for Shane to visit here in the summer, because he is so much more grown than you, but I am afraid the sudden change to this climate would not be a good thing for you until you are a little older."

How she wished to be older then. If her age was all that kept her from her father's house, why, it was absolutely too unfair to bear! She wished for some clue that would help her become more acceptable in Daddy's eyes. Or rather, in Carlotta's eyes, for Oona sometimes wondered whether it was Carlotta who didn't want a pesky little kid around.

There was nothing she could do but write more letters, filling them full of fine grammar and mature topics such as the latest literature and the state of the economy, each of them ending with a fresh request to be allowed to come, please, just for a short visit. Finally her persistence paid off. Daddy had actually written his own letter to her, by his own hand. He hadn't left it to Carlotta. Oona read it over and over, putting aside her confusion at his odd comment that he "hadn't heard from her in so long that he could not imagine she wanted to come visit him in California!" That didn't matter now. The important thing was he said yes!

Her chest filled with exploding fireworks. Was it possible for a heart to explode with joy?

So, the end of summer it was. Anything else she might have had planned could go suck an egg as far as she was concerned. Everything would be different from now on. She was going to see Daddy. In California!

She presented her ticket and was admitted to the vaulted terminal that led on to the platform for the

20th Century Limited, Westbound Train 25, the train which would carry her on the first leg of a three-day journey (barring any delays). As the soles of her shoes met the wooden platform, the weight of this journey began to settle across her shoulders, pulling her body out of the perfect posture she cultivated so carefully. She stopped and looked all around, amazed to have made it here, ready to travel across the country, the only daughter of the great Eugene O'Neill on her first solo adventure.

Like a long-held dream crystallizing before her eyes, everything she hoped life would hold for her–love, security, acceptance, family–depended on this visit with Daddy. She caught her reflection in the window of a boxcar, then she unclasped her handbag and retrieved a lipstick, using the glass as a mirror as she applied a fresh layer of coral red. Her favorite lipstick set off her blue traveling suit perfectly, and the effect calmed her. Mother always told other people that Daddy used to think his daughter was a beautiful child. Would he still think so? She pressed her lips together, clicked the lid onto the tube, and dropped it back into her bag.

Hers was the first train out of this platform today, being the main line to Chicago which would deliver passengers to connections to points south and west. In Chicago, Oona would disembark and switch to the Santa Fe Railroad's *Super Chief* train to Los Angeles, The journey would take the Atchison, Topeka, and Santa Fe Grand Canyon route through states Oona had only seen on the big screen, or read about in

Willa Cather's stories. The news had thrilled Carol to no end.

"So many celebrities take that train to cross the country, they call it 'The Train of the Stars,'" Carol said, her voice dreamy, as if the image of the voyage appeared in her mind covered in a layer of silky gauze. "Oh, I do wish I were going with you!" Her friend was happy for her, but she and Oona were close enough friends that she felt no need to hide her envy. She had jumped off her fluffy pink bed and swayed side to side in front of her book case, searching for one in particular.

"Here it is!" She pulled a thick volume from a middle shelf and dropped it on the bedspread with a triumphant thump. "This will be the perfect read for your journey."

Oona smoothed a hand over the book cover showing a droopy man and his weary family gazing at a long trail of beat-up cars making its way over a barren prairie. "*The Grapes of Wrath*," she read dubiously. "Is there romance?"

"Not really. But I cried and cried endlessly," she said, waving her arms as if addressing a crowd. Her eyes widened and she waggled her eyebrows. "And just wait till you read the *end*!"

"Sounds swell." Oona waggled her own eyebrows to mirror Carol's, and the girls dissolved in giggles.

"We will make that thoroughly glamorous journey together some day, Carol," Oona said. "Pinky promise."

Now, Oona patted the side of her bag and felt the book's reassuring outline. She found an unoccupied bench and sat in the middle of it, hoping to send a subtle message that the whole seat was taken. Then she began watching people, listening to snippets of conversation. The best stories were always the ones overheard. Plus, the sound of other people's voices, voices from outside of herself, was strangely reassuring. She inhaled, feeling her lungs fill completely for the first time since Daddy's letter.

The air was thick with the smell of hot metal tinged with a faint whiff of urine. Anxious passengers milled around the platforms in their best traveling clothes, checking and rechecking their billets against the signs hanging from chains above the tracks. They clutched their bags until they were relieved by the porters weaving their carts through the gathering crowd. A small family found a space on another bench and Oona watched the father deal with a porter who carried off their small trunks while the mother tied a rope around her toddling son's waist, tethering him while she soothed a fussing baby with her pinky between his bright red gums. Oona imagined what their home might look like. Probably comfortable and clean, she thought, but also cramped with two cribs and piles of baby clothes in various stages of launder.

Another man sat at the end of the family's bench, eating a pastrami sandwich. He spread the waxed paper wrapping across his lap as a napkin, and a rye seed from the crust of the bread stuck to his lip as he chewed. While she waited for it to fall off, Oona imagined the man's wife had packed that sandwich for his trip, but the thought of it in his bag wouldn't leave him alone and he couldn't wait to eat it. When he told her about it some time after he returned home, she would be peeved that he hadn't saved it till further along in his journey, but she'd be so glad he was home safe that she would pat him playfully on the shoulder, and most likely make him another sandwich.

She checked the clock, then her watch. That morning, she'd been so anxious about running late, she'd rushed to get ready and wound up making it to the station an hour early. She checked her purse for the ticket for the hundredth time, looked at the date on the pocket calendar for the thousandth, opened her purse unnecessarily and snapped it closed again. She fought the urge to tell strangers she was going to see her father.

Finally, a conductor threw open a door and called into the terminal.

"All aboard to Chicago and points West, boarding now. This way, please, this way!"

The train's interior was another world. With the latest in fashionable Art Deco style, all done in velvety blues and grays with gilded trims, the effect more sumptuous and elegant than the lobbies of most uptown buildings. Oona couldn't resist running a finger over everything as she passed through to her sleeping car, carrying her travel case close and nodding 'how do you do' to everyone she passed.

Out the window of her Pullman car, America passed by. The tracks rolled on endlessly, each spike hammered down by some calloused, anonymous hand. So much beauty, yet so much pain. Here were small towns with windblown, abandoned main streets and there were ambitious little cities where few boarded and not a soul disembarked. None resembled the iridescent bubble that was New York City. Harsh scenes flashed by, frame by frame, telling without words the devastating story of the Dust Bowl and the Great Depression. A stark reality lived deep in the hollow, hungry eyes of skeleton people wandering through shantytowns, dressed in ragged clothes and rat skin hats. Children played kick-the-can and stick ball in the narrow lanes, and Oona recalled reading that flour mills had begun printing cheerful patterns on their sacks when they learned the rough fabric was being repurposed as dresses and overalls for their customers' children. Oona absently stroked the soft fabric of her own sleeve cuffs and wondered at the stroke of some magic pen that had put her on the other side of the glass from so near a fate.

At night, Oona read the book Carol had given her, *The Grapes of Wrath*, and the desperate truth of it all settled in her heart as an impotent fear, setting off dreams of a very different life, of milking cows and carrying the tins for miles to town, along a narrow dirt road, like her mother had done before she left it all. Before she left her first daughter behind with her parents and went in search of a new life in Greenwich Village, where she'd met a young man, a promising playwright named Eugene O'Neill, and jumped at the chance to start over.

Despite the desperate faces and ramshackle homes that flickered in and out of view, the journey to California was a marvel. In only three days, Oona thought as the middle of America whizzed by her window, she would be in San Francisco. The vast spaces between where she now lived and where Daddy made his home with the woman he chose over his family seemed as large as the gulf between their hearts. It had been so long since she had seen him, so very long since she'd heard from him in a meaningful way. She knew him from articles in the paper and pictures in magazines, and even those were few and far between.

The days when she would carefully clip any mention of Eugene O'Neill— a new play, a well-reviewed production—and paste them in that scrapbook now seemed in the distant, childish past. How tired her friends had grown of hearing her talk about him, and about how he would come see her if only he weren't so very busy. He was an important man, after all. A genius. The family of a genius must be understanding and accommodating. It was their part to play for the sake of the art. But her friends, even those whose own parents were divorced, couldn't understand a father so busy he couldn't come for school functions, for the holidays, for her birthday.

She let herself imagine the moment they would see each other again. Surely he would smile at her and say how proud he was of his little girl now all grown up, how he realized and regretted missing so much. He would finally see her again in person and then things would be different. He would notice all she had done to make herself worthy of his admiration. He appreciated ambition and self-sufficiency. She had ambition, even if she didn't quite know where to focus it. He could help her with that, once he knew her better. And she tried to be self-sufficient, as much as she could be. She'd make him as proud of her as she was of him. She spent the days watching and thinking, trying to memorize the things she would tell Daddy when she saw him. She wondered what he would think of her Park Avenue accent? It had gotten very convincing, what with the close proximity to Gloria and Carol.

When fellow passengers made conversation with her, whether in the dining car or other cars, Oona listened politely to their stories before announcing, "I'm going to see my father!" By the time she reached California, she'd talked so much about him, without mentioning his name, that they were obliged to wish her a lovely visit with her daddy along with their good-byes.

⚮

A man in a linen suit held a card with "O'Neill" neatly printed in black block letters.

"Miss O'Neill?"

Oona smiled. *Daddy sent a car!*

"Yes! Oh, yes, that's me!" she said.

"I'm Henry. I'll be taking you the rest of the way, to Mr. O'Neill's residence." He picked up her bag, and reached for her travel case.

"Oh, no, thank you," she said, gripping the case tighter. "I'll just keep this with me if that's all right." The case held all her favorite lipsticks, and she'd kept it close by the whole way to California. It was too precious to ride in the trunk of a car.

Hank tipped his hat and opened the car door with a grand sweep. "Are you sure you're here for Miss O'Neill?" she asked discreetly. "Oona O'Neill?"

"Yes, Miss O'Neill. And is this your only luggage?" He cast a politely dubious glance at her suitcase.

She nodded. *Should I have packed more?* She was used to traveling light, for weekends in Point Pleasant, since she had a few things that stayed there always. Her stomach twisted: perhaps she wasn't as prepared as she thought. All at once, the distance between herself and her home grew even more vast than she realized.

"I'm sure you can obtain anything you may need once you're settled in at Tao House."

Oona couldn't place Henry's accent. All around her were palm trees and clear, blazing sunshine that gave the impression she may have gotten off the train in a different country altogether. She inhaled sharply. Even the air was different here, light and lemony, like a balm.

Gloria was somewhere in California, too, visiting her mother for the first time since she was small, since the infamous custody trial. The coincidence meant she had at least one friend in this other-worldly place. She wondered if Gloria found it as strange as she did.

The hot car seat burned through her cotton dress. She leaned back and inhaled the scent of warm leather and Hank's Aqua Velva. She closed her eyes, just to rest them for a moment, and missed the entire drive, waking up to find the car stopped outside her father's home. After imagining the place for so long, it could have been a dream. But it was solid, not blurry at the edges like dreams were. She blinked awake and gathered her things, no time to check her face, then followed Henry up the path to the front door. It opened as if by itself before a small woman appeared in the doorway.

Carlotta.

She was as beautiful as her photos, with shining dark hair and penetrating, sharp brown eyes. She stood stiffly, her chin raised at an elegantly haughty angle, and aimed an air-kiss over each of Oona's shoulders.

"Welcome to our home, child," she said. "How was your trip?" Her words were clipped and her voice extravagantly showy.

Oona peered around the foyer and down the main hall.

"It was fine, thank you," she said. "Where is Daddy?"

"He will be out very soon, child. He asked not to be disturbed until he takes his afternoon break."

"Oh," Oona said, "I see." Her legs tingled.

"Now let me show you where you will stay," Carlotta said.

Oona followed as Carlotta swept through to the end of a hallway. "This is the guest room," Carlotta said, dispelling any idea Oona might have that a room had been set aside for Eugene's only daughter when he had this house built.

"Thank you, Carlotta."

But Carlotta had already left, closing the door behind her with the abrupt finality of a judge's gavel. Oona looked around the tidy little room and wished she could go back and start over. She wished she were back on the train, when the joyful front-door reunion she had imagined was still a possibility.

❦

Daddy appeared just before dinner, with tired eyes and a drawn, far-away expression, but he patted her back when she hugged him, and Oona's eyes shone as she heard his voice for the first time since she was a child.

He didn't look anything like the photos she had pasted in her scrapbook. Instead of sharing the stories she wanted to share with him, the carefully planned narratives she'd added to a mental list of Things Which Should Impress Daddy, she kept quiet and listened while he complained about how poorly the day's work had gone.

"Too many distractions!" he said. Carlotta looked at her pointedly, then looked away. Daddy gave her shoulder a preoccupied pat, and she smiled up at him, but he had turned away.

At the dinner table, Oona's face set with determination. Surely she could change his mood. She had taken extra care getting ready to see him. Her dress was crisp and fresh, her shoes polished of traveling dust, and her makeup perfect. She wore a sheer berry lipstick, pretty yet not too grown up.

"Well. Oona." His long, thin fingers fiddled with the silverware. "I hope your journey was fine."

"Yes, and we know you will want to get back East soon, to spend the rest of the summer in Point

Pleasant," Carlotta said, covering a snicker with her napkin.

"I don't mind The Old House so much," Oona said brightly. "Point Pleasant has its own sort of charm."

Eugene inhaled sharply and glanced sidelong at Carlotta before looking down again at his plate.

Oona's chest tightened, and her stomach followed. *No, please, not now.* She glanced out the window, over the view of a valley grove full of fruit trees toward Mount Diablo in the distance, searching for solid ground.

"Yes, Agnes's family home," Carlotta drew delicate quotes over her plate and smirked.

"It's quite nice there, really," Oona said. "I rather miss it when I go away." *Is it hot in here? It feels pretty hot.*

"Well, dear," Carlotta said. "If you're missing it too much, we would understand if you feel you'd like to go back early."

The room seemed darker than it had moments ago, complete with little stars dancing in front of her eyes. "Daddy?"

"Oh, your daddy agrees," Carlotta said. "Isn't that right, Gene, dear?"

"Oona, have you heard from Vassar yet?" Eugene said, wiping his mouth and replacing the cloth napkin across his bony lap. He didn't look well, but his face blurred as Oona's vision grew watery.

"No, Daddy, not yet," she said. The room was spinning now.

"All right," Eugene said, chewing slowly. "Well, when you do, have them send me the bills."

"That's right," Carlotta said. "I'll send the payments to the school. Directly."

Oona nodded, and then began to list forward. She swallowed and made a small catching sound in her throat. Carlotta looked up, then glanced at Eugene, who hadn't noticed anything amiss with his daughter at the other end of the table. She leaned across to Oona, mouthing the words, "Are you quite all right?"

Oona shook her head almost imperceptibly. *Why? Why now?* She'd waited so long for the chance to do this, to sit at the table with her father, just simply to talk. The slight head movement made her swoon. Closing her eyes made it worse, but opening them... Carlotta stood.

"If you're done with your meal, child, I'll show you where you can find everything. Get you settled in for...however long you're staying." She put an arm through Oona's and helped her up, leading her out of the room before Eugene noticed anything amiss. In the hall, she stopped while Oona leaned against the wall, taking deep breaths.

"Your father does not like to be disturbed or worried," Carlotta whispered loudly. "I thought it best to get you out of there to deal with...whatever is happening...in private." She dabbed her own forehead dramatically with the back of her hand. "We don't want a repeat of what happened last time." Carlotta was never going to let her live down the kidney incident.

"Thank you, Carlotta," Oona said. The walls were slowing down and the stars fading. "I would have died if I'd fainted in front of him."

"You're a sensitive soul then," Carlotta said. "Like your father. Here, take these towels and get in the bath. You'll be better after a soak, and I'll tell your father you'll come for your hour when you're done."

"My hour?"

"Yes, child, your hour," Carlotta retrieved a small container from the medicine cabinet and handed it to Oona. It was a beautiful little glass vial with a turquoise horse shoe encrusted on its brass lid. "Smelling salts. You must open that and take a sniff when you feel woozy, please." She bustled to the cabinet and pulled out a basket of toiletries. Oona opened the vial and took a whiff, and her eyes opened wide. Carlotta placed the basket beside the tub.

"I trust you brought slippers?"

"Oh," Oona said, suddenly worried. "I like to go barefoot."

"Barefoot?" Her shoulders shuddered as if Oona had announced a predilection for wallowing in slop. "That won't do. We will have to find you some slippers." Oona tried to picture the contents of her bag. Had she brought ankle socks, at least?

"Your father has set aside an entire hour in the evenings while you're here, to spend time with you," Carlotta went on. "It's different today, since you've just arrived and there's nothing to be done about that, but the remaining days, however many they are—but no more than ten—he'll see you before dinner, in the garden, or on the verandah." She finally stopped whisking about and Oona's woozy head settled like a spent spinning top. "Isn't that so wonderful of him?" Carlotta said. She didn't sound like she thought it was so wonderful. "He's extremely busy, you know."

"Yes, Carlotta. I know. Thank you." The color began to return to her cheeks. Steam rose from the tub as it filled with a growing mound of bubbles, and a surge of gratitude toward Carlotta replaced the jittering feeling in her belly. Maybe a bath could change everything. She needed to wash this day off and start over.

In the tub, Oona hugged her knees to her chest and tried to turn off the questions filling her mind. Sparse islands of weak bubbles floated on the surface of the tepid water like survivors of a shipwreck, and she shivered, watching the goosebumps rise on her skin. How long had she been sitting here? And now what? She'd set so much store on this reunion with Daddy, and already it was going downhill, on the first day. What could she do to turn things around, to keep this whole visit from turning out like tonight?

☙❧

The days passed like dry sand slipping from her fingers. It was as if her father couldn't bear to look at her for too long, and when he did look at her, his jaw was tense and his hands clenched, even if she hadn't said a word. Before coming here, she could blame the physical distance between them for the misinterpretations and the coldness that grew with each passing year. If only she could get to him, see him in person, they would talk and laugh together, filling every moment with shared understanding like two sides of the same brain. But this was nothing like that. Nothing she tried worked. Nothing she said was right. What was it he wanted to hear?

Carlotta made an occupation of reminding Oona that her father was a very busy man, an artistic genius, that his process must not be disturbed. She spent her days replying to correspondences and keeping the home running well. Oona couldn't imagine her mother ever having done any of this for her father. Perhaps if she had...

Oona had learned what she could about Carlotta over the years, most of it from the newspapers. She had renamed herself after a glamorous California town. As Carlotta Monterey, she'd been a promising actress, and she'd starred in one of Eugene's plays before Oona was even born. Before meeting Daddy, she had been married to an artist named Ralph Barton, a well-known illustrator at *The New Yorker.* They hosted legendary parties for the toast of Manhattan, including movie stars and politicians and socialites. At least, that's what the papers said, and Oona pasted the articles in the scrapbook she'd started when she was five, the one with "Daddy" written on the cover in wobbly blue crayon.

The week was nearly unbearable, filled with day after day of waiting for her hour with Daddy, then trying and failing to draw him out, to get some small inclination that he thought well of her, that he might love her. The only subject in which he seemed truly interested was that of her career after graduation. Carlotta echoed his sentiments later at dinner, with even more force, as if the words were hers all along.

"You should give up these silly ideas of acting and art, and become a nurse," Carlotta declared just as Oona took a bite of her food, looking not at Oona but at her husband. He'd folded his newspaper and taken up the subject anew, like a planned scene from one of his plays.

Oona's heart sank. Nursing? If either of them really thought she was cut out for nursing, it was the final nail in this visit's coffin. Not only did they not know her at all, it was as if she was still a small child in their minds, as if they were shocked when she arrived at their door as a grown young woman.

It was one of their last dinners before she would go home. How had things turned out this way?

"I think I could go on the stage, but Mother thinks I would do well in the movies—"

"What?!" Carlotta said, her brows nearly lifting off her forehead.

Oona had learned Carlotta's histrionics could be somewhat amusing if she didn't take them too personally. Right now, it was hard not to.

"That sounds like a lazy Boulton idea if I ever heard one," Daddy said.

Oona had also learned that at least one thing was the same here as it was back East: parents did not shield children from the messes they made in their own lives.

"You have a daughter, isn't that right, Carlotta?" Oona said. Carlotta went quiet. "How is Catherine?"

Like both Daddy and Mother, Carlotta had also left a daughter to be cared for by her mother, the child's grandmother. Sometimes it was hard to keep it all straight: Daddy had a son, Eugene Jr., from his first marriage, a time that was nebulous and mysterious in Oona's mind because it was so long before she was born.

The last Oona had heard about Carlotta's daughter Catherine was that she'd gotten married at sixteen. The subject was a sore spot with Carlotta, who seemed to prefer pretending she had sprung into being the moment she and Daddy got married. A small guilty pang hit Oona's stomach the moment she mentioned Catherine. Hadn't Mother left her own first daughter, Barbara, behind with her own parents when she went to New York to become a writer? Abandoning children seemed to have been an epidemic in their set.

Oona joined her father in the garden for their walk. Though he'd been busy and distant and mostly cold all week, there had been a few moments when she'd thought she may have caught the edges of a smile. Did that barely perceptible crinkle at the corner of his eyes mean he remembered? Did he recall she was the child he once loved, in another life, in Bermuda? But tonight, his hands were purposefully clasped behind his back as he walked a step further away from her, as if blocking out both their places on a stage in his mind. It must somehow be her fault. Had she disappointed him simply by doing the one thing she could not avoid, by growing up?

"Carlotta says you told her you would never be caught darning socks. That you said you were going to marry a very rich man."

"She told you I said that?" *What in hell...?*

"She told a friend and a friend told me," Eugene said.

It was like a game of telephone around here. Bewildering.

All week, a young woman named Jane Caldwell had been visiting in the afternoons to help Daddy type up his work, which had relieved Carlotta of that duty. On that last day of Oona's visit, Carlotta had taken the free time to compose herself into a picture of wifely devotion, settling into a rocking chair positioned in the flattering light near a bright window. Across her lap was a homely scrap of muslin and in her hands a threaded needle and a single sock. Oona had to swallow hard to keep from laughing at the ridiculous tableau of elegant Carlotta as a domestic goddess.

When Oona had come nearer, it appeared the sock had no hole, but Carlotta still ran the needle and thread through over and over the same spot, humming and tilting her head up in her inimitable, haughty way. Even while pretending to fix a sock, her vanity would not allow her to tilt her head downward. After all, the motion could cause a double chin and terrible wrinkles. Every actress worth her salt knew that.

Carlotta had somehow sensed she was being watched. "Just darning your father's sock," she sighed.

Oona cleared her throat, surprised at having been discovered. "You do so much."

"Indeed."

Was Daddy referring to that conversation?

"Daddy, I did not say that."

But could she tell him what she really said? That she'd actually told Carlotta, in the most oblique way possible, that she would never be like her? She hadn't been sure Carlotta even caught it. Maybe Carlotta was just narcissistic enough to think Oona meant "I could never be like you" as a compliment. If she told Daddy now, would he get her real meaning? That she'd meant she'd never be a woman who steals another woman's husband, one who keeps a child from her father.

That could be worse than what he thought she'd said.

How extraordinarily frustrating it was that people could say anything they wanted about you, and in doing so could put you in the position of having to defend yourself, of having to prove the liar wrong. If you didn't nip it right then, it could grow and grow until it was a matter of public record. Like the terrible stories of Gloria's custody case.

She'd always dreaded the life-changing power of misunderstandings. It was one reason she was so guarded with her inner thoughts. People were voracious for the words of other people, as if they were raw materials to be twisted into something self-serving for a fleeting moment, with no regard to the consequences.

"I asked her about it," her father said, "and she said it was true. That she'd even written it down in her diary."

Oona hid a scoff by clearing her throat, then instantly regretted it because it made her seem evasive. Her hands closed into fists, but she carefully controlled her expression. "A person can write any-thing in their diary." *Especially a psychopathic nar-cissist. Read a psychology book, Daddy. Some are even known to go back and change what they wrote later, to suit their delusions.* "Like a novel. She should be careful, Daddy. People are very interested in the diaries of notable people once they're gone." She looked at his shaking hands and unsteady gait and wished she could take those last words back. But surely he couldn't believe she would say something like that! Did he know her at all? Only one week ago, she'd been beside herself with excitement over coming here. Right now, she couldn't wait to get back to New York.

"Are you calling Carlotta a liar?" Eugene said.

She bit her tongue. "No, Daddy. I wouldn't. But I did not say that to her. What I said was that she was very good with you," she knew then she would say have to say it, "but that I was nothing like her."

Carlotta was a woman who stole a man from his wife, from his children. She controlled Daddy's life, deciding every detail including whether he ever read the letters she sent. She was petty and vindictive, and she didn't care how her actions affected the children she left in her self-centered wake. Oona couldn't say any of it out loud. But it burned through her, leaving a fresh clarity deep in her mind.

Nothing like her. Never.

I'll never be like Carlotta Monterey.

Chapter 9

A GLASS OF MILK AND
A PACK OF PICAYUNES

Truman made his petulant face and waved down a cigarette girl. Oona leaned her arms on the table and looked around the Cub Room of the Stork Club, and stifled a yawn.

"I guess it's just you and me tonight," Oona said.

Carol was on a date, and Gloria was at a theater premier with Aunt Gertrude. The cigarette girl, a new one she didn't recognize, displayed her tray in front of Truman.

"Do you have any Picayunes?" he said, pronouncing each syllable like the ringing of a tiny bell. He couldn't resist asking for the obscure brand, even though he knew most of these poor girls had never heard of them.

The girl scanned her supply. "Oh, no! I'm sorry!" she lamented in a soft Midwestern accent. For a moment it seemed she might offer to run out into the night and find him some.

"Come on, Truman, leave her alone," Oona said, touching his arm.

"It's all right, darling, it's all right," he said, and the girl relaxed. "I'll take Lucky Strikes, or whatever you need to get rid of."

Oona sipped the last of her glass of milk, which the owner Mr. Billingsley provided for free to certain young guests whose names would get his club mentioned in the society pages, also for free.

Truman leaned back against the booth and tapped out his cigarette on the Stork Club ashtray so that the ashes fell right on the stork's top hat. Oona held her cigarette with glamorous expertise—she'd obviously been practicing—but she never actually took a puff. Her ashes formed a nice little beach for the stork to stand on. She'd let him slip some of his sweet brandy into her milk, and now she felt nicely dozy and melted around the edges.

"No wonder people drink," she said. "Say, have I ever told you about my father Eugene O'Neill?"

Truman sputtered.

"What's so funny?" Oona said. Her words began to slur.

"You said 'Eugene O'Neill' like you've never met him."

"Well," Oona said. She sat up and straightened her skirt, hiding the cigarette under the table. The house photographer was making his rounds. "It's not that far from the truth."

Truman put one elbow on the table and rested his chin in his hand, the cigarette still between his fingers, as he watched her pose for a snap. He could hardly wait until he had a name big enough to get his picture in the papers.

The photographer moved on and Oona retrieved her cigarette, took a big gulp of her spiked milk.

"I take it the visit didn't go well," he said.

She shrugged and leaned closer. "You just want me to spill the beans."

"You insult me!" Truman said, a slow grin spreading. "Do I love it when my girls open up to me? Of course. I would give them anything, tell them anything, to make them share their beautiful secrets. They're like treasures, like precious, amusing baubles, that I can put in my pocket for safe keeping, to bring out on a dreary day."

Oona smiled dreamily, and Truman's shoulders fell.

"But there is something confounding about you, darling. You are too real, too of-this-planet, and damn if that doesn't ruin all the fun for me. How could I use my powers on you? Do I respect you too much? The very idea makes my brain itch." He shook his head. "No, damn it, if you want to open up to me, you will just have to do it without the encouragement of my tawdry games." His gaze dropped to the jaunty stork standing one-legged on his ashy beach.

"He left when I was a baby," Oona said. A precariously long stem of wasted ash fell from her cigarette into the ashtray. Her stomach growled, and the brandy milk made the words melt deliciously from her crimson lips. "And I wrote to him and I asked him all the time, all the time, so many times, to let me come visit him. *Just let me come visit, Daddy. Can*

I come visit you? Why can't I just come visit you? He doesn't even have to come here, you know? I'd make it easy. Any time, I would go, I mean it, I would go. But he didn't even reply to my letters. His *wife* did." She forced her eyes open wider to see if he was still listening. "And finally he did write, and they let me come, and it was terrible. It was terrible for a whole week, and then it was over."

Truman leaned in closer, pulling a deep drag off his cigarette. He blew a thin stream of silvery-grey smoke that spread into a cloud and hung over them like an apparition. Oona took another sip and went on.

"His father—so that was my *grand*father—he was a traveling actor, and his mother, well, she was an addict." She frowned like a sad clown. "Morphine. Or something. I dunno. He never had a childhood of his own because of that, so I try to understand. I really do. I give him chance after chance. But Truman. Guess what, Truman? I'm not goin' to be a kid forever you know. Soon I'll be grown up. And then I won't need a daddy anymore anyway." She stubbed out her cigarette. Truman slid her glass away from her.

"Come on, let's dance," he said.

"I haven't fixed my lipstick!" She shook her head slowly, side to side. She fumbled for her purse, then gave in, nodding. Once Truman got a spot near Winchell, it took a lot to get him out of the *sanctum sanctorum*. "Okay, okay, Truman," she said, "let's dance."

He offered her his arm and led her though the crowd and to the center of the dance floor.

"You really can be so gallant when you want to," she said, resisting the urge to bop the tip of his cute little nose with her finger. She couldn't quite make out which of the Trumans she saw in front of her was the real one anyway. "If you cross your eyes just so," she said, "the candles on the tables look like a backdrop of stars."

"Very poetic," he said. He pressed his palm to the small of her back, steadying her.

"I suppose The Stork Club is my home now," Oona said close to his ear. "And this is my house party."

They danced two slow dances, and Truman turned away anyone who tried to cut in. Then they went to lean against the bar. They caught each other's reflections in the mirror behind the bar.

"Look at you," Truman said. "Those dark teary eyes and that stoic chin, so vulnerable yet so tough, and so utterly guileless. You can spill the beans to me any time you want to, darling. But when it comes to you, something is different. No matter how much I adore being the bearer of gossip, I would never gossip about you."

"I would never gossip about you, either."

"I would certainly *listen* to gossip," he said, "just so we're clear."

"Oh, of course," she said, "same here. Obviously."

They looked out over the dance floor.

"Oona, when I grow up," he said, "I'm gonna be your daddy."

"Sure," Oona said. "Every writer would like to be Eugene O'Neill."

"That's not what I meant—"

"You-u-u," she said, pointing blearily in the direction of his face, "should get better idols."

He didn't laugh. She drew back to look down at his face and blinked hard, surprised by his small, earnest smile.

"Your dreams will come true, Truman," she mumbled. "One thing I know, it's writers. And you will be a great one." She hiccuped.

The band finished one song and went straight into another. "Moonlight Serenade." The floor was filled with moony couples, swaying to the smooth melody. Oona swayed, too, the music and the brandy creating a rhythm of their own.

"Someday, I'll bet you're going to be even more famous than my father," Oona said, giving him an encouraging smile. "You mark my words."

She didn't say she hoped that if his work was as important to him as it was to her father, he wouldn't have children. She leaned against the oak bar and fiddled another cigarette through her fingers, then pulled a telegram from her purse and put it down in front of Truman.

"I do keep trying, Truman. Daddy still hasn't replied to my letters since I've been back," she said, "but Carlotta finally sent this telegram." Truman peered at it and read it out loud in a mocking tone:

"Your father is very busy with the cycle, etc. Also house guests expected soon. Not a good time. P.S. Will NOT pay for acting school."

"Why does she have to be so damned *emphatic* all the time?" Oona said. "Must have learned it in *acting school.*"

Truman almost spat his drink and Oona held a deadpan expression as long as she could. Then they laughed as if it was the funniest thing either of them had ever heard. The bartender put two glasses of milk in front of them, and they rolled their eyes at him.

"Just doing my job," the bartender said.

"Mooooo," Oona said.

"Sorry, buddy," Truman said.

"Yeah, sorry, buddy," Oona repeated. "Oh! I've got the results of my fall exams in there, too."

She rifled through her mail each day—with eyes trained for a San Francisco return address in her father's small, heart-stopping handwriting. Instead, she got love letters and gifts from young men who hoped she wouldn't forget they existed. Today, she'd received the exam results which were actually meant for her mother's eyes.

"Have you read it?" Truman said.

"Not yet," Oona said. "I will. *After* I fix my lipstick. A girl doesn't read that sort of thing without her lipstick."

Truman's mouth dropped open, and he looked as though he'd just seen the most impossible magic trick. He blinked, his lids like camera shutters, capturing the moment.

People milled around them—waiters picking up drink orders and couples coming and going from the dance floor. The room was suddenly buzzing about a politician who had just arrived with his entourage in a blustery cloud of cigar smoke. Truman gave the situation a once-over and decided the guy was nobody to get excited about. He turned back to Oona.

"Carol told me the most outstanding story about you," he said.

Oona looked at him without turning her head. The house photographer had paused to record her presence once more, for tomorrow morning's paper. She sucked in her tummy and smiled. Truman went on.

"Really, darling, the *most* outstanding. The one about Little Oona and her daddy's fancy new Cadillac and how she couldn't hold down two servings of kidneys and she ruined a divine mink blanket."

Just like that, the buzz evaporated and Oona was suddenly completely sober.

She couldn't imagine a situation between Carol and Truman that would have brought up that story, one she'd told Carol in confidence. She turned her head away and half-closed her eyes. The photographer asked for another shot, another angle, thinking he'd caught her in an extra-obliging mood. She gave him a half-hearted smile and turned back to Truman. If she left it long enough, let the moment lie there cold, his attention would most likely be caught by something across the room, something even more shiny than her embarrassing childhood story, and drop the subject.

She was right. His eyes perked as another group entered the dining room, then drooped again when they were no one, and she sensed him drifting back to the likely inspiration point of his question—himself. She helped him along in that direction.

"Truman, darling," she said, "do you think a prerequisite to becoming a successful writer is that a person must have had a tragic childhood?"

"Ha! If so, I certainly qualify!" Truman dusted the edge of the bar with his fingers then turned and leaned against it. He crossed one foot in front of the other and cocked his head, his pose matching hers. Backlit that way, with the brilliantly colored dance floor lights reflecting off the bar back mirror, they could have been a page out of a glossy movie magazine, an image of two beautiful actors playing themselves in their own sad life story.

PART
Two

*C*hapter 10

SALINGER AT THE SEASIDE

Point Pleasant, Late Summer, 1941

Oona stopped as she passed the bathroom window to watch the sea breeze blow through the smokey plumes of a blooming fountain grass. Mother stood at the mirror, pulling rollers from her hair.

"It's good to be back at the Atlantic Ocean," Oona said. "The Pacific is not very pacific at all, really."

"It's lovely in some places," Agnes said. She pressed the skin at her jaw and drew it back, frowning at her reflection. "I would imagine not so 'pacific' at... where you were staying." She still wouldn't bring herself to say the ridiculous title her ex-husband and his wife had given their latest home, at least not with a straight face. *Tao House*. Oh, please.

Oona had spent the afternoon reading a script on the beach. Auditions for a production of Pal Joey were coming up, and she was determined to win some small role in it. If the reviews were decent, Daddy would have to come around to the idea. They were dressing for a dinner party at the house of Mother's friend Elizabeth Murray. Oona chose a floral printed summer skirt and matching rose-red Merino wool sweater set since the evenings were getting chilly. Agnes wore one of her best dinner dresses, a long blue sheath with satin trim, old but still serviceable, and her dependable cape was draped over the bed, ready and waiting. She wore a small enamel pendant Eugene had given her after Shane was born, and it lay in the hollow of her throat like a pearl in a shell.

"Elizabeth has a younger brother," Agnes said, fastening an earring. "And she's invited a young writer she's quite excited about."

"Oh goody," Oona said. She chose the reddest lipstick she had, the one she'd bought at a drug store at one of the stops on the way back from California. One coat, blot with tissue, and another coat. She pressed her lips together and then pushed them out. Perfect.

"Darling, might a lighter shade be more appropriate for the occasion?"

"What is most appropriate is what looks best on a person, Mother," Oona said, stepping into her pumps. "Individual style is all the rage, haven't you heard?"

"Oh, well, what do I know?" Agnes said, smoothing her hair down over her ears. "After all, I've never been known as a great beauty."

Oona stopped adjusting the waist of her skirt. "That is not true."

"But it is," Agnes said. It was rare for her to drop her shield, and her expression was suddenly vulnerable. "Certainly not a great beauty like Carlotta."

A knot twisted in Oona's chest. It had never crossed her mind that Mother would think such a thing—that Daddy had left her because she wasn't beautiful enough. Sure, Mother had her faults. She was messy and self-centered, put too much store by social status and always seemed to have something to prove. But her looks? Even now, she was still undeniably beautiful. And anyway, that would be a horrible reason to leave your wife, your family.

No. Her father was a temperamental artist who demanded an impossible combination of complete attention and total isolation, and a woman who would devote herself entirely to his artistic needs. *That* was what Carlotta had offered him. That and the promise of the childless existence he craved. Carlotta could only wish to be so naturally lovely as Mother.

Oona was trying to form these thoughts into words when a little alarm clock went off, jangling them in her head right out of order.

"Time to go," Agnes said. She sniffled, and brought a handkerchief to the tip of her nose.

Oona took her arm. "Mother," she said. "You are more beautiful every day."

Agnes lowered her head, then raised it and looked again. She caught Oona's eye in their reflection and smiled wanly.

"Look!" Oona said brightly. "Just look at us. Where do you suppose I got these cheekbones from, hmmm?"

Agnes laughed as she dabbed a small tear. "Certainly not your long-faced father."

Oona pulled a hang-dog expression and transformed for a moment into the image of her dad, an image still fresh in her memory of him sulking around his California mansion like some tortured main character from one of his plays.

Agnes laughed out loud, then leaned closer to the mirror. "Maybe I should try a dab of that red lipstick?"

☙

Elizabeth Murray greeted Agnes and Oona at the front door, wearing a crepe de chine evening dress the precise color of the ocean at dusk. She hugged Agnes like a good old towny neighbor and friend, then took Oona by both hands and stepped back to take stock, nodding approvingly. Her piercing eyes flashed and she smiled broadly.

"Come in, please, come in!" she said, stepping aside to let them pass.

"This is Oona," Agnes said. Her tone revealed a hint of reference to a previous conversation, and Elizabeth raised her eyebrows and nodded. She drew a pair of spectacles from a hidden pocket and perched them on the end of her nose.

"My, my. Aren't you an absolute dream?" she said. "Let's have a spin." She waved a hand and Oona complied, turning around to allow the older woman to pass judgment. "Divine," Elizabeth sighed. "Come along now, there's someone I want you to meet."

She led them down a narrow hall covered all around with a nautical wallpaper, ceiling included, then she led them into a parlor. Comfortably worn velvets and Irish lace covered the comfortable furniture and picture windows, and all sorts of sand-colored treasures from the nearby sea—bowls of seashells, fat pink starfish, green and blue sea

144

glass—were displayed on the tables and built-in wooden shelves. Gas lamp sconces lit a portrait of a lady in a windswept beach dress and a dog of indistinguishable breed which hung over a modest fireplace lit with the glow of dozens of candles. Two young men mixed drinks at a rattan bar cart, and Elizabeth made the introductions.

"Agnes, Oona, please meet my brother William," Elizabeth said.

"Her obviously much *younger* brother," the first young man said, coming forward to shake the ladies' hands. "Lovely to meet you both," he said, but his eyes were fixed on Oona.

"Okay, that's enough, that's enough. Thank you, William," Elizabeth said, waving him off. They mocked each other playfully, and he glanced at the other young man and went back to mixing drinks. "And this," Elizabeth continued, "is our dear friend Jerome Salinger."

The tall, lanky young man stood in his spot near the fireplace, looking rather dumbfounded, and raised a large hand by way of a greeting. Agnes smiled and nodded 'how do you do,' then joined William at the drink cart.

"What can I get you, Ms. Agnes?" William said, sending a wry glance toward his friend.

Young Mr. Salinger stared at Oona, frozen in place, until finally Elizabeth was compelled to bring Oona to him. "Jerry, this is Oona. Oona O'Neill." Elizabeth's eyes twinkled merrily as she looked expectantly from Oona to Jerry and back again.

"Oona," Jerry said, clearing his throat.

"As you can tell, our Jerry is a sparkling conversationalist," Elizabeth said. "Seriously, he's quite good with words, I assure you. He was just published in *Colliers*. I am a great fan of his work and predict great things for him."

Finally, he offered his hand and Oona accepted, giving a soft but forthright shake. His deep brown eyes fixed on her with a melting warmth before he looked away again. His handshake was strong despite the weak introduction.

"Jerome. It's a pleasure to meet you." His hand was cool and dry, and as he withdrew it, his thumb grazed the inside of her wrist, then her palm. Not a very original move, but a thrill shivered up her arm nonetheless.

"Please," he said, "you can call me Je-Jerry." He laughed at himself and Oona looked at him in such a direct way that he couldn't help returning her gaze.

Throughout the dinner and into the evening, Oona felt the warmth of his deep, mysterious eyes on her. She waited until her mother and Elizabeth were caught up in some bit of gossip or discussion of literary news, and then stole a glance at him across the table. There was something deliciously gratifying in finding, each time, that he was already looking at her, with a dopey, smitten look on his handsome face. There was something familiar in his manner, in the tension in his hands and the flex of his jaw, the ambition already setting itself in his brow. Something in her was drawn to him in the most visceral way, but something else, something that felt stronger but also wildly unreasonable, wanted to run.

Elizabeth finally noticed all the glancing and staring and eyelash fluttering.

"Jerry, why don't you tell us about your story in *Colliers*? I've read it, many times of course, but perhaps Oona would like to hear about it. She's Vassar material, you know."

"Oh, I've read it," Oona said. Her mother's head swiveled toward her questioningly. "It's true. I have!" Oona said. "You don't have to look so shocked."

Agnes raised both hands and exchanged a glance with Elizabeth.

"Should I dare to ask what you thought of it?" Jerry asked. He drained the last of his drink and looked at the empty glass as if it had betrayed him.

"It's called 'The Hang of It,' isn't that right?" Oona said.

"Yes, that's it," Jerry said. "I can't believe you've read it."

His eyes danced as Oona talked about his story. "My favorite line was, 'I hatecha, Pettit!'" Oona said. Jerry joined in, and they finished the line together, laughing. "*You hear me? I hatecha!*"

The empty lobster shells were removed and dessert brought round, then more cocktails for everyone except Oona. She glanced around the table, the only sober one in the room, and her eyes landed once more on Jerry, who was again looking at her. She knew exactly what would happen next. He would ask her to step out with him for some air, or to take a drive, perhaps to the boardwalk. Cigarettes were passed around and lit, and the air above the dining table grew foggy, smoke curling around the crystals hanging from the chandelier.

If she half-closed her eyes, the scene became strangely familiar. A group of writers and literary patrons discussing the letters of the day, describing their work to each other with feigned humility that often broke into blatant self-promotion before subsiding back down into mutual flattery. The sound of her mother's voice, unabashedly mentioning her ex-husband's name, and then Jerry's voice in reply, so much like the cadence of other conversations, some time long ago. So familiar, but also out of reach. Something about Jerry's presence intensified the uncanny effect, but she couldn't put a finger on what it was. His long, handsome, slightly morose face swam in front of her, and those eyes—discerning, critical somehow—that seemed to be considering several other lines of thought at the same time, even as he spoke.

The room began to spin and she lightly touched the edge of the table for balance. She dabbed her face with her napkin.

"Excuse me," she said, pushing back her chair. The two young men moved to stand. "No, no, please," she said, and they sat again. "I'll be right back." The room spun again when she stood, but she covered it well and the table conversation continued as she left the room. .

Leaning against a shining burl-wood foyer table, she focused on her reflection in the mirror above it. Her cheeks were colorless and damp, and a flush of heat rose up her neck. She fished around in her pocketbook for the glass vial of smelling salts, trying to think how long it had been since she'd used them. "Please, please, please, be in here."

"Are you talking to your purse?"

She looked up, giddy, just as she pulled the little vial from the depths of her bag. Jerry was standing beside her.

"Smelling salts," Oona said, a bit embarrassed. "I get lightheaded sometimes…"

"Ah," Jerry said. "I wish I could say I always have that effect on women." He walked toward the front door.

She turned away and pulled the stopper, took a discreet sniff, and her head cleared. Once she'd dropped the vial back in her bag, he returned to her side, carrying his coat and hat with an air of determination. She pulled a tube of lipstick from the bag.

He stood by watching her in the mirror as she twisted the tube and a ruby red bullet rose from the gold case. She brought it first to her bottom lip, expertly gliding the color with a slow, excruciatingly precise swipe from one side of her smooth, full mouth to the other. She pressed the sharp pointed tip to each peak of her Cupid's bow and drew the color out. She pressed her lips together like blowing a kiss, and finally she blotted the center with the pad of her ring finger.

"There. Lipstick makes everything better," Oona said, dropping the tube in her bag and snapping it shut. When she turned from the mirror, he was leaning against the wall, fairly panting. "Oh, gosh! Are you all right?" Her brows drew together in genuine concern. She put a hand on his elbow and searched his face.

"Uh huh," Jerry said, then cleared his throat. "Just peachy."

"Well, all right, if you say so. But let me know if you need some of my salts."

"I'll do that," he said, coming to himself a little and prying his gaze from her mouth. "Listen, I was wondering, would you like to step outside? It's a bit chilly, but a damn nice evening." A wince passed over his jaw and he tried again. "A darn nice evening."

She smiled. *Just as she'd predicted.* "Sure. Let me get my things."

"I would offer to get them for you, but today's girls like to do these things for themselves, right? Shall I get your cardigan? Do you even want your cardigan? You can decide for yourself if you want your cardigan, of course." By the time he'd almost finished dithering, she was already at the front door, wearing her cardigan, pulling on the matching wool gloves. Her expression was eminently patient and unperturbed, so he took a deep breath, opened the front door, and followed her out into the breezy late summer night.

At first, they walked in silence, his hands deep in his pockets and hers behind her back, but soon he began asking her about herself, her family, her plans for the future. Honestly, slightly older men had no more subtlety than younger boys. Still, there was something to him. She couldn't put her finger on what it was that seemed to draw her out, so she put herself safely away after every reply.

They came to an ice cream shop and stopped for a scoop, then sat on a bench at the edge of the rocky beach. The ocean breeze was calm and cool, almost cold, and when he put his arm around her shoulder, she relaxed against him with a natural motion that felt like the satisfying snap of puzzle pieces fitting together.

They walked all the way down to the water. The moonlight set off her dark eyes and raven hair, as she knew it would. When he reached to brush a wind-blown curl from her cheek, he didn't cringe at the trite cliché, she didn't stop him, and then her eyes closed, but only part way, as he leaned in and kissed her cheek.

"You only close your eyes half-way when a fellow kisses you. There's something poetic in that," he said.

"Actually, I've always done that," she said. "In moments that are both thrilling and scary. It's a kind of self-protection. When your eyes are half-closed, they're also half-open."

They walked back up the beach and up and down the streets where only the tourist shops were still open at that hour, talking easily. She let him hold her hand, and let him talk about himself and his work, about a story he was working on. They found themselves back in front of Elizabeth's house. They slowly climbed the flagstone steps, and a lace curtain moved and then fell back into place. Jerry and Oona looked at each other and laughed.

"I hope you'll let me see you again," Jerry said. "I'm already half in love with you."

"Oh, no!" Oona said, laughing. "I'm going back to the city soon."

"Then so am I," Jerry said.

"Well then, if I'm there, and you're there..."

"We might run into each other?"

"Exactly! See how that works?"

They laughed, and Oona hoped that would be the end of that. But that troubled her, because she couldn't figure out why.

At first blush, he was exactly the right kind of young man for her: a writer, published, with a bright future. A person with the kind of mind she could understand, those ambitious literary minds, smashing boundaries, constantly turning and churning on ways to say what was in their heads, ways to convey the human condition through searing prose, while she was listening, always listening, just outside the room.

Maybe it would be better to be free going into her senior year. Maybe the boys at school wouldn't be so silly and boring. She could hope. Whatever the doubt was, it was strong. *Why is it so hard to trust yourself?* Even if she could trust herself, which impulse should she trust? The one that said Jerry seemed like a fascinating, lovely person? Or the one that couldn't find words to express itself, but made her feel inexplicably lost when he turned his eyes away from her?

They sat on a faded porch swing sanded smooth by years of salty Atlantic air. Conspicuous shadows continued to rustle the lace curtains. Above their heads, tiny silver moths dashed around a yellowing lightbulb, crashing into it over and over, refusing to learn any better. "What can I do to make sure I run into you then?"

"You can find me at the Stork Club quite often. I sort of work there."

"You work at the Stork Club?"

"Yes, the owner Mr. Billingsley likes to have nice young people around, you see. The society papers write about the goings on there, and it's free advertising."

"Free advertising."

"Yes."

"For whom?"

"Well, for everyone involved, really. Look, I'm under no delusions about why they like to write about what I'm up to, who I'm seen with, et cetera. It's not like they ever fail to mention my father's name when they write about me. But it helps me, too. I'm going to be an actress after I graduate."

"Does that mean you're *not* going to Vassar?" He seemed relieved to hear it. "In my experience, Vassar girls inevitably came out of school with heads full of tripe."

"Is that so?" A tiny red flag waved in Oona's head. "Anyway, that's what my father wants. But I somehow don't think it's for me. I've just come back from visiting him, and he was not as thrilled about my plans as I'd hoped he'd be. That's what I gleaned from the one hour a day he set aside to allow me into his presence." She bit her tongue, and stopped short of mentioning Carlotta's input.

Opening up to Jerry was too easy. It was both frightening and thrilling, so even though she knew she would see him again, she needed some space and time to figure out what it was about him that made her feel the need to keep her eyes half-open.

"Listen," she said, getting up from the swing, "if you really want to see me again, you can find me back in Manhattan. Then I'll know you're serious and not one of those fellows who forgets you once the moon goes down."

Before he could reply, she opened the front door, throwing him a shattering smile over her shoulder as she stepped inside.

*C*hapter 11

WHEN GLORIA CALLS

Manhattan, October 1941

I t was good to be back home. Not her own home—
Carol's—but it felt more like home than Mother's
empty apartment, and after visiting Tao House, she
knew for sure: Daddy's house wasn't her home at all.

She sighed and settled comfortably into the
rose-scented bed next to Carol's and straightened
her stack of new magazines—*Harpers, Mademoiselle,
Vanity Fair*. This may not be home, but all was right
in her little corner of the world.

"Gloria sent a telegram," Carol said from her seat
at her vanity table. A cloud of powder floated around
her as she brushed through her hair. "She said she'd
try to ring again tonight."

"Oh good!" Oona said, flipping through the pages
of alluring images. "I can't wait to hear what she's
gotten up to!"

Oona had still never met anyone else quite like
Gloria. Though only a year older, she had the aloof elegance and slightly bemused expression of someone
who had seen it all and wasn't that impressed with

much of it. She gave the impression she thought, no, she *knew*, she could not only do anything she wanted, but she could do it better than it had ever been done before, if only she could get a bit of space to do it.

And that was why when she finally got the chance to visit her mother Big Gloria in California, she secretly plotted not to come back. She was finally free, and Hollywood had proven to be far too much fun. Somehow, Oona and Gloria both ended up with the chance to visit an elusive parent in California that summer, but only one of them had returned.

"You're peering at that magazine like you're studying for an exam," Carol said.

"It's a story about Gloria," Oona said. "Oh, it's awful."

"Oh, that." Carol had seen the article. "Her name sells papers. They trot out that story every time something happens in her life. It's disgusting."

Gloria had been photographed on the arm of some new beau, and that was all the press ever needed to inspire a rehash of the custody case which had indelibly labeled her the Poor Little Rich Girl.

"Did you ever think about how some people probably shouldn't ever have children?" Carol said.

Oona brought the magazine up over her face.

"Well, I have. Especially since I met Gloria. The girl is a dream, but it's in spite of her name, not because of it." Carol bit into a sandwich. "But Oona, that story doesn't even mean anything."

Oona lowered the magazine. "What do you mean?"

"She's not even dating that guy. Not seriously anyway."

"Carol, what do you know?" Oona said.

"She told me. She's no longer interested in these eligible bachelors everyone thinks she should marry. She's got other ideas."

"Like what?"

"Like *men*. Men who already know their way around the world. That's what she says. 'Older men.' To be like a courtesan to a great man, to be a muse, that's where it's at."

Oona felt queasy. "But, how old?" She was currently fighting off the advances of several older men herself. Fresh stacks of testosterone-soaked messages awaited her as she went out and as she came in. It was dizzying. She crossed her legs.

"Gawd, Oona, I don't know," Carol said. She tucked the last quarter of her sandwich into her mouth. "I don't suppose there's some magic number of years. Do you know what Gloria said? She said, 'What does age matter—gods don't have ages.' Isn't that profound?"

Oona squinted and shook her head. "Who are the gods in this scenario?" she said.

Carol ignored her and went on. "Anyway, she says she's decided—she's not coming back to finish school. Aunt Gertrude will be *livid* when she finds out. Big Gloria knows everybody out there. I'm so jealous I could scream. But I'm happy for her, too, you know?"

Oona had stopped listening, though she kept nodding along while her mind reeled. In the magazine she held was a picture of Gloria as a round-faced, confused little girl, running from a courthouse as photographers hounded her about her mother, whom the article called "negligent" and "immoral." Those harsh words mingled in her mind with the terrible ones Oona's parents had carelessly flung at each other during their ugly divorce.

She and Gloria shared more than looks. They shared the kinds of pasts that seemed to have no solid timeline, marked by scary moments and times of emptiness, loneliness, and determination. They had parents who saw their children as pawns in a game where the most selfish one wins. They'd both lost their only constant mother figures—Gloria's nanny Dodo, and Oona's nanny Gaga—both sent away at the whim of parents myopic with indignant rage. Even Carol, who had lived in foster homes until her mother married well and brought her to Park Avenue, didn't share that same bottomless longing Oona recognized in Gloria.

Gloria never gave in. She just kept going. Oona wondered if she too would ever learn to leave the past behind that way. Like the trains on the lines where her grandfather made his fortune, Gloria kept on moving, ever forward.

And now Carol said Gloria had a new plan. So when the phone rang in Carol's room, and Gloria's voice was on the other end, it could only be exciting news.

"En*gaged*?" Carol shrieked, and Oona plugged her ears. "Engaged!"

"Engaged to whom?" Oona asked. Her heart raced. Gloria had been right. The world was just waiting, and she had gone out to meet it. "Engaged to whom?"

Carol swiped at her as though she were a gnat, then held the phone sideways so they both could listen.

"His name is Pat. Pat de Cicco. He works for Howard Hughes. We met when I was dating Howard."

Oona mouthed the word 'dating' and drew quotation marks in the air around it. Carol aped a shocked expression and went back to listening.

"The wedding will be in January, and Carol, I want you to come out and be my bridesmaid. Say you will! I'll be back in town for a while next week, but then you must come out and stay, to help me get ready."

Oona was quiet, and Carol didn't reply right away.

"Carol?"

"Yes, darling, I'm here," Carol said. "Oona is here with me."

"Oh Oona! Of course I would have loved for you to come, too, darling, but I know you have so much going on there, with school and all."

"Yes, Gloria," Oona said, trying to cover the shock. Let alone being a bridesmaid, had Gloria not planned to invite her at all? She took a strengthening break and cleared her throat. "And I'm just back from California, too. I don't think my father would like it if I travelled again so soon." Having let Gloria off the hook, Oona sat back and picked up her magazine, pretending not to listen while Carol got all the details.

Finally, Carol rang off fairly buzzing with excitement, as if she might take flight and flap around the room Peter Pan-style at any moment. Then she looked at Oona, and they both looked away.

"I really am very busy anyway," Oona said, controlling the shaking in her voice. "I've agreed to see Peter Arno and Jerry Salinger, and lots of soldiers are waiting their turn as well. And Mr. Winchell lined up a photo shoot for a soap ad. Can't miss that. And of course, some of us still have school." She deserved an Academy Award for this performance.

"I'll write to you every day," Carol said.

"No, you won't. And it's okay, Carol. I'm going to make good use of my time, free from the burden of babysitting you," Oona smiled. "But don't forget our promise."

"Which promise?"

"We pinky-promised to make that trip to California together some day," Oona said. "Remember?"

"You really are swell, Oona. Of course I remember! Pinky promise!"

"Good. So you go to Gloria's wedding and have enough fun for both of us."

"Oh, don't worry," Carol said, scrambling for paper and pencil to start a packing list. "I will."

♋

When Gloria returned to Manhattan for a short visit, flashing a gorgeous engagement ring and a big, victorious smile, Oona couldn't wait to hear all about the wonderful world of Los Angeles. They made the rounds of the clubs, finishing with an uncharacteristically quick showing at the Stork Club, then stopped at Hamburg Heaven (Gloria had missed their French fries), and headed back to Carol's house early, closing Carol's door behind them by one o'clock.

Gloria's adventures in California turned out to be nothing like Oona imagined. She started the sleepover by announcing she'd kept a list of the men she'd dated. Carol ran and got a Dixie cup from her bathroom and poured an ounce of sweet brandy from a bottle Truman had given her for her birthday, and they passed it around.

"All right now, Gloria, tell us all about it," Oona said. "I may be heading to Hollywood myself some day, you know."

"Really? I thought your goal was the stage. 'Trodding the boards' and that?"

"Yes, but Mother has designs on getting this face on the big screen." She lifted her chin and composed her face into her best Heddy Lamar.

"Ambitious mothers abound in Hollywood! But seriously, darling, I think you should give it a shot," Gloria said, a funny look in her eyes. "If you think you can hack it, then why not?"

Oona brushed her hair in front of the mirror. "Well, Daddy doesn't like the idea…"

"Oona is very obedient to her invisible parents." Carol said. She threw a pillow and Oona batted it down as Gloria and Carol giggled. "But they can't agree on what to do about Oona."

So it was going to be one of those nights. All evening, she'd found herself feeling like a third wheel on Carol and Gloria's joyride. She fished a book from under the bed and got comfortable, leaning against the headboard and propping the open book on her bent knees.

Gloria enjoyed the most eye-opening time that summer, completely on her own and away from her aunt and grandmother for the first time since she'd come to live with their side of the family. The way she described it, Los Angeles was like a merry-go-round, a thrill a minute. She had dated so many men she'd literally lost count before she met her fiancé.

Oona eavesdropped, intrigued, while pretending to be engrossed in her book. The allure of California was undeniable, knowing that was the world where her father existed and her mother wanted her to succeed, but inside, if she was honest, she was terrified of the place, and Gloria's torrid stories were not helping. She might have gotten very good at putting up a great front as a good time girl who hung around clubs and was pursued by older men, but she was still green and inexperienced. She had no desire to sleep with so many, many people. The idea of the actual act, and doing it as some sort of recreational activity, both excited and disgusted her. It was confusing. She tried to cut in and change the subject.

"Did you have a good visit with your mother?"

"I barely saw her," Gloria looked down, then back up again with a new smile. "I was too busy dating and having lots of affairs."

Carol shrieked. She couldn't get enough.

Oona's eyes went wide. "Yes, Gloria, you mentioned that—"

"Howard Hughes was divine and Errol Flynn was just so wild!" She laughed, then leaned in. "Girls, the Manhattan rules simply don't apply in Los Angeles. No one cares whether you're a virgin when you get married. Once I'd gone the whole way, I mean the whole way, with the first, it was simple as pie."

Simple as pie. Oona swallowed hard. The rule had been: she could have as many beaus as she wanted, as long as they had good prospects, but if she wanted to marry well, she'd better remain a virgin. Mother hadn't told her much about sex. She'd left all that to school hygiene classes and magazines. But she wanted Oona to marry well, on that she was clear, and if a girl wanted to make a really advantageous match, she either had to be a virgin or make sure not to do it with anyone who would talk about it. Reputation was everything, and the worst rumor Oona heard circulating about herself was that she was a tease. There had been a certain security in being able to fall back on the understood rule of a girl saving herself for marriage. She could always tell the boys she wasn't a tease, that it was just the way things were.

She missed most of the rest of Gloria's description of her California escapades, and only caught pieces of Carol's snoopy questions, while her mind worked on this. As Gloria's tales grew more graphic, the room spun faster and faster, like a horror carousel, and she slipped off the bed to take a surreptitious sniff of her smelling salts.

She and Carol had talked about the mechanics of it, of course, about the risk of getting pregnant, which Oona called 'in the family way.'

"Babies don't make a family," Carol had said, dissolving in tears of laughter. It was funny to her that

Oona would think of it that way, rather than as a disaster.

Maybe she was a prude, compared to Gloria, at least. Lately, she found herself flirting automatically, trying to get the attention of every man she met whether she fancied them or not, as if it were some kind of game. That didn't mean she wanted to sleep with them all. But what did that make her? What did wanting *them* to want to sleep with *her* mean?

The game suddenly seemed much more dangerous than she'd ever realized.

Chapter 12

WINCHELL'S TABLE

October 1941

A group of reporters jostled for positions at the curb when Oona arrived outside the Stork Club. The owner, Mr. Billingsley, had recently started sending the club limousine for her when it was available, which was a very welcome improvement from her previous transportation choices—the bus or her own two feet. Her favorite doorman was at his post, and he held out a protective arm as she stepped from the car. The rows of buttons on his long black coat glowed with polished golden brilliance. It was a bright, cold Saturday night, and it was going to be a good one. She could feel it.

That summer, with her long journey to California and time at the Jersey coast, had brought with it a new sense of determination. Ready or not, she thought, she was a young woman now. The world was at war, and the United States stood on the edge of joining in full force. The city vibrated with uncertainty and hyper-activity, as if all the clocks in the world had colluded to make time run faster.

Having her name in the papers had never seemed that unusual, until now. Now she saw what it meant in a completely new way. She could take advantage of it, use it for some good purpose. She hadn't asked to be born into a famous name, but she'd be a fool to deny the value of it, to pretend it didn't help. It was the most valuable thing her father had given her.

But now it was time to claim the name O'Neill as her own.

The group of reporters pressed in, and the line of people waiting for their turn to get inside followed their lead.

"Behind the rope, please," the doorman said. "Come on, back it up, behind the rope."

"Thanks, Eddie," Oona said as she smiled for the cameras. "Say, is Mr. Winchell already inside?"

"Yes, Miss O'Neill. He's in the Cub Room. He wanted me to give you this." He reached into the pocket of his long black coat and retrieved a paper napkin. Oona read the note scribbled on it:

Miss O'Neill—

Come straight to my table when you get here.

W.W.

P.S. Oh, yeah: please.

"Someone should buy Mr. Winchell a notepad, eh Miss?" Eddie said. "Imagine a big shot journalist taking notes on napkins."

"Oh, that's nothing, Eddie," Oona said. She straightened the collar of her coat and fluffed her hair. "Sometimes he gets *really* professional and uses a matchbook!" Oona said. "But I wouldn't dare ask him to change! Stick by me while I deal with the vultures, would you, Eddie?"

The press was calling her name and shouting over each other.

"Oona! Oona!" and "Over here!" and "One shot, please Miss O'Neill!" Oona smiled for a picture. She'd answer a few questions, then she really should get inside. Mr. Winchell was waiting.

"Miss O'Neill! Miss O'Neill! Have you told your father about your plans to be an actress?"

Just once, could they not ask about Daddy first? "I don't know if I—"

"He's still your guardian isn't he?"

"Yes—"

"Until when?"

"Until I'm eighteen—"

"And when will that be?"

"When will I be eighteen?"

"Yes, dear. When will you be *eighteen*?" He enunciated like a nursery school teacher.

"I'll be eighteen next May and—"

"And..."

"—and, well," she thought fast, biting her tongue. Mother said to be nice to the press. They hold your future in their hands. The first things that came to mind were Carlotta's words. As she said them, Oona imagined her stepmother's reaction when she read the syndicated society column the next day. She smiled a secret smile and finished her answer: "And a girl ought to earn her own living."

The reporter scribbled furiously, shaking his head at his own good fortune and journalistic skills. Oona watched his eager hand jot down her words and smiled as he finished it off with a satisfying smack.

Maybe that *will earn a response to my letters.*

Oona walked the tiled path to the front door and the doorman reached for the gold chain. As he swung open the door, he stepped out as a silent warning to any who might try to get too close, either to Oona or to the entrance into New York's hottest nightclub.

She checked her coat and proceeded through the already crowded dining room, past the dance floor and to the door of the private room where there stood a bulldog of a man everyone called St. Peter, since he guarded the gates. The whole room turned to follow her as she passed, like a field of pale sunflowers. She gave St. Peter a smile as she passed through and waited just inside the door for a moment, as if by instinct, allowing the room to notice she'd arrived. She'd learned a lot in the few weeks of being one of the club's favored glamor girls.

At Walter's table, she slid into a seat beside him and planted a kiss on his cheek.

"Say, what was that for?" he said, rubbing the spot with a napkin he'd been writing on.

"Why, Mr. Winchell, are you blushing?"

"I never blush."

"Well, if you really want to know, it was for that 'P.S.' on your note. Keep that up and I'll have to kiss your other cheek, too."

"You were pretty steamed last time I summoned you without a 'please.'"

"Manners do make the world go 'round."

"No, darling Oona, that's 'money.' Money makes the world go 'round. Which brings me to why I wanted you to come straight to me—"

"But Mr. Winchell, aren't you going to ask me about my visit to California?" As she spoke, Oona surveyed the room. It was good to be back, and after the decidedly non-glamorous version of California she'd just experienced, the good old Stork Club felt like coming home—to the safe and familiar confines of her own personal snow globe.

Walter Winchell sighed and rubbed his eyes. "How was your visit to California, Oona?"

"Terrible!" Oona smiled brightly. "I mean, California is wonderful. But the visit? Not so much."

"Oh, well, I'm sorry to hear that. I *have* heard a lot of talk about that stepmother of yours. Is it true she won't let your pop's old friends talk to him without her permission?"

"No comment," Oona said.

"Okay, never mind that. For now." Walter rubbed his hands together. "Listen, word around here is you have a good shot at 'Debutante of the Year.'"

"No!"

"Yes. Listen, just let me talk a minute, okay? I have a call in three minutes."

Oona closed her mouth and nodded.

"Debutante of the Year. That's what they're calling it this time. They almost canceled the whole event after Pearl Harbor—I guess 'Glamour Girl Number One' was too frivolous for war time. But all of this isn't." He gestured over the room full of glittering tables covered with shining silverware and full cocktail glasses. "Anyway, they changed the name and it's on again. And they're interested in you."

Oona covered her mouth, her eyes wide. Debutante of the Year! She hadn't even let herself imagine it.

"It'll mean some changes. You'd have a table up front a few nights a week where the vultures can get their questions, ten minutes max, but then you wouldn't have to work that mob scene outside any more. The house photographers'll feed more and more of your pictures to the tabs over the next few months, get your recognition up. You'd have to be exclusive here for the next few months, until the fellows vote, but frankly it's a done deal. They want you. You're gold."

A young man approached the table and opened his mouth to ask Oona for a dance, but Walter waved him away. "Not now, kid, she's busy," he said, and the fellow turned on his heels. Oona smiled after him apologetically.

"Now listen," Walter continued, "Billingsley wants to talk to you about it tonight. That's why I sent you that note. I wanted to give you the live news, so you're not blindsided. So you can go in with the lights on, see? I already called your mother, as soon as I got wind. She thought it was grand, of course. And I called the *Mirror*, told them to get something ready to run tomorrow. They're waiting on my word, and I'm waiting on yours. I think you should take it. But it's up to you. But you'd be bananas not to take advantage of the opportunity. Strike while the iron is hot and all that."

Oona started to ask a question, but Winchell raised a finger. Oona frowned.

"You should get some benefits, meals, a little pin money, a clothing account, stuff like that there—you want a nice image, but not too fancy. It is wartime, after all. I know you're no Dumb Dora, kiddo, but even so, I'll back you up. Billingsley gets plenty of press off your face and your name, and your...well, everything you've got going on there." He made another note on another napkin. "They can afford it. And make sure you get a couple bottles of that *Sortilege* perfume he's always handing out around here like water." He cocked his head meaningfully toward the bustling room full of Manhattan's most noteworthy clientele—politicians, society staples, movie directors, writers, Hollywood stars pretending they wished to remain incognito. A glass of milk with a cute straw appeared on the table in front of her while Mr. Winchell talked a mile a minute.

"Better take your cow juice and let the people watchers watch you for a while," Walter said. "Billingsley will find you."

She stood. This was a lot to think about. If she won the club's title, the publicity would be immense. Without having spoken to Mother about it, she knew she'd want her to do it. Who knew what it could lead to, what doors it could open? And how fabulous would it be to be known first by her own name, Oona O'Neill, and not just "daughter of Eugene O'Neill"?

"Oh, and Oona," Winchell said. She turned. "When it's all set in stone, I want to be the first to know."

Oona laughed. "Oh, Mr. Winchell," she patted his arm. "We both know Mr. B will make sure of that."

He put his hand over hers. "Never let them get the best of you, kid. You're smarter than them any day of the week, and you have something they want. Make 'em work for it."

"Got it, Mr. Winchell," Oona said. She gave him her best debutante smile and headed to the main dining room.

The comings and goings of the Cub Room were known to be a 'who's who of anybody who's anybody,' and necks usually strained for a glimpse behind the guarded door. When Oona appeared in the doorway, all heads turned once again, and all eyes followed as she wound her way between tightly-placed tables. Her new shirtwaist dinner dress was fresh from the tailor that afternoon, and it fit her perfectly in all the right places, accenting the hourglass proportions of her figure just like the magazines said it should. She loved the way it moved with her, transforming her every motion into a liquid shimmer.

She felt at loose ends standing there, like never before. A generation ago there would have been more guidance for a girl in her shoes, some little pamphlet, perhaps, titled "How to Be a Café Society Debutante." No time for that now. It was unseemly to take frivolous things like a café society debutante title too seriously in times like this, in war time. But there was no denying that for her, it could open up all kinds of opportunities. With her name in the papers and syndicated stories about her win, she would have a name of her own. Mother wanted a film career for her so desperately, but Daddy refused to support her if she chose acting school instead of Vassar. Maybe he was right, but then again he wasn't here, nor did he bother to reply to her letters. He only spoke up when she chose something he disapproved of, and by then it was too late. At least Mother seemed to think she could do this, and be good at it. Daddy knew her so little that it actually made *sense* to him when Carlotta said she should be a nurse. A nurse! She who passed out at the scent of incense. Every time she thought of it, she imagined herself flopped in a dead faint over the bed of some poor recovering patient, her nurse's cap dangling by a bobby pin while the invalid tried in vain to scream for help.

Carol was off juggling boyfriends and the hapless fellows she used to make those boyfriends jealous. The last time she'd seen Gloria was before they'd each gone to California to visit their respective parents, and now she was engaged and planning a wedding. Truman had pulled one of his regular disappearing acts, the kind from which he usually emerged with outlandish tales of other, more interesting worlds while also behaving as though he had been there with his old friends all along.

But none of them were here now. Tonight she was on her own, except for the soldiers and her regular stable of beaus who kept their eyes out for their chance at a dance. All there was to do was dance. She turned from the bar to survey her prospects, and there he was. She blinked.

Jerry.

The first thing he said to her was, "This place is crawling with phonies," but he smiled into her eyes with the wonder of having just seen a shooting star.

She stood and hugged him around the neck. "Well, I'm not a phony," she said.

An audible moan of disappointment rippled through the group of men who had been working up the nerve to approach her exactly the way this other guy did, as if they had every reason in the world to think this beautiful girl would want to dance with them, if not for him.

Oona let him go and stepped back, looking him up and down. *So handsome.* The dark eyes, the wry smile, the long, intelligent face. What was it about him that drew her in so easily, but then just as quickly made her stop? Like the first time they met, she felt she already knew him, but somehow knew she'd never really. A girl's leading man wasn't supposed to make her heart flutter and sink all at the same time.

He stepped closer and into the light.

"You've cut your hair," she said, reaching to touch the shaved nape of his neck. She stopped, her smile faded and her blood grew cold.

"You enlisted," she said. She looked away, determined not to show tears. A girl had always to be bright and cheerful for the soldiers. Let them know you are proud of them. Just keep smiling.

"Let's not talk about it just yet," Jerry said, drawing her hand away and holding it gently. He looked into her eyes. "Come on. Let's dance."

❧

September 7, 1941

Mr. Billingsley,

As headmistress of Brearley School, I must ask why it is that you allow an underage schoolgirl to spend so much time in your nightclub? A girl her age should be safely home in the evenings. I am informed that you have several daughters yourself, so I would think this fact should be quite evident to you.

Regards,
Millicent Macintosh
Headmistress, The Brearley School

December 30, 1941

Dear Oona,

Gloria's wedding was an absolute dream. Her dress was like a giant whipped cream confection. She never looked so beautiful. And the food!

Being Gloria's bridesmaid at the wedding might sound like the height of glamour and excitement, but we've been going to all the best places and meeting such interesting people. Errol Flynn, Oona. Errol Flynn, who I would make myself a scandal for in a heartbeat, was a groomsman. I know how you like him, on the big screen anyway. But there he was—in the flesh! I hope my thoughts in the church during the ceremony won't get me struck dead by lightning the next time it rains. Luckily, the weather here is endlessly perfect, so I'll probably be fine.

I have to tell you something without writing it in words. Gloria dated Errol, before she dated Howard Hughes and before Pat. I mean dated *dated.*

That was stupid. I may as well just say it. I think Gloria had slept with most of the men in that church. They were probably all crying inside to see her married off. I don't think there can be a more wonderful situation than to get married with a church full of heart-broken men there to watch.

I promise I'm not jealous. What I am is inspired. We're all three of us about to be let loose on the world, and we're expected to marry well. Everyone keeps asking me if I'm next. There are loads of New Year's parties coming up, so let's just see what happens...

Chapter 13

THE GIRL DOWN THE HALL

Christmas 1941

Carol was away for Gloria's wedding, and her mother Rosheen had gone, too. The whole scene in California had been so much fun that Rosheen took a suite of rooms at a Beverly Hills hotel so they could stay on a while longer and see where Carol's fortunes might lead.

So Oona went back to her mother's apartment for the Christmas break. They planned to spend some time at Point Pleasant with the Boultons, and Oona hoped to see Shane. There was no way of knowing whether he would turn up or not, but he'd written to say he would try.

After school on the last day of fall term, she went by the Marcus's apartment to pack some of her things. She stepped around a pile of slush the street sweeper had deposited on the corner, then turned into the wind and ran the rest of the way to the building. The doorman let her in as usual, and she stomped off the snow that clung to her boots before heading to the apartment, but the moment she reached the door, she was barefoot.

It was always strange to be in Carol's room when she was away, even after essentially living here for the past year, but today was especially strange. Something was different. The atmosphere in the apartment was hollow, lonely. She was happy that Carol could go to California and be a bridesmaid in Gloria's wedding, but all of it—the wedding, Carol's extended trip, her opportunity at The Stork Club—also meant that nothing would ever be quite the same again.

If only she'd realized it the last time they'd all been in this room, doing each other's hair and trying on lipsticks, putting on a full face of white powder makeup, even if the plan was only to stay in and discuss their literature assignments or help each other study for entrance exams. She would have committed it to memory so she could replay it like a movie some day when they were all old and gray and had forgotten what it was to be young and beautiful together, like she used to do with her fading memories of Bermuda.

Gloria and Carol were done with school. Gloria hadn't bothered to finish. "Why should I?" she'd said. She'd been so ready to start her grownup life, she decided not to come back after her wild California summer with her mother. And then she'd gone and gotten engaged. It all happened so fast.

Life was proving to be something that did not wait around. Oona thought of the boys she knew who were away somewhere across the ocean, fighting and dying. Every day there were new names. She remembered them, dancing with them, flirting and letting them hold her a little too close, because soon they'd be going away, so what did it hurt?

Very soon she'd graduate from Brearley. So soon. She'd need to make a life for herself. Daddy and Carlotta had made it clear he would not support her after she graduated, except to pay for an education in the career they wanted her to pursue. They could do as they chose with their lives, but she could not. Writing plays was fine for Eugene O'Neill and acting had been acceptable for his wife, but Oona acting in plays was somehow proof of low ambition and lack of character. Her mother had her own plans and expectations, her father opposed them all, and they loved jousting over her life. Somewhere between what they all wanted for her was the life she might want for herself.

She finished packing her things and carried the bag out, closing Carol's door behind her. As she started down the hall, she heard a noise coming from Elinor's room. Carol's sister was at home. The door was open, and Oona glanced inside as she passed.

"Have a Merry Christmas, Elinor," she said.

"Merry Christmas, Oona," Elinor called.

The sound of her name from Elinor's lips struck her as odd, both because it sounded so much like Carol's voice and because Oona couldn't remember ever hearing her say her name before. She was struck with an illuminating pang of guilt. She's spent so much time at this house, but mostly holed up in Carol's room. They'd even taken their meals in there most of the time. It had seemed luxurious and glamorous then, but now she realized as if for the first time that another girl had been there all along, almost their same age, just down the hall. How insensitive of them not to try to include her.

She stopped and went back, peeking into the room. Elinor was drawing something in a sketchbook, but she looked up and smiled encouragingly. She wore a tortoise headband on her dark hair, and her eyes sparkled like deep amber.

"Come on in!"

Oona walked into the girl's room for the first time. It was like walking into a room at a chic midtown hotel, beautifully decorated in muted pastel tones grounded by sleek, modern wood furniture, much more elegant and sophisticated than the fluffy, flowery decor which Carol preferred.

"I'm just taking a break from my psychology homework. Did you know pathological narcissists often lie in their own diaries? They keep diaries because they think they're terribly important, but they do it with a mind to how it will sound to somebody reading it some day! It was simply too much to take in, and I needed to stop and think about that for a while."

"I have actually read about that!" Oona said, remembering how she'd used that fact to defend herself with Daddy. "It makes complete sense when you think about it—from a narcissist's perspective."

"That's true! And by that token, an honest diary would actually go against their personality."

They were both quiet for a moment, and Oona wondered if Elinor was thinking the same thing she was: this was the first real conversation the two of them had ever had. Elinor set her sketchbook aside, and Oona saw what she'd been drawing, a beautiful drawing room in an Neo-European style, complete with potted palms and vases of delicately-drawn flowers. She hadn't known Elinor was such an artist. Oona still liked to think she might be an artist herself one day. Like Gloria's Aunt Gertrude.

Elinor patted the end of her bed and Oona sat down.

"So, do you have any...any big plans for the holiday?" Oona said, looking around the room. It had a similar elegant and comfortable style to the room in her sketchbook.

"Well, mother is in California with Carol for Gloria's wedding, and she said I could come out there. Daddy is working though the holiday, so I might go."

Oona nodded.

"I suppose Carol will be finding a fiancé, too," Elinor said, "now that Gloria's getting married."

"Do you think so? We made this ridiculous pact..."

"What sort of pact?"

"It was Gloria's idea, before she went to California. She was upset about breaking up with some fellow at Princeton or Yale or Harvard or who-knows-where." Elinor laughed and Oona went on, "And we said to her, 'He's just a silly boy after all. What do you expect?' We'd already vowed to each other that we'd only marry true geniuses," Oona said, "but then the breakup gave her the idea that genius wasn't enough. That she wanted to marry an *older* genius." It occurred to her that she'd never spoken those words out loud to anyone, and hearing them took the grown-up solemnity right out and made them sound very childish indeed. "Though from what I hear," she went on, "Gloria hasn't stuck to it!"

They both laughed.

"I'm sure he convinced her he's a total genius," Oona said, "and Carol…"

"Ah, Carol!"

"Well, her judgment is sometimes—"

"Questionable? She told me she met William Saroyan."

"And she's madly in love, I'm sure." They smiled because they both knew Carol. Every man was a new opportunity for romance. "I love her dearly. Who knows which older man is going to convince her of his giant genius." She bit her lip. Usually, she reserved the suggestive double entendre for impressing Carol and Gloria, and maybe Truman if he was being good and dear and not distant and petulant. But Elinor's eyes widened as she got it, and then she fell back laughing.

Elinor was so different from Carol. Even just sitting here with her for these moments, Oona felt the difference. When she spoke, her words didn't float on air, didn't seem buoyed like helium balloons. Carol's conversation, while fascinating and endlessly entertaining, could leave you feeling as if you'd been spun like a top. Elinor's conversation was stable, solid, real. She gave no impression that at any moment she might float off and fly around the room and land on the dressing table. She seemed more like the older sister rather than the younger, but maybe that was only because Carol refused to get older.

"Do you mind if I ask," Oona said, "were you and Carol in the same foster home before Rosheen, I'm sorry, before your mother married Mr. Marcus?"

"I don't mind. And the answer is 'no.' What I've gathered is that Mother had Carol, then she met another man and had me. When they brought me home from the hospital, my father supposedly told her, 'Now we can put the other one up for adoption.' Isn't that rich?" She told the story as if it were the most natural thing on earth. "So Mother supposedly asked him very kindly to hold me a minute, and then she took Carol and left!"

"No!"

"She seems to think it's a charming story actually. And that's not all..."

Oona listened as Elinor told about how her father in turn put her in a foster home, but that it was a nice place with a sweet family. Only after Rosheen had been married several years to the fabulously wealthy Mr. Marcus, who had taken Carol in like his own daughter, did she tell him that she had another child. Mr. Marcus, being a kind and apparently forgiving man, welcomed Elinor into the family, but in the process little Elinor had been taken from the only home she'd ever known. Oona's head spun to think of it, and of the carelessness with which parents could treat their children.

What did this mean about Carol? When they'd first met, she'd actually tried to convince her that

Elinor was the older sister. Was there anything Carol said that she could trust?

"I can't believe Carol never told me all that." It was like Carol told herself the way she wanted things to be, and then believed them herself, so it wasn't really lying when she told them to you. Oona had suspected it at times before, but then Carol was so much fun, and such a fascinating companion. She could convince anyone of anything, then reverse course the opposite way and make you believe you were headed there all along. But Oona hated to doubt the only girl who had tried to befriend her when she was the new girl, hoping to fit into a big-city society that felt as foreign as a faraway country.

"The thing about my sister," Elinor said, folding her hands in her lap, "is that she's a sort of collector. Like I collect charcoal pencils and sketchbooks, she collects people. She and Truman both."

Oona was silent. Truman *had* been Elinor's friend before he met Carol. Perhaps no one saw the dynamic of Carol and her friends quite the way her own sister did. Carol and Truman...collecting people? Was she a collectible to them? A curiosity?

"You've always seemed a good egg to me, Oona," Elinor said. "I haven't forgotten how you helped convince Carol to finish school when Gloria dropped out and ran away, and she wanted to do the same. I will always remember that!" she laughed, then grew more serious. "Don't worry. Sometimes friendships can change. You and Carol, and Gloria, you will always love each other. But everybody has to grow up some time."

Oona nodded, staring down at her lap, at her own hands. Apparently, motherly advice could sometimes come from a girl your own age, a girl you've largely ignored for years and to whom you've barely said two words. She looked up and smiled.

"Do you mean to tell me you've been right here down the hall with all this wisdom, all this time?" she sniffled, smiling wistfully.

"Yes," Elinor said simply, looking around with a little shrug. "Right here."

"Well, I wish I'd found you sooner," Oona said.

Chapter 14

WE NEED TO TALK ABOUT OONA

January 1942

Oona arrived early at Tavern on the Green for her lunch with Carol, Gloria, and Truman. Carol's note had said the reservation was under Gloria's name, and they would meet in the Elm Tree Room.

"Oona O'Neill," she said to the host, "I'm meeting Miss Van—no, sorry, Mrs. DiCicco."

The host nodded before she finished speaking, apparently recognizing the name, and led her to the bank of booths situated beside a wall of floor-to-ceiling picture windows with a fine view of Central Park. Oona took her seat close to the window, leaving room for one of the others on her bench, and then adjusted her new hat. It was a beautiful one, worn at an angle, in a peacock blue that she would never normally choose for herself but couldn't resist when it reminded her of Aunt Gertrude. Its wide brim covered the side of her face and much of her new shorter bobbed hair, and she smiled to herself, wondering if her friends would recognize her when they arrived.

She waited until the reservation time and sure enough, heard her friends' three voices in a low chatter as they approached. She tilted her face away toward the window with the plan to turn toward them at the last moment and surprise them with her new look. But they were shown to the next booth, behind her, instead. Gloria and Carol slid in with their backs to her, and Truman's voice sounded like he'd taken the seat opposite. The high backs of the booth benches came above her shoulders, but she found she could make out their conversation clearly. The host called Gloria "Miss Vanderbilt" and Gloria didn't correct him, but after he left, she said, "Vanderbilt still gets a better table than DiCicco..."

Oona wondered for short moment whether she should say something, but then her love of eavesdropping won out. The host dropped by to ask if she was still waiting on her guests, and she shook her head vaguely, hoping to buy more time before a waiter asked for her order. Then she pressed her back to the bench and trained her ears on her friends' conversation.

The new Mrs. Gloria Vanderbilt DiCicco had come to Manhattan for a few days to receive in-person congratulations from the East coast set and see friends before settling into the holy estate of matrimony. Aunt Gertrude hadn't approved of the match with Pat DiCicco, one Gloria's mother seemed to have encouraged largely to get back at her mother and sister-in-law, and she hadn't come to the wedding. All Gloria knew or cared about was that she was her own woman now, and no one could tell her what to do any more.

Carol tagged along on the quick trip for the hell of it, but her mother had rented a penthouse at Sunset Towers back in Hollywood after Gloria's wedding, and Carol was eager to get back to the wonderful world of hobnobbing with celebrities. They looked so much better in the California sun than they did in dark, steely New York.

Oona noticed a shadowed spot on the bright window where her friends' table was reflected per-fectly, like a television screen. Now she could watch and hear. If she had any doubts about revealing her-self, they were gone now.

A waiter took their order, but when he tried to ask Oona, she raised a finger and pointed to the first thing on the menu without speaking. The waiter nodded solemnly, as if he'd seen weirder behavior in New York City.

Gloria quickly exhausted Carol and Truman's indelicate honeymoon questions and now she pulled a folded page of newspaper from her handbag, and placed right it in the middle of the table, moving the bud vase and salt and pepper shakers out of the way. "Will you both look at this?" she said, poking the page.

"What is it?" Carol said, squinting at the paper.

"Is that...?" Truman gasped.

"It *is*." She folded the paper back and laid it on the table. "Just listen. 'Oona O'Neill, daughter of play-wright Eugene O'Neill, with actress Lynn Fontanne at the American Theatre Wing Stage Door Canteen in New York, where they are planning the charity premier of *Moontide* at the Rivoli Theatre. All proceeds will benefit the American Theatre Wing War Service." She dropped the paper and shot an incredulous look around the table. "Well, what do you know about that?"

"Shy, gorgeous little Oona," Truman said, tilting his head and affecting the tone of a spinster auntie. "Where is she anyway..." He looked toward the front door. The waiter brought their salads.

"Oh, that," Carol said, poking at her plate. She frowned at a cucumber sprinkled with oil and vinegar and put her fork down. "It does look quite mature and respectable, doesn't it? Volunteering at a theater to raise money for the soldiers? Maybe it will soften her father up. He doesn't like her plans to be an actress one bit. Carlotta wants her to be a nurse, and he generally thinks what she thinks."

Maybe she felt herself drifting toward sharing too much of what Oona had confided in her, because she retrieved her fork, stabbed a lettuce leaf, and shoved it into her mouth.

"It's really quite remarkable, though, wouldn't you say?" Gloria waved her hand over the paper.

"Glo, sweetheart, hold on just *one* moment, will you, darling?" He reached toward the waiter who was standing nearby and gave the back of his vest a gentle tug. "Yes, Garçon, would you please bring out a large plate of French fries for this divine little moonbeam here *tout de suite*?" He waved a hand in Carol's direction. Oona realized Truman was too short to see much over the top of the booth, so she sat a little taller, but not so high that she lost the reflection in the window. Eavesdropping took a great deal of stealth.

"Of course, right away," the waiter said. He clicked his heels and pivoted, crossing the dining room like a chorus line dancer exiting stage left.

"Gracias. Por Favor..." Truman said after him. He sat back in his chair and watched the waiter walk away, then leaned in, whistling. "Mamma mia..."

"Well, now you are just saying words," Gloria said. Oona stifled a laugh.

"Truman, behave," Carol said. "How would you feel if he treated you like that?"

"Like what?" Truman said.

"Like a big box of glazed doughnuts," Carol said.

"Oh, like *that*. Why, I'd feel wonderful!"

"He's probably an actor," Carol said.

"Well, if he's not, he should be," Truman said, making googly eyes.

"Excuse me, darlings, but could we get back to this gigantic picture of Oona in the paper?" Gloria said.

"Why, Gloria, what is the big deal?" Carol said, straining her neck to look toward the kitchen. "It's certainly not the first time Oona's had her picture in the paper."

"That may be so, but have you noticed? Our Oona is really coming into her own as of late. Maybe it's because I don't see her as often as you both do, but it's not just the regular sort of blossoming." Gloria displayed a new level of comfort with talking freely about her unmarried younger friend now that she herself had accomplished what the rest of them still aspired to—a glamorous marriage. Her hair was pulled back in a chic chignon that spoke to her status as a wife, no longer a mere debutante. She'd barely been on the market a few months when she'd been snapped up, but not before having a great deal of decadent Beverly Hills fun while it lasted. Now that she had a 'Mrs.' in front of her name, Oona could tell she considered herself a woman of the world, entitled to voice her own thoughts like never before.

The conversation continued with Oona as their main topic. They came to the same conclusion: left to her own devices while her friends were otherwise occupied, Oona was quietly succeeding at something none of them were doing. With no money or support at all, she was being pursued, courted by society. Sure, she was the daughter of a famous playwright, Gloria put in, but that didn't account for all this. Truman added that the surname certainly opened some doors, but Oona had something that let her capitalize on it once she was there, something of her own—that light, affable air and quick wit that people found irresistible. Carol interjected that Oona held her own in any situation, and in their group she had always been somewhat of a mother figure, or like a cool young aunt, one who would teach you how to smoke without inhaling or exactly how to handle a stressful situation by clamming up and playing it reserved, without ever showing how scared you really were.

"Where is she anyway?" Truman mumbled again. "And who is that? The top of her hat is fabulous."

Oona froze. She peaked at the window and saw him crane his neck to look around the room, then worried for a second he might find her reflection in the window between their booths like she found theirs, but it seemed the lucky phenomenon was a trick of the light that only worked in her position.

Carol applauded the arrival of her French fries like a gleeful child. Truman batted his eyelashes as the waiter glided by. But they were not finished discussing her. Oona bristled. They hadn't said anything bad about her, but there was something strangely terse in Gloria's demeanor.

"I just think it's...interesting, that's all," Gloria said. "How she's managed to rise into the spotlight like this."

"For one thing," Carol went on, popping a fry in her mouth and speaking around it, "Oona has the very sophisticated ability to smile serenely through just about anything. The prettiest, most inscrutable smile you ever saw in your life. It's not just any smile, but a stunning one, an enigmatic one, that sets all comers back on their heels and shuts them up like nothing I've ever seen." She finished off a fry and picked up another.

Gloria and Truman looked at her.

"Moonbeam, have you ever considered taking up writing as a profession?" Truman said.

"Honestly, darling," Gloria said, "did you *just* come up with all of that, just now?"

Carol shrugged. "These fries are *wonder*ful," she said. Oona smiled, looking down at the plate of exotic jams and assortment of cheeses she'd apparently ordered.

Gloria shook her head. "Well, it's obvious they're all using her, aren't they?" She picked up the paper and dropped it again, tapped it with an oval finger-nail, "You see it, too, don't you?"

Truman had gone back to watching the door. "They may be, but that's how it works around here, isn't it?" he said vaguely. "She's not stupid, and neither are you, Glo. Oona is practical, not cynical. She is merely using them just the same as they're using her. It's a perfectly beneficial *quid pro quo*. Everybody wins."

"Everybody wins," Carol repeated.

Truman leaned closer to her and patted the table lightly. "Carol dear, don't parrot me." Then he leaned the other way, "Gloria. Darling. Glorious one. We all know how it works, *you* of all people know better than any of *us*. Hell, we're all just humble acolytes at your feet! Don't play dumb. Oona certainly isn't."

Carol seemed to recognize a tenuous thread of contention in Gloria's point and Truman's interest. Her gaze went oblique and fell on the nearest window. "When I think of the hours and days Oona and I have spent together over the past few years! Bosom buddies since the day we met in that dance class. I don't deserve her, and that's the truth. I hardly thought of Oona at all while I was away for the wedding. Why is it that I forgot people when they are out of sight?"

Gloria and Truman got quiet as Carol spoke, her voice soft and full of unexpected emotion.

"Oona is a divinity. I've tried to copy her. I can't do it, I tell you. I don't know how she does it," she said, as if speaking to herself. "The way that pretty face of hers turns to marble, ever so slightly chilly, just around the mouth, and her eyes half-shut as if the world doesn't deserve her full gaze…Well, it says more to the other person than a litany of scolding words. I wish I could do it. I've tried, a few times, when people upset me. Tried to be cool and composed and rise above it all, like her."

Gloria and Truman listened with closed mouths, for once.

"But before I know it, I'm spewing every venomous thing I can conjure up as fast as the words can come to me. And well, once you've done that, any attempt at that demure smile is a lost cause, isn't it? You're exposed for what you are at that point, aren't you?"

They all sat in silence for a few moments, until Truman couldn't stand the quiet any more.

"Do you want to know what I heard?" he asked, in a voice uncharacteristically low.

"Would it matter if we didn't?" Carol said, snapping out of her reverie.

"She means of course we do," Gloria said, twirling her wedding ring.

Truman leaned in. It seemed to be becoming his most favored position. "Well, word is that our Oona is quite the tease." His voice went up an octave at the end, which seemed impossible but was true. Oona covered her mouth to keep from speaking out.

Gloria and Carol exchanged a glance.

"What was that?" Truman said, pointing a finger back and forth between them.

"Never mind, Truman," Gloria said. "We'd rather keep you innocent a little longer."

He crossed his arms and huffed. Carol could never bring herself to let Truman down when he felt left out, and he wasn't above using this to his advantage.

"It's just that in our experience," she said, "boys call girls a 'tease' when we have the nerve to turn them down. Look here, watch." She wriggled in her chair. "This is how they imagine it should go." She leaned closer to Gloria and squeezed her arms together to accentuate her bosom. "Oh, gee, Harry baby, thank you so much," she said, her voice girlish and breathy, "for the fifty-cent hamburger and the milkshake, which *you* mostly drank! *How* could I *ever* repay you?"

Gloria put her arm around Carol's shoulder and stared down her cleavage with a lecherous grin. "'Not to worry, sweetheart, not to worry,'" she growled, "'I have a few ideas...'"

"Ugh," Truman said, shuddering. "Disgusting."

The waiter stopped by to crumb the table, and they all tried to swallow awkward giggles until he finished.

"Anyway, I think she's smart not to rush into anything," Carol said. "She and I talk about it all the time. So many girls waste themselves over the first soft-boiled fellow who calls them gorgeous." Truman's eyes darted surreptitiously at Gloria as she went back to twirling her wedding ring. "Oona is picky. She makes herself rare and hard to get. And now *everyone* wants her even more."

Gloria jabbed the newspaper article. "Even the gossip columns!" she said.

"Even the gossip columns," Carol said.

Truman sat back and raised a hand for the check, which they all knew he wouldn't be paying. "Well then," he said, "she must be doing something right."

The waiter stopped at Oona's table next, and before she could raise a finger, he spoke. "Can I bring you anything else, Miss O'Neill?"

The chatter from the other table stopped.

Oona slumped. The jig was up. But then she turned and got up on her knees, her peacock blue hat rising above the seat back. Truman gasped, and Carol and Gloria turned to see Oona looking down at them. She crossed her arms on the top of the booth.

"Hi there, friends!" she said, her eyes flashing and a tinge of sarcasm in her voice. "And may I congratulate the new Mrs. DiCicco!"

Chapter 15

BONAFIDE CELEBRITY

February 1942

Now that she was on the fast track to becoming The Stork Club's Debutante of the Year, it was as if a spotlight followed her every move. Every afternoon after school, she sat at a designated table in the Cub Room in a state of permanent photo-readiness, a small mirror on her lap to check for lipstick on her teeth or a dark wave of hair out of place. She smiled her best smile while the cameras pressed in on her, sinking in relief and letting her stomach out for a few seconds when they turned away.

As if by magic, a fresh glass of milk with a flamingo pink and white striped straw had been placed beside her hand. She wrapped her fingers around it precisely so her dark pink polish would show and lifted it beside her face, cocking her head to give her best side. She smiled before the flash went off, looking just over the photographer's head to avoid being blinded and to assure her teeth were captured at their most dazzling. With every blinding flash of the camera, Oona pictured the resulting image printed in the paper and wondered if Daddy would see it, then gave herself a mental kick for doing so. This was her moment, not his.

"My gads, Oona," Truman said as they walked out of the club one night and were greeted by more photographers. "You are a bona fide celebrity."

He watched as Oona nodded to the cameras and kept walking. "If my lovely friends are my 'swans,' then you are the mysterious black one, the one who swims at a bit of a distance from the others, you know? Part of the bevy, but aloof, set apart. The one who seems to understand the world beyond their own island, their beautiful Manhattan, with her eyes set out there, on the horizon, always searching."

"Gosh, Truman," Oona said. "I'm not sure I rate all that."

"Of course you do, Oona. I love that name. 'Oona.' Have you noticed you're the only one I don't call by a silly pet name? Only Oona."

"All right, all right, that's enough," Oona laughed. "I already forgave you for gossiping about me behind my back. No need to butter me up any more, okay?"

"Okay. But I did mean all that mush just now. Oona. My black swan."

"Enough."

"Okay."

"Jerry called this afternoon," Oona said. "He won't make it to the club tonight. He's working on a new story."

"His loss," Truman said. "The handsome Mr. Salinger might find himself heartbroken, letting you out on your own."

"Oh, no. I understand. He's going to be a famous writer, same as you I can *smell* it."

Three young soldiers approached and passed them on the sidewalk and tipped their hats. One of them caught Oona's eye, and winked.

"Well!" Truman said. "How rude!" He tossed the end of his scarf over his shoulder with a petulant snap. "How does he know you're not with me?"

Oona laughed. "Oh, gosh, I don't know, Truman."

Truman pouted, fiddling with the fringed end of his scarf. "And what's worse, not one of them winked at *me*."

❀

Posing for photographs and dancing with Stork Club patrons had become Oona's job. Her dance card stayed full on the evening she was obliged to turn up, perfectly dressed and in full makeup, hours after getting out of school. The next day, while people read about her latest night out, she was in algebra class, trying not to doze off.

"You know, I don't think she even see it," Truman said to Carol, pretending not to see Oona as she stopped at the table, conveniently positioned by both the bar and the dance floor, for a quick sip of something cold. Oona was a terrific dancer and only becoming more gorgeous every day, spinning and gliding around out there under the bandstand lights as besotted men waited their turns.

"Sees what?" Carol said. She pulled at the neckline of her dress, taking it even further off the shoulder like Oona had showed her in front of the dressing room mirror. Her favorite boyfriend from California was in town and he'd said he might join them, and she knew better than to be dancing with anyone when he arrived. William Saroyan, she called him 'Bill', was so terribly jealous. She loved it. The back of a teaspoon served as a handy mirror to check the effect, and it amplified her cleavage beyond reality, which pleased her just fine.

Oona shook her head. Truman continued to speak as if she weren't standing there listening, his lips pursed in a droll little line. He was already drunk. "I don't think she even sees how much Jerry resembles Nobel Prize Winning Father of the Year Eugene O'Neill."

Oona's smile melted and she put down her drink.

"Don't be vulgar!" Carol said.

"Like that dress?" Truman said. Oona looked toward the dance floor as if she weren't listening.

"Oh, go on," Carol said. "You know you like them." She sat up straight and expanded her chest with a deep sigh.

"You mean 'it.' And to think I thought you might be a born writer! Get your pronouns right, Moonbeam." He teased Carol, but his eyes were on Oona.

"I said what I meant," Carol purred, leaning her chest over the edge of the table.

Truman pulled his gaze from Oona's profile and leaned in towards Carol for a closer look, then raised his head squarely in front of her face.

"And so did I..."

Several young men tried to ask her for a dance, but Oona begged off politely. "I just need to catch my breath, fellas!" she said, leaning against the bar. In the mirrors behind the shining bottles, Oona checked her hair and pressed her palm to her glowing cheeks. Mr. Billingsley appeared at her side.

"How's everything tonight, Miss O'Neill? Can I get you anything?" He made a little bow. "How about another glass of milk, hmm Miss O'Neill?" *Could he possibly say 'Miss O'Neill' any louder?*

"Mr. B., I swear if you send me one more glass of milk, I'll turn right into a cow!" Oona said.

"For the pictures, Miss O'Neill!" He snapped his fingers behind his back, summoning a waiter and two photographers. "Milk. And one of those cute straws," he told the waiter, "for Miss O'Neill!" He leaned closer to her ear. "When you're a little bit older, we can dispense with the cow juice," he said. In a moment, the glass was in her hand.

Truman was still talking. "I mean, not only do they look alike," he said, his words slightly slurred as he made a long face, "but look around! Where is he? Hmm?"

Oona ignored him, but a niggle of anxiety swam into her belly.

"Say, Truman," Carol said, "why are you so obsessed with who we date anyway?"

"I'm not obsessed. What is it to me? You girls do what you want. Throw your lives away if you want to. Don't cry to me when you're poor and sad and married to your dads."

Oona turned away. Was he right? Was that what bothered her about Jerry? Before she could think, the photographer popped up again. She took one conspicuous sip, gawd she was getting sick of milk, then set it down on the gleaming oak top and surveyed the crowded dance floor. The big band was particularly swinging tonight, and just as they wound up a rhumba, a mellow saxophone came in, low and smooth as a lover's sigh, and the band responded, segueing into a slow melody. "Moonlight Serenade." It never failed. Couples drew closer, locking eyes as the ladies melted into the gentlemen's arms. Oona leaned against the bar and sighed. *So romantic.* A hopeful young man picked up two drinks and headed towards her to try again, but her dreamy eyes widened as they landed on a familiar figure across the room.

"Well, would you look who's here…" Oona said, her eyes sparkling toward the doors. She gave Truman a pointed look. Jerry entered the dining room and stopped, taking in the scene with a look that began as wide-eyed amazement but quickly morphed into casual disinterest. Oona recognized it immediately—his desire to be above all of this, to broadcast disdain over all the manufactured glamour in the place, refusing to admit it appealed to him on a level so deep it made him queasy.

She hurried through the dining room to meet him and took his hand. "Jerry, you came!" she said, "Let's dance!" He surprised her by dropping the practiced bored expression and leading her out onto the dance floor as the slow song ended and the band struck up a new swing tune.

The bandleader stood in the spotlight to one side of the stage, cradling the microphone with one hand.

"You'll be hearing a lot of this next one soon, Glenn Miller's newest record, 'Don't Sit Under the Apple Tree'!" He counted off, snapping his fingers to set the beat, and the trumpets came in with an upbeat intro held up by smooth saxophones gliding below them. The clarinets, bassoon, and bass jumped in, and Jerry jumped in right along with it. The bandleader sang the lyrics, and Jerry soon picked up the backup, shouting 'no, no, no' in all the right places while never missing a beat.

"You sure are a jive bomber, Jerry!" Oona said.

"I'm a what?" he said.

"A 'jive bomber,'" she said, closer to his ear. "A great dancer."

"Oh, right," he said. He added a shrug to his moves, tried to look cool, but a blush rose in his cheeks and he cracked a smile.

When she and Carol used to draw up their lists of requirements for potential boyfriends, dancing skills were always at the top of hers, right under 'good kisser,' 'beautiful eyes,' and 'makes me laugh.' Where had Carol run off to, anyway? She wanted her to see Jerry had come.

The next song was another rhumba. They moved together, and he put his hand on the small of her back and pulled her close. He smelled wonderful, like fresh warm sheets and burning candles.

"I'm so glad you came tonight," she said.

"I got some leave and I'm spending it on you," Jerry said. "Anything to make you happy."

"The whole gang will be here tonight! Carol is back in town, and she's making Gloria come. And you can meet Truman—"

"Oh goody," Jerry said.

"Come on, Jerry," Oona said, "If we're going to see each other, that means you're going to see my friends. We're sort of a package deal." She tried to look him in the eye, but he blinked and looked away. "What? What is that look for?"

"Nothing, nothing," he said. "Well, okay, it's something. It's just that—well, don't you find them all a little bit…what's the word?" He let go of her hand to snap his fingers. "Phony?"

She dropped her arm from around his neck and stepped back, but he glanced around and reached again for her hand.

"That's not a very nice thing to say, Jerry," she said. If he felt that way about the people she liked, how could he not think the same about *her*? "I happen to like them. And you don't even know them."

"Do you?"

"Of course I do." Actually, she had her own doubts about each of her friends, but now he'd put her in a position to defend them. "Maybe you're the one who's phony. Has that ever occurred to you? I guess not, since you're so busy being better than everyone." Her calm expression never faltered while she spoke, always aware of the eyes on her.

"Come on, Oona."

She looked down at his hand around her wrist. He let go.

Mr. Billingsley swept onto the dance floor and stood beside them. "Everything all right here?" He looked at Oona. "Everyone happy?"

"Sure, Mr. B.," Oona said. "Just fine." Jerry's jaw flexed and he gave a half-hearted smile. "We're just talking about...the price of tea." She gave him a false smile. "I'm bullish," she said, "but Sergeant Salinger here, well, he's quite bearish."

"I see, I see," Mr. Billingsley said in a friendly tone that didn't match the look in his eyes. "Listen to the lady; that's my advice." He gestured a signal to a waiter who nodded and went to the bar. "Sergeant Salinger, I must borrow your lovely dance partner for a short while. There'll be a drink for you at the bar. I trust when she rejoins you, you will have changed your attitude?" His eyebrows raised. "About the price of tea?"

"Actually, when she rejoins me, I have news for her," Jerry said.

Oona stopped and turned towards him. "What news?" She walked back to him.

"I'm shipping out," he blurted, then lowered his head. "I got my orders. They're sending me to training. In Georgia."

Oona dropped into the nearest chair, and as if on cue the band picked up the first, mournful strains of "I'll Be Seeing You."

Chapter 16

DON'T INHALE

Oona had been making more frequent trips down to Mother's apartment, running by several times a week to check Mother's mail and see to her bills. More and more, Mother let these things slide, and with school ending soon, Oona didn't want to miss anything important from Brearley. Daddy might just crack up into a pile of red hot rocks if she didn't make it to graduation.

"Miss Oona!" Mother's doorman clapped his gloved hands together instead of getting the door. Oona gave him a puzzled look.

"What's up?" Oona said, about to reach for the handle herself.

"Well, Miss O'Neill, it's just…your mother arrived today." While he spoke, he handed her a stack of messages. "She's been ringing down here looking for your return."

Oona's eyes went wide and she yanked the door. "How nice," she said, smiling at the doorman as she breezed by. "It will be so nice to see her again, after so long." She stopped short of sharing the many months it had been since she'd seen Mother: since the end of last summer, before her senior year began.

Oona found her mother pacing a dull line into the living room rug, cocktail and cigarette in hand. She turned when Oona entered, her mouth already forming words, but then she stopped, her jaw hanging slightly open and a somewhat disoriented look in her eyes.

"Hello, Mother!" Oona said cheerfully. "Lovely to see you." Mother could take that however she'd like.

"Hello, dear." Agnes gave her a peck on the cheek, then took a puff from her cigarette. She stared at Oona as if for the first time in her life.

"Mother, you shouldn't actually *inhale* the smoke, you know. Remind me to teach you how to smoke without actually smoking." She brushed by toward her room, casting a smile over her shoulder as she went. Agnes followed.

"I need to speak with you about school, and about this Stork Club business—"

"All right, but I only popped by for a moment to change," Oona said, flicking through dry cleaning hangers in the wardrobe. "What's up?"

"'What's up'? What kind of talk is that? Don't tell me you're a fan of Bugs Bunny, dear. Honestly."

"How do you know what Bugs Bunny says?" Oona laughed lightly.

Agnes took a sip of her drink, a puff of her cigarette. "Oh, I spent the night with a young…friend… the other weekend, and he—actually, never mind that." She brought the subject back to her point and set her cocktail down roughly. It sloshed on the table.

"Would you like to know what your father has said about this whole business? Not directly to me, of course, but through the illustrious Mr. Weinberger, Esquire. Well, I'm going to tell you what he said!" She unfolded a sloppy stack of papers from her purse and read Eugene's words:

Oona is no genius but merely a spoiled, lazy, vain little brat who has, so far, by her actions only proven that she can be a much sillier and bad-mannered fool than most girls her age.

A thin, icy dagger slipped through Oona's chest, but her face remained stoic, unmoved. When she spoke, her voice was hollow. "He must not have heard about my charity event yet. For the Theatre Wing war service. And I roll bandages at the armory once a week. I suppose a story like that isn't syndicated to California—"

"Do you really think that page of the paper would have gotten through Carlotta and made it to your father?" Agnes laughed bitterly. "I'll tell you which article she did share with him, and I know because he's been raging to all his friends about it. He doesn't realize some of them don't love Carlotta quite as much as he does."

Oona didn't reply, but waited, so Agnes flipped through her messy little stack of papers and read from a newspaper clipping: "When asked by one reporter if she were 'lace curtain' or 'Shanty' Irish, the young spitfire answered, 'Shanty Irish, and proud of it!'"

Oona winced. She'd known Daddy wouldn't like that, but she'd said it anyway. She hadn't regretted it, until this moment.

Agnes went on. "Carlotta read it to him, and then his friends started calling, and don't think she wasn't pleased as punch to inform them of how she wouldn't dream of keeping news about his children from him and so she had no choice but to read the article to him, of course." Little beads of spittle flew from Agnes's mouth and landed on the pages in her hand.

Oona began sorting through the stack of messages the doorman had given her. *Jerry Salinger, Peter Arno, Jack Topping, Orson Welles...* She gathered them back up and dropped the stack on the foyer table beside today's newspaper, and as she did she noticed a familiar name in the headline:

Famous Heiress and Sculptress
Dies in New York-

Gertrude Vanderbilt Whitney
Victim of Heart Attack

Oona's heart pounded in the back of her head, in her ears. Aunt Gertrude was dead. Her eyes closed half-way, and she bowed her head. Agnes kept reading passages from the letter, all her father's bitter, hateful words conveying his anger at Oona having had the nerve to ask him to pay for acting school while simultaneously dating half of

Manhattan. Oona's head swam and she only caught parts of it. The worst parts.

"He says he does not wish to hear from you until you've proven you've *come out of this silly, brainless stage.'*

"*Tops in empty-headed, nitwit bad taste and vulgarity...*

"And listen to this! *I'm afraid the young lady is mentally and spiritually a Boulton. Could one say worse?*"

Agnes read on and on. Oona took shallow breaths and braced herself against the table. When her mother paused in reading the horrible letter, she opened her eyes only to see the terrible headline again, blazing in front of her face.

Her mother continued to rail against her father until Oona couldn't take it anymore.

"Mother," she finally said, her voice flat and empty and cold, "why would you read that to me?" She raised her head and turned to face her mother.

"What?" Agnes said. "What do you mean?"

"I said, why would you read that? To me?" She fought tears.

Agnes faltered, and while she fumbled, Oona cleared her throat and continued. "Anyway, it's old news. Apparently he has contacted everyone he knows, both on the stage and on the screen, and forbade them to hire me." Oona paused, watching Mother's lips pull tight against her teeth. "Oh, yes, I've received my own forwarded messages from Daddy. Much more hurtful than *that* one, if you can imagine it. Yet I keep on shuffling through the mail, day after day, hoping he has found it in his heart to grant me a bit of grace."

Mother was, for once, speechless. Oona's eyes stung with the pressure of self-control. The moment suspended between them like the deceptively calm eye of a gathering storm and the room threatened to spin, but the sound of her own voice grounded her.

"You know, I really don't understand," Oona said. "Am I not doing exactly what you wanted me to do when you brought me back to this city?" The color rose in her cheeks as she stepped closer to her mother. Gertrude's simple words rang in her mind: *They are mistaken.*

She'd bitten her tongue so often and for so long it had never had a chance to heal. What was the worst that could happen? Could it be any worse than living every moment trying to live up to the expectations and demands of two parents who she never saw? Who never truly saw her? The first time to stand up for herself was like rising from the depths of a churning ocean.

"You moved us to Manhattan. You put me in those ridiculous society dance classes. You called on your friends, and had them call their *better* friends. Why was that? What for? What was it you said? Oh, I do remember. You said, 'Those Cushing girls are rising above their station thanks to their mother's training. The Vanderbilts don't bother to train their girls—others train for them.'"

Agnes stubbed out her cigarette as if she hated the ashtray.

"Am I supposed to believe it was all for my own benefit? Please, Mother, let's at least be honest with one another. Surely I am not to blame for doing so much better at the game than either of my parents would have liked, for their own rather oblique reasons.

"My father, and his wife, want very, very, *desperately* much for me to be self-sufficient." The sarcasm dripped from her cool red lips. It felt wonderful. "You want me to run in glamorous circles and to marry well. I promise each of you, I intend to fulfill all of those demands. Yes, I'll grant your wishes for *my* personal life—since you've all made such a cracking job of your own." She had walked across the entire room, the serene smile never leaving her face, and she now stood in front of her mother. "But I will do it in my way, on my terms." Agnes abruptly sat down on the edge of the bed as Oona passed the wardrobe. "Now you'll have to excuse me, Mother, but I really must retrieve my green dancing shoes and be on my way. I wouldn't want to keep even *one* of my *many* inappropriate suitors waiting."

"Wait!" Agnes shouted after her.

Oona stopped with her hand on the door. She squeezed the knob to hide the shaking in her hand.

"I'm planning to go out to California myself, to Hollywood," Agnes said.

"Okay."

"And I want you to come out there once I'm settled. We have to get started if you're going to get into the movies."

"The movies."

"Yes, after you graduate, of course."

"I'm auditioning for *Pal Joey* after graduation."

"That's fine, that's fine." Agnes's face broke into a needy, childlike expression. "But if your father asks, tell him I said you had to graduate first."

Oona turned away, replying as she walked out the door.

"He won't."

Bainbridge Army Airbase, 1942

Dearest Oona,

I just knocked off my post for the day and took up another one—in front of this typewriter. I leaned back in the chair, pressed my knuckles, and then lit a cigarette. I can't put it off any longer. I have to finally sit down to write a reply to Elizabeth Murray. Ever since she introduced us at the dinner at her house, the woman will not stop badgering me for details about my progress with you. How is it going? Is she in love with you yet? Will I propose?

Elizabeth already knows how I feel about you, Oona. I've already irrevocably committed that to paper in previous letters, and I'd like very much to be able to report that you have declared deep, undying love to me during one of my visits up to the city. But that has not happened. You have proven yourself impossibly slippery, and the damnedest part is I am completely in love with you despite myself and my better judgment. Despite your vapid friends and the shallow quotes they attribute to you in the gossip columns. Despite the revolving door of other suitors you swear are simply 'school chums' or 'family friends.' Despite your love of all things bright and sparkly and beautiful and, to me, fake.

The worst part is you make me face the fact that deep down I want all those things, too. And I tell you, I don't appreciate that one bit. I would give you anything you want if I could. If you'd have me. But you'd have to let me close enough to figure out what exactly it was you want, for a start. Instead, it's as if the moment I make the smallest break through the wall around you, you disappear completely until you've built it back up stronger than before.

At basic training, I've spent most of my scant free time writing these long, ardent letters to you, and most of my leave traveling to and from Manhattan in the hopes of spending even one eve-ning with you. I couldn't let Elizabeth think I was failing to win you over. She is one of my most ardent supporters. I answered her instead with a clever little literary shrug, "Little Oona is hopelessly in love with Little Oona." That's a good one, don't you think?

As I type those words, I imagined Elizabeth reading them. She would see right through my deflection. She always says men's egos are the most delicate bits of gossamer floss in the universe. I can hear the woman now, scoffing as she tosses my letter aside to write her likely reply: "She isn't falling at your feet, so something must be wrong with her. Is that it, Jerry?"

I've watched you navigate your world like a beautiful spider on the finest of threads, developing in the dark corners of my mind a real and true hatred for the fake, phony people, a disdain for those who hold the keys to everything I want, the ones who made the girl I love dance for her supper. More than that, I hate the part of myself that wanted to be one of them.

I admired your father so much. He came from a family of poor immigrants and rose to the top of the literary world. Once there, what does a person do? Can they ever again be part of the place they came from? I grew up on the perimeters of what I imagine was your world, almost, but never quite one of them. My family did well enough, living comfortably on the

*profits of my father's deli import busi-
ness. My life has never been a struggle.
If I hate anyone, it should be myself, but
I didn't ask for an easy life. Now, I'm
obliged to go to war to get some grit.
At least I'm trying. How much easier
it was before I met you, to turn myself
inside out, to turn the hatred outward.*

*You flit from your tony private school to
upscale nightclubs to Madison Avenue
photoshoots as if it's your birthright.
And maybe it is. It's all so damned confusing, inhaling the ambition to rise to
your level, exhaling the urge to knock
you down to mine.*

*I used to take you to your damn Stork
Club, because it was the only way to
spend any time with you. Every night I
beat my head against the pristine wall
you built around yourself. And I'd do it
every day for the rest of my life if only
you would tell me you love me.*

*Love,
Jerry "the creep who loves you" Salinger*

September 1942

Dear Oona,

> *You had better come back from your triumphant four-line stage debut in New Jersey soon. I saw the review of Pal Joey in the paper, with a big picture of you and Peter Arno backstage at the Maplewood Theater! I must get your autograph. Has your father warmed to the idea of having an actress for a daughter?*

> *Without you here to watch over me, I'm getting into a lot of trouble. The fun kind. Gloria was in town. I've seen Bill quite a lot. He says I can call him 'Bill.' Imagine me calling a famous playwright like William Saroyan 'Bill.' Ha! And to think, I used to think he was dead! He won a Pulitzer; did I tell you that? Just like your father. He's putting me in one of his plays. Gloria thinks it's a wonderful idea that I see him. She thinks I should marry him!*

> *Bill and I have the most romantic situations. We kiss and kiss, and take care of things in that way Gloria told us about. Then I say something that makes him cross, and we have a big fight and I say*

I don't like him anymore. Then the next night he might see me out dancing or with friends at dinner, and I make sure to flit by him so he'll want me again. He comes when I call. All I have to do is say something very dirty very sweetly, and he turns to mush.

I heard Jerry shipped off to Georgia for basic training. Does he care about you and Arno? It's not like he's made you any offers, is it? Or has he? We really must catch up.

Do you remember when Truman introduced us to sweet brandy? I drink that now. I think sweet brandy and I are simpatico. My stage name should be Sweet Brandy.

When are you coming back? Without you here, half my brain is missing. Maybe a smidge more than half.

Love,
Carol

Chapter 17

ROOM KEYS AND TAXI MONEY

Manhattan, 1942

Another summer gone, another day spent. Oona clutched the knot of her head scarf and held the collar of her coat close to her neck as she turned down Park Avenue into the whipping wind. It was strange not to be going back to school this time of year.

After so much media hype leading up to her role in *Pal Joey*, now that was over, too—part of the past. Some of the windows displayed flags or framed pictures of lost soldiers. Three years. War time should never feel like the status quo. How much longer would it go on? If all of life moved this fast, it might be over before you knew it.

"Mail for you, Miss O'Neill," George the doorman said as she entered Carol's building. The night was dark and blustery, and she stomped the fresh snow from her shoes. "And a message." He held his face stiffly as he handed Oona her correspondences. At the bottom of the stack was an envelope fat with what they both knew was a room key.

"Thanks, Mr. George," Oona said, taking the stack of notes and letters from his hands. George treated her like one of the Marcus family. She knew he had a daughter around her age. Maybe that was why he always looked at her with that fatherly look mixed with a hint of pity. She shuffled through the mail automatically, looking for something from Daddy. Her shoulders fell. *Nothing.* Nothing had come from him since a single postcard in spring. Today's mail consisted of a thick envelope from Jerry, a thin envelope from Jerry, then the normal invitations to dinner, to the club, to drinks at a hotel bar...

It was starting to get quite old already, accepting invitations to dinner or dancing to end up fighting off unwanted hands under the table or too low on her waist. Keys left for her, stuffed in hotel envelopes, which George was obliged to collect until handing them over with downturned, decidedly judgmental eyes. She'd never used the keys, not once, but it seemed such a waste to throw them away. Some of them were so pretty, and probably cost a lot. So sometimes if she knew she'd pass a certain hotel in the course of her day, she'd stop by and drop them off at the front desk. She'd met some of the most interesting people while doing that, so at least there'd been *some* benefit to her suitor's crude offers.

Did this move actually work with some girls? Surely a man couldn't think for the price of a steak dinner a girl would trip all over herself to *sleep* with them. Not even in these times. The envelopes often contained taxi money and a cryptic note, one that wouldn't mean too much if read by anyone else, but that Oona would understand. Some double entendre based on a dumb joke or dull story from the night before. At least Jerry was somewhat amusing, in his churlish way. Maybe she'd try ringing him up when she got upstairs.

On the other hand, why was she bothering with any of these boys? Jack Topping had lobbied hard for her to be his date to his birthday party at El Morocco, enough for that society columnist Dorothy Kilgallen to officially pronounce them "oonited." Clever, but not true. According to the society gossip in today's paper, which may or may not have been true either, Jack Topping had wasted little time getting his name connected with no less than two other girls after his enormous birthday bash. It hadn't even been a month since he'd practically begged her to be his date. The love lives of high society seemed in a continual game of round robin.

And what about Jerry? She saw his name on the envelopes in her hand and instantly dreaded reading them. His letters lately were so cryptic, inexplicable, as if they came from two different people: He loved her. He couldn't stand her. He had to have her. Her friends were a bunch of phonies. Would she give his best to her friends? He hoped she wouldn't wait for him. Would she wait for him? He took her silence to mean would not. He took her reply to mean they would marry and have a dozen children.

Till now, she'd tried to be understanding of his ways. After all, he must be under a lot of pressure, training to serve in the war while trying to keep writing and publishing his stories. The changeability of his manner in his letters might be a picture of the agitation he felt about his future, his insecurity—that he was trying different tactics with her—but if he wanted her to fall in love with someone who understood she didn't deserve his love, he had the wrong girl. She already had that with Daddy, thank you very much.

She was tired dealing with him, and they weren't even going steady. What would it be like to be married to a man like that? A mercurial man who gave love and took it away on a whim.

Going to the Stork Club had become more of a habit than anything else. That evening, she'd accepted all dance requests, letting them pull her close, their hands too low on her back, their eyes everywhere, their faces a dizzying whir until they were all the same man, someone she recognized. She danced every dance until the room spun with leering faces and grasping hands, but then one of the hands had reached out and taken hers, stopping her spinning.

It was Orson.

"Mr. Welles, I haven't seen you since—"

"Since you stopped returning my calls. What happened, that bastard Peter Arno got his hooks too far in?" He led her back to the Cub Room, to his table. She waved at Mr. Winchell as she sat down.

"It was someone else actually. A writer." Her head still spun a little, but in a pleasant way.

"A writer. Exactly the opposite of what you need," Orson said.

"How would you know what I need?"

"Oh, my darling girl, I know exactly what you need."

He had tried to coax her to his hotel room. Orson could have any woman he wanted. She didn't have one particular beau. She was a free agent, could do what she wanted. But which of these young men could be trusted? Sometimes she thought maybe Orson could be the one. She'd put him off tonight by promising to go to dinner with him on Saturday. Beyond that, she couldn't let herself think.

Now she took the envelope bulging with a room key from the bottom of the stack where George had discreetly placed it and knew right away who it was from—the boorish junior publicist she'd had dinner with last night. She turned it over in her hands, feeling Mr. George's gaze on her, and her cheeks flushed.

*Why should **I** feel embarrassed?*

She wasn't the one propositioning people she barely knew, sending room keys by way of poor, hungry little messenger boys all over town. A spark of defiance ignited in her chest, and she handed the envelope back to George.

"I don't need this one. Thank you, Mr. George," she said. "You can send it back—feels like it's from the Intercontinental—or whatever you think best. And, George, please do the same with any others like it that might come in the future, too."

George's barrel chest puffed. "Yes, miss. And if I may, I might just bring it back to the Intercontinental myself. Maybe find the room and use the key, give whoever waits inside a piece of my mind, and this good hard fist to the jaw..."

"Thank you, George," Oona laughed. "You're a dear."

George closed the door and the sound of the cold wind collapsed behind her. She pressed the elevator button and closed her eyes to wait. Once inside, she leaned against the elevator wall, thinking she was much too young to feel so very, very tired.

Chapter 18

UNDER A WAXING MOON

In Carol's room, Oona sat on the floor surrounded by her day's mail. She needed to stop. To take stock. To breathe.

Things obviously weren't going to work out with Jack Topping. He wasn't thrilled about her plans to be an actress, and Mother didn't like that, but she did like Jack's money. Oona wished someone would ask her what she liked. Just once. Maybe she was going about it all wrong. Maybe no one ever *would* ask her what she liked. Maybe the onus was on her to speak up.

Jerry's letters kept coming. They weren't exclusive with each other, but sometimes you couldn't tell that from his letters. Well, some of them, because it wasn't unusual to receive two in one day, like she had just now—the first telling her off for her shallow Café Society life and the next apologizing and professing he could never love another girl as long as he lived, and he'd die if she didn't love him back.

Could she ever really be with Jerry? Could she be with a writer at all? Truman had been right. Jerry made her think of her father, and she didn't want to think of him any more than she already did. Once she saw how alike they were, she couldn't unsee it. And the last thing she wanted was a repeat of her own family's past. She wanted something spectacular, something to make up for the emptiness of her childhood, to fill the space where home and family should be. What if that was out there right now, ready for her to walk up and discover it, waiting for her?

Jerry wrote things like: "What am I doing with a girl like you?" He wanted her world, the world of her father. And at the same time, he despised it for its phony posturing, its heavy price. He loved her, and then he hated her for making him think he couldn't afford her. Yet he couldn't afford to lose her, either. Was she supposed to feel responsible for *his* feelings? Her own were a burden enough.

She reread a passage from his letter, the nice one:

I realize I enlisted in the army to be like Hemingway. To experience something hard and gritty I could put down on the page and show the world. Then they'd know. Then they'd have to admit me to all the places that shut me out. They'll be forced to acknowledge me, these self-satisfied editors and agents and publishers with their cold rejections, pat phrases like 'this doesn't do' and 'unfortunately not to our standards.'

I'll prove them wrong, make them regret ever rejecting me. Then I'll be the one to sit in tony bars and slick salons with a bottomless glass of something amber and expensive, and on their tab. And I'll be the one to tell them, "No, this doesn't do."

She had no doubt it would happen just as he imagined, if that was really what he wanted. But whether she'd be by his side when it happened was a separate question altogether.

Jerry was right about one thing. The more time she spent at The Stork Club lately, the more she realized she had to face facts. She couldn't go on pretending she fit in Café Society forever. She'd never be like the girls who won Debutante of the Year titles outside of wartime, never be a real society woman, not like Carol and Gloria. The real debutantes would be back with their coming out parties and white gowns the moment the war ended and lavish public celebrations were no longer unseemly.

Even if she had money, she would never truly be one of them, and if she were honest with herself, she wasn't sure she wanted to be. If she ever did have money, she'd want to be like Gloria's Aunt Gertrude had been—helping artists and writers, really making use of her good fortune. Quietly contributing in a real way. Social climbing was another of Mother's dreams, not hers.

The other young women around her were all playing the same game. Their mothers turned a blind eye, strict in public but indifferent in private, offering little guidance or supervision, perhaps not wanting to know or see what their daughters would do to fulfill their jobs of finding a good catch. So the girls ran wild in New York City, making choices on the fly with the hopefulness of youth and the heady understanding that they already possessed the most obvious power, the thing everyone else wanted, the strongest power in the world—beauty. No matter what other talent or achievement they possessed, beauty was the most important thing they had to offer.

She picked up the phone and dialed the exchange for Jerry's barracks. A gruff voice answered, "Who d'ya want?"

"Sergeant Salinger, please."

"Salinger!" the voice shouted before coming back on the line. "Hold on, please, miss."

When Jerry came on the line, his voice was not the one Oona had just read in his nice letter, still in her hand. The difference was jarring.

"Jerry?"

"Yeah, it's me. Sorry, I was in the middle of a new story. Don't get much time."

"Oh, well, that's all right then. I'll ring off—"

"No, no, you're on the line now," he cleared his throat. "Sorry, it's wild here. I am glad you called though."

"I got your letters," Oona said, and laughed lightly, still unsure of the mood.

"Yeah, I guess maybe I should cut that out," he said, "seeing as how I hardly hear back from you."

"Well, I do reply, Jerry. It's just that I can hardly keep up. I'm not as fast a writer as you, I guess."

"Say listen, Oona, I've been meaning to ask you something, and it's pretty damn important. To me anyway," he said.

"All right, go ahead."

"Do you have any idea what a pain in my ass it is?" His voice came through gritted teeth.

She didn't know how to respond. What exactly was he talking about?

"Well, do you?" His voice raised, and she held the phone from her ear. "Seeing you in the paper, swishing around Manhattan with other men, twice your age? Posing for pointless pictures in the God-and-Walter Winchell section of the damned phony Stork Club?"

Oona swallowed hard. *Enough.*

"Do you want to know what I think, Jerry?" she said. "I think anyone that makes you feel like an out-sider is a phony. At least I'm being as truthful as I can be about what I want."

"Don't you mean what your mother wants?" he shouted. "You have no idea what you should want."

Oona was quiet.

"Listen, Oona," he said, his tone softening "I shouldn't have—"

"Oh no, Jerry! Don't apologize!" Oona said. Her voice was high and tense, completely controlled. "In fact, I want to congratulate you!"

"*Congratulate* me?"

"Yes! Congratulations, Jerry!" Oona said slowly. "You've met *one* of your goals in life!"

"What the hell are you talking about?"

"You did it." Oona said, her voice infuriatingly calm. "You are just like my father."

She hung up, setting down the receiver with a precise motion, then she picked up again and slammed it down.

Chapter 19

ORSON WELLES, FORTUNE TELLER

Manhattan, 1942

Oona looked across the table at Orson, watching him bring his drink to his lips. She caught his eye, and he held her gaze. A thrill ran up the back of her legs, and she took a sip of her sparkling drink. He'd suggested she must be getting tired of the food at The Stork Club and had taken her to dinner at El Morocco instead, but Oona was obliged to make an appearance at the Stork on a Saturday night, so they'd stopped for cocktails and smokes. The main room buzzed with its usual Saturday excitement, and all eyes had followed them as he led her through, his hand at the small of her back, to the exclusive Cub Room.

Orson. He lit a cigar across the table from her. Her insides melted just looking at him. What was it about him? Even their names matched each other.

He'd released his film *Citizen Kane* the previous year. It may not have been a hit at the box office, but she still heard critics speaking highly of it. Gloria and Carol would agree, he was definitely a certified genius. If he asked her to marry him, she was afraid she'd say yes in an instant—afraid because she knew if she did marry him, it would be for the wrong reasons.

Not that he was asking. He waved off the staff photographer as Walter Winchell glanced at their table and jotted a note on a napkin.

Orson made no bones about the fact he wanted to sleep with her, and she was long past playing shocked. She had many, many beaus, and the reason she wasn't still with many of them was that when it came down to it, none of them felt right. At least not right enough. But Orson felt as close to right as she'd ever come. Maybe if she just got it over with it would be okay from then on. But what if it weren't?

Why do I have to think so much?

"I have a fantastic room at the Waldorf," Orson said. "I'd love to show it to you."

"Is that right?" Oona cringed at the saccharine sound of her own voice.

"Yes," he said plainly, "I find you extremely attractive."

Oona tossed her hair. *Dear god, stop me.* "You're very attractive as well."

They were both silent as he let the idea sink in.

"I don't know..." She absolutely could not go with him tonight. If she did, that would be it. There was no doubt about it. But what if it were a mistake?

Did other girls torture themselves like this? Other girls besides Carol and Gloria, that is, because they definitely did not. They were actually beginning to think she was stuck on herself for being so protective of her precious—

"Wait a minute," Orson said. "Are you trying to tell me you have never..."

"I'm not trying to tell you anything," Oona said. She stopped short of telling him that she wanted to—very much. That it was all she could think about sometimes, but that because she was a thinker, she thought about how once she'd done it, that would be it. There's only one first time for anything. What would he think if he knew? And was it even his business? Was it his business to know about every sloppy make out session or awkward episode of groping in the back of a taxi?

The moment to speak passed, and she hoped he'd taken her silence as a feminine air of mystery.

"All right, all right. I get your game," Orson said. "You're a real firecracker. You know that? Listen, I'm going back to California again soon, but if you ever do come out to Hollywood, I can help you meet people, you know, show you around. Protect you from the dogs, if you know what I mean. If you want, that is."

He laid his cigar across the ashtray and reached across the table. "Give me your hand," he said.

"What for?"

"Just give it, please," he said, waving his fingers. "I'm going to read your palm."

She placed her hand on his and he traced the lines slowly with one finger. Her toes curled inside her shoes.

"Hmmm," Orson said, knitting his brow with carnival side-show intensity. "You will marry an older man."

"Oh really?" Oona batted her eyelashes, and instantly regretted it.

"Yes, an older man. And that man is...Charlie Chaplin!"

Once he'd said it, he seemed pretty pleased with himself, searching her face for her reaction. Her eyes turned faraway and pondering, half-way closed.

Her hand still lay open in his. She opened her eyes and leaned closer, as if trying to see in her own palm what he claimed to see. She took in a sharp breath, half-relieved that he wasn't trying to seduce her any more. Moments ago, the idea of being with him, alone in his Waldorf hotel room, had been too much to imagine. But now he had switched the script, making a vaudevillian show of predicting she would marry someone else. If he'd suddenly changed his mind about showing her his 'fantastic room,' all he had to do was say so. She sat back in her chair, unsure whether to be relieved or devastated.

$\mathcal{C}$hapter 20

LONG DAYS JOURNEY

Autumn, 1942

The Stork Club, again. The nightclub was so familiar, *too* familiar. A vague restlessness had worked its way into Oona's daily schedule, rising with the moon as the days slipped toward evenings.

Her past was so much a part of every new day that Oona's life almost didn't feel linear any more. Bermuda lived in the part of her brain that also held the lyrics to her new favorite songs, and memories of Point Pleasant mingled with each new dance step she learned. The past blended into the present day like a piece of cloth woven from scraps. If the moments of her life were a tapestry in progress, then Daddy was the shuttle on the loom, always flying between the threads just out of her reach.

"Oona, would you please play quietly? Daddy is trying to work."

"If you will be a good girl, and let Daddy work, perhaps later we will have a nice picnic on the beach."

"Daddy hasn't had a good day, Oona Dear. Perhaps tomorrow."

Now she sat at a table at The Stork Club, across from Carol and her huge brown eyes, and it could have been a year ago, or yesterday. Another new cigarette girl swayed around the room, and the band played a primal drum beat for a woman in beads and scarves who gyrated while revealing herself from behind two feathered fans. The makeup-stained elastic band of her blonde wig showed behind her ears with every snakelike contortion. Oona sighed.

"Bill convinced Mother to let me visit him in California." There was a decidedly wicked twinkle of secrecy in Carol's eyes.

"Bill?" Oona said. "Saroyan? Are you seeing him again?"

"Of course I am, darling, and I'm terribly in love. Anyway, Mother agreed I could go! But only if I take along a chaperone—"

"Yes," Oona said.

Carol stopped talking and cocked her head. "I haven't even finished asking you yet."

"Are you about to ask me to act as chaperone for your torrid visit to see the horrible and not-dead Saroyan in California? If so, then 'yes.'" Oona said, then raised a finger. "Oh, hold on to that thought a minute," she said, pointing toward the ceiling.

It was that time of the evening when The Stork Club dropped money-filled balloons for the shameless guests gathered below. The balloons might contain anything from one dollar to $100, or more if Mr. B. was trying to make a really big splash. Only the women could participate. They stood on tiptoes, or on tables, reached over and around each other, and since the club had become a tourist attraction, few left the melee without at least a scratch from some blindly grasping hand, or a stomped finger earned by snatching a bill before it got caught under some frenzied woman's heel. Mr. B. would need to rethink this whole idea soon, before somebody sued.

One balloon, smaller and duller than the rest, drifted down, bouncing off bigger, brighter balloons on its way down. Oona spotted it up high as it left the net and kept an eye on it as it fell, all the way down and right into her hands. She popped it against her shoe buckle. Inside was a one-hundred-dollar bill.

She flagged down the nearest waiter. "Break this into smaller bills for me, will you please? Thanks, Andy."

Carol kicked her way through the sea of balloons. The popped ones lay deflated and gutted and some still full of air and buoyant, having been given cursory shakes and cast aside as empty, and therefore useless trash. She fluffed her puffed sleeves as she came to stand beside Oona. They surveyed the wreckage.

"So when do we leave?" Oona said.

"A few weeks," Carol said, frowning at the crumpled remains of an empty balloon in her hands.

"All right. I'll tell Mother," Oona said. The waiter returned with the change. "Thanks Andy, and here's a twenty for you." The waiter's mouth dropped open. Oona smiled, then turned to Carol. "I'll be right back."

Oona dashed up the stairs to the ladies' washroom, her heels clicking on the tiled floor as she flew through the door. The attendant looked up, surprised.

"This is for you, Ms. J.," Oona said, and gave the woman three crisp ten-dollar bills.

"Miss Oona..." the woman said. Her eyes glistened. "...ah, sweet girl."

"Don't mention it!" Oona said. She pulled a Kleenex tissue from the box Ms. J. kept on her shelf of ladies' essentials and handed it to the smiling woman. She wrapped her in a big hug, kissed her on both cheeks, and then she dashed out as quickly as she'd come in, leaving the woman shaking her head and smiling after her.

She took the stairs back down to find Carol tugging a protesting Truman by the scarf.

"But I hadn't finished my story!" Truman whined, holding his hands out toward a group of tipsy stragglers he'd cornered for one final tall tale of the evening.

"That may be so, Truman darling, but they had finished listening," Carol said.

"Come on," Oona said, heading for the door. "Carol and I have a trip to plan!"

❧

Preparations for their cross-country trip made the time fly, and Oona soon found herself in a tight but comfortable pullman berth, ready to ride across the land as Carol's chaperone. It was too good to be true, but rather funny, as well, that her seventeen-year-old presence was required in order to make the whole production seem somehow more honorable. Oona had read his letters. His intentions were not 'honorable' in the least. Whatever the case, he'd sent money and Carol bought the tickets. They would wait at the hotel Bill booked for them until he could leave from the base, and then Carol was to meet Bill's family. Somewhere in there, Oona thought, she might be able to see her father in nearby San Francisco.

Carol bustled around town in the weeks before the trip, having new dresses made and old ones altered, making sure her hair was blonder than blonde.

They watched the bustle on the platform as the train pulled away.

"I'm going to pretend I'm a Harvey Girl, going to find my fortune," Oona said. "Like in Samuel Hopkins Adams's book."

"You're going to pretend you're a poor girl excited to become a waitress?" Carol said, shaking her head.

"It sounds romantic."

"Romantic."

"Yes. Striking out on your own to make a new life for yourself. There aren't that many ways for a girl to do that, in case you haven't noticed," Oona said. *What am I saying? Of course she hasn't noticed.*

Carol pulled back a curtain and looked out the window, turning to see both directions. "Imagine it, Oona. Gloria's own grandfather built these railroad tracks."

"Well, his company built them. I highly doubt the commodore ever swung a hammer."

"Still, if not for him, we would be taking a horse and buggy to California."

"Speak for yourself!"

The train was full of soldiers wearing nervous, chivalrous grins, the terror of offering their young lives for God and country madly blunted by basic training, cigarettes, and alcohol. Most were barely out of high school, with glowing, pimpled faces and hands that shook, exposing the flimsiness of their bravado. Some others, the golden boys, were more practiced at projecting confidence. Former football quarterbacks and Eagle Scouts, they sported a shiny baked-on enamel confidence, no visible scratches in sight.

The states rolled by Oona's window like a beautiful movie. Each new vista emerged perfectly set, like an epic opening scene. Oona imagined the views framed on the big screen and set to it music. The wide-open plains got orchestral treatment with plenty of violins and timpani rolls. Streams called for piccolos, rivers needed a rhythm section and in some parts, banjos. But the most beautiful of all were the mountains. She switched seats when the red rock came within inches of her window, sending shadows that made her dizzy (the music for that scene would have been ominous—bassoons and oboes, maybe the low end of the piano keyboard). The vast valleys of New Mexico called to her from the other side of the railroad car. Every instrument of a full orchestra, playing the highest notes at fortissimo, even that wouldn't have conveyed the overwhelming grandeur of that view.

Carol went to the dining car and came back with three young soldiers trailing behind. Each carried a plate or cup or a sandwich wrapped in crinkly waxed paper. Carol carried only her smile. Her cheeks glowed pink and white like strawberries and cream, and Oona realized for the first time what it was about Carol's face that she'd been trying to figure out. Of course, she was beautiful. A stunner. Men could not yank their eyes off her. And no one else looked anything like her. But now, with the mountain light hitting her pretty mouth just this way, she saw it. For all the world, Carol always looked like a little girl who had just pulled her thumb out of her mouth, like a child who only breaks from her thumb-sucking habit in order to ask for a lolly, or to call for her nurse. Her front teeth jutted prettily, adorably, just as they probably had when she was an irresistible little girl, as they had when her mother introduced her to her new beau and won his heart over on the spot. She was a living doll, grown up too fast and with a body she couldn't control.

The soldiers, heartbreaking with their fresh crew cuts and their earnest expressions, placed Carol's purchases on the table as Carol positioned herself to best effect, draping an arm over Oona's seat. Oona smoothed the waist of her dress and sat up straight. The cut of her travel dress emphasized her own figure to perfection, and she knew it. She arched her back, just slightly. Carol arched hers with a casual theatricality. The train car groaned and the soldiers sank, helpless, into the nearest empty seats.

In Omaha, Oona hopped off the train. While passengers loaded and unloaded, she ran to the post office window. She pulled an envelope addressed to San Francisco from her handbag, kissed it, then handed it across the counter to the sleepy postwoman.

"When should that reach its destination?" Oona asked.

The woman looked at her blankly. Silvery dust had settled around her eyes, highlighting the lines baked in by the prairie sun. "Before you do," she said.

Oona eyed the envelope until it disappeared into a burlap bag behind the counter.

Next, they stopped in Leavenworth, Kansas, and the girls stepped off the train for a fast walk and meal at the local Harvey House. They said Harvey Houses brought fine dining to the West, and even though fewer people rode the trains since the war started, they didn't disappoint. Oona ate her steak and potatoes with gusto. It had been a few years since Oona made her trip to visit Daddy, and she'd looked forward to coming back here ever since. The loos were a big improvement from the train, too, and the girls used them to freshen up for the next leg of the journey.

Back on the train, Oona chose an open seat in the general seating rather than the coach car. She looked forward to reading her book in peace and watching the scenery change. Her spirits lifted with each mile they traveled from New York, leaving the insulated routine of the city further and further in the distance.

Carol left for the dining car the moment they boarded, though they had just eaten a full meal at the Harvey House. "These darling GIs are going to buy me a soda, Oona. You coming?"

"Yeah, doll. You coming?" one of the soldiers said.

"No, thanks. I'm going to put up my feet for a while. You all go on."

"Well, all right. You stay here and be a big old dud, I suppose," Carol said, blowing Oona a playful kiss.

One of the soldiers got down on one knee beside her. "I'm gonna find you the biggest slice of cherry pie they have, nice and red, just like your pretty lips."

Oona placed her hand on his chest and looked him in the eye with her sweetest expression. "Why don't you eat it yourself," she said. The other men hooted as the soldier put a hand to chest and hung his head, pretending to be stricken.

Just as the conductor called for "all aboard," one last woman hurried up the steps, lugging small bags in each hand. She carried a cloth satchel knotted to a stick over her shoulder. Her frizzled hair was piled on her head like a weaverbird nest held all over with stark black hair pins that stood out against the sun-bleached strands. Over her shoulders she wore a rough shawl with shades of a desert sunset embla-zoned across a geometric design. She unwrapped a fur of some indistinguishable animal from around her neck as she looked over the car, assessing the seating options.

She chose the first bench seat near the door, across the aisle from Oona, and quickly settled her-self with a collection of small bags all around her on the bench and under her seat. Then she pulled paper and a fine pen from what looked like a man's attaché case, arranging it on the table in front of her, and began scribbling intently before the train pulled away again from the station. She had a busy, substantial air about her and seemed to take assumed ownership of the car as she set about shuffling papers and flipping through a ledger, comparing numbers from a long sheet with those in the thick black book while mumbling to herself, things like, "Not if I have anything to say about it…" and "Oh, ho, ho. I should say not, haha!"

Oona smiled and turned to her window. The view as they left the station became once again vast and boundless, with dry, barren fields giving way to rows of carefully tended grains, fall vegetables, and potato vines. Scrawny mules and wild, rust-colored dogs ignored the passing train, unimpressed with the roar of the engine and the smell of burning coal and the faces in windows that flashed by day after day.

The crooked remains of a shanty town came into view as the train picked up speed, and two men emerged from the rubble. They ran alongside the train, matching their speed to the train's as it gained, and Oona turned to watch them leap and grab the edge of a boxcar as it rounded a bend and whipped sideways like the tail end of some enormous prairie snake.

The whistle blew, long and high pitched, and Oona thought of the Willa Cather book in her coat pocket. What would her favorite author write of these prairies if she saw them right now, just as Oona saw them? She moved the velveteen curtain further aside and leaned her head on the glass, trying to peer as far out over the horizon as her eyes would go.

"Oh, ho, ho!" The woman across the aisle slapped the pages of the ledger, shaking her head as if the book itself insulted her intelligence. Curious, Oona discreetly turned to watch.

Light the color of apricots and forget-me-nots shone through the windows, the last of the day's sun, highlighting the woman's profile to reveal the outline of what must have once been a very beautiful face, now turned to soft beige leather. Whatever it was she was working on, it seemed to amuse her to no end. Feeling Oona's eyes on her, she looked up from her pages. Oona glanced away, then back again, and smiled.

"Ah hell," the woman said. "Was I being too loud?"

"Oh, no, not at all," Oona said.

"Yes, I was. But you're too well-mannered to say," the woman closed the ledger and stacked the papers. Clearing the table, she motioned for Oona to join her on the other side of her table.

"I'm afraid I can't ride backward," Oona said. "I get a bit woozy."

The woman cleared the seat beside her and patted the cushion. Oona looked around. No sign of Carol. She wondered for a moment if anyone else could see this lady, or if she had conjured a character from some book. Either way, the lady across the aisle was a bouffant composure of fur and fabrics and turquoise and business too fascinating to resist.

"I'm Effie," the woman said, offering a hand. "Effie Jenks."

"I'm Oona," she said, settling in the corner of her seat. As usual, she left off her last name, just in case a fan of her father recognized the name.

"Oona, huh?" The woman said. "Tell me, what kind of a name is that?"

"Irish," Oona said. "It means 'one.' Or some people say it means 'lamb.'"

"Maybe it means 'one lamb' then, hmm?"

"Maybe," Oona said. "Say, what were you working on so hard?"

"Oh, that. Just my portfolio. I own some land, y'see, and I'm on the way to meet with my manager."

Oona nodded, thinking of the meetings she used to overhear when Mother was selling some of the property near Spithead. She'd learned a lot about real estate at a young age, but mostly about selling, not buying.

"But I do want to hear all about it. And all about you, too."

The woman seemed pleased to be asked. She settled her hands in her lap and looked straight ahead as if thinking where to begin. Once she started, her words came like pellets from a shotgun.

"My husband died last year, and long story short, I own a bunch of old dead gold mines in a town called Bland, if you can believe that. But I'm getting ahead of myself, and you said you wanted a story."

"I did."

"I was a Harvey Girl. You ever heard of that?"

"Yes!" Oona couldn't believe her ears. Just like the book!

"Like the girls at the restaurant at that station we just left. Fred Harvey set up these fine restaurants along the Santa Fe Railroad, and the dining cars, too. Then he hired girls like me to make the experience like fine dining in any fancy city out East.

"We made good money, and food and lodging were provided. We made enough to send home. Lots of girls came out of the dust or from places where they wouldn't have had a chance to improve their lives any other way. It was like a miracle for those of us who got hired. He took care of us. I sent all the money I made back to my family and it kept them alive.

"Now we weren't allowed to date the customers, but of course that didn't stop them from asking. People started calling the Harvey establishments a 'matrimonial bureau,'" she laughed, a big round laugh that brought a sparkle to her eyes. "Stay out here long enough, you'll meet all sorts of women ranch owners, business owners, and the like. They married the men who came out here to make something of themselves, and it makes good sense when you think about it. The men had that in common with us Harvey Girls: we were all brave and intrepid enough to take a chance on the unsettled west."

Oona thought of her father's play *The Fountain*, but she held her tongue. Daddy's play about the search for the Fountain of Youth depicted a different version of the 'Wild West' than most history books conveyed. He'd finished it the year she was born, and she'd kept a copy in her book collection through every move, every new boarding school. She'd even slipped one into Carol's stepfather's library.

A young woman with a tea cart stopped by their table.

"Ms. Jenks! It's lovely to see you, ma'am!" she said.

"Molly girl, how are you? Doing the dining car run, are you?" Effie pointed to the plates of cake and cookies and raised her eyebrows at Oona. Oona nodded. The delicate slices of dense fruit cake and rich butter cookies with ruby-red jam centers looked like they could have come from the window of a fine Manhattan bakery. The waitress deftly set the table in front of them.

"I'd better get this perfect, seeing as I'm serving you, Mrs. Jenks! Only a Harvey Girl legend, that's all!"

"Balderdash," Effie said, but she couldn't help adjusting a crookedly placed fork when the girl turned her back. Then she proceeded to heap spoons of sugar into her teacup.

They ate in silence for a few moments. The pastries tasted even more beautiful than they looked, the tea aromatic and invigorating. Effie looked faraway out the window.

"I've been places I never imagined I would go. All started by being brave enough to take my life in my own hands. I married a good man, Thomas Henry Jenks was his name. He had kings and knights in his family tree. His first cousin was Jerome K. Jerome, the English author and playwright? Have you heard of him, dear? Probably not, but that's fine..."

Oona dabbed the corners of her mouth with the cloth napkin and started to speak, but then pressed her lips together instead and blinked encouragingly.

"My husband was friends with Herbert Hoover, Theodore Roosevelt, Taft—he was invited to the White House! And here I was, daughter of Danish immigrant peasants. But look at me now!" She pulled the shawl around herself and raised her chin, then filled the car with her laughter again. She sipped her tea as the train slowed to cross a river gorge. The trestle rumbled beneath them and the sun painted the water to a showy necklace of diamonds and rubies, worn with pride.

"One thing I can tell you, Oona girl, is there's nothing wrong with marrying a man with money, so long as you love him. Love is wonderful, but money helps. Times are hard for everyone. This damned Depression we've been through..." She shook her head with the stories she could tell. "But it's harder for a woman to get her own money any other way than marriage. Some day that has to change, but we're living in now, and now is what we have. The important thing is that a girl knows herself and her own value. He might have money, but you have something, too, and not only what you might think it is either. A man needs a partner in life, not just a pretty thing to set on his mantel. Without a good partner, a man can get himself in all *sorts* of trouble."

Oona nodded. Not since Aunt Gertrude had anyone encouraged her to think of herself as more than a pretty face. What an amazing life this woman had lived, was still living! Had she had someone who believed in her? Who encouraged her to go into the world bold and brave? Or was she the product of harsh circumstances in a generation with no space for fear or doubt, lest you get left behind in the dust?

"Oona, huh?" Effie said, swallowing the last of her syrupy tea. "I don't think I've ever met another Oona," she said. "Nope. You're special. You're the only Oona."

❦

Carol didn't reappear for several hours, and when she did, her lipstick was smudged and her entourage had grown.

"Well, now I feel guilty," she whispered, dropping into the seat next to Oona.

"No, you don't," Oona said.

"You're right. I don't," Carol sighed. "There are so many handsome men in the world."

"Right, but we're on the way across the country to see one in particular, so maybe sit on a block of ice or something till we get there."

The soldiers spent the rest of the afternoon trying to impress the girls with their most heroic stories from back home and their big plans for the future. By the time they went back to their bunks, Oona was half in love with each one of them, and Carol was in love with the attention.

"Listen, Oona," Carol said. "I have to write Bill a letter. His letters are so highbrow and literary, I need some help."

"Okay, I guess," Oona said.

"How about you let me crib some lines from one of Jerry's letters? They're always so clever and so...

tender. Tenderer than God, which is a bit too tender if you ask me. But I need to sound smart to impress Bill or he's going to decide I'm just a dumb kid and drop me."

"Okay, okay!" Oona said. She pulled out one of Jerry's latest letters from the depths of her book bag. After a slew of apologetic letters, then a few more angry ones, the last one before they left New York had been the most ardent yet. Coming on the heels of the mean ones before, it had had the opposite effect from what he might have hoped: she was almost ready to stop giving him any more chances.

"Good grief! How does he have time to write these letters?" Carol said, taking the fat envelope and leafing through the pages.

Oona shrugged.

"So romantic!"

"Do you think so?" Oona said. "I don't know. But then I don't find mercurial highs and lows as romantic as you do."

"What is this signature?" Carol said, reading the last line. "'Drippleton Mashingworth'?"

"He always signs the really dramatic ones with some made up name. The last one was a humdinger, and he signed it 'Thiero Santi Winslow.'"

Carol looked confused.

Oona shook her head and turned to look out the window. "Don't ask me."

Outside, an abandoned farm came into view. Dry brown stalks of some unidentifiable grain leaned as one with the wind created by the train as it passed. As the train car pulled even with the falling-down fence, a large white dog appeared from behind a stand of hawthorne. The creature looked up at the train, its eyes hollow with hunger and its ribs clearly visible under mangy fur.

All at once, a memory of a memory washed through her mind, awakening an old pain that never really slept. She leaned her head against the window and thought of Bermuda, and of a dog that had once been part of her family—when they were still a family.

Bermuda, 1929

*D*addy's favorite dog Finn MacCool wandered the grounds of Spithead with the same drooping aimlessness as Shane and Oona. He poked around, restless, the tethers fraying from days and nights left flapping in a rough new wind. Nothing was solid. Nothing stayed the same.

Oona's big brother Shane, at nine years old, seemed already to feel the weight of the coming years descending on his narrow, freckled shoulders.

Agnes was leaving. She hugged the children quickly and turned from them with distracted finality. Her bags were packed, and she had a trunk this time. She was going to New York for Daddy's premier whether he wanted her there or not.

"When you come back, will Daddy come with you?" Shane asked as Agnes strode from room to room, lifting papers and books in search of some mislaid document.

"Yes," she said. "No." She stopped in the middle of the room, casting around, hands on her narrow hips. "I don't know," she mumbled.

"Oh, but Muvver, say 'yes,'" Oona said. "When you see Daddy, will you tell him I want him to come home?"

"Yes, Mother, tell him Oona misses him terribly and wants him to come home," Shane said. "And tell him Finn misses him terribly, too." He ran to the book shelf and retrieved a framed photo of his father standing with the wolfhound he used to love, on the day they'd taken family photos in the garden. He shoved it into Mother's hands.

In the months that followed while their mother was gone, Oona haunted the halls of Spithead, listening. Her hair grew too long and her dresses too short. Wherever Shane went, she tried to follow, padding along on tiptoes, quietly as she could, but he would catch her and send her along back up to the house. Finally, Oona tried a new tack.

"I'm not a baby, Shane. Take me with you. I can help."

"Help with what?" Shane patted Finn's side. The dog's lips pulled back and his tongue hung out, giving him a laughing look. Oona patted his head.

"Whatever you're going to do. I'm good at helping." Oona looked up at him, pushing her fringe from her eyes.

"I'm not going anywhere to do anything," Shane said. "I'm just going away from here. Some place where I can think."

Oona had been trying hard to be extra quiet. All Daddy had wanted was some peace and quiet to work. A place with no toys strewn all about or children asking endless questions. Before he left, he had taken to working in a shack on the property rather than be in the house with them. With her.

"I can be quiet," Oona said. "Quieter."

He looked into her eyes and gave in, sitting down in the grass beside Finn and patting the ground. "You're all right, Oona. It's not you."

"Then why do you want to go away from me?"

"I don't. You don't get it." He let her lean against his sunburned arm. "You're the only one around here I want to be around."

First Gaga had been sent away, then Daddy left, and now Mother had been gone so long with no idea when she was coming back. The new nanny was a stranger. There was no one left at this house to make it their home. No one but his little sister. And Finn.

"When Mother brings Daddy back, I'm going to be so quiet, like a mouse," Oona said.

"You don't have to be quiet if you don't want to. God damn it. You're a little kid."

"You shouldn't say guhdammit."

"Why not? Daddy says it, and worse."

"Don't say that!"

"Why not? He can't hear me."

Oona half-closed her eyes. She skimmed the surface of the grass with the palm of her hand. A pelican flew overhead, dipped low and swooped up, headed for the docks. "Still, we have to practice being good. For when he comes back."

Shane looked at the top of his sister's head. He couldn't bear to see her half-close her eyes like that, just like Father. "Okay, Oona," he said. "I'll try."

Oona smiled. Shane's eyes looked like Daddy's.

"But before I start, you want to hear a poem?"

"Yes, please!"

"All right, well here goes." A naughty expression danced around his mouth.

> A wonderful bird is the pelican.
> His bill can hold more than his belican.
> He can hold in his beak
> Enough food for a week,

He paused, grinning.

But I'm damned if I see how the helican.

Oona's face froze, her eyes wide and her mouth big and round, and when the giggles broke out, Shane's smile broke through the sadness that had settled into his young face.

CR80

Neighbors near Spithead had begun to wonder how long the O'Neill children were to be left on the island with neither parent anywhere on the horizon. Oona heard them at the front door, questioning the housekeeper, who knew little more than they did but made efforts to assure them all was well. The Hubers in the next house, whose children sometimes played with Oona and Shane, questioned their children for updates. When they spied the cook coming or going, they'd send members of their own staff out to make small talk with the ulterior motive of bringing the conversation around to what the hell was going on over there.

One neighbor, Mr. Stokes "of the Philadelphia Stokes," prevailed upon the much-loved butler of another neighbor, a young Mr. Timoney, to give him a hand with a difficult situation. Oona heard Timoney talking about what the man said: Mr. Stokes had been keeping a close eye on the goings-on over at the O'Neill household, he said, and was keen to know whether Timoney knew what the O'Neill's giant nuisance of a dog had done to the poor defenseless chickens in the coop? Why he'd torn those poor birds to shreds and left nothing but the feathers, that's what. He, for one, had had enough of that damned wolfhound Finn MacCool. Who gave their dogs such a name, anyway? The horse-like creature never liked him, barking whenever he came into view with all the vim and vinegar that he could muster. But it didn't end there. The damned thing barked and howled nightly, and nobody over there seemed to give a damn. Damn, damn, damn.

Timoney said Mr. Stokes had handed over his own pistol, and gave Timoney a grim command.

"But sir, the dog is just being a dog, sir," the butler said.

"Listen here, I've had about all I can of that damn dog. I want you to go over there and take care of it." Old Mr. Stokes of the Philadelphia Stokes said.

"Take care of it, sir?"

"Yes. You can take my gun."

"It's not a wild dog, sir. It belongs to the O'Neills."

"Yes, but neither of the O'Neills are home and the blasted dog is running wild. The boy can't manage it. You go over there now and just take care of it, will you?"

Oona consoled herself. It wouldn't happen. A person would never shoot a dog just for being a dog.

But one day, in the late afternoon, she watched from her window as Shane wandered to the back yard to water the chickens.

"Hey, Finn!" he called, rounding the side of the house. "Finn, where are you, boy? Time to water these chickens." He knew each hen by name. With both their parents gone, he'd taken to watering them in the afternoons before throwing a stick with Finn. Then he'd pour a bucket of water over himself and Finn for good measure, to wash off the hot salty day.

An ocean breeze lifted the palm fronds high above and an afternoon cloud slipped over the sun. The air was too quiet as he drew closer to the coop. No excited clucking, none of the normal commotion. Oona strained to make it out. At the edge of the yard, a gruesome scene took shape. Not one chicken had been spared.

"Finn?" he said, his voice low. Then he ran, shouting all around the yard, "Finn!"

Oona dashed from the house and across the yard to find Shane lying beside Finn, his face red and matted with muddy tears. One arm was draped across the great dog's back, and Shane's eyes stared unblinking into his inanimate face.

Oona knelt beside her brother. She patted his head, his tangled curls drenched in sweat, and her heart shattered into her belly.

☙❧

Several weeks later, Agnes finally returned. The children rushed to her, hopeful for comfort and good news about Daddy, but her face was drawn and tight. They took her to see Finn's grave. Standing over the plot of freshly turned soil, she spoke of the happy time when she and Daddy had come here with Shane and this dog and a little girl on the way. This place was to be their sanctuary. Their perfect island of peace. All at once, there seemed no use in waiting to break more bad news.

"Your father has decided to marry that woman he met in Maine," she said, as much to hear the words herself as to tell the children. Life as they knew it before really was over. It was just the three of them now.

Shane cried until he again ran out of tears, and he looked toward the ruined coop where feathers still clung to the chicken wire. Oona held her mother's hand and thought of Finn. Daddy had loved Finn. But he left him. And now Finn was gone.

They placed a small marker where Finn was buried, and they all stood there together in stunned, impotent silence.

Dear Daddy,

I am writing from the train on my way to California. We're passing through such lovely country. I wish you could see it with me.

The train is full of young men on their way to serve in the war. I don't know if you heard about the charity movie premier of Moontide at the Rivoli on Broadway? I was asked to help with the planning and was pleased to do it. When I accepted the job, I thought first, "Daddy would think this is a fine thing to do," and it made me want to do it all the more. Did you see my picture in the paper?

Daddy, I write so often, and I hear back from you so rarely. Even if you don't approve of my publicity, that doesn't seem a reason to be so angry. I can explain if you'd let me. Please see me in person so I can do that. I only have one Daddy, and that is you. It breaks my heart missing you so while knowing you think things about me that are not true. If you knew how good I am, when so many want so much from me, you would be proud. I'm sure of it. Please,

Daddy, let me come visit you and explain it all.

I will be staying at the St. Francis Hotel in San Francisco, and I'll wait to hear from you. Just name the day and I'll be there.

Love,
Oona

Chapter 21

A GIRL WITH BLUE RIBBONS

San Francisco, October 1942

William Saroyan met Carol and Oona at the Oakland train station outside San Francisco. They stepped off the train and onto the platform, smiling and laughing as a half-dozen soldiers trailed behind, carrying their luggage—mostly Carol's, as Oona had under-packed once again—and serenading them with an alarmingly off-key rendition of "I Will Take You Home Again, Kathleen."

He grabbed Carol by the waist and kissed her roughly. "What's all this then?" he said, waving an arm at the young men, who shared a look between them and quickly took their leave.

"Those are our friends," Oona said, watching the backs of their heads disappear into the crowd. Those boys had made them laugh every day and cry in their sleeping car every night, those lovely young men, boys really, who were heading off to war. Who knew which of them would return?

"Is that right?" His jaw tensed as he herded Carol out of the station, with Oona close behind. His eyes bored through Carol's head.

But once they were in his car and the doors closed, he started shouting louder than Oona had ever heard anyone shout before.

"You were awfully chummy with those men!"

Carol looked out the window, a small smile on her face. Oona elbowed her, and she shrugged, smiling again.

"Who do they think they are? What right do they have to treat my woman like this? So familiar! Like a movie star, they followed you. Did they pay for your ticket out here, so they can drool all over you? Why would they feel they can do that, if they weren't encouraged, huh?"

When he caught her eye in the rear-view mirror, Oona got the clear message that he somehow blamed her for all this.

Bill didn't deserve the lovely lines Carol had cribbed from Jerry's letter. This was the great William Saroyan? What a jerk.

He ejected her from her room moments after getting to the Senator Hotel, handing her a few sweaty small bills and shutting the door in her face with a dismissive, "Kindly scram."

Oona went to the lobby and sat there for a while. What was she meant to do in this strange city, and when might she be allowed back in the room? Bill hadn't said, and Carol seemed too lost in the bad romance novel in her mind to be of any use.

She wanted something to eat and a hot bath. The lobby was full of people checking in and out, milling around with their suitcases and hat boxes and all the things people seemed to think they couldn't live without. She thought of her cosmetic case upstairs, holding all her lipsticks. Bill had better not touch them.

A man entered the lobby just then, and a little girl followed close behind. She was holding a red lollipop in one hand, and her hair was in two braids tied off with blue ribbons. She cradled a baby doll in her other arm, and as she came to stand beside the man, he put a hand on her shoulder. The gesture was so natural, so protective, Oona wiped tears from her eyes before they could fall. As the man and his daughter made their way to the elevator, she found herself walking to the lobby telephone booth. She strained close to the mouthpiece and pressed the receiver to her ear as the operator made the connection. After several clicks, the operator said, "I'll connect you now," and Carlotta's voice came on the line.

"Carlotta? Hello, it's Oona."

"Oona? Oh. Hello, child."

"Is Daddy there?"

"He's very busy at the moment. This is his work time."

"Oh, well, did he get my letter?"

"Which letter?"

"It was postmarked from Nebraska. I've come to California with Carol, as a chaperone, and—"

Carlotta laughed.

"Did he get it?"

"Did he what, child?"

"Did he get the letter?"

"I don't know."

Oona twisted the telephone cord around her fingers and squeezed hard. "Well, all right. Listen, Carlotta, do you think I could come and visit while I'm here? I'm not far away at all, and I really want to speak to Daddy in person. If I could just—"

"No, I'm afraid that's not possible."

"What?"

"It's not possible. In fact, your Daddy doesn't want you to call at all here anymore."

"I don't understand."

"Please don't argue with me, child. I am merely relaying a message."

Oona didn't reply. Words wouldn't come to her lips. She pressed the receiver harder against her ear, hoping to hear a trace of Daddy's voice in the background.

"Good bye," Carlotta said, a strange cheeriness in her voice now.

"Good bye," Oona said. She replaced the receiver on its hook and stood in the phone booth until she could feel her hands and feet again.

CRSO

She could not believe she was doing this, showing up uninvited and unexpected at Daddy's front door. But he'd left her no other choice. She slept on it, fitfully, once Bill let her back into room, and woke up determined. She had to try, even if it was only to see for herself that what Carlotta said was true. No thinking, no planning. She'd only overthink and get cold feet and change her mind.

The front door of Tao House opened. She looked over Carlotta's shoulder and saw Daddy at the end of the hall. He dismissed her with a wave of his hand. She engaged every muscle in her face, begging them to conjure the smile she had as a small girl, the one that could sometimes soften him toward her, make him take her on his lap and hold her around the shoulders for a few moments.

But then Carlotta said one word, a simple "No," and closed the door.

Words crashed inside Oona's head, clogged her throat, rattled her teeth. Her palms pressed against the door and she lowered her head, the image of Daddy's face blurring behind her tears.

CR8O

Oona stared at the hotel ceiling, trying not to close her eyes, not even blink. Each time her eyelids shut, the same image projected there behind them: Carlotta at the door, Daddy at the end of the hall, the door closing, shutting her out.

She searched her memories, mined every moment of her life she'd held onto thus far, trying to figure it out. How had it come to this? How could she have failed so miserably? All she wanted was her family back. To feel again the way she had as a small child, when Mother and Daddy were both there, in Bermuda. When all she had to do was smile and Daddy would turn kind for a moment. She smiled for the cameras now instead, always hoping he might see the picture in his morning paper, on the other side of the country, and remember.

She'd fashioned her group of friends into a sort of substitute, but now even that was falling apart. They were all going their own ways, and soon they'd have families of their own. Why was it so hard for her to have something so simple? Carol had been her closest friend, but every new day brought fresh concerns about her. What used to seem like innocuous confidences started to take on a more nebulous tone: "Make sure you don't tell Truman. He'll just say it's a lie," or "Gloria said Pat is a brute, but if you ask her, she'll say she didn't—best not to bring it up." Why was she so cagey? And what was she doing with this insufferable man?

On his last day of leave, Bill sent Oona away, again. She wandered around a corner drugstore as long as she could, trying not to imagine what was going on back at the hotel. She got a bite to eat, looked in shop windows, and then took the long way back. When she returned, Carol was alone.

"He's in the adjoining room," Carol whispered, apparently all full of propriety now. She blotted her hair with a towel, but her makeup was in place. She hummed the theme from *Wuthering Heights* and tilted her head to the light, just like Merle Oberon as Cathy, as she languidly rubbed cream on her limbs.

Oona put her shopping bag on the bureau, which was covered with things she didn't recognize. Bill had certainly made himself at home.

"What exactly is Bill's problem with me?" Oona asked.

"He thinks you're a bad influence," Carol said absently.

"On who?"

"On me."

"*I'm* a bad influence...on *you*?"

"Shhh," Carol said.

"Where would he get that idea, Carol?"

"I have no idea."

"Remind me, Carol: Why am I friends with you again?"

"Oona, listen. I have to tell you something," Carol said. "Bill has asked me to marry him!"

Oona sat down. *That's it.* This whole lark to California had been a huge mistake. First Daddy wouldn't see her, and now Carol actually wanted to *marry* this man?

"But first, he wants me to get pregnant."

Oona's face froze.

"It's because of his family. To show them I can have children. It's a cultural thing."

"I'm pretty sure that's not true, Carol." Oona's head spun. Was Bill tricking Carol, or was Carol tricking her?

"I don't know, but I want to marry him, Oona. He's established. He's a writer. He won a *Pulitzer.*"

"Oh, a *Pulitzer*? Well, why the hell didn't you mention that one hundred times before?" She covered her eyes and laughed as though she might cry. Carol couldn't say Bill's name without also saying the word "Pulitzer." It was obnoxious. Her father also had a Pulitzer. A Pulitzer didn't mean a damned thing about a person. "He's asking you to do this, and *I'm* a bad influence? I wouldn't even eat dinner with that man if it weren't for you." She sprang up and flew across the room, stopping with her hand on the front doorknob. "You're *not* marrying him, Carol, because I am going to kill him!"

"Shhhh, Oona, please! He'll hear you!" She sat on the edge of the bed like a rag doll. "He's everything I could want. I love him so much I'm going to be sick thinking about it."

"Oh really? Maybe you're pregnant already." Oona held her head and had to sit down.

"Oh, you're impossible." Carol wrung her hands as tears gathered in her eyes.

"It's ridiculous," Oona said. "The most ridiculous thing to ask someone." Maybe this was the big difference between herself and Carol. Oona knew she wanted to have children, but she would want to give them a real, honest family with a father who would be there for them. Not like the one she had. Bill was too much like Eugene O'Neill, in the same way she could see Jerry was. Their ambition to have their names followed by the word "genius" overrode anything and everything else. Including their families.

Carol lived on dreams and fibs and justified so much to herself by chalking it up to the dramatic vacillations of romance. Romance was the center of her life. Romance was love, and love was pain. Oona's idea of love was different. She didn't know what love would turn out to be when she found it, but somehow, she knew it was not what Bill was asking of her beautiful, impressionable, possibly insane friend.

"Carol, please. Promise me you will not marry Bill," Oona said, with the last of her energy. She thought of one last point to try. "It's not too late for it to have been a little fling, right? Like Truman always says?"

Carol brightened, a little. "You're saying I should have a full affair, and then end it?"

"No, Carol," Oona said wearily. "That is *not* what I'm saying. Not at all. Don't put words in my mouth—"

"It's not a terrible idea," Carol said, her eyes going distant, then she snapped back. "But I want to marry him. I want to get married."

"You want to *be* married. Like Gloria." She waited for the point to settle.

While the wheels turned in Carol's head, Oona thought back over the days since they'd arrived here. Why would Bill think she was a bad influence on Carol? How much had Carol told him about her problems with Daddy? Had she told him he wouldn't see her? Oona knew how writers thought. If the great Eugene O'Neill wouldn't see his own daughter, Bill would conclude she must have done something to deserve it.

She retrieved her shopping bag from the bureau, and noticed a telegram amongst Bill's things. The sender's address was Tao House. She snatched it off the bureau and read it:

Telegram Service
To: Pvt. William Saroyan
Camp Kohler, Sacramento, California

Heard Oona traveled with your new girl. I would watch out for that girl—I'm referring to my stepdaughter!

From: Carlotta Monterey
Tao House, San Diego

What the hell?
"Oh, and Oona," Carol said sheepishly. "There's one more thing."

"What is it?" Oona's voice was thin, defeated.

Carol answered fast: "Bill thinks you're older than I am." Then she dashed back to the bathroom.

Oona sat down on the bed, speechless. She expected the room to spin or her stomach to lurch in it's usual way, but somehow, it just didn't.

Change was coming. Inevitable. Unavoidable. Necessary. Like growing up.

$\mathcal{C}$hapter 22

PILE OF THINGS

San Francisco, late October 1942

B ill left them at their hotel where they were to wait around, amuse themselves, until he was able to get away again. He was back within a day. Did he ever actually report for duty? He collected them from the hotel with the plan to ride out to the rocks near a river he knew. Carol rode in front, and Bill kept a constant eye on Oona in the rearview mirror.

He'd invited another man along without asking the girls, a fellow called Ross he said was his cousin, in the apparent hope he would hit it off with Oona and keep her out of his way.

The cousin pressed against her the whole way in the back seat of Bill's hot, sticky car, and once she'd peeled herself out, she spent the day in the river's irresistible rushing water. At twilight, the men took the car and went off in search of provisions, and she and Carol explored the shore, finding a dreamy lagoon hidden in a cove. They stripped to their underclothes and waded into the water, then took of the underwear, too, balling it up and throwing it all to the shore. Like two nymphs free of the gaze of male eyes, they floated on the surface and then dropped their feet to sink to the bottom, over and over. The cool water felt wonderful, sparkling and quiet. Oona closed her eyes half-way, tuning her ears to the lapping of the water around her face as it stroked her hair in waves spreading out over the surface like a mysterious black island.

The quiet was broken by the high trill of Carol's laughter, her voice calling to someone. Oona put her feet on the riverbed and stood, hunched to stay under the water. The men were back already, and Carol waved to them, beckoning them to join.

"Carol! What are you doing?" Oona said. "We don't even know that man." The men quickly shed their clothes as they came toward the water. "Wait!" she shouted at them. "Wait right there!"

"What's wrong with you?" Bill said. He was drunk. "Is Miss O'Neill a prude?" Carol giggled.

Oona stood up, completely naked, and calmly walked up the shore to retrieve her clothes. The cousin tried to approach her, but she waved him away, and he moped against a rock while Carol and Bill disappeared behind the edge of the cove. Oona drank half a beer and lay back to watch the clouds. She tried pretending she was on a desert island, alone, but the sounds of Carol and Bill splashing and giggling and moaning kept disturbing the peace.

The sun went low, and Bill and Carol reappeared, wrapped in damp towels, Carol's pale skin pruney and mucky and decidedly not sexy.

Back in Bill's car, they rode in silence for a while. The plan was to make their way to Los Angeles next. Bill had some appointments set up, something about making one of his plays into a film, and there was the chance she and Carol might be able to see Gloria, who was staying at the Beverly Hills Hotel. They settled in for the drive, but Oona soon felt Bill's eyes on her again, in the rearview mirror. It made her skin crawl.

"What's your friend's problem, Carol?"

"I don't have a problem, Bill," Oona said. "And I can speak for myself."

"Is that so?" he said. His brows drew together menacingly. "So what is it? Why didn't you want to swim with us?"

"I decided I didn't like the water that much after all."

"Don't like the water?" His patronizing tone made her want to punch the back of his neck. "What about bathtubs? I suppose you hate bathing. A girl should keep herself clean, you know." He laughed mockingly.

The sound of the tires on the road slowly drowned under the roaring in her ears. She knew he must have seen her publicity photo in the paper, the one where she had posed in a bathtub. She'd worn a swimming costume in the water, taking the straps off her shoulders to sit in the tub covered in bubbles. It was to be playful and fun, glamorous. But the photographer's assistant had dug out underclothes from the laundry hamper and dropped them beside the tub without her seeing. She'd been mortified when she saw the layout, how it implied she must have undressed in front of the photographer. She'd hoped Daddy hadn't seen it. Add it to the pile of things he held against her. He would be furious, but even he could not have been as furious as she had been. It had been syndicated to papers everywhere.

But had Bill really just said that to her? He must have, because he laughed, but what was worse, Carol laughed, too. The sound reverberated in her head, rattling around with his words.

A girl should keep herself clean.

Who did he think he was?

"You're right, Bill," Oona said. "Just another reason why Carol should stay away from you."

She was glad then that she was stuck in the back seat where she could shoot daggers at the back of his head. His eyes in the rearview mirror told her how much he would love to slap the stubborn boldness right off her face.

When they reached the hotel, she went to the new room alone and locked and bolted the door. Carol could stay with Bill tonight. And his boring cousin, too, if she wanted to. She'd had enough of Bill and the person Carol was when she was with him. She'd wasted enough time 'chaperoning' this ridiculous situation.

It was time to do something about her *own* future. Would Daddy reply to her letter now? If he knew how much she wanted to please him, to make him proud, he would understand. She'd only taken advantage of opportunities when they presented themselves. What else was she to do with no one to turn to for advice? The Debutante title, the role in

Pal Joey, the charity work with the American Theater Guild, all seemed like things that might make a father proud. If only he would have answered her letters all these years. Maybe he would know her better now.

She could tell him all of that if she could get past Carlotta, if she could see him alone without her buzzing in his ear. Who knew what she said to him about her? About Shane?

Oona's body shook from within. Her fists opened and closed, opened again, tingling with the desire to hold the letter she had to believe her father was writing to her right now.

☙❧

Her father's reply did come, through his lawyer, via Mother. She'd already heard he still accused her of trading on his name. What was she supposed to do? Change it? It was her name, too. Hadn't he used his own father's name when he was getting started as a playwright? And hadn't his father paid for his first book of plays to be published, even though he didn't approve of them? Oona knew these things were true, Mother had told her, and yet Daddy conveniently forgot he was guilty of doing exactly what he accused her of.

Carol eventually came looking for her in the late afternoon, the next day. Oona's eyes were red and swollen.

"What did he say?" Carol asked, untying a new silk scarf from her hair.

Oona waved a hand toward the letter on her vanity.

After reading her father's words for the fifteenth time, she had crumpled the letter in her fists and thrown it in the wastebasket. But after circling it widely for some time, she retrieved it in a rush, flattening it out against the wall before folding it back into the envelope and propping it up like an accessory between two golden tubes of lipstick.

"'*Oona*,'" Carol read.

"*You should have written first and explained your present plans and ambitions in these war-torn days. Then I could tell you if I wanted to see you. As it is, all I know of what you have become since you blossomed into the night club racket is derived from newspaper clippings of your interviews...*"

She looked down at Oona, who sat at the vanity, filing her nails. The ferocity of the motion belied the indifferent expression she struggled to keep on her face.

"*...all the publicity you have had is the wrong kind, unless your ambition is to be a second-rate movie actress of the floozie variety—the sort who have their pictures in the papers for a couple of years and then sink back into the obscurity of their naturally silly, talentless lives...*"

She paused, tried and failed to catch Oona's eye, and continued.

"*...The thing I cannot forgive you is that you never wrote me to tell me about anything or to take advantage of my experience and ask my opinion—*"

"But you did write!"

Oona tilted her head and examined her nails closely.

"...whilst all the time you were riding on my name! I could have warned you against every stupid blunder you have made—from the standpoint of your own self-interest I mean..."

Oona bit her cuticle.

"To get back to your request to see me: you don't want to see me. Your conduct proves that. So let's cut out the kidding. And I don't want to see the kind of daughter you have become in this past year..."

"Oh, Oona, but this is so unfair of him! He doesn't even know you!"

Carol's eyes flew over the typewritten page. "Do you think maybe Carlotta wrote it?"

Oona threw the nail file against the vanity top and stood up. She began reciting the last part of the letter from memory as Carol looked back down at the crinkled page.

"Here's hoping you change as you grow out of the callow stage. I had hoped there was the making of a fine, intelligent woman in you, who would remain fine in whatever she did. I still hope so. If I am wrong, good-bye." Tears streamed down her face. To add humor to the tragedy, she finished with the soaring voice of a true thespian. *"If I am right, you will some-time see the point in this letter and be grateful— in which case..."* her hand drew a little flourish, *"au revoir."*

Carol came to her, held Oona's hands still with her own, pressed her forehead against hers.

"Oh, my sweet, darling friend," she said. "I am so sorry."

Oona sank into Carol's arms and let all the tears, and all the years, fall like the driving rains of a sea storm finally reaching the shore.

CRSO

Alone again in the hotel, Daddy's words echoed in her mind—*floozie, stupid, talentless... I don't want to see the kind of daughter you have become.*

What was this impossible devotion her father demanded? What did he believe he'd done to warrant it? Nothing in his behavior toward her in the years since he left could possibly justify the level of fatherly worship he seemed to believe was his due. The cruel audacity of chastising her for accepting a train ticket—not a flight!—but a train ride, when he himself lived in one castle after another, was simply too ridiculous. New cars, swimming pools, and all that alcohol didn't come cheap either.

In all the years of her childhood, all the adults she'd known had lived as if theirs were the lives that mattered, as if their children were accessories to be put on when they matched the occasion and otherwise ignored. Oblivious to the consequences to their inconvenient offspring, they schemed and planned their next moves, passing days and months in altered states of mind, while their children continued to grow up, to grow into people parsed together from bits and pieces they gleaned from any adult who seemed, maybe, perhaps, to be doing well enough. They were expected to become people of whom their parents could be proud, but there was no one to teach them, to guide them, to offer a solid role model. Money and the security it offered ruled their actions, but for children raised by a series of nurses and nannies and sitters who could disappear at the turn of a parent's favor, there was no such thing as security.

Oona raged through her room, throwing one item for every indignation he'd purposely tossed on the fire of his abandonment since she was a baby. Nothing was ever his fault. He had traded his family for a lying manipulator and turned her mother into a hollow shell all for his own selfish purposes. He'd resented the responsibility to care for and support the children he carelessly dumped in pursuit of his own ever-changing desires. The coward! He'd allowed his shrewish wife to destroy their family and build an impenetrable wall between him and his children. He wanted the innocent child he left fatherless to stop reminding him of his responsibility to her, and then he tore her down when she made the most of what she had.

The list had not ended, but she'd run out of things to throw. She found a hairbrush on the bed and gripped it with both hands.

Her father had ignored her for years, wouldn't allow her to visit him for the flimsiest of reasons, and then had the nerve to criticize the person she had become? But the worst offense of all was that he had succeeded in remaining almost entirely absent and negligent in his role as father while somehow keeping her on a tether he could yank at any time and make her run to him. Somehow it was worse to know he was there and didn't want her to forget him than it might have been if he'd just left her alone long ago, made the abandonment complete.

And he'd done it to all his children. She knew Eugene Jr. was a tortured soul because of him, and Shane's lost expression from their lonely days at Spithead never went away, his mournful eyes forever on the verge of tears, on the few occasions he'd fought his demons well enough to turn up as promised.

The hair brush flew. It hit the center of the shabby wall mirror, sending shimmering shards in the most surprising, satisfying explosion.

As the pieces fell to the hard floor, broken and transformed, Oona stopped in place. Panting, she pushed her hair from her eyes. The swirling air settled around her as she caught her breath, each one deeper and steadier than the last, and the vortex in her head slowed. She felt it collapse, leaving behind a strange quiet. Something was shifting, changing like light through a prism. She'd wasted so much time trying to make her father love her. How could she criticize Carol's choices when she wasn't going anywhere herself? Was it really only a few months ago she'd been named Number One Debutante, her pictures in all the papers? Now here she was, spending day after day playing indulgent nanny to a version of Carol she didn't recognize, one whose behavior seemed inspired more and more by a desire to be someone else, someone more like Gloria. To *be* Gloria.

They'd both been enamored with their glamorous, adventurous friend and her alluring way of living life one day at a time, confronting what may come minute by minute, with no fear of the future. She existed only for the moment and expected good things would happen. They'd wanted that for themselves. But Carol had lost herself to it, could see no further than this arrogant, self-serving man and his pretty, impermanent words.

No use looking back. What was the *point* of looking constantly back when what you found there made you only miserable? Her life had arrived—it was here, right now. She couldn't wait around for permission to live it any longer. It was up to her to make it into something different. Perhaps she could get up the nerve to write to Daddy's lawyer, to ask him to tell Carlotta to tell Daddy that his *daughter* said it was far too late for him to try to raise her now. The idea alone gave her strength.

She bent closer to the shattered, shimmering bits of mirror scattered across the floor, a mosaic of colors reflected from the deep olive of the walls, the gold brocade of the drapes, the glossy black of her hair, the creamy beige of her legs. She stared at the effect through half-closed eyes. Then she opened them wide and took it all in. She smiled.

She picked up the jagged pieces one by one. Then she straightened her shoulders and got to work setting everything in order.

PART
Three

Dear Orson,

I hope this finds you safe and sound, back in Los Angeles. I'm on my way there myself from San Francisco, and I plan to stay. I'd like to take you up on your generous offer to show me around.

You can reach me at the return address, my mother's new place. She won't mind you writing to me as she's very keen for me to get into the movie business. I hear her place is a temporary mobile home. We all must do our part! By the way, the war relief fundraiser I helped organize was a moderate success. It did not, however, impress my father one bit. Oh, but I've promised myself not to keep mentioning him! I should have written in pencil.

Sincerely,
Oona

P.S. Carol has been using your name to make that awful Bill Saroyan jealous whenever he gets a bit cool. I do hope she outgrows the fibbing stage soon. Then I can send the scamp off to kindergarten with a clear conscience, knowing I've done my part to raise her well!

Chapter 23

HOLLYWOOD TRAILER PARK

Hollywood, October 1942

The hit song from Bing Crosby's new movie *Holiday Inn* seemed to follow people around everywhere they went. "White Christmas." It rang from the store fronts and the cafés, played in lobbies and offices, floated through the air as if piped in just for her ears. The song pined away for just the type of setting Oona had left behind in New York, and gave her a small pang of doubt every time she heard it. Even now, it played on the transistor radio in the bedroom of the tiny mobile home, the only place Mother could get to work on her new novel due to wartime housing restrictions.

"I'm so glad you came to me," Agnes said brightly as she bustled from the closet to her nightstand and back to the closet in her stockinged feet. "Soon, you'll get a huge part in a movie, and your face will be on big screens all over the country."

Oona turned in her chair, looked at her hands. She traced the lines Orson had followed when he read her palm. Had coming here been the right choice? But then, what was there for her back in Manhattan? Mother had insisted Oona must strike while the iron was hot, while her name was still in the papers and there was interest in what *New York City's top debutante, daughter of playwright Eugene O'Neill* would do next. This time next year would surely be a whole different story, with an entirely new Christmas movie and new young women for journalists to write about.

Christmas in California would certainly be different from the last few in Manhattan, and it remained to be seen whether that would be a good or bad thing.

Oona was at the tiny vanity table, catching up on the beauty regimen she'd all but abandoned in the last few weeks of travel. She wore a cotton robe as a dressing gown and her feet were bare on the rough, nylon rug. She'd already plucked away an astounding number of stray brow hairs and removed layers of nail polish which had been poorly applied while riding in the back of Bill's car. She dipped her fingers in a bowl of acetone and watched as the chipped red color softened and dissolved away. It was rather poetic, really. Starting fresh. A new beginning.

She considered her face in the mirror. In her short time as Carol's 'chaperone,' she'd acquired a decidedly Irish version of a suntan—a wash of rosy glow across her cheeks and the bridge of her nose. It was no use. No amount of powder would counter it. She gave up, replacing her powder puff on the vanity.

The mobile home might not be the ideal living situation, but it was in Hollywood, near the action.

If nothing else, it offered quick access to town, to the places where the movers and shakers were. Agnes was getting by week-to-week, and certainly couldn't afford a hotel, so this place would have to do for now. In the grand scheme of things, it was a small sacrifice that would pay off in the long run. At least, that was the plebeian type of thinking Agnes tried to employ when a cockroach ran out of the kitchen drawer or the water ran ice cold in the shower.

Agnes came to stand behind Oona at the dressing table and nodded appreciatively at the effect in the mirror.

"Oona," Agnes said.

"Mother," Oona said through lips pursed for lipstick.

"Dear, I just want to say that I know may not have been entirely…available…for you in Manhattan." Oona sat up and returned her gaze in the mirror. Agnes raised her chin. "But we are here now, and I will do whatever I can to help you make it out here. Despite what your father thinks about it."

"Mother," Oona said, "I hope we can both try to learn to make decisions without thinking first of what Daddy will think."

"I hope that for you, Oona. But it's too late for me." She went to the wardrobe and brought out a new dinner gown, blue crepe de chine with a full skirt and cinched waist, and laid it across the bed. "What do you think?"

Oona didn't know where Mother had gotten the money for that dress, but she stopped short of protesting when she saw the hopeful look on her face.

"Thank you, Mother. It's glorious."

"I'm glad you think so. It has to be perfect. Hollywood is calling!"

The phone rang.

"Minna!" Agnes said, mouthing at Oona, "Minna Wallace!" and "Agent!" Her voice went up a full octave. "How are you, babe? Yes, yes, Oona arrived safe and sound. I know you're anxious to meet her!..."

Feeling the fabric of the new dress between her fingers, Oona couldn't help laughing at how on-the-nose it all was. Like a scene from a movie, the timing was perfect. Hollywood, quite literally, was calling.

Dear Jerry,

Every time I sit down to write to you, I get a feeling in the pit of my stomach that is not the way a girl should feel when writing to a beau. It's not new, but I'm starting to understand it better, as I'm starting to understand myself better. When I write to you, I feel the same trepidation and insecurity I feel when I'm writing to my father. My thoughts go to what I can say or do to make you happy, trying to write only those things that won't make you upset or angry. I figured out very recently that is not the way it should be. I'm afraid of it, and in large part it is because I've realized something, and now that I have realized it, I can never forget it, though I wish I could. I'll try to explain in this letter.

Jerry, you are a truly gifted writer. I'm so happy to hear you're still writing even while you're serving. You are going to take your place among the greats, I know it. Like I've always said: I can smell it! Like my father, you draw characters that do more than tell a story. They represent the mysteries of the human condition with such dazzling honesty. Your characters are your children, just as my father's characters have been for him.

This is what scares me.

I've spent my entire life to this point trying to get my father's attention, his love. A girl needs to feel loved by her father. What the child psychologists say actually is true: if a girl doesn't have the love of her father, she will forever look elsewhere for the security she misses because of it. Without knowing why it's happening, she searches constantly for something to fill the empty space where that love should be. Carol and Gloria and I used to talk so much about it, and I used to deny it was true. But when I realized how much your genius reminds me of my father, it all became completely clear to me.

I think I'm saying that this is why I've been hesitant to let our relationship grow too close. I've been protecting myself from falling for someone who will never truly be able to love me the same way in return. It's all very confusing and feels too enormous to grasp all at once, but I do know for sure that I cannot go from trying to be loved by my father to trying to be loved by you.

You say you love me, but my father loved my mother once, too. I know that may sound unfair, comparing you to my father, but now that I've realized it, I can't unsee it. I don't know what to do, because I do care for you a great deal. I didn't like it when you tried to change me, and I'd never expect you to change. It's just no good. It never works.

Please take care and stay safe, and don't forget to go looking for Hemingway (and his fake chest hair) in Paris once this dreadful war is over.

Sincerely,
Oona

P.S. Don't think for a <u>minute</u> I didn't recognize bits of myself in "The Long Debut of Lois Taggett." At least you called her 'intelligent,' so I suppose I can let it slide.

Chapter 24

BIG TIME HOLLYWOOD PARTY

Hollywood, Early November 1942

Mother had arranged to introduce Oona to some Hollywood friends at a party at the home of some producer and his third wife. Oona had met so many new people already, she worried she may to lose track of names. There were new pressures to replace the old, or in some cases add to them. They seemed to come from every side, pressing in just firmly enough to hold her together.

She had accepted the way things stood currently with her father, but knew she must find a way to get a message through to him. Even if he didn't want to speak to her, she would not be able to rest until she'd had a chance to clear the air, to know at the very least that their separation was not based on misunderstanding and lies.

Then there were the men. So many men, in their powerful suits and jaunty hats and smelling of expensive aftershave. They each drove a car more fantastical than the next. She'd never seen the likes of them, even in Manhattan. They all played some part in the world of filmmaking, and they all wanted a piece of her.

So far, she'd avoided the kinds of entanglements Carol and Gloria had found themselves in. Soon, though, she'd be considered an old maid in society circles. These beautiful glittering creatures treated first husbands like a sort of social appetizer. Yet, marry they did, early and often.

But this 'starter marriage' lifestyle didn't sit right. She had played the game, same as her friends, and done it well. She'd juggled countless beaus in Manhattan and managed to keep ahold of herself even without a parent around to look out for her. Men came on to her with blithe entitlement, as if they expected her to willingly tear her clothes off and jump on the nearest bed. But she'd learned to juggle them with the skill of an experienced woman twice her age—the benefit of having been an observant child who peeked around corners, listened at doors, read discarded letters. The nursery had not felt comfortable, never natural. At least not since Daddy left.

Then there was still Jerry. His latest letter found her at Mother's house. He wrote like a man who hoped for more than another romance. He was sorry for reminding her of her father, but she drove him crazy. He would do better, be better. He wanted to marry her when the war was over. His words were so tender, so much more real than ever before.

But she couldn't forget the reservations he created inside her, in a place she couldn't quite reach but which seemed the root of who she was and what she should choose for herself. She reread his older letters, avoiding the mean ones, trying to shake her trepidation when it came to him. But it remained, frustrating and baffling.

She stopped replying.

But she couldn't stop replying to Carol. Bill tells her she has to be pregnant before he'll marry her, and that's all it takes. She agrees to it. *Why did I let her use Jerry's letters?* It was a betrayal on her part. Jerry was almost as private as she was herself, and she never should have done it. The only consolation in the whole thing came when Carol wrote and told her Bill had almost broken things off after reading some of her letters because they didn't sound like the girl he thought he was dating, that he hadn't realized she was a clever literary sort. He'd *almost* broken it off. But 'almost' wasn't good enough, and she resolved not to help that relationship advance any further.

It might be too late. Carol was determined to get pregnant if that was what Bill and his family wanted. What did Carol see in him? Of all the men in the world, and she could have any of them, she chose *him*? Just how far was she going to take her 'Heathcliff in Wuthering Heights' fantasy, anyway?

She noticed the cares lining Mother's face. Shane was not doing well, drinking away his life, falling further and further out of reach, and Oona learned Agnes had lied to her first child Barbara about her real father her whole life and had been exposed. Her hopes now rested heavily on Oona's shoulders.

Oona stood under the pressure and felt for a crack she might break through. She held up the beautiful new gown Mother bought for her. Tonight, at the party, she would have to put on a good show.

This was her shot.

C3∞

Ice cubes clinked in crystal tumblers, and the main parlor hummed at a frequency only emitted by people who told stories for a living. "White Christmas" wafted into the hallway. The song had followed them, even here, but Oona didn't mind. It calmed her, somehow, as she paced in a side hallway, listening closely and taking deep, slow breaths.

The hosts' house was more of a mansion, tucked away in the Hollywood Hills. Oona had yet to lay her astonished eyes on one thing that was not absolute perfection. Her eyes ached from being wide open since the moment she and Mother had arrived. She checked her makeup in a hall mirror, walked toward the doorway, walked back, checked the mirror again. The Lancôme lipstick had been a good choice for this light.

Good.

She went back to listening from behind the doorway, waiting on Mother's preassigned cue.

Mother was nothing if not dramatic.

"Why, it's in her blood!" she heard Mother say, holding up her drink as if toasting to Oona's paternity. She was holding court with a cluster of MGM moguls in dinner jackets and their sharp little wives in Easter-egg shifts who nodded regally under a cloud of smoke and hot air. "Her father is, well, who he is, of course," Agnes went on, emboldened by two very stiff martinis consumed in rapid succession, "and *his* father before that was an actor, celebrated in his signature role of Edmund Dante in *The Count of Monte Cristo*." She excluded the part of the story where James O'Neill had risen from the impoverished life of Black Irish peasants. Halfway through her third cocktail, she was full of excited animation. "The silver screen seems a most natural choice."

Oona pinched her cheeks and fluffered her hair. Ready.

"And besides—just look at her!" Agnes raised an open hand toward the doorway as Oona glided through, on cue, and stopped. The sudden, calculated halt of forward motion allowed her hair to bob prettily before bouncing into place. Her full skirt swirled gently, unfurling about her legs like a moonflower. Her face was pure, composed elegance.

There was a collective gasp, and silence. And then conversation burst from every direction as Hollywood descended on fresh meat.

☙❧

Oona sat in the center of a blue velvet sofa surrounded by a braying array of Hollywood elites. A slick comer to her left shifted his legs closer and let his knee fall against hers. She adjusted her position just slightly the other way, only to find the head of a gawking old screenwriter with a burgundy nose and matching cravat hunched beside her, directly at chest level. She stood up and turned toward them, a crowd that had grown three rows deep, men of all ages, shapes, sizes, and colors. They all waited, cocktails in hand, for the next line from her ruby lips.

"Go on, Oona, give us one of those snappy lines like we read in the paper. We want to hear it from the pretty horse's mouth, right fellas?"

"Come on now, gentlemen, you must know how it works with society reporters," Oona said. She felt ready and alert. "They say, 'Miss O'Neill! Oh, Miss O'Neill?' And I say, 'Yes, George' or 'Peter can go next.' And they say, 'Now would you say so-and-so…,' some inane question about my father, usually. And I say, 'Well, something like that, I suppose,' and they cut me off while I think about it, and then they say, 'Close enough!' Then they tap their pencils on their little notepads, and before I can stop them, they're on to the next question!"

Oona's audience laughed as if she were Martha Raye or something. She fought the urge to roll her eyes. "The next day, I read about what I'm supposed to have said, and I don't recognize half of it!"

More laughter, and a hand on the back of her leg. She shifted out of reach.

"So you didn't say you were 'Shanty Irish and proud of it?'" said a voice from the crowd.

"Oh yes, I did say that." The men roared with laughter. A ball of heat rose in her chest.

"What about the thing you said about the state of the world?"

Oona smiled. She took a breath.

"Well, that was a silly question for them to ask in the first place. I did think just what I said: that it would be silly of me to comment on that, sitting there in The Stork Club with a ridiculous huge bunch of roses. Honestly, who really wants to hear the political opinions of a fake debutante? Anyway, my reply would have belonged in a different section of the paper."

The crowd was silent for a moment, seemingly unsure what to make of that, especially coming from this young woman who was, after all, the daughter of Eugene O'Neill. Oona sensed the quiet realization spread amongst them—they didn't quite know who they were dealing with.

Her lips spread into a wry smile and she held her ground, letting the silence sink deeper into the crowd of stupefied men.

"I must say, I *am* tired of having words put in my mouth." She started to turn away.

"Are you sure you want to be an actress then?" someone said. The crowd tittered.

Agnes appeared at her side. "Oh yes, she certainly is sure." She placed a hand on Oona's waist, guiding her out of the crowd. "You can get in touch with her agent if you're interested."

"Who's her agent?" a voice shouted.

"I'm working on that," Agnes said. "But give me a call tomorrow, and I'll let you know!"

All at once, Oona felt her store of politeness drain away. Between Daddy's last cold, dismissive letter and Jerry's purposefully hurtful ones since she'd stopped replying, and now this, her reserves for dealing with self-satisfied men were depleted. Someone laughed in another room, and Oona looked toward the door.

"Have a good evening," Oona said over her shoulder. "Gentlemen."

The night was young, and she'd already had enough of these hucksters. Amusing a bunch of overbearing blowhards was tiresome, and it was not her job. She went to leave, but someone addressed her.

"I heard you're a fan of Willa Cather." It was a woman's voice. Oona turned around, and Agnes gripped her elbow like a talon.

"That is true," Oona said, finding the face in the crowd that matched the voice. The woman reached out a hand.

"Louella Parsons, dear," the woman said.

Oona knew the name immediately. This woman was one of the two in this town who could make or break an actor's career with the stroke of a pen.

"I'm sorry, did I startle you, dear?" Louella said, a note of sincere concern in her voice. "I couldn't help myself. It's my job to know things, you understand, and it is exciting when one makes a connection."

Oona hid her confusion behind a composed smile, and Agnes relaxed her grip.

"A connection, Ms. Parsons?" Oona said.

"Yes! I wonder, did you know Ms. Cather started off her writing life reviewing arts and music for a midwest newspaper?" She paused, the consummate gossip columnist holding a room captive on the tip of her tongue.

Oona nodded vaguely. Was this tidbit meant to be some sort of big revelation?

"Yes, I remember reading it. I must have been twelve or so, but let's not do the math, shall we?"

Louella laughed, and the wives, who had come looking for their husbands, joined in. "Anyway, Cather wrote a review of the local performance of *The Count of Monte Cristo*, staring none other than—"

"My grandfather..." Oona said.

"Yes!" Agnes interjected, "as I mentioned, it's in her blood!" Her smile waved like a flag across the bottom of her face.

"Indeed!" Louella went on. "Cather was quite taken with his performance and gave him the most glowing review!"

Oona's eyes darted over the hungry faces watching Louella's tale, waiting, like baby birds, to be fed whatever crumbs she might drop.

"Old O'Neill might hold that against old Cather," said one of the men Oona had left behind on the sofa, and there was more laughter. Mother joined in nervously. Was everyone in on the joke but her? The man went on. "Perhaps that explains it, Oona!"

Oona swallowed lightly, straightened her back. "Explains what?"

"Explains why he's so against you going into the acting business." He stood up, drawing closer to her. "To play a role, and play it well, an actor must reach a certain level of understanding with the work, with the minds that create it. Perhaps your father is afraid that if you become an actress, you'll come dangerously close to understanding too much about him."

Oona flinched as the man spoke, his sour whiskey breath puffing into her face. The room filled with uncanny silence, straining to hear his words, then gasping for her response. She stepped back gracefully, then let a wry grin spread slowly over her face.

"All the more reason for me to pursue acting," she
said, projecting her voice, so the room could hear, "If
it can promise a miracle like that!"

In the three beats it took for her response to process, Oona wound up to employ the most effective
acting technique she'd gleaned in her short stage
career thus far. She offered a broad, toothy grin all
around the room, then she turned on her heels, and
left them laughing.

ᘓᘔ

Dear Carol,

> *It's me again, your best girlfriend. Do you miss me terribly? I'm determined not to write even <u>one</u> curse word in this letter, so it might be a short one!*
>
> *I have realized there won't be a time in the next few days when I can sit down and write one proper letter to you, and even if I did get an hour, I wouldn't be able to sit still. My mind is racing all the time with how fast everything is happening. I'm going to take this letter along with me for the next few days and jot things down for you as I go.*
>
> *Today is a Friday. It's as if this town had been waiting for me to get here. Of course I know that's not true, I'm not THAT conceited! But if I thought I had a lot of opportunities in New York, I was mistaken! Writers, directors, agents, and actors (!) call for me and send messages all day long. The telegram service is sick of my mother's front door. I have at least one date almost every night. Orson has taken me out a few times already, too.*

Signing off for today.

Hello again. It's Saturday now. Honestly, Carol, there's just so much to tell you, I don't know where to start. Many job offers, none of which seem like something I'd want to do, but Mother thinks I should just pick something with a good movie company and do it. It's so much pressure. Then all these men want to take me out on dates, show me around, show me off to their friends. I can't help thinking it's because I'm Eugene O'Neill's daughter. Is that crazy? Even now, with my own name, I can't shake the fear that in the end, they'll all decide I'm a fraud and abandon me.

Maybe 'abandon' is too dramatic a word. It felt right in the moment, though. Syntax plus diction equals drama!

I've been to every hot club in town, multiple times. They're wonderful! The people here are different from New Yorkers, though the best of them are shunting back and forth between the two at the drop of a hat, it seems. My father was angry at me for taking one train ride with you, but these people go East to West to East like they're hopping a bus downtown.

I'll write again after the party tonight.

All right, I'm back.

Listen, Carol, is sex really the center of the universe? These people act as if it's the main goal of every hour of every day. They all want to sleep with me. It makes me nervous. I'm no prude, you know that better than anyone. But per-haps my vision of Hollywood glamour is being shattered a bit. In the movies, the passionate kiss is the ultimate moment. They never really show what comes after. I want what comes after as much as any girl. Just not as an extracurricular activity (like Gloria does! Ooh don't tell her I said that. And if you do tell her [because I know you will] just make sure to tell her it's only because I'm jealous).

I've just had a message from my new agent. Her name is Minna Wallace. She wants me to come to her house for a dinner party and meet someone, but wants to tell me who it is in person in the morning. Okay!

Carol, next time we see each other, we must have one of our nice, inno-cent talks about literature. Like we did when we first met and we were so young and green. When I would analyze Willa Cather and you thought the playwright William Saroyan was dead. Now you're planning on having his baby! And when we do have that talk, can we debate the merits of brackets inside parentheses? It will be a nice break from worrying whether Hollywood girls shave the hair 'down there' or whether I can truly break into the movie business without auditioning parts of me that don't belong on camera!

We can also talk about exclamation points, I guess. We're both getting a little too reliant on them.

Love you,
Oona

Chapter 25

HOW TO FAIL A SCREEN TEST

Hollywood, November 1942

Oona rolled her hair and smoothed it with a dab of the Brylcreem she found in Mother's bathroom. It was a man's product, but her hair had been so difficult since coming to California. She took a lot of trouble to make sure it was perfect, smooth and flowing and luxurious, like Veronica Lake. She didn't know what this director, Mr. Eugen Frenke, was looking for.

She walked the whole way to the address Minna gave her, checking her pocket often for her vial of smelling salts. After coming in from the bright sun, the studio was pitch black. She gave her name and suddenly she was led to a chair, a light flashed on above her, and the screentest was underway. A high-pitched male voice came from the dark behind a camera she could now make out a few feet in front of her face.

"This movie is called *The Girl From Leningrad*, okay? So you wear this scarf, like babushka, yes?

And you sit on the chair and we make pictures of you pretty face. Okay? Okay."

"He doesn't want to see my hair then?" Oona said to a girl who dabbed more powder over the makeup she'd carefully applied.

"Your hair is very pretty, dear," Mr. Frenke said.

"Yes, very pretty," a woman's voice said. She came into the light and introduced herself. "I'm Anna, Eugen's wife, and that's Eugen. Thank you for coming." She disappeared into the shadows again.

The makeup girl waited while Oona perched herself on a stool on the soundstage and then wrapped a scarf over Oona's head, tying it under her chin. All the while, Mr. Frenke and his wife chattered. Oona couldn't tell when they were speaking *to* her and when they were speaking *about* her.

Oona fiddled with the scarf under her chin. Her eyes had almost adjusted to the lights now. The cameraman looked through his viewfinder and then pushed the camera stand closer, slowly at first, but Oona had become so focused on listening to the Frenkes that she didn't notice him moving in closer still. When she finally tore her wide-eyed gaze from the director and his wife, convinced they had already decided she was hopeless, she found the camera inches from her face.

"All right, baby. Such a pretty girl. Look right here, would ya?" The voice came from behind the camera. Oona looked toward the camera and smiled at the lens. "Okay, now look away." She did so instantly. She had a vague idea that film people liked girls who cooperated and took direction well. This was her only opportunity to show Mr. Frenke something he could work with. The unique combination of her father's name and a pretty face had gotten her here, but now there was nothing between her and a film camera that could bring her face to the whole world.

If she didn't screw it up.

"Are we starting now?" she asked.

"Hey!" Frenke shouted. Oona clenched her bottom to the seat and her stomach dropped. But he wasn't speaking to her. He waved his arm in the air toward the camera. "Why are you so close? Move! Move back from her face!" Then he turned back to Oona.

"Yes, darling. We start now." He pointed to the camera and said, "Action."

"Action," Anna said.

A clapperboard appeared before her and slapped closed with a loud snap. Oona gripped the vial of smelling salts, took a small breath, and smiled.

"Is it running? Yeah?" Mr. Frenke's voice turned high and sing-song. "Okay, start from here."

Oona turned, and her neck followed his direction at an awkward angle, but this man was the expert.

"Over here?"

"Come on, we're waiting for you. Do something!" Frenke said. His wife began to sing. *Do they want me to sing, too?*

Mr. Frenke threw out more commands, and his wife repeated them as Oona floundered to grasp what they wanted.

"It's a silent film," said Mr. Frenke.

"Is it silent? Well, shall I look over here?" Nervous, she fell back on her Park Avenue accent, then cringed at the sound of her own voice. It didn't fit in this situation at all. She turned the opposite direction.

"No, look over here. Say something."

Why should I say something if it's silent? She didn't dare ask.

"I don't know what to say," Oona tried to conceal the desperation bubbling up her throat, but it came out in a slightly pleading tone. "Give me something."

"You should say something, do something."

"I'm sorry, oooh, I'm sorry"

"Don't be so sorry," Mr. Frenke sang, as if speaking to a little child. His wife began to sing again, but Oona still couldn't tell if she was meant to sing along or if the song was meant as some sort of emotional support.

And then it was over. Her big shot at a screen-test, and it was over in minutes, leaving her sitting on a bench in the dark as the crew followed the Frenkes out a side door, lighting cigarettes as they went.

She sat there silently, her head whirling. *What just happened?* Then the cameraman stuck his head back through the door: "He'll call your agent, sweetheart."

Afterward, back at Mother's empty mobile home, Oona didn't know what would happen or what to do next. It had been a disaster as far as she was concerned. How ridiculous she must have looked, fully made up with a scarf over her perfectly coiffed hair, trying to pretend she was a Russian peasant. She cringed when she thought of it, and she could not *stop* thinking of it. If she'd known that was what they wanted, she would have tried to fit the part. Mother would be so disappointed.

She did the first thing she could think of: she took out a fresh stack of paper and a pen and started a letter to Carol.

Dear Carol,

I don't know if I'm cut out for this. It's all too much. Anyway, I'll write again if anything new happens (besides casting directors and screenwriters trying to sleep with me—it's getting old, if you can believe that!)

Love,
Oona

P.S. Tell Elinor I said hello. And don't say you will but then not do it, because I'm going to check after you!

*C*hapter 26

THE SECRET GUEST

Beverly Hills, November 1942

What does a girl wear for dinner at her agent's home with a secret surprise guest? Oona stared at the meager selection hanging in the closet and decided on the one Mother bought. She'd be fine as long as the mystery guest hadn't been at the party a few nights ago.

"I hope you can forgive me for all the secrecy, Oona," Minna said as Oona arrived. Our guest of honor is keeping a low profile these days…"

"It's quite all right, Minna," Oona said, shrugging off her coat. "I understand." A fire crackled in a small parlor off the foyer, and she rubbed her hands together. Winter in Los Angeles was nothing compared to Manhattan, and she wasn't one bit cold, but rubbing her hands together came naturally when near such a beautiful, flickering fire.

"Of course you do. Now if you'd like to have a seat in the parlor, just in there, I will go check on the food. You make yourself comfortable in one of those chairs." She turned to go. "Actually, take the one that faces the door, would you? Wonderful. Thank you." She hurried away before Oona could ask any more questions.

She did as she was asked, and was soon mesmerized by the fire. The colors were enchanting, flicking up and up like tongues lapping up their own beauty. She'd always loved the fireplace at Old House. A fireplace really made a house feel like a home. Why hadn't they ever lit fires at Carol's apartment? Was there even a fireplace there?

She was lost in these thoughts and a bit dreamy-eyed from the warmth when a shadow fell on the carpet beside her chair. Minna's voice brought her back, but her eyes were still quite dazzled from staring at the fire. She blinked, sighing contentedly.

"Oona, I'd like you to meet someone very special."

Her eyes adjusted to the romantic light of the parlor, and it was only then she realized Minna might not have come in alone. She stood, unselfconscious and with an air of excitement at finally learning who the mystery guest might be, and when she turned, she was face to face with a man—a very handsome older man. He smiled, and his clear blue eyes sparkled, reflecting all the colors of the firelight.

"Oona, this is Charlie Chaplin," Minna said. "Charlie, I'd like to introduce Miss Oona O'Neill."

The man bowed his head cordially and a lock of quicksilver hair fell across his forehead. When he looked up at her again, there was an instant recognition, as if some long ago question had finally been answered. She offered her hand, and he took it, drawing it to his lips and placing a courtly kiss on her smooth skin.

They stood that way for a moment, a moment that extended into forever.

"A pleasure," Charlie said.

"The pleasure is mine," Oona said. She could not stop looking at him, at his eyes, and the droll little smile that played around his mouth.

"Well," Minna said. "Why don't I let you two get acquainted, shall I?"

Oona took her seat, and Charlie took the one opposite her. His every move was measured and precise. The room became another world, as if she were watching a movie from within. No one *really* moved that way, with such perfect expression and economy of motion, not in real life.

"So, tell me all about yourself," he said. He gazed at her with keen interest. Her heart beat faster, pounded, but not too much—just enough to take her breath.

"Oh please, won't you start? Won't you tell me about yourself?" she said.

"Modesty forbids, my dear. Please, won't you..."

Oona bowed her head. "Well, I arrived here in California rather recently. My mother wants me to be a movie actress," Oona said, glancing again into the fire.

"I have heard this, yes," Charlie said with complete seriousness.

His eyes were almost too much to take, the most amazing shade of blue, full of expression and life and charm, and so completely focused on her. A thrill shivered down her back.

"I had a screen test with a Mr. Frenke just yesterday, him and his wife."

"Oh, yes, Eugen Frenke is a friend of mine—his wife as well."

"I suppose there's no name I could drop that you haven't already heard of."

"That may be true."

His smile settled something in her that had agitated continually for as long as she could remember, until that moment—like a constant noise you stop noticing until it suddenly switches off.

"I'm afraid it didn't go very well." She forced herself to look away. Firelight flashed on her black hair and lit her eyes. Her cheeks flushed. She felt oddly perfect, comfortable, unrecognizable.

Herself.

"I don't see how that could be possible." He spoke with the most delightful precision. It was as if he were tuned in to the pulse inside her chest.

"Well, I couldn't understand what they wanted from me, you see. I wanted so much to please them."

"There must have been some mistake. You'll simply do it again."

"I will?"

"Yes, and if they won't have you back, I will. I'll test you at my studios," he reached out, and she thought he may take her hand, but he picked up his glass from the table between them and reclined into his chair, smiling again. "I will set it all to rights."

And she believed he would.

She held her hands to the fire, then turned them over…

Her palms!

Orson had read her palm, and he'd said she would marry his friend Charlie Chaplin. The heat rose to her cheeks. She thought of telling the story, but couldn't think how to bring it up: "I was on a date with your friend, and he predicted I'd marry you," seemed a bit forward.

She had very nearly figured out the right words when Minna came to call them for dinner.

It would have to wait for another time.

Dear Carol,

How are things back in Manhattan? Does anyone notice I'm gone?

Well, Minna is very excited about my prospects. She says Charles Boyer wants to test me for a film. And Orson says he heard there's interest at MGM. But tonight is the dinner I told you about, the one she's being so secretive about. I wonder who the guest of honor is. She says she won't tell me so I won't get too nervous, but that just makes me more nervous than I would have been! I wonder who it could be.

I hope Bill is not being as big of a jerk any more. He's lucky to have you, and I'll be happy to let him know that if he needs telling. Has he gotten a post yet? Or is he still living in a fancy hotel and feeling sorry for himself? Sorry, sorry. He just rubs me the wrong way. But I guess as he rubs you the right way, that's all you care about. Haha! You have to admit that was a good one.

*I'll wait to seal this until after I get back,
so I can add a postscript if the mystery
guest was anyone exciting.*

Love,
Oona

*P.S. I just met Charlie Chaplin! What
blue eyes he has!*

Chapter 27

SHAKING THE TREE

Hollywood, November 1942

Oona was wide awake but pretending to be asleep, wondering how long Mother would wait before her curiosity grew too strong. The aroma of fresh coffee and slightly burned toast drifted down the hall, and she'd held off running to the loo almost as long as she could. One or the other of those needs would soon drag her from bed, but Mother lost the waiting game and knocked on Oona's door and leaned into the room, brandishing a steaming Jade-ite mug.

"Good morning, starlet!" Mother said in a gravelly, singsong voice. Her sleek hair was tousled and limp and last night's mascara had formed raccoon rings under her eyes. "Rise and shine, Miss O'Neill, you're wanted on the set!" She laughed in a high-key way.

Oona rolled to her back, stretching and yawning. Sunlight streamed in through the spaces in the blinds, throwing golden stripes over the white coverlet. Her hair was tamed in two thick black braids and she wore the one nightgown she had packed for her trip with Carol. That train ride already seemed like years ago.

"Mother, have you even been to bed?"

"For a bit," Agnes said, waving the question off. "I was too excited to sleep after Minna phoned and finally spilled who you were meeting, and you were already asleep when I got in! Tell me everything. How did it go?"

Oona had been seeing Charlie's blue eyes every time she closed hers. She'd dreamed about them, how the firelight had cast that magical, unreal glow over them. In her dreams, he'd been as an apparition, gliding from his chair to hers and lifting her into his arms. She shook the dream from her head so that Mother wouldn't see it on her face.

"It was wonderful actually. He is like no one I've ever met in my whole life," she drew up her legs and hugged them close, sighing. Mother looked at her expectantly. "He said he met you before, in New York," Oona said.

"That's true, I did meet him once, at a theater party in Greenwich Village. It was 1920, and he had had his great success with *The Kid*. It was pandemonium everywhere he went. He had visited Provincetown Playhouse, and he admired your father's play *The Emperor Jones*—enough to offer to play a bit part, uncredited, just to experience a theater stage again, I think. Perhaps he was just making polite conversation. I remember he seemed genuinely interested in people and their specific talents. Everyone with whom he held a conversation thought themselves very special. He had that way about him. How I miss those days." Her eyes went distant. "Anyway, I had to talk him out of it. I knew if we let him do it, people would find out he was there and come just to see him. Your father wouldn't have liked that one bit."

The fact that Charlie was there when her father was getting his start was fascinating, and not at all concerning. The spark she'd felt for him the previous night was too great, too special and entirely unique to be put out by something so trivial as Charlie having met her mother before she was even born.

Perhaps it was fate.

 infinity

Before parting at Minna's house, Charlie had told Oona to come and see him at the studio to discuss a part in his new film. The next day she was at United Artists' lot before the sun rose, but she soon realized this would be harder than she thought.

There were girls up and down the street in front of the studio, each saying different versions of the same thing: "Mr. Chaplin said to come see him" and "He's expecting me, we have an appointment" and even "Say, what do I gotta do to get in there, mister?"

She went home and called Minna, who called the studio to set things right, and then Oona resolved to try again the next day. Before she could do that, Minna called again. Oona took the call, standing at the telephone table and scrutinizing her reflection in the mirror as she pulled the rollers from her hair. Did Mother have any decent scissors? Her hair desperately needed a trim.

"I called Mr. Chaplin to shake the tree a little, told him MGM was interested and what did he plan to do about you. He said he'd just come from dinner with Orson Welles, who talked you up to the moon, and to send you over to his house first thing tomorrow to see about some acting lessons."

Oona almost dropped the phone. "Thank you, Minna! Thank you so so much!"

"Go get 'em, kid!"

"All right, I will!" Oona hung up the phone, grinning and declaring to her reflection. "I will."

☙❧

Dear Oona,

I had to sit down and write even though we just got off the phone. Charlie Chaplin?! It's too much!

About your screen test with Mr. Frenke, I hope you don't mind me asking this, but could it be that your father was up to his tricks again? Please don't be angry with me, but he did interfere with your prospects before didn't he? If I'm out of line, just forget I said anything.

I'll write again soon. Bill has been giving me fits and making everything much too difficult. We chase each other around the city like a cartoon cat and mouse. But I love it. The drama!

Love,
Carol

ᘓ৪ᘎ

Oona filled a glass with ice. She was pouring it over with cold coffee while reading Carol's latest letter when something Carol said stopped her short. How had it not occurred to her till just then? Daddy had done it before, hadn't he? When the newspaper articles announced she would pursue an acting career in Hollywood, he called in every Hollywood connection he had and instructed them not to hire her. It had been over before it began, all the doors that had flown open from the New York debutant publicity were slammed shut in her face just as fast, and she hadn't even known what happened until months later when Orson told her.

But had he done it again, when he wouldn't even hear her out? When he'd allowed Carlotta to slam the door in her face? The idea was too harsh to consider, and yet it was more than likely the truth: Daddy must have told Frenke to go ahead and give his silly, talentless daughter a screentest if she must have it, but not to make it easy. Let her flap and flounder in front of the camera. Then she'd see. Then she'd know just how far his reach extended.

Perhaps his ego didn't allow him to think Mr. Frenke might have better, more important friends than him. Friends like Charlie Chaplin.

Charlie Chaplin. One of the most famous and powerful men in the world. Hollywood royalty. It would drive Daddy crazy if he knew Charlie was interested in hiring her. After everything Daddy had done to block her plans—or rather, Mother's plans, but still—if Charlie Chaplin thought she had something, there'd be nothing Daddy could do to stop it. If Charlie wanted her to star in his next film, then there could be no doubt, could there? She would know then that Mother had been right to push her toward this career.

But what if he didn't?

Well, Mother would have to accept that, too. And after that, she supposed she could go back to school. Maybe Vassar would still have her after all, just as Daddy wanted it.

*C*hapter 28

FEVER DREAMS

Charlie Chaplin's acting classes began at his offices at United Artists Studio. He gave Oona a scene from his upcoming film to learn, even performing in character so she would see exactly how he wanted it played.

Oona learned the scene, practicing the lines in the mirror just as he had showed her until the delivery seemed just right. However, when it came time to show him how well she had prepared, the words would not come. The moment he entered the room, in his linen suit and sharp white shirt, his overwhelming presence and the cool scent of him first filled the room, and then her mind, and she forgot everything.

"Come to my house this evening," he said. "I will show you some of my films. When we had no sound, no spoken dialogue, the story was told with action. You might find it enlightening." He took her hand and squeezed it encouragingly. "Bring your mother along if you wish, of course."

That evening, Charlie sent a car for them, but Agnes had not been at home all afternoon. She would

328

kick herself when she got Oona's note, but only if she got home before Oona, which wasn't entirely likely.

The car wound up the hillside, and her heartbeat quickened as the house on Summit Drive came into view. The gracious façade seemed more like a home than the other mansions she'd caught in glimpses along the way, somehow simultaneously imposing and welcoming. Two handsome young men, around her age, met her at the door to Charlie's. Both had Charlie's mop of wavy hair and a trace of his twinkle in their eyes.

"Welcome, welcome," said one. "I'm Sydney—Charlie's son."

The other wrangled for a spot in the doorway. "I'm Charlie Jr.," he said, smiling.

"Pleasure to meet you both. I'm Oona O'Neill."

The two men stood in the doorway, staring and smiling.

"Mr. Chaplin is expecting me."

"Of course!"

"Apologies! Do come in!"

They parted, exchanging glances as she passed.

"Can we get you anything, Miss O'Neill?" Sydney said, jockeying in front of Charlie Jr.

"Yes! A drink, or something to eat?" Charlie Jr. said. Sydney elbowed him and smiled wider.

"Ow!" He elbowed his brother back, but harder.

"Thank you, but no..." Oona looked over their shoulders, around the grand foyer and through the doorways.

A knowing look passed between the young men. "Dad is in the film room," Sydney said, crestfallen.

"Just down this hall. I'll show you to it," Charlie Jr. said.

"I'll come, too," Sydney offered. "My brother gets lost easily."

She followed them down several hallways, up a flight of stairs, and down another. She glanced into the rooms as they passed, each one appointed with beautiful furniture and art, but nothing austentatious. It reflected Charlie himself: bursting with self-effacing good taste and the intangible quality of comfort and security.

Sydney opened the door quietly, and Oona looked at him, wondering whether she should go in. He nodded, and she smiled and mouthed 'thank you' to the brothers as she entered the room, and Sydney closed it again behind her.

Charlie was seated in a wingback chair, his legs crossed with elegant ease and his chin resting on one hand. A film projector clicked as sixteen millimeter film wound its way through, and flickering images of Charlie's famous image played on a screen just beyond. Another chair sat several feet away, also facing the screen. Oona waited, transfixed. The camera panned to a close up of Charlie's face. His battered top hat was slightly askew and his eyes darted from one corner of the screen to another while his brush mustache danced as if it had its own role to play.

She stepped closer, fascinated by the story his face told, conveying layers of emotion, humor and pathos and understanding, deeper and more fully human than any complete movie she'd ever seen, any book she'd ever read.

"Ah, my dear," he said, noticing her silently standing behind the other chair, her eyes glistening in the blue and gray light. "Please, take that seat."

He got up and changed the film in seconds, winding a new tape and securing it in place with flying hands while beginning his lesson.

"This film is *His New Job*. It was the first film that had ever displayed my own name on it. Such a triumph!" he said, playfully mocking his younger self.

As it played, he pointed out small details of his and his costars' performances, showing how they moved the story along with their hands, their posture, and with every small movement of their faces. "This girl here?" he pointed to the stenographer in the background of the scene, "Gloria Swanson! Uncredited! Look how she does exactly enough to embody the role, but not so much that she overtakes the visual story. Control, precision, communication, all very natural." He stood beside the projection, performing the scene in tandem with his on-screen image. Oona followed his every movement, hanging on every word.

Next, during *The Tramp*, he pointed out little techniques that had made him a star. He spoke of his character as if it were a real person. "Here, when he is tempted to steal the money of the damsel in distress, The Tramp does a subtle bit of stage business just before snatching her cash from her hand. He scratches his right palm. This refers to an old superstition which says that if your left hand itches, money is going out. But if your right palm itches, money will be coming in. So the gesture suggested The Tramp is convincing himself that this money was coming to him, so it was all right to take it, but he believes his delusion only for the briefest moment, because he instantly repents when the damsel begins to cry, and he hands the money right back."

"All without saying a word," Oona said.

"Without saying a word," Charlie said.

"It's like a Dickens story," Oona said.

"Do you think so?" Charlie asked.

She realized then that he must have heard that comparison hundreds of times in his career. When she glanced over at him, he was watching her face, his own expression vulnerable, as if it were the first time he'd ever heard those words. He hung on every nuance of her reply, and Oona felt for the first time as if the words she spoke were infinitely valuable simply by virtue of having come from her lips.

☙❧

Jerry's letters continued arriving at Oona mother's place despite what Oona had told him in her last one. She'd forced herself to stop replying, and it was more clear now than ever, as his words grew meaner and more petty, that she had been right: he was too much like her father. She was glad to have told him so. Perhaps it would serve him well in his writing career; it certainly had worked out for her father in his, but it would not work with her. She would let him see the news of her growing association with Charlie in the paper, though the fact that this would not be unlike what her father did to her mother was not lost on her.

What did that say about her? Maybe she was more like her father than she wanted to admit. Maybe in his absence from her life, he had somehow increased his influence on her in certain ways, even more than he would have had he been around. If that was so, then not only was Jerry too much like her father, but so was she. All the more reason they should never be together. They both wanted something more, something different from the hand they'd been dealt. They both wanted her father's attention, just for different reasons.

With the benefit of time and distance, and Jerry's erratic stream of letters, she wished she'd cut the whole thing off when she received his first unpleasant one, when he'd written out of anger when she hadn't replied fast enough for his liking: "You do not tell the truth. You are a liar. Liars do not go to Heaven. Only girls with braces on their teeth go to Heaven. And Rita Hayworth." She knew now that half of Jerry's love for her was a love of who her father was. How could she blame him when half of her feelings about herself were based on the same thing?

All of this took on new clarity against the contrast of how she felt when she was with Charlie.

The decision to consider pursuing a relationship with him came to her all at once, without reservation, and with full understanding of how it would seem to anyone but her. He was a fascinating and handsome man, brilliant, beloved the world over, and though it didn't affect her growing feelings for him, he was more famous by far than Eugene O'Neill. At least on this count, Daddy couldn't hold his name over her.

ⴳⴳ⅃ⴲ

When she left New York with Carol, Oona had packed for a short stay of perhaps a few weeks, and she hadn't even packed enough for that. Now it had been months. She washed and rewashed her things in Mother's sink and hung them to dry over the bathtub each night.

She visited the house on Summit Drive several times a week for acting lessons, sometimes with Mother in tow. Oona looked forward to each meeting with Charlie, but the past few months seemed to be catching up with her. She'd developed a cough, slight at first, but then a damp heaviness settled in her chest. It grew worse every morning after nights of fitful sleep where Daddy's long, stern face floated in and out of her vision, silent and out of reach. At their first lesson, Charlie had offered the use of his swimming pool whenever she liked, and she took him up on it, arriving early for her next lesson in the hope the air high in the hills might help. But she had no bathing suit. Ensuring Charlie's sons weren't around, she sunbathed in her shorts and a bra, reasoning that it could pass for a bikini top.

She sat on a folding chair, feverishly flipping the pages of a magazine. There was an article about the latest in bathing suits, and she tore out pictures of the ones that might suit her. When she got some money, she would buy herself one like these, and a hat with a big floppy brim. And sunglasses...

"Hello, my dear!"

Charlie's voice echoed around the pool deck. Oona jumped, pressing the magazine and jagged ripped pages to her chest.

"Ah!" He turned away while she covered up. "I am here for your lesson. Shall I wait in the film room?"

Oona started to reply, but was overcome with a wrack of coughing.

Charlie put the back of his hand to her forehead. "My dear, you are ill!"

"No, no," Oona said, swallowing painfully. "It's just the past few months catching up with me. I will be fine. If I could just have some tea, or—" she coughed again, harder this time. The pool grew blurry, and then dark.

When her eyes opened again, she was in a bed under soft, creamy sheets, leaning against a pillow that felt like a cloud under her head. Charlie sat in a chair beside the bed, and when she woke, he took her hand. He made sure she took her aspirin and drank a full glass of water, placing the glass back on a silver tray on the bedside table. He stayed with her, talking and amusing her with stories, until she fell asleep again.

The next afternoon, her chest was heavy, her breathing a chore. Sunshine and tea didn't help, and she couldn't eat. She curled on a lounge chair in the sun, and Charlie's staff shook their heads in the shadows: another young woman taking full advantage.

She had chills and felt hot at the same time, and beads of sweat formed on the back of her neck.

Falling into a feverish dream, she heard ringing and followed it into her childhood bedroom, her little room in Bermuda. It was a call from Daddy. She answered the phone, and then he was there with her instead. Still she pressed the phone to her ear, straining to hear every word he said.

He was sorry for not seeing her. He'd heard that Carlotta sent her away from his front door, and he'd told her she must never do that again, that he loved his daughter unconditionally and would see her any time she wanted. The telephone turned into a letter held in her hands, written in Daddy's tiny hand-writing. The words got bigger and bigger until the end and the ink turned red: "*None of us can help the things life has done to us. I love you, my only daughter, my only Oona...*"

But when she woke, the pool was deserted. The sun was going down, and the shade was colder and damp. Her teeth chattered, and she wrapped herself in a towel.

When Charlie came home and found her that way, his concern was obvious. He disappeared and returned with a housemaid. They carried aspirin and water, blankets and pillows. "So you won't have to move until the doctor comes."

The doctor did come. He wrote a prescription, promising to have it delivered that evening, and gave her a tonic for the meantime. In a little while, Oona began to perk up, a bit of color returning to her cheeks.

Charlie sat down beside her, worry lines around his eyes relaxing into relief. Then he noticed the book on the table beside her—a book of plays by her father. He gave her a long, appraising look and cleared his throat.

"You know, I had a friend years ago, an artist. A cartoonist for the New Yorker."

"Not Peter Arno?" Oona muttered.

"No, not your former beau," Charlie said, settling into a wicker chair. There was a white patch of zinc smudged on his nose. He'd never gotten his after-work swim. "My friend's name was Barton. John Barton."

"Oh but, Charlie..." She knew that name. John Barton had been Carlotta's husband.

"They'd split up, and he was in a very bad way about it. I used to go to their apartment when I was in New York. They threw the most marvelous parties! Well, I convinced him to come along with me on a tour I was making of Europe, and along the way he and Carlotta exchanged letters and resolved to reunite when he returned to New York."

"And what happened?"

"Carlotta met your father."

"No."

"Indeed. By the time Peter returned, Carlotta had her hooks in a much better catch."

Oona cringed at the sharp memory of that time. Behind her sunglasses, her eyes closed on the broken visions of endless lonely days as a small child in her bedroom in Bermuda, looking at picture books about happy families and putting her dolls to bed before crying herself to sleep, wishing someone would answer her question. *When is Daddy coming home?*

"Eugene and Carlotta returned to New York, and it hit him most fully then that he would never get her back. He committed suicide."

"No, Charlie."

"Oh, yes. I'm afraid so. And I'm also afraid I've never quite forgiven the man who stole my dear friend's happiness. Barton was much too tender. He had no idea the person Carlotta really was. But with the benefit of time, it's more obvious now than ever that she truly is one of the most diabolical people I have ever met."

Oona's chest went cold. Memories of Mother waiting for letters, then crying, raging. Shane's sensitive, boyish face slowly taking on the quality of pumice stone, hard and rough yet still vulnerable, absorbing. Daddy willingly cowering behind a wall he let Carlotta build. To keep them out.

"I'm awfully sorry about your friend," Oona said.

"My darling Oona," Charlie said, reaching out to place his hand on hers, "I am sorry about your father."

For the first time in her life, Oona felt no urge to defend Daddy. She lowered her head, and when Charlie drew close, she leaned into him, letting him put his arms around her, as the tears came.

Dear Oona,

How goes it, dear sister? It goes all right with me at the moment. Cathy sends her love as well. I'm actually writing because I have a tale from my lovely wife that might soothe you in some way. Or maybe not. I hope it does.

The basic story goes like this (but I'm not the great storyteller our father is, so you'll have to forgive if my prose goes astray): I had given Cathy a little money before I sailed for work in December, and asked her to send a few Christmas gifts to Dad and Carlotta. She wrote a letter, too, telling him some stories about my new job and, oh, I don't know, about my adventures and the like, I suppose.

She received a reply—from Carlotta. Carlotta basically told her she didn't give Dad the letter and that I'd better be the one to write in the future since 'second-hand' news might upset him and keep him from being able to work! What a delicate genius, our father. Even the idea that you and I exist outside of his own imagination can apparently throw him into a spiral.

Cathy was beyond livid, of course, and can't understand how we can bear it. Or how Dad allows this to happen. What she said, which I found revealing and also quite funny, was, "Who does she think she is—St. Peter, opening and closing the gates?!" I tell you, I very nearly did a spit-take. She said, "Doesn't he have any feeling of responsibility to you? Does she open all his mail?"

I told her it must have been a good letter she sent! That's why Carlotta hid it. I wonder how many of our letters he's ever received. For one thing, I know for sure, I sent him a telegram after he won the Nobel Prize. But when I visited him last, he said how he was hurt that I'd never written to congratulate him. What does that tell you? I don't think he believed me when I told him that naturally I did.

Of course this made me think of you and your current situation. For most people, being barred at the door to their father's house after coming such a long way would be the last straw, dear sister. But you wrote to him <u>again</u>. Since the divorce, he has had every opportunity to see us if he'd wanted to. I wonder if he realizes what he's

*done, now that our childhoods are over.
Though sometimes I feel mine ended
the day he left us.*

*You have a heart made of some other,
much finer stuff. But I've always known
that, and it has given me some hope at
times when things seem dark.*

*Please don't take on so badly about
our father's behavior. Don't do to yourself what I've done to myself. You've
never done a thing wrong to him. I can
vouch for you!*

*Your loving brother,
Shane*

Chapter 29

FEVER

January 1943

Charlie insisted Oona stay at his house to recuperate fully. "No offense to your mother's fine home," he offered tactfully, "but I believe you will be more comfortable here. Don't you agree, doctor?"

The somber man nodded gravely.

"You're fever has not broken," Charlie added, "and there's no use exposing your mother—"

"Mother," Oona mumbled. She tried to sit up, but Charlie and the doctor eased her back to the pillows. "I have to go home. Mother..."

"I've called her, dear," Charlie said. "She knows you're here. She sends her love and knows you are in good hands. Don't worry."

"She should be over the worst of it soon, then she will be all right after some rest," the doctor said, snapping his black bag closed.

For the next few days, Charlie was there whenever she woke. Her fever finally broke, and he personally brought soup and soda crackers, light coffee with swirls of cream, and sugar cubes in a delicate silver bowl. The clouds slowly cleared from her mind, and she saw that he had been there with her all along, sleeping on an armchair beside her bed.

"You were very ill, my dear," he said as she sipped a cup of delicious clear broth, feeling its energy surge into her veins. She wondered at his kindness. Pushing the blanket aside, she moved to get up.

"I am so sorry to have been a burden, to you and to your staff."

"Burden? What burden? You were no trouble at all. Only I've been very worried." Listening to him, the most wonderful sensation took over, one that felt as though she could believe him, that it was all right to rest. Searching his eyes, she found only deep concern and something she could only hope for, something she didn't dare name yet. But whatever it was, she knew she could rest with him. As if she could breathe, really breathe, deeply, and from a place inside herself that had been smothered closed for a very long time. He smiled at her and took her hand, and she was free. Free to be only Oona, nothing more, nothing less, nothing else but herself. And that was enough.

⊂⊃⊗⊃

While she recovered and regained her strength, he brought the projector to her room and played his films on the wall, over and over at her request. Sitting beside him in the dark, she watched the younger version of Charlie brilliantly expressing every human emotion, with just the tilt of his head and lifting of an eyebrow. There was no explaining his charisma, his innate talent. He reached out from the screen and made her laugh and cry, sometimes both at the same time. It seemed impossible that anyone could watch these movies and not feel for him what she felt. Her heart hurt with love for him. It was a glorious agony, wishing she could have been there all along, to know Charlie then, to have been his first love, but also completely content that fate had brought her here at this exact time instead, so she could know him now.

One evening, as the closing credits to *City Lights* flashed in the dark and the film strip sputtered, she turned slowly to him, brimming with awe to be sitting in the same room, in such close proximity to the recipient of so much the world's well-deserved admiration. The brilliant character he had silently portrayed on the screen was an avatar of everything pure and boundless she sensed at his very core. Her breath caught in her chest. He turned to meet her gaze, and in the cosmic depth of his blue eyes she found a simple, astounding understanding, a symbiotic connection her heart had longed for her whole life. She leaned closer to him, closed her eyes completely, and kissed him.

"I love you, Charlie Chaplin," she said, pulling back. Her eyes sparkled in the darkness.

"My dear," he shook his head gently and stood, "your illness has made you delirious."

"I'm not ill any more, Charlie," she sat up. "I'm perfectly clear. I'm more clear than I've ever been in my life."

Charlie sat down at the edge of the bed. His every move was as if composing a shot in one of his films.

No wasted movement. Every gesture had meaning. This silver in his hair glinted in the sunlight, and she reached for his hand.

"Charlie, I've been searching for what is missing inside myself, looking everywhere, in every corner. It's sad really, but I've always looked outside myself. I guess that's because the place where love should be has been so empty. But you've filled that empty place, Charlie, like no one else has ever done. It makes me feel strong. And it makes me sad in a way, too, realizing what I've been missing until now."

Charlie looked at her hands holding his, but didn't speak.

"I know what it must look like, me pursuing you like this. But it's just that I'm finally sure of something, for the first time in my life. Of who I am and what I want for *my* life. And that is you. I don't want to be a movie star. I never have, not really. I made it what I wanted because it was what the one parent who spoke to me wanted. And that's the truth. It feels wonderful to say it out loud.

"Acting has been your life, and you were made for it, but for me it's ridiculous, and I see now that it doesn't fit. All I've ever wanted was to fit, like I did when I was little and still had my family, whole and complete. But then it was gone, and I was powerless. I've tried to cobble together a family out of friends and beaus and reporters and photographers, but it's all a sham. Do you know what, though, Charlie? It's all okay now, because all of that brought me to you."

Charlie had begun to cry, slowly shaking his head. She held on to his hand.

"You don't know what you're asking for," he said. "Do you realize who the world thinks I am? They say I'm a monster who marries young women and mistreats them, one who would deny his own child. That's who they make me out to be now. Have you read the stories? Can you imagine what the press would make of me? Of us?"

"I have read the stories. I know all about your wives, about this woman who filed suit against you. I don't care about any of that, because I know you, Charlie. I see what you really are."

He turned to her then, and the hope in his small, sad smile nearly broke her heart. She knew then, for certain, that he loved her, too.

"All I could ever want is to be your wife, and to create a beautiful family with you, a beautiful life. We'll do it right, not like anyone has done before. Not like anyone expects from two people like us. All the ugliness out there can't touch us if we protect each other."

"It is not easy to let one's guard down," he whispered into her dark hair, "when life has made you wary."

She looked into his eyes, wishing she could wipe away the haunted look she found there. She let go of his hand and wrapped her arms around his neck. "Please protect me, Charlie," she said, "and let me protect you."

There was no use putting off the inevitable.

Charlie lay down beside Oona in her bed, in the room decorated by one of his former wives. The sheets were freshly laundered, to remove any trace of the illness she'd suffered over the past several weeks. Oona rested her head on his chest, and though it felt natural to be so near to Charlie, she wasn't used to the closeness, the intimacy of lying with the man she loved. She held her body stiff, but as close as she could be to him.

He stroked her hair. He was silent for a long while, and she was about to ask him what he was thinking when he took a deep breath and spoke.

"If you are lying here regretting what you said, you must know I won't hold you to it. You could still go now, and I would determine within myself not to bother you. If you left, I would be heartbroken, but you have the whole of your life ahead. If I love you as I fear I do, then I must let you choose."

Oona sighed and dug in closer, pulling the covers to his chest and under her chin. She smiled.

"Dear one," he said, "aren't you concerned? You really do not know what you're getting yourself into with me. Have you considered my age?"

"I suppose I should regret the difference in our ages, but I simply don't," Oona said. "I try to look at it frankly, but I don't perceive it. I am glad for whatever years each of us have lived, because if we hadn't met precisely when we did, it may not have been so perfect a connection as it is now."

He stroked the marble skin of her arm. "Then you must know that whatever happens from now on," he whispered, "I cannot lose you."

They were both quiet for a moment, his breath washing over the back of her neck. The moon shone clear and luminous through the window above them.

"Where in the world did you come from?" he said, his voice husky and warm.

His words fell on her head as his chest rose and fell.

"From Bermuda," she said, and closed her eyes, fully. She yawned, and drifted to sleep.

☙❧

In the morning, Charlie got up—shaved, bathed, and dressed—before Oona awoke. He was pacing a line into the carpet when her eyes opened.

"Oona, if we are going to continue with each other, it is only right that you know a few things."

Oona sat up, blearily pressing her forehead to make sure she was really awake. What was he going on about? Was he going to tell her one of the stories Charlie Jr. and Sydney had already told her by way of 'entertaining' her while she recuperated? They'd already gone out of their way to tell her about their father's previous wives. Maybe Charlie wanted to explain about a very 'adult' party he had tried to throw for a visiting friend, young female companions included, which had turned into a bust when the girls ended up fighting over who got to be with Charlie. She settled in for a beaut of a tale, trying to hid a bemused smile, and if that was the case, she would tell him exactly what she'd told his sons: "That was before he met me."

But Charlie sat down beside her. "You know about Joan Barry," he said, all seriousness, and Oona wiped the smile from her face. "The young woman who that bitchy Hedda Hopper keeps fluffing up so she can print stories about me?" He paused, tense, and Oona nodded. "Well, then you know that she and I did see each other for a time, but I soon learned that she is unstable. It's very sad, but she also became dangerous. She used to come here at all hours and just stalk around the grounds shouting for me. All sorts of horrors.

"Well, I thought I was finally rid of her, free of her threats and constant attacks. But I'm afraid she has turned up again. And Oona, she says her baby is mine."

"Okay," Oona said. "And is it?"

"I'm telling you it's not possible. But she has Hopper and others who are against me on her side, and she's not going to let it drop."

"Well," Oona said. "What are we going to do?" If Charlie said the child was not his, she believed him, simple as that.

Charlie sputtered, his brow furrowing.

"We?" he said.

"Yes, you and me. Tell me what you need and I'll do it."

He seemed unable to speak. She held his gaze, and his eyes filled with tears.

She squeezed his hand. She couldn't help anything that happened before. Half of Charlie's life to that point was before she was even born. But she was here now, exactly where she should be. He needed someone on his side, and she knew she definitely needed him. They were perfect for each other. She'd never been more sure about anything in her life. Everything she'd ever done or seen, loved or hated, felt or avoided, all of the things that made her who she was told her she had been made for this man, and he for her.

Regaining his composure, he went on. "I'm afraid you'll have to move to an apartment for a while. If you're feeling well enough, I'll find you a suitable place. With the scrutiny and photographers coming back around after her latest interview, I—"

Oona finished his sentence: "—can't have a beautiful young woman sunbathing beside your pool just now."

Charlie exhaled. "Exactly."

She sprang into action, and by the next day, her few belongings were moved to a furnished apartment on Olympic Boulevard.

She spent the night alone, staring at the ceiling. The bed was comfortable but nothing like the lovely one she'd enjoyed for the past few weeks. Now that she'd spent the night sleeping in Charlie's arms, she wondered how long she could last alone in a strange room by herself. But she would do it, for Charlie.

The next morning, the doorbell rang, once, twice, then repeatedly. Who could possibly know she was there? Maybe they were looking for someone else. She got out of bed and padded to the door, wearing the new oversized pajamas Charlie had given her while she recuperated. Thinking of him, she didn't remember to check the peephole before opening the door. She swung it wide open to find a camera in her face and a tall man in a gray suit standing on the stoop.

The man spoke quickly.

"Miss O'Neill, I'm an officer with the attorney general's office, here on official business. We're investigating the paternity suit brought against one Charles Chaplin. Do you know anything about that?"

Oona put on her most innocent expression.

"No..."

"Don't you live with Charlie Chaplin at his home?"

The photographer stood steps away from her front door and began snapping pictures.

"Of course I don't live there. I live here."

A camera flashed, dazzling her eyes. She squinted and hid herself behind the door as the men came closer.

"What is your relationship with Mr. Chaplin?"

"Why, he's a good friend."

"A good friend," the officer jotted on his pad.

"Yes, and I took acting lessons from him. My association with him is entirely on the esoteric side. He is teaching me to be an actress, and he is truly a great teacher." Her hand went to her mouth automatically, and she studied the men's faces, but their disinterested expressions did not reveal whether they were buying her story. The officer scratched out notes with his little pencil while the cameraman moved for a different shot.

"Say, now, what about Joan Barry?"

"What about her?"

"Well, your 'good friend' Chaplin is accused of fathering her child and deserting them both, refusing to support them. He's going to be brought up on Mann Act charges. What do you know about that?"

Oona opened her mouth to speak, then closed it again.

"How about this then? We'd like you to come down and visit the district attorney's office, to answer some questions."

"Well, I'll certainly let my mother know about that," Oona said. She gave them a disapproving little smile as she shut the door, then she went straight to the telephone and called Charlie.

☙❧

Hedda Hopper had it out for Charlie. The Joan Barry story was the latest she had grasped with both fists.

At the house, Oona recounted the exchange with the investigator at her door. "He asked about my relationship with you, and so I said you were a very good friend, and that you were giving me acting lessons," she explained cooly. "He tried to push on, but I wasn't intimidated. He didn't know who he was dealing with. I've dealt with tougher inquisitions than he can imagine." She thought of Walter Winchell, and blessed him for his training on how to handle prying questions. *Never let them get the best of you, kid. You're smarter than them any day of the week, and you have something they want. Make 'em work for it.*

Charlie explained Hedda's other, much deeper motive—rooting out Communist sympathizers for the FBI.

As he talked, she thought about it. How had the newspaper photographer known to be there when

352

the investigator showed up? It had Hedda written all over it.

"I'm not a Communist, Oona," Charlie said. "I understand the struggle of the poor, I was them once. But I love this country. If I say we should be supporting a second Russian front, it does not make me a Communist. But something has to be done about the Nazi's and this little shit Adolph Hitler."

She saw in his conviction where his loyalties lie, and hers were with him. She would do whatever it took to help him through this unfair campaign against him.

Chapter 30

SUDDENLY, EVERYTHING

Oona put aside all the negativity surrounding Joan Barry and resolved to be happy. She was in love, and they'd never get this time back. They should be blissful, finding joy in every moment, wringing every ounce of happiness from every moment of every day. She tried to ignore the newspapers, where Hedda Hopper interviewed Joan Barry under big, splashy headlines, always accompanied by a dark, guilty-looking photograph of Charlie.

They were not going to let this go.

The more the press continued to make him out to be a cruel and heartless man, the more Oona resolved to support him. She believed him when he said it wasn't possible for the child to be his. The man she knew would never deny his own baby.

Oona and Charlie spent peaceful evenings at the Summit Drive house before his driver took her home. He tried to throw himself into his work, reading new scripts and writing new scores for some of his early silent films. Everyone around him tried to soothe the agonizing pain of having his legacy torn down, his image destroyed by irresponsible reporters.

They tried and failed. When the lawyers sent him new reports of Miss Barry's claims, only Oona could reach him.

"You seem to understand the tortured soul of an artist, darling Oona," he said.

Did she? His words ignited memories, images of herself in the years that had led her here, to Charlie's side. She had set her mind at such a young age on winning the heart of one artist that now she was practically made for the role. She'd stored up fierce love and unconditional devotion all her life, waiting for the chance to share it. Sometimes she worried it would overflow, break the banks of her heart and flood the world, but she managed to control it. All these years. Now, she'd found the one who needed all of that love, and wanted it. No matter how busy, no matter how burdened, Charlie never denied her. His face lit up when she smiled.

It was all she had ever wanted.

"Oona," he said one evening soon after Oona's 18th birthday, they sat together in the parlor watching the last of the flame flicker out in the hearth. She'd been lying on the sofa, her head on a cushion, almost dozing off, while he sat near her, stroking her hair. "Oona, darling, look at me."

She sat up and turned to him. He twirled a lock of her hair in his fingers.

"I want you to be my wife."

"You do?"

"Yes," he said. His face broke into a smile. "I do."

She sat up and looked at him expectantly.

"So?" he said.

"So…"

"What is your answer?"

"You haven't asked a question."

"Oh!" Charlie slid to one knee. He took both her hands, assuming the traditional Prince Charming position. "Oona O'Neill, will you do me the honor of becoming my—"

"Yes!" Oona said. She threw her arms around his neck, and kissed him with all her heart.

☙ ❧

Carol married that awful Bill.

Oona could not believe it. So she called Truman. He couldn't believe it either. How many times had he told his girls: have affairs with whomever you wish, but never marry a poor man. Had he taught them nothing? At least Oona hadn't let him down, he said, and Oona scolded him. She loved Charlie. And his money wasn't the reason she was marrying him. "Doesn't hurt though, does it?" Truman said.

The thought of Carol marrying Bill still made Oona shudder. And Gloria's husband Pat was not much better. Oona remembered the night the three of them had made that silly pact. They would only marry real, certified geniuses. It seemed so girlish, so long ago now, though it had only been a few years. They were important years, the years that made them, for good or bad.

She would never say this to either of them, but she couldn't help feeling that of the three of them, she had made the most perfect match. She had really hit the jackpot of love the day she met Charlie.

Oona and Charlie had a wedding to plan. Each night after he got home from the studio, they volleyed ideas back and forth across the dinner table with all the intensity and strategic thinking of a championship tennis match. Every idea they considered dead-ended into the reason it wouldn't work or the disastrous way it could turn out.

Charlie had been married before, so a church wedding was out of the question. They didn't want a big affair, so no hotel. Oona couldn't ask Daddy to give her away, so no family and friends. Oona was not the first very young woman Charlie had married, so publicity announcements were probably not the best idea.

Charlie wanted to keep the story as long as possible from Hedda Hopper. Somebody had to get the scoop, he said—as if that were an average sort of problem every couple in the world had—so at least let it be Louella Parsons instead.

Oona set down the notepad she'd been using to jot down wedding plans. The page was covered in scratched-out lines and big black *X*s. They weren't getting anywhere.

"Sometimes I can't believe it's already been eight months since I came to California," she said, "and then other times I can't believe it's only *been* eight months."

"Eight is a lucky number," Charlie said. He finished a mug of coffee and dabbed a napkin to his mouth.

"It's a nice curvy number, don't you think?"

"A nice curvy number, like you," Charlie said, and he waggled his eyebrows in the way that always made her laugh, made the world laugh.

She did laugh, but then frowned at the page on her lap.

"Why don't we elope?" she said, throwing up her hands. Charlie shook his head.

"Because you deserve more than that."

"I don't want anything more than to be married to you. I don't care about the minutiae of how we achieve that end."

He paused, looking off toward one corner of the room. Oona knew that meant his wheels were turning.

"Charlie," she said, turning his face back toward her. "Do you love me?"

"I love you most terribly."

"All right then, let's do it."

"Good, it's decided."

"When?"

"Tomorrow."

"Tomorrow!"

"Yes. Tomorrow. Tomorrow will be eight months exactly since we met. It's perfect. You make some calls, put on a nice suit, and we'll meet up first thing in the morning."

The startled look in his eyes gave way to amusement, and relief. "Yes, dear." He smiled, and she pressed her forehead to his.

"Ooh, I do like the sound of that!" She kissed him on both cheeks and rubbed the lipstick stains off with her thumbs. Then she planted another in the middle of his forehead and ran off to pick a dress to wear for her wedding day.

CRSO

If everything went according to plan, they'd be married and on their way to their honeymoon before anyone got wind of it.

As she slipped her good navy-blue dress over her head, trying not to disturb the rollers in her hair, Oona went over it in her mind one more time. They'd meet at a friend's house, the driver would know where to go, and then ride together to the marriage license office. Her bag was packed and waiting by the front door, but Charlie had said to pack light. They could get everything they needed once they were married and safely hidden away on their honeymoon. *Perfect*, Oona thought. She certainly knew how to pack light.

She smoothed on the perfect shade of red lipstick and blotted it with a square of tissue. Shouldn't there be jitters? Nerves, dizziness? Something? She checked her purse for her smelling salts. The smelling salts reminded her of Carlotta, which in turn reminded her, for the hundredth time that morning, of her father. She shook her head, her dark curls swirling around her face and settling on her shoulders, then she put on her hat and pinned it in place.

The car arrived, and Oona took a last look around her apartment. It had been a place to live for a short while, but after today, she would have a home. She closed the door behind her with a firm click and set off to meet her groom.

The next hour would be crucial to pulling off the elopement before the press caught wind. Charlie had asked his friends Harry Crocker and Catherine Hunter to serve as witnesses, and they were waiting at the appointed meeting place, which was one of their homes. Oona didn't know whose house it was, but it was thrilling to think that soon those kinds of details would be her business to know, when she became the lady of Charlie's house. She'd have to start a new address book with all his associates' details, so she would never miss sending birthday or anniversary wishes "from Mr. and Mrs. Chaplin."

They arrived at the Santa Barbara County Courthouse in the town of Carpinteria before they opened for the day. Charlie held her hand until the doors were opened, and Oona kissed him. "Here we go!" she said, sliding out of the car. She smiled at him through the window and headed inside by herself.

She was first in line. The nameplate on the counter read "Ira Altschul, Clerk of Courts," and a man in a blue collared shirt with black sleeve garters looked at her wearily, as if he'd already worked a full day. "How can I help you?"

"I'd like a marriage license, please," Oona said, as if ordering a tuna fish sandwich.

"All right." He retrieved the right application form and slid it toward her. "But aren't you missing something kind of important?"

Missing something? She had all the documents in her hand. What did he mean? "A pen?" she said, hoping she hadn't forgotten something that would throw the plan off the rails.

"A pen!" Ira said. "No, dear, not a pen. I mean the *groom*. You can't get a marriage license for one." He seemed very pleased with himself.

"Oh, of course!" Oona began filling out the form. "He's just outside, parking the car. I'll just get this started, and then he'll be in to finish up. Is that all right?" She smiled sweetly and wrote fast.

"If you want this issued now, I need you both present."

Damn. Oona kept writing. "Well, sure. That's no problem. I'll just go and get him, shall I?" She turned, hesitating. The moment Charlie showed his face, the word would be out. Their presence at the courthouse would be in the afternoon papers across the country.

She quickly finished filling out as much of the information as she could. Name, date of birth, mother's name, father's name…She paused, then continued. groom's name, date of birth, mother's name—

"I'll just go and see what's keeping him." People had begun slowly filing into the lobby. Oona rushed out the doors and down the stairs to the car.

"They need you to come in as well," she said. "Hurry!"

Charlie and Harry got out. Catherine offered to stay with the car. "Do a loop around the block if the police come by. This isn't a parking space," Harry said.

Charlie pulled his hat down low and entered the courthouse building. Oona led the way back to the counter. Ira had stepped away, and was shuffling through a file cabinet. Charlie started scribbling.

"Here you go, Mr. Altschul!" Oona said softly, and the man turned back. His eyes went wide.

"Well, I'll be damned." Another clerk joined Ira behind the counter, staring from Charlie's face to the application and back again. "Say, Mr. Chaplin, I'm a big fan. Watch this!" He proceeded to turn and walk away, his feet pointing in different directions as he waddled along, miming a spinning cane at his side. "I'm The Tramp, see? You see that?"

"Yes, yes! I see! Very good!" Charlie said, trying to keep his voice low. "Listen, good fellow, I'd consider it a personal favor if you'd rush this along. Could you do that, my friend?"

Ira laid a finger beside his nose and nodded conspiratorially, then he took the form, typed up a license, and witnessed their signatures. The other clerk stood by, a starstruck look on his face.

"I suppose this is pretty hush-hush, eh, Mr. Chaplin?" he said.

"Ideally," Charlie said, "my good man." He glanced around the lobby, which was growing busier every minute. Oona noticed two secretaries pointing and whispering. One of them had her hand on the telephone.

"Let's go, dear," Oona said. The three of them headed for the door.

As they hurried through the lobby, Harry spoke up. "Better if you go out first, Oona. Once you're in the car, we'll follow."

They made a comical scene, Catherine hopping out to change seats and Harry taking her place behind the wheel while Oona and Charlie slid into the back seat and hunched down. The secretary had wasted no time. As Harry drove the car away, reporters screeched to a halt outside the courthouse and jumped out, already holding cameras at the ready as they ran to claim the best spots by the door.

Oona and Charlie watched out the back window, and laughed.

So far, so good.

Harry took all the side streets, racing to outrun the reporters who would soon be on their trail. It seemed to Oona that they drove forever, but when they turned onto Maple Avenue and arrived at the home of the justice of the peace, she realized not even an hour had passed.

The officiant introduced himself, Linton P. Moore, justice of the peace and Methodist minister. Charlie and Oona stood in the man's living room with Harry as best man and Catherine as maid of honor. Someone snapped photos. Oona tried to focus on the moment, to take it all in. They'd made it. It was happening. Charlie was all hers. The moment was on them and time suspended, settling on the gold ring Charlie held between his shaking fingers. It gleamed as it slid into place.

And then it was over. Within three short minutes, they had recited simple vows, both of them trying not to cry. "Mr. Chaplin, you may kiss your bride." Charlie drew her close and kissed her.

Oona beamed. Now it began: a new life, with a new husband.

A new name.

CRED

The news reporter's tobacco voice fairly shuddered from the radio with the thrill of sharing the news.

"Today is June 16, 1943, and it is rumored today that Charlie Chaplin's latest bride is the former Miss Oona O'Neill. The new Mrs. Chaplin—and I do mean new, she is just barely eighteen years old— is American literary royalty, a princess of sorts, one who has risen like cream to the top of New York City Café Society, winning the coveted title of Number One Debutante, and catching the eye of more than one rich, eligible bachelor."

Oona slid her foot out from under her and rose from the couch. She walked slowly toward the radio and kneeled inches from the speaker. She could almost see the society page photos the reporter described as he listed Oona's supposed suitors.

"...and the greatest of these: no less than Mr. Orson Welles himself. Miss O'Neill—again, daughter of renowned Pulitzer Prize-winning playwright Eugene O'Neill—has appeared in one or two little plays on the East coast, and her dear friend and fellow society queen, the former Carol Marcus, recently married none other than famed playwright William Saroyan. Carol was most recently seen on the Pacific coast when she was a bridesmaid for another of the girls' bosom buddies, none other than the ultimate Poor Little Rich Girl herself, Gloria Vanderbilt—she of the tumultuous and scandalous custody battle between her mother Big Gloria and her Aunt Gertrude Vanderbilt Whitney, sister of Little Gloria's dearly departed father Reginald Vanderbilt..."

Oona couldn't blink. She stared at the radio dial as if it might reveal the reporter's face, and then shook her head. They hadn't missed a name to drop, throwing in Peter Arno, Jack Topping, and a few men she'd never even met, speculating for shock value and good measure. No one was off limits.

The reporter went on, like a train whistle blowing steam, but Oona couldn't listen to any more. The last sentence she heard before she flicked the radio off made the blood rise to her cheeks: "Indeed the new Mrs. Oona O'Neill Chaplin could have had her pick of the world's most notable, handsome, sought-after men..."

"Yes, I could have had my pick," Oona replied, mocking the radio voice, "and that is exactly what I got."

❦

That night, she bathed in a gardenia-scented tub and oiled her limbs. Her new name played in her mind in various forms: Mrs. Charlie Chaplin...Mrs. Oona Chaplin...Mrs. Oona O'Neill Chaplin... She brushed out her hair and carefully applied her lipstick, but no other makeup, letting her bare face shine with joy. Wrapped in the softest bath towel she'd ever touched, she padded down the hall and entered Charlie's bedroom. He was lying in his bed with his arms behind his head, his chest bare.

She came to him, standing beside him as he looked up at her as if seeing an angel. She smiled.

"Just for tonight," she whispered, "for our first time, let's only do things neither of us has ever done before."

His eyes traveled from her lovely face down the length of her body. "That may be more difficult than you imagine, my dear. Don't forget who you've gone and married."

"Well then, husband," she slid between the sheets and draped one leg over him, her voice low and coy, "you'll just have to get creative."

He moved from under her leg and turned to her, then took her face between his hands, holding her gaze, and kissed her with all the uncertain tenderness of a first kiss. His hands were gentle, his eyes hungry. When they joined together, he drew back to look at her face. "Something I have never done before?" He lowered his face close to her ear, burying his face in the dark depths of her hair, and whispered, "I love you, Oona."

The Office of Harry Weinberger, Esq.

June 10, 1943

Dear Mrs. Chaplin,

As requested by our clients EUGENE O'NEILL and his spouse CARLOTTA MONTEREY, you are hereby notified that in light of your recent rash behavior and ill-advised marriage to Mr. Chaplin, your father has excluded you and all your subsequent progeny from the terms of his will.

Mr. O'Neill assures us, via Mrs. O'Neill, that this decision is final, and he will not entertain negotiation. She further relays his wish that you refrain from attempts to contact him in the future.

Best regards and well-wishes on your nuptials.

Sincerely,
Mr. Harry Weinberger, Esquire

From: Imperial Officer Jerome D. Salinger

> Somewhere on the front having learned from the newspapers why the goddamn girl stopped replying to his dopey letters

Mrs. Oona de Luna Chaplin,

> *I hope you are enjoying your wedding night, having so carefully saved yourself to be deflowered by a crusty old man with empty walnut shells in his saggy, soiled drawers. Speaking of drawers, I shall draw for you here a picture of how I imagine the bridal chamber looked:*

Chapter 31

HONEYMOON...KEEP A-SHININ' IN JUNE

Santa Barbara, June 1943

Oona read Jerry's letter at her dressing table, but as she turned the page, she covered her mouth so Charlie wouldn't hear her gasp. On the back of his ugly note, Jerry had drawn an old man running around, naked, swallowing monkey gland supplements in order to make himself ready to join his wife in bed. He'd drawn Oona, too, as a giggling young girl waiting in the corner.

She couldn't believe what she was seeing, but then on the other hand yes, she could. She'd been right about him after all—and he had just proven it. He may be a brilliant writer, she'd called that as well, but he was also a monumental jerk, and in that moment, she stopped feeling guilty for jilting him and thanked her stars that she had never agreed to wait for him.

For this letter to come on the heels of the one from Daddy's lawyer, basically informing her that he no longer considered her his daughter, seemed like perfect symmetry. Individually, each letter was an awful depiction of the true characters of two men who had held pieces of her heart. Taken together, they fit like the final pieces of a puzzle that seemed ugly until it was complete. Now, it was almost beautiful. They were breaking her heart with their selfish carelessness. But the heartbreak brought revelation, like the first rays of sunlight across a frozen plain: now that she had Charlie, her heart simply could not shatter as it might have done before.

☙❧

Santa Barbara, July 1943

They honeymooned in secret in a rented Santa Barbara home while the press went mad trying to figure out where they were. Oona went out only once, for a few items of clothes. She chose carefully, selecting well-fitting, comfortable, classic tops, cropped pants, and dresses, nothing too trendy. Just a few good pieces she could mix and match. Charlie told her to buy whatever she wanted, but what she wanted more than any fine piece of clothing was to show him she had a level head which she would not lose simply because she'd married a millionaire.

However, there was one small thing she could not resist.

One afternoon while Charlie was tied up talking to his lawyer about the Joan Berry case, she got tired of hearing about whether he had or had not had sex with the woman on the day in question. Now that he was her husband, and his body hers alone, the woman's ever-growing claims were a bit harder to hear than before. Anyway, she'd heard the sordid details a hundred times, and there was no new news on the case since Charlie agreed to a paternity test, so she wrapped a scarf over her hair and took herself out to the closest department store.

The driver dropped her at the front entrance to a large unfamiliar department store. She walked straight to the beauty department and stared into the case as if it were full of jewels.

"May I show you anything, miss?" said a powdery-chic older woman behind the counter. She smiled, revealing shiny gray teeth behind her wine-colored lips, and her cheeks folded into burgundy fans.

"Oh, it's actually missus as of just recently!" Oona said, smiling and brandishing the gold band on her finger.

The woman nodded approvingly. "I have to say, dear," she warbled, "you war brides are getting younger and younger, if that's possible!" She cackled, and Oona smiled, holding her tongue. "Anyhow, what can I help you with today?"

"Lipstick," Oona said. "I'd like to see what you have in red."

"Certainly." The woman pulled out trays from several brands—Estee Lauder, Lancôme, Chanel, Max Factor—and placed every red shade on the counter in front of Oona, whose eyes went wider with each new tube.

"Any of these would look well on you," the woman said as Oona twisted the tubes up and down, up and down. She waited, then asked. "Which would you like?"

"I'll take all of them, please," Oona said, opening her purse.

"All?" The woman's penciled eyebrows rose, underlining an accordion forehead.

"Yes, please," Oona said brightly. "Every last one."

As the woman wrapped her purchases and rang up the sale, Oona thought of Carol, of their fun times carousing around the fine department stores of Manhattan, remaking themselves, and of Gloria, the girl people mistook for her sister, who had never failed to ask her what shade of lipstick she was wearing so she could buy one for herself.

ᬀᬀ

One night, Charlie entered the bedroom in a new and strange get up.

"Are you a bear tonight?" Oona said, trying to play along, but secretly hoping this wasn't his way of announcing some strange kink now that they were married. When he came into the light, she saw what he was wearing—a glossy, full length mink coat.

"Aren't I simply divine?" Charlie said. He posed like The Tramp, with one hand inside the coat Napoleon-style, then spun around.

"Ummm," Oona said as he came closer, "I suppose that's one way to put it?"

"Oh, don't you like it?" he said. "I'd hoped you'd love it." He let it slide off his shoulders and held it out. "It's for you."

Oona leapt from the bed and gathered the coat in her arms, unbelieving. She stroked it with the tips of her fingers, lightly, as if not convinced she could trust her own eyes.

"I saw it and I thought, 'Oona must have it,'" he said. "You deserve the best of everything, my love."

Oona felt the fine soft fur, looked inside at the satin lining and found her name beautifully embroidered in silk thread. She slipped it on over her new satin peignoir, sliding both arms in as Charlie set it on her shoulders. She turned to him, stroking the lapel, then she held the coat open for him to come inside.

His next honeymoon surprise came a few days later. They had driven to a quaint market area and parked, then strolled along until they came to a small jewelry shop. Oona peered in the windows at the sparkling displays while Charlie admired a row of pocket watches. Inside, he encouraged her to try on the pieces she liked, watching her reaction to each one. Then they thanked the shopkeeper and went on about their day. They enjoyed lunch at a small café, fed bits of bread to the pigeons in the park, and then returned to the car to head back to their rented villa.

Oona had been working on her driving, and she'd taken the wheel for the short ride back. They'd just pulled away from the curb and into the street, and she was focusing mightily on the road, when Charlie pulled out a diamond bracelet and dangled it in the sunlight.

"What is that?" Oona said.

"Why, I don't know a woman who doesn't know what that is, my dear," he said dubiously. The brilliant stones shattered the light into hundreds of tiny sparkles all around the car interior, and Oona had to force herself to keep her eyes on the road.

"Yes, but where did it come from?"

"Why the jewelry store, of course!" he said, as if that were the most droll question he'd ever heard.

"But when? How?"

"Well, I saw you liked it, so I just put it in my pocket."

Oona looked at him wide-eyed, then began looking for a place to pull over. "Now, listen, Charlie, I don't know if that's such a good idea," she said, thinking that with his legal troubles, he did not need any more negative press. But what was he thinking? "Maybe we should stop and think this over..."

Charlie tried to keep a straight face, using all the old acting business he could muster to keep up the story, but her reaction broke him. "Darling, you believe I stole it, but you're still on my side?"

She shifted the car to park and looked at him, suddenly flushed with relief. "Of course, Charlie. I'm always on your side. Through anything."

He looked at her quizzically and was the adorable tramp again, despite the years and the silver hair.

"Well, not *any*thing, you understand?" she said.

"Yes, dear," he said, "I understand." He slipped the bracelet around her wrist and kissed her sweetly as she shook her head, and the entire drive back she felt him watching the tiny rainbows dancing over her skin.

❧

They stayed away on their honeymoon for two months, so long that the town of Carpinteria had taken on the comfortable atmosphere of home. But the press had figured it out, found their peaceful hideaway. They wouldn't be safe there much longer, and they reluctantly made plans to return to the real world, to the house on Summit Drive.

One morning, Oona sprang from the bed, running from the room without a word.

Charlie jumped up and followed. "What is it?" he shouted in a whisper. "Did you hear something?" He moved the edge of the curtain and looked outside, scanning the garden.

While they had enjoyed an idyllic time here together, they were on constant alert for the possibility that Joan Barry might figure out where they were. She had been bold and nimble enough to break into the grounds on Summit Drive, so this house would be easy for her to breach if they weren't on their guard.

Oona's low, guttural moan filled the hall. "Oona!" Charlie said.

She sank to the bathroom floor just in time, moaning again, but she couldn't reply to his calls. Every time she tried, a wave of nausea hit.

He rounded the doorway just as her stomach emptied into the commode.

"Don't look at me," she moaned.

Charlie came into the bathroom, a small smile on his face. He dampened a washcloth and held her hair from her face.

"I said don't look at me..."

"Oh, my dear," he said. "I don't wish for you to feel ill. But this is the happiest news you could have given me."

Oona wiped her lips and looked up at him as if he were mad. "Happy news?" A fresh wave rolled through her stomach. She hadn't felt nauseous or needed her smelling salts for such a long while. It had been wonderful. This was happy news?

He continued smiling, an expectant look on his face. Then, slowly, the truth dawned on her. Her eyes flew open wide.

"We're going to have a baby!"

He stood, an amused look on his face. "I'll order some tea and toast." He bustled off.

After he went, Oona washed her face and hands, and then stood staring through her reflection in the mirror, her hands protective on her belly as she whispered the words.

"A baby!"

Chapter 32

NEW YORK, NEW LIFE

New York, 1944

In the late spring, Charlie and Oona made an attempt to escape his seemingly endless legal troubles by taking a trip to Nyack, New York. Since the elation of learning she was expecting their first child, Charlie had said he longed to take her away from California. Then maybe they could both work in peace: he on his new screenplay, a story called *Monsieur Verdoux*, and she on growing their happy, healthy baby.

Charlie was a member of the Odd Fellows, a fraternal order which he believed shared his ideals. Oona read a member's pamphlet on the train. On the cover was an emblem encircled with the motto: "We Command You To Visit the Sick, Relieve the Oppressed, Bury the Dead and Educate the Orphan," and the words "Friendship, Love, Truth." Their beginnings were in England, and members had included men, women, and people of diverse creeds. Presidents, prime ministers, kings… Musicians, architects, ministers… Unlike the masons and other fraternal orders, they seemed open and inclusive. Names like Winston Churchill, Robert Melville Bailey, and Georgia Dwelle impressed her, some others on the list not so much. But the order's mission struck her as admirable, and Charlie was pleased to be a member. She hoped putting some distance between themselves and the ravenous press back home would offer some relief. They settled in to stay near the lodge, in a home owned by another member.

But trouble proved to be like water, flowing to the lowest point. Charlie had become depressed, bitter at the campaign against him for an act he swore he hadn't committed. They waited for the results of Joan's baby's blood test, but in the press, Charlie had already been found guilty.

They came down to Manhattan on a weekend, and met Carol and Bill for dinner at El Morocco. Oona and Carol squealed when they saw each other.

"Oona, darling!"

"Carol!" Oona said, squeezing both of Carol's hands, then strained to keep her smile in place: "Bill."

Hugging her friend, it was as though they had never left, and yet so much had happened in the few years since they ran around this town together, full of vim and vinegar and in love with themselves, in love with how the city seemed to love them. The restaurant was the same as always, with its rush of famous faces and sparkling trays of drinks held aloft by skillful waiters, yet different somehow, now that time had done its work of buffing memories to a smooth shine. Hollywood life may be glamorous, but having lived them both, Manhattan nightlife still could not be beat.

They were seated at a table in the center of the room, and Charlie's presence caused a rustle of interest. Bill bristled at the attention Charlie received, casting glances around the room for a familiar face.

But once the excitement of Charlie's appearance died down, drinks began arriving for Oona and Carol, drinks which had not been ordered by their husbands. Soon they were visited by a stream of young men, ones who had been Oona's and Carol's beaus only a few years ago, some they barely recognized.

"Ah, the one that got away!"

"Jack!" Oona said. "How are you? This is my husband Charlie. Charlie, this is Jack Topper."

"My good man," Charlie said with a confident nod.

But when Carol's male friends visited the table, Bill became agitated, which in turn seemed to give Charlie pause, and soon he too was upset as well. Bill pointed out a woman he had dated before marrying Carol, while he and Carol were in one of their 'off-again' phases, and the men's conversation drifted more than once to the women of *their* pasts.

"What *is* going on with all these men?" Charlie finally said, after a handsome man in uniform had gone back to his own table.

"Yes," Bill said, his blue eyes flashing, "what are you two up to?"

"We're not up to anything, Bill," Carol said. "These fellows are our friends."

Bill went quiet, but his eyes grew dark. This must be the look Carol had told her about, the one she'd already learned meant she was treading on thin ice and had better watch out.

Oona squeezed Charlie's hand under the table and caught his eye, reminding him of their understanding that no matter what might go on between them, they would never call each other out on the mat in public.

Poor Carol.

"I need to freshen up my lipstick," Oona said, sliding out of the booth. Her growing belly had just begun to really show, though she was well along, and she stood carefully.

"I'll come," Carol said. "I need to powder my nose."

"What's stopping you from doing it here?" Bill said, his voice hard, then turning to Charlie, "She drives my friends crazy, grooming herself at the dinner table. You could choke to death from that white powder flying around."

"All right now, Bill," Charlie said, giving Carol an understanding smile. Bill had too much to drink already, and Charlie detested drunkenness. "Ladies, we appreciate your dainty loveliness. Run along to your toilette. We'll wait for you right here." He gave his most charming smile, but as the women turned to go, Charlie took Oona's hand. "However, dear, mind you don't get swept away by one of your old boyfriends."

In the ladies' room, Oona dug around in her purse for the right lipstick. Carol combed her hair and caught Oona's eye in the mirror.

"I really think it's wonderful how jealous they are. To me, jealousy is a mark of passionate love."

"Don't tell me," Oona said. "'Like Heathcliff.'"

"Yes!" Carol sighed.

"Oh, I don't agree at all, Carol," Oona said. "At least, not any more. If anyone has a right to be jealous, it's me. Charlie's past love life is longer than my whole life so far." She blotted her lips. "Jealousy is one thing, and sometimes it's warranted. But I want something deeper."

How could she put it, how to explain it? That she wanted to be so confident in Charlie's love that she was immune to jealousy, and she wanted that for Charlie, too. Trying to find the words helped her understand it more clearly herself.

"Believe it or not, Carol, I think I'm learning that love is something more than longing and desperation and jealousy and jumping into bed."

Yes, she thought. As upside-down as it seemed, that was it.

BREAKING NEWS!
Shocker!
Charlie Chaplin Is Not the Girl's Father!
Blood Tests Prove The Tramp Is Not the
Father of
Joan Berry's Daughter After All
Despite proof, judge still orders child sup-
port payments for the youngster
until she comes of age.

Chapter 33

SECOND MARRIAGE, SAME MAN

Beverly Hills, 1951

Oona was pregnant, again. This would be their fourth child, and friends had begun to teasingly wonder aloud if the Chaplins may have converted to Catholocism.

After Charlie's vindication from Joan Berry's accusations, he had tried to put the whole sordid situation behind him, which was difficult since he had been inexplicably ordered to provide child support. The fact that his experience in the courts inspired new legislation in the matter of paternity cases did little to erase the damage done to his reputation by Miss Barry, her lawyers, and the press.

This situation had been part of their marriage from the beginning. Oona knew the truth. Nothing the outside world said could touch the depth of her love and loyalty, her determination to be the soft place for her family to land. She ran her household with the diligent devotion stored up through years of longing for a home and family of her own.

Carol phoned frequently and while listening, Oona often imagined the telephone wires growing red and hot. Carol was the most terrible gossip, and Oona knew her friend's propensity for embellishing had only grown with time. Still, she loved to hear Carol's voice and imagine her telling her stories like she used to, traipsing across the bedroom of her Park Avenue apartment as if giving the performance of a lifetime.

Though Carol hadn't come out and told her so, Oona suspected that Bill had not only hurt her emotionally, with his controlling personality and gruff demeanor. Between the lines of Carol's stories, Oona sensed something else, a shuttered fear.

During her last visit, Carol's children seemed to have retreated into themselves, their eyes taking on the distant, hollow look of children who had seen and heard too much, too close to home. Oona recognized it, but Carol insisted she was wrong. Bill was just a passionate artist, a genius. She sent the children away to school, and if she could figure out what it was he wanted from her, perhaps maybe things would be all right this time.

When she finally left him and come to Oona, Carol took to her bed in the Chaplin's guest room, making cross-country calls to Gloria, Truman, and anyone else who would listen. Bill was terrible, a monster, and she wanted nothing to do with him. Oh, but also, inconveniently, she loved him.

CRSO

Oona wished for her friend to have what she had—a marriage worth holding on to no matter what trial may come—but she'd never liked that Bill Saroyan. Ever since they got off the cross-country train to find him there, already glowering, she hadn't liked him. She shuddered, remembering the sinking feeling she got looking at the back of his neck from the back seat of his car. He would drive, saying snide things to her, and Carol would giggle, though Oona understood now, with the wisdom of a few years away from adolescence, that it was probably only because she hadn't known what else to do. Still, she had hated the back of the man's head and wished she could sock it every time she saw him, though she smiled and nodded at his bombastic talk for Carol's sake.

How she still regretted letting Carol use Jerry's sweet letters to write to him. But then, Bill had nearly broken it off with Carol when he read them, thinking she was one of those clever literary sorts and not the simple sex kitten he imagined. Maybe she should have let her copy more of Jerry's long letters, word for word! When Bill had raved about that 'damn good young writer J.D. Salinger' as if he'd discovered him, it had been an utter thrill to reveal to him that he hadn't thought so much of Salinger when he received love letters written by him!

Small victory.

Despite Carol's dramatic stories of her difficult life with Bill, Oona knew Charlie had been moved by the man's emotional reaction to Carol's ultimate decision to divorce him. The situation put him in mind of his friend Barton, he said, and how the loss of the woman he loved lead to his downfall and tragic suicide. He was afraid. If he didn't help this pathetic man get his wife back. What if it happened again? He'd finally learned the value of a good woman through his magical match with Oona, and if Carol were anything like her, Bill shouldn't let her get away. So when Bill begged him to help him win her back, Charlie had agreed. Oona had absolutely no proof of the things she suspected, and though Charlie valued her judgement, her reasoning against Bill fell flat. All she could do was to be there for Carol, and try to do what she could to change her mind without insulting her friend and driving her away.

Unfortunately, Carol had ultimately decided to take him back, to marry the jerk again. And now, Oona and Charlie were obliged to host the wedding reception.

Once again, it was the two of them in front of a mirror. "Honestly, Oona darling, are you ever not pregnant any more? Do I need to inform Charlie of what causes that?"

"Thank you, but no. He is well aware," Oona laughed.

"I really think what you have is the perfect love, Oona. I really think so," Carol said. Little lines were beginning to form between her brown, and she rubbed at them with her pinkies, which necessitated the application of more powder.

Oona gave Carol an enigmatic smile. She still wore the same shade of red lipstick she wore when they were the belles of New York, only now she had countless brands to choose from lining her vanity.

"If I had a bit of interest in keeping track of the passing of time, it would seem absolutely ages ago that we were girls."

"And yet, here we are, already on the far end of our twenties!"

"It's sort of comforting, though, watching you apply that same shade of lipstick, like the familiar waft of a mother's perfume," Carol said. She smashed the powder puff on her face and waved her hand at the cloud the exploded around her head.

"You really should have been a poet, Carol," Oona said seriously.

Oona did feel the passing of time. It was amazing, how something like the color of lipstick or the smell of perfume could take you back and remind you that you didn't just appear as you are, fully formed, from out of nowhere. She was whatever she was for a reason, had gotten here to this exact moment after trekking a course *from* somewhere. So what in the world was she doing right now, staying quiet when she knew she must speak up?

"You don't have to marry Bill again, Carol," she said.

Carol blinked, staring at Oona's sweet smile, the expression of a sister, concerned and lovingly condescending.

"We aren't all so lucky, to get it right the first time, like you have." Carol's whispery voice returned. "I believed in love. At least, what I understand of love. And yes, I *do* still believe in a *Wuthering Heights*, Heathcliff-on-the-moors kind of love, an overpowering and overwhelming love, so much that I would marry the same horror—*twice*!" She held up two frosty, pink manicured fingers. "Despite you warning me the first time!"

"I did warn you, didn't I?" Oona looked out the picture window and into the treetops which always made her feel like she was in a tree house. She stroked her pregnant tummy, felt her baby, their fourth child, give a delicate kick.

"You did, you warned me. When I was seventeen and wanted to marry him the first time, and Gloria thought it was a wonderful idea, and I cried to you about how I couldn't resist the beauty of his words, you tried to tell me. 'He's just plying his trade,' you said."

"But you didn't listen to reason," Oona said. "You listened to Gloria. Even now, you listened to Charlie instead of me."

"Well, that's not fair!" Carol said. "We all listen to Charlie!"

Oona laughed, bringing a wide smile to Carol's face. They went to the window and sat in two chairs, their feet up. The children's laughter drifted up from the pool below. After a few moments, Carol spoke again.

"I just can't believe it when love isn't enough, because it's supposed to be enough. It's Heathcliff, loving his soulmate Cathy so much that he was driven mad wanting to hold her again, even after she was gone.

"Everyone today says it's not enough, that it's not real love, and I start to wonder if maybe they're right. Maybe I'm stuck in another time. But I can't think that for very long. Because then I see you and Charlie, and I know I'm not wrong. It *should* be enough. My problem is that I keep giving my love to people who don't believe like I do."

"Carol," Oona said. "I think that may be the truest thing you've ever said to me."

"I always want to be true. I always want to be better than what I am. At the heart, don't you think people really are who they pretend to be?" Carol said. "You and I, darling Oona, we know better than most anyone that aspiration is everything."

Oona thought for a moment. "Do you know, Carol, I remember the first time you said those words to me? We were in Gloria's bedroom—actually, her dead uncle's bedroom—at the house party at Old Westbury. She was sitting on that awful masculine mahogany bed, and you and I were lying on those cots we thought were so glamorous just because they'd been brought out for us by a Vanderbilt-Whitney maid. We'd been talking about boys, about men, about how to *do it* without actually *doing* it, which by the way, Gloria should not have known about at the time!" They laughed, and Oona blushed. "How silly we were! To think aspiration was more of the truth than what we all really were right then, which was a trio of fatherless girls desperate for a man to love us. And we're still the same. Those aspirations of love we all had came straight from that desire, from being girls who had everything but the one thing we needed."

"You're right, of course, Oona," Carol said. "You're always right."

Oona brightened. "Oh yes?" she said, "Because it's not too late to ignore my husband's advice and skip this terrible idea of a second marriage to the man I told you not to marry the first time."

"I'm sorry, Oona. I have to. It's simply what comes next in my story, and I have to live it out."

"Carol," Oona reached out, stroking her friend's still improbably blonde hair. "I will never understand you, but I'll always love you."

While Oona oversaw the party for Carol's second wedding to that awful man, she mused about the way things turned out. Her two friends had had multiple affairs, some with married men, while she'd been busy having babies. She'd lost count of Gloria's conquests, though it was an excellent pastime to try, and Carol only told her half the truth at any given moment, so who knew how high her count was?

A strange question occurred to her: Was *she* the solid one? Then the straightforward answer: yes, actually, she was. The truth of it pleased her, but the loneliness of it scared her. Perhaps there was some answer to be found there. That fear of being alone, of being the odd one, the one left without, maybe *that* was behind the choices her friends made. Perhaps it had been behind her choices, too.

She tried to shake off the thought. If a person doesn't go in for too much psychoanalysis when she's happy, then too much self-reflection could only mean there was some unhappiness left to uncover, and to face. But she couldn't quite let it go. This blasted wedding wouldn't let her.

Her friends seemed to use affairs as steps, to get in and out of other situations, out of bad marriages and into new ones. Their husbands and their lovers generally all did the same. Faithfulness and loyalty weren't part of the equation. How did they live that way? Charlie used to be something like that, and she supposed she might have turned out that way, too, if she hadn't met him when she did. But she had, and she and Charlie had fallen in love—a big, real love, that made happily ever after seem possible.

When her father went away, someone had come between him and her mother. The other woman then wedged herself between her and her own father. She would never let that happen to her children. The best thing she could do for them as their mother was to have a solid, happy marriage. Her parents had been unwilling to bend, to sacrifice anything. They ended up sacrificing everything. And now, neither of them was happy. Her father lived behind a wall constructed by a power-hungry wife, and her mother lived her whole life since the great Eugene O'Neill looking for the kind of love she could only have for him.

She and Charlie were different. Charlie adored her and she him. She was his home. As long as she was beside him, life was everything the former 'Oona O'Neill, Number One Debutante' had dreamed of, wandering New York City and watching the families in the parks. She had a brilliant man to love her and only her. Side by side, nothing could take away her happiness.

Chapter 34

JUST A BOOK

Beverly Hills 1952

The sun had begun its melting descent into the ocean, and a deep shadow fell across the novel in Oona's lap which had made the afternoon disappear. She drew a towel around herself and picked up her books. Time to check in with the nannies about the children's dinner. Holding the ends of the towel, she padded inside.

Quiet. That was good. But also a little bit strange. She climbed the stairs and walked by the doors to the children's rooms toward the nursery, looking for Kay. The head nanny was good at many things, but keeping the children quiet while they dressed for dinner was not usually one of them. To be fair, though, no one could be expected to keep children quiet *all* day.

She peeked in on Victoria, the baby, miraculously sleeping. She would be up all night again. Oona didn't like the littlest ones to have a nurse too soon. Despite what the experts suggested, she wanted to coddle them herself as long as she could. They were babies for such a short time.

She closed the door again and continued down the hall. Passing Geraldine's room, she heard a small gasp, then giggles. She stopped just past the oldest child's door, so her bare feet couldn't be seen from underneath, and listened.

Whispering. *What is this girl up to?*

She reached for the doorknob just as another voice came from inside Geraldine's room. It sounded like Michael. As she leaned closer to the door, he said, "What does goddam mean, anyway?" She turned the knob and threw the door open.

Her three older children looked up, instantly zipping their mouths. Eight-year-old Geraldine sat cross-legged at the foot of her bed. Six-year-old Michael knelt to one side, little Josephine, only three, mirrored him on the other. They all leaned over a book Geraldine held across her legs. They turned in unison at the sound of the door opening, and Geraldine smacked the book closed.

"What is that?"

"Just a book," Geraldine said.

Oona crossed the room slowly, hiding her amusement the best she could. She'd had a moment of dread before opening that door, wondering what she might find her children getting up to. Some Hollywood kids started drinking and doing drugs before their tenth birthdays. But here were her funny children, snickering over a novel. They were up to something, though, so she couldn't let them off the hook just yet.

She picked up the book from Geraldine's lap. *The Catcher in the Rye* by J.D. Salinger.

Oona laughed out loud then, and the children looked at each other.

"Is this a good one then?" she asked.

"Yes, Mother, very educational," Geraldine said.

Oona raised her eyebrow as she perused the cover, playing dumb. "'J.D. Salinger,' hmm?" She flipped through the pages as the children eyed each other, Geraldine shooting them warning looks. "Perhaps I'll borrow it then, since it's so educational." She gave the children one of the looks that had become part of her personality now that she was a mother of four, the 'I'm watching you,' look, and slowly walked back out of the room, leaving the slightly relieved children to wonder whether a punishment would come later, after Mother read all those 'goddams.'

She read the book while Charlie was at the studio and the children were at school, read it in an afternoon in her favorite reading chair, placed in the perfect spot beside a window in her bedroom. The dappled sunlight streamed in to light the pages, a pacific light so brilliant, and so completely different from the pale sunshine she and Jerry had known together.

She devoured the book, finally shutting it with amazement. He had done it. Jerry had found the voice of his heart and put it down on paper in the most frank and revelatory way. It was the pitch-perfect voice of their generation.

"*Well done, Jerry,*" she thought, closing the book, "*to write like that...so perfectly.*" Nothing he had written before had inspired such a sense of awe in her. He really was as talented as she'd felt he was. She held the book to her chest, knowing some of his inspiration, because she'd been there. Knowing she'd been Sally to him once, and hoping he could know somehow that she saw his words and saw the inspiration from their time together. They hadn't been meant for forever, but they'd been meant for a singular, exceptional impression of time. Sally's confusion and fear, her rejection of Holden, even in the sadness of those things Jerry had shown he understood. He had worked it all out on the page, at least on some level, depicting the parts of himself that had driven her away, and the parts of herself that had kept her from committing to him.

She opened the book again and started it all over, from the beginning.

Beverly Hills, 1952

Dear Daddy and Carlotta,

I hope this will find you both well. I want you to know that Charlie and I and the four children will be traveling abroad soon to support Charlie's new film. It is a very personal work for him, and I know you understand that concept, Daddy. Life imitating art. The lead actress is Claire Bloom, and she and I have become dear friends. If you see fit to watch the film, you will see me in a scene, as I stood in for her during editing when Charlie needed to reshoot a scene.

Geraldine and Michael are excited for the trip, as we're making a family vacation out of it. Josephine and Victoria just enjoy any kind of adventure. We will be quite the entourage. Charlie suggested we stop in Bermuda to visit the old family home. The children might find it interesting anyway, though it will be hard for me. They say it's good to face those things that have caused us pain, and if that's so, Spithead would be the place to begin for me.

I've kept up with all your work, Daddy, and I read all of it. I see the stories of my grandparents and my uncle in them. I see my mother. And of course, I see myself. I should say, I see how you must have seen me.

It is so sad to watch the cycle repeating itself. The O'Neill curse, which could have ended with us, lives on. I worry for Shane, enough to entreat you that if the inspiration ever strikes you to reach out to one of us, that you make it Shane. He was broken the day you left us, and he was never able to recover. All he has ever wanted was your approval. Maybe time will reveal to you how much your sincere love could change the lives of your children. With Eugene Jr., your oldest, gone now in such a tragic way, perhaps you might consider reaching out to your other son. As for me, I will continue to hope you might have a change of heart, to see me and Charlie and your grandchildren when we return to the United States.

Very sincerely,
Your only daughter,
Oona

$\mathcal{C}$hapter 35

ALL ABOARD

Beverly Hills, 1952

Oona sealed the letter to her father and looked across the room to Charlie. He'd been watching her, and his face reflected a full range of emotions—empathy, sadness, anger, love. That face which had been the silent voice of a generation, now was an open book telling of his tender regard for her. He got up and came to stand beside her, his hand on her shoulder.

"It breaks my heart, seeing how you keep trying to reach him. You, the woman who has changed my entire world with your steadfast love, through good and bad times. In the nine years of our marriage, you have been the steady, practical voice that makes the world make sense. You simply give your love, and that love has opened me up, enabled me to do the same in return."

She wiped away tears, and he stroked her hair.

"All this time, and you keep trying to reach him. You continue giving him chances. He ignores every attempt, even pictures of your babies." He shook his head. Oona's shoulders fell, and he tempered his own growing anger. "He doesn't deserve it. He doesn't deserve you."

Oona placed the letter with the other outgoing mail—birthday greeting, thank you notes, anniversary cards. She always sent Daddy a card on his birthday. He never responded. Never reciprocated.

The family was getting ready to leave on a six-month tour to promote Charlie's new movie, *Limelight*. He'd made the film in honor of her, as a public declaration, he said, for the love of his life. The four children buzzed with anticipation of the journey, the longest family vacation in their memory, and he had high hopes the film would be well-received here and abroad.

"Despite the disdain I feel toward them," Charlie said, "on my old friend Barton's behalf, I feel I must offer one more time: Shall I try to contact him?"

"No, Charlie," Oona said. "It would only upset him, I'm sure. If Carlotta even put your call through." She'd heard snatches of news of him from friends and through his lawyers, that her father was ill and Carlotta was keeping him more and more isolated.

"He may come to realize how poorly he has behaved. Perhaps when we return to the States, after he has seen *Limelight*, or at least heard about it, he will have a new perspective. The movie will show him, like it will show the world, how truly I love you. Why, I do not know of one other man more perfectly suited to his wife than I."

The film was for Oona; it was about her. She heard him talking about it with his closest friends, late at night when he thought she was asleep. It was a gift to the woman who saved him. The woman who saved him while letting him think he had been the one to save her. It was so much for her that he'd searched for an actress who resembled her. Claire Bloom had studied Oona, taken dance classes with her, all in preparation to play the ballet dancer Tracy, the girl paralyzed by the circumstances of her life. His own character, the washed-up clown Calvero, nurses her back to health and happiness while his own career, and yes, his life, proceeds to its inevitable end just as Tracy is ready to stand on her own again. It was a dramatic depiction of how Oona had come to him, how he had nursed her back to health even as the career he loved slowly left him behind. It broke her heart to hear him say that he knew he wouldn't always be there—the difference in their ages would catch up to them eventually—but he'd build her up with the same kind of love she'd offered him, to make her strong enough to go on when he was gone.

✤

Once the family and their entourage were settled on the train to New York, where they would embark on the *Limelight* movie promotion tour, Oona pulled letters from Gloria and Carol from her bag. She opened Gloria's first, saving Carols' for after, since it would no doubt contain juicy details about anything Gloria told her in hers. Gloria was married again, but she'd had so many affairs, both with married men and single ones, that she said she counted them to help her fall asleep rather than counting sheep. She signed off with a sly comment about Charlie's troubles with the House Un-American Activities Committee, just in case Oona needed a reminder.

Then Carol's letter. Oh, Carol. Once again divorced from Bill, she was now seeing a married man after having several other affairs, also with married men. Oona put the letters away, suddenly tired. Her life at that moment couldn't be more different from those of her childhood friends.

It was as if they really felt themselves faultless in all these affairs with married men. It was the one thing she couldn't abide, and the one thing both these friends couldn't seem to stop doing. The thing that formed an invisible barrier between them over the years, as their romantic relationships came and went and Oona's stayed. She did not judge them, not really. Their paths were just different, but the passing years drew divergent roads on the map of their lives, taking them to very different places.

Despite the vast differences in their backgrounds and experiences, she had truly believed they all started out with the same goal: to find a good man to love, and who would love them back forever. Even when Gloria had blithely declared they should commit to marrying 'certified geniuses,' Oona never dreamed they would include geniuses who already had wives.

While she remained married and devoted to one man, her friends were living as if there were no tomorrow, no consequences, no wives at home, waiting for their husbands and the fathers of their children. Sometimes she let herself wonder what it would be like to live that way, like nothing mattered but what you wanted in that precise moment, like other people's lives were inconsequential compared to your own, like right and wrong applied to everyone else but you.

Like Carlotta.

And there it was. Oona stared out the train window, watching the past go by. She had seen her parents' marriage torn apart by infidelity. The details were never hidden. It was ugly and cruel and wholly unfair. Even if Charlie were to leave her tomorrow, which she truly believed would never happen, she meant what she'd said years ago even more now than she did then:

She would never be like Carlotta.

⊗℘

September 19, 1952

The RMS Queen Elizabeth began to pull away from its pilings in the misty morning hours and Oona quietly joined other passengers on the port side. Children jostled for spots to watch as the anchors weighed while the crew loosed enormous ropes from their mooring. The docks were lined with well-wishers, waving scarves and hats and shouting final goodbyes to friends and family, but this voyage had attracted a larger crowd than usual. The morning paper mentioned that Charlie Chaplin and his family would be onboard, and Oona smiled at the sea of eager faces, some in bowler hats and carrying canes, hoping to catch a glimpse of The Tramp on deck as the ship sailed away.

Charlie had been hesitant to leave the cabin. "The lawyer says a former studio employee is filing some sort of suit against the studio, and they may try to serve summons before I leave the country," he said, "and then we would be called back from this journey. We can't have that!" He'd promised to join Oona topside once they were safely underway. She watched for him, anxious that he not miss the crowds who had gathered for him, and finally he appeared, making his way to the bow, to an area specially reserved for the ship's guest of honor. As he appeared, a small figure barely visible in the sun's glare off Hudson Bay, Oona joined him at his side. Only then did the crowd know for certain the diminutive was him.

Charlie's friend and assistant Harry Crocker was along for this leg of the tour. At lunch the next day, Oona sat back and watched as Charlie laughed and joked with him, having the grandest time with their other table guests. How wonderful it was to see him like this, relaxed and free in the way only a journey by ship seemed able to provide. What was it about being completely surrounded by the open sea that dissolved any troubles left behind, back on land? Charlie had launched into an impression of one of the immigration agents who had come to interview him before their trip, in order to get his traveling papers. He pulled a long, serious face, transforming instantly, and to hilarious effect. He switched back and forth between the agent's voice and his own.

"If this country were invaded, would you fight for it?" he mimed, his voice deep and monotone. The table erupted in laughter, then he answered as himself.

"Of course. I love this country—it is my home, I have lived here for forty years."

"But you have not become a citizen."

"I don't believe there is a law against that. I pay my taxes here. And a hefty sum, too!"

His impression of the agent's reaction sent everyone nearly off their chairs with laughter. Then a ship's officer approached, whispering something near Harry's ear. Harry excused himself, his face turning suddenly gray, and followed the officer out. Watching him leave, Charlie's face turned sallow, and Oona took his hand. Soon Harry returned.

"The United States has revoked your reentry papers, Charlie. They will not be reinstated until you agree to appear before the court and answer further questions about your political beliefs."

Charlie lowered his head.

Oona remained calm until they reached their cabin, but once inside, she fumed. How could they treat him this way, in such a completely underhanded and unfair fashion? Would it ever stop? Charlie was devastated, she could see the sadness through the anger in his eyes. It came to her then, as she stood in front of him and he wrapped his arms around her waist, pressing his head against her: she would have to be strong now, strong enough for both of them.

She appeared at dinner that evening cool and elegant in a black satin ballgown with a tiered skirt, a diamond brooch, and her dark hair neatly coiled into a chic bun at the nap of her neck. Photographers captured the event, and Oona held her head high, determined that no one would know from her face that they had just received news that threatened to change her family's life.

Chapter 36

MISSION

1952

The Chaplin family arrived in London to a welcome that was just the balm they needed after the long and unsure journey. *Limelight* had been shunned in the U.S. by movie-goers who were afraid to be labeled communist sympathizers for entering a Charlie Chaplin film, but in Europe, Charlie's cinematic gift to his beloved wife was an overwhelming success. Charlie's anger at how the country he loved had treated him had grown with every mile of the voyage, and now he resolved not to return. Oona stood by him with her usual outward calm, concealing the turmoil inside. She had more than Charlie's feelings to think of. She had four little children now. Protecting her family was all that mattered.

The four children had looked forward to this family trip, to seeing the place Daddy came from. But they'd left home for the long voyage with the knowledge that they would be coming back again, to their home in Beverly Hills, the only home they'd ever known.

"Here is what we have to do," Charlie said one day. Bolstered by the welcome they received, he seemed emboldened to take a stand for himself and his family. "I will stay here, that part is obvious, but you will have to go back and settle our finances. The children will stay here so you can focus on the task, because it will be a big one. And when you get back, we'll find a new home together, whatever you want."

Oona remembered the pain and fear of losing her childhood home, the confusion, the destabilizing feeling of picking up and setting down, learning not to get too attached, that every place she laid her head after that might be temporary. Her children wouldn't suffer that, no matter what she had to do. They would have both their parents, and they would have a new home, a solid one from which they would never be turned away again. She looked directly into Charlie's eyes.

"Just tell me what I have to do."

"Dear, are you sure?" Worry tightened his lips and he took her hand.

"I can do it, Charlie. Honestly," she said, squeezing his hand reassuringly. He relied on her so much. She knew her being gone, alone and so far away, would be a terrible strain for him. So she smiled and added in her lightest tone, "How hard can it be?"

Charlie leaned closer, and they made a plan.

CR80

In November, Oona boarded a flight to New York International Airport, then another to Los Angeles. Her luggage was uncharacteristically numerous, but rather light, and she wore the beautiful mink coat Charlie had given her on their honeymoon. It smelled as much of him as it did of her, and it bolstered her confidence. She was strong. She could do anything. She would get in, take care of business, and get out. It was that simple.

The stewardess brought her a martini, and Oona took a deep sip and repeated these things to herself. She was Oona O'Neill Chaplin. She could handle anything. She stuck her hand into her travel case for the hundredth time to check for the documents and letters Charlie had given her. The folder was just thick enough that she'd had to remove the tray of lipsticks to make room. She smiled remembering Geraldine's face, finally breaking into a grin after months of sadness, when she'd watched Oona remove the shining gold and silver tubes and store them away in a drawer, "Just until I get back!" The papers were, of course, still there, and she snapped the case closed and settled back to finished her martini. Yes, everything was going to be fine. Just fine.

As the plane approached the Los Angeles airport, she plucked from her Hermes handbag the one lone lipstick tube which had made the cut and carefully reapplied. No mirror needed.

Everything went to plan, but on the last leg of the journey, in the back of the black car on the way to Summit Drive, Oona's heart began to pound. What if she did something wrong? What if someone tried to stop her? She had no idea what had been going on here in their absence. The government had been serious enough to cruelly wait until they had left

U.S. waters to inform them Charlie's reentry papers had been revoked. They had it out for him, and they were not going to let it go. They knew people who had spoken out against lifelong friends out of fear of losing their own reputations or even being prosecuted themselves. McCarthyism didn't seem to be going away as Charlie had initially, perhaps naïvely, hoped.

But what was she really worried about? She wasn't there to steal anything. She was there to collect what belonged to them, what was theirs, before it was taken from them. What scared her, she realized suddenly, was the unknown. Just as the revocation had come out of the blue and changed their lives, something else could be waiting around any corner, no matter how well she did her job on this crazy mission.

Charlie had never failed to pay his taxes. His love for America was blatantly clear, regardless of his sympathy for the plight of people it considered enemies. She loved that about him. His compassion was what allowed him to capture the pathos of the 'everyman' on black and white film, in a time when actors couldn't even use their voices. From the beginning, he'd used his image to give voice to people who felt forgotten. Even in his wealth, he never lived decadently. The boy who grew up poorest of the poor, performing for his keep as a boy in Victorian London, never forgot what it was like to be almost destitute, to have nothing.

And that was why he'd hidden his money on the grounds of his own house on Summit Drive.

Thank God for Charlie. That money, if she could find it all and take it back with her to London, would allow the family to find a new home regardless of what else might happen.

So there was no room for fear now.

Her heart slowed automatically as the car climbed the hill, crawling slowly up Summit Drive, and the house came into view. This place had been her first real home since Bermuda. It was the place where Charlie had proven to her that a man could be both strong and tender. That a genius could be a genius without tearing the people who loved him to shreds and casting them aside. Indeed, he could be even greater for holding on to his humanity rather than despising it. In this house, Charlie had healed her childhood heartbreak and, it occurred to her as the gate swung open, she had done the same for him.

Starting now, she must find ways to detach herself from this house. Home was where Charlie and the children were. She steeled herself. But the moment she stepped inside the front door, the tears came, rising up from somewhere deep, like a fountain. Memories flowed with the tears and she let them come, let them roll hot down her face and into her hands. She cried them all out, until she was done crying.

And then she wiped her face.

She walked straight through the house, through the wide back door, and down the path that lead into the back yard.

⚬⚬⚬

One million dollars. Cash. Oona couldn't believe her eyes. She separated the thousand-dollar bills into neat, thin stacks and laid them out on the floor, and stood over the carpet of cash, a spool of black thread in one hand and a fine sewing needle in the other.

She lingered in a patch of sunlight and tuned her ears to the home's familiar sounds. The silence reverberated with absence, with the lack of children's high-pitched laughter, the low tone of house staff conversations, the symphony of Charlie's booming voice. They would have all of that again, in a new place. Her eyes roamed around her old bedroom, and as she looked, it became her 'old' bedroom. Soon they would make a new home, away from the constant accusations and interrogations. She was so close to finishing her mission and leaving the hysteria and vicious attacks against her husband behind her. They would do it together. Her children would have some peace.

One by one, she sewed each stack of cash into the lining of the fur coat Charlie bought for her after their wedding, the one that had made her feel secure and loved and completely safe for the first time in her life, ten years ago when she'd met her soul mate and her life had changed forever. The coat, splayed open across her bed with its satin lining carefully separated at the seams and peeled back, had been a symbol of Charlie's love for her, not because it was expensive or fine, but because when he chose it for her, he knew she hadn't had even had a proper coat when she came to him. When she was sick and cold with fever, he had cared for her. And when he knew he loved her, he had wrapped her in the finest gift he could think of as a symbol of his protection, of the shelter of his love. The fur coat was like the hug of a father, the lover's embrace, the soft place to land when the world was too hard and too cold.

She recalled the days when she had traipsed around Manhattan with Carol, thinking how terrific they were and how the world probably couldn't wait for them. How she'd stopped in front of that furrier and watched the woman dress the mannequin. How she'd wondered if she'd ever have a fine fur coat like that, one that had been chosen by a fine man who loved her without condition and asked only that she love him back in the same way.

As she sewed, she remembered the close call she'd had earlier, at the bank. Smiling to herself, she thought of how closely they'd inspected her signature before turning over the contents of the safety deposit boxes. Things had seemed a bit dicey for a few minutes before they'd had no choice but to do as she'd requested.

At that point, the whole venture had turned rather thrilling. Once she'd found the money safe and sound, buried where Charlie had marked the spot on his hand-drawn map of the grounds, the anxiety had lifted completely, and she'd swept into United Artists Studios on the next phase of her mission feeling rather like an international spy. She saw to it that Charlie would have his film reels, every one that was stored there.

It seemed Charlie was having a less thrilling time back in London. His telegrams were getting increasingly desperate. He wanted her back with him—at this point she could leave the money if she must, just get back to him safe and sound. She hated that he was suffering so much in her absence, but it was secretly gratifying to know he missed her so much that he couldn't go a day without telling her so.

She finished sewing the cash and then carefully stitched the hems. When she put it on, it hung more heavily, but she'd done a good job. People might think she'd put on a bit of weight, or more likely, that she was pregnant again!

She took one last tour of the house. Tears came and went in waves, as she noticed a corner where Geraldine had danced or Michael had sat in the sun with a book, his radio beside him, where the babies used to sleep in the nursery, or the secret places where she and Charlie used to make love, day or night. They might never be here again. It was all right, even though it really wasn't.

It had to be. What choice was there?

The next day, after another bout of tears, she watched her luggage, now heavy with Charlie's carefully packed original films she'd retrieved from the studio vaults, as it was loaded into the belly of the plane. She wanted to see them go into the plane with her own eyes. That done, she headed back into the airport to meet the security officer who would accompany her through the terminal.

She hesitated when the officer offered to take her travel case, but then relented. It was important to look calm and unflustered, so she handed it over, all the better to have a free hand with which to hold the front of her heavy coat closed.

Her heart began to pound as they approached customs.

"Are you sure I can't take your coat for you, Mrs. Chaplin?" the officer said, watching her dab at beads of sweat forming on her brow.

"Oh, no," Oona said lightly, her red lips spreading into a disarming smile. "I am perfectly fine."

She handed over her passport with the proper documentation, everything in order, then stood there with a disinterested expression until it was all handed back to her. Other agents had gathered to see the young wife of Charlie Chaplin depart, perhaps for the last time. If they were so intent on staring, she'd give them a show. Their curious heads followed her, and she raised her chin as she swished by the counter, daring to let her coat fall open slightly, and smiled, a woman with a million-dollar secret.

Bermuda, 1929

Little Oona sat on her bedroom floor surrounded by her toys. Mother had told her to pack up only her favorites to take with her on the ship to The Old House. They would be staying there for a little while again, Mother said, and if she left something important behind there'd be no coming back for it for a good while.

She picked up a teddy bear that wore a dashing blue bow tie. She tapped its feet on the floor and spoke with a deep voice: "I must have quiet. Don't you understand?" In her other hand, she held a porcelain fashion doll with a beautiful blue silk gown. Tapping its feet on the floor, her voice went high. "Shush Baby! Can't you be quiet? Daddy is working."

A pink-cheeked baby doll lay on the floor, staring unblinking at the ceiling.

"Why can't you be more quiet, baby," Oona said in the high-pitched voice.

"Oh, yes!" she said in the deep voice. "Can't you be more quiet? I must have quiet!"

Agnes appeared at her door.

"Have you chosen a toy, Oona?"

"Yes, Mother."

Oona held up the porcelain doll for her mother to see, but the doorway was already empty.

She put the porcelain doll down, and looked at the baby doll. Its soft brow stirred a gentle fluttering in her chest. She picked it up and cradled it, then hugged it tight.

"It's all right, baby," she said. "It's all right. We're going to a new home."

She patted its back and smoothed its curls, then laid it on the bed beside tomorrow's traveling clothes.

Switzerland, 1952

Lausanne, Switzerland: Film star Charlie Chaplin and his wife Oona O'Neill Chaplin, daughter of famed playwright Eugene O'Neill, have purchased the palatial Manoir de Bain in Corsier-sur-Vevey, Switzerland, on the shore of Lake Geneva. The family has been living in exile in London while they decided where to settle down. Mr. Chaplin was denied return to the United States after leaving the country on the QE2 for a film tour to support his newest film Limelight.

The neoclassic style Manoir will be home to the Chaplin family of Charlie, Oona, their four children, and a fifth baby due soon.

Chapter 37

HOME

Vevey, Switzerland 1952

Crates of furniture from Beverly Hills began arriving at the family's new home, everything that had filled the Summit Drive house plus pieces from the studios: the sofa used in *Limelight* was a favorite of Oona's and she spent early evenings on it, reading aloud to the baby who would be born any day.

Oona found a local gardener to teach her everything about the gardens. She became an expert on the soil and weather of the banks of Lake Geneva. Soon she was name-dropping flowers and plant species like Carol did celebrities and Gloria did lovers.

Charlie focused his energy on the creation of a film room. His original films needed special housing to protect them from air and moisture, and once it was done, the room became his place to find himself again. When he thought too much of how his adopted home had turned on him, and pushed him away, his chest filled with indignation that eventually turned to anger which in turn came out as a short-temper with his children.

"Why don't you share this with the children?" Oona said, and he let the four children watch his films, too. But only his films.

As Oona observed the young heads bob with laughter over their father's on-screen antics, her heart broke for what they had gone through. They'd been uprooted from their home, and they tried so hard to be brave about it all. A new mansion home was a distraction for a while, but it couldn't erase the only place they'd ever known. The new baby would be born in Switzerland, an entirely different childhood awaited him and any more children they would have.

Finally, the last shipment of their belongings arrived at the front door of their new home. Oona directed the placement of every piece, smiling as each was uncrated, a small connection to the family's old life. Once the last piece was placed on the mantel, Oona added a framed family portrait in the center of the arrangement, then stood back to assess her work. Her hands pressed to her lower back as the baby kicked.

She walked around the house, giving it one more look to make sure everything was in place. The children were playing in their new bedrooms. The nanny would bring them down for dinner with her and Charlie soon. Chef had made a lamb stew and fresh bread, filling the house with the warm aroma of comfortable abundance.

She thanked the exhausted movers as they gathered their equipment and folded up their giant furniture covers, then she took a look around.

Finally.

It was official. This was their home. She marched to the front door and stood there for a moment, like a sentry, sending a warning look to the world outside. Then she quietly shut the door, and set the lock.

The children trooped down the stairs and she gathered them up and herded them to the sitting room. She arranged her family in a tight composure on the sofa, then sat next to Charlie.

"We're going to have our picture taken now," she said, "All of us together in our new home. Everyone look, look at the camera!" The children fidgeted, jostling for a seat close to her, and Charlie moaned as one of them knocked an elbow against his head. Oona smiled over the commotion, placing a protective hand on her belly.

In that moment, all was right. All was good. She had built the family of her dreams, made sure they had a home, that they were all together, safe and secure, secluded from any danger.

No storm could ever reach them here.

THE END

Afterward

Oona and Charlie lived at the Manoir de Ban in Cousier-Sur-Vevey, Switzerland, near the banks of Lake Geneva. They added four more children–Eugene, Jane, Annette, and Christopher—to their family after leaving the United States, and the couple defied the odds and naysayers, remaining happily married for thirty-four years.

Oona never stopped trying to reconnect with her father, but all attempts were thwarted. He passed away on November 27, 1953, one year after Oona moved to Switzerland. Sadly for Oona, they were never reconciled. After his death, details of his life were revealed to her through sources including Eugene's friend and editor Saxe Commins and Eugene's final doctor, also Carlotta's doctor, neurologist Dr. Harry Kozol. They and others confirmed what Oona had long known to be true: Carlotta endeavored till the end to keep Eugene from contact with his children, most especially Oona. Eugene had learned in his final years that the trust fund Carlotta always claimed came from an aunt was actually funded by another man, one with whom she had kept up contact and engaged as a personal advisor. Dr. Kozol wrote in his notes that he had showed Eugene, who was under his constant care, a Boston Globe photo of Oona and her children, adding "but I had to do it surreptitiously. Carlotta noted the same paper, crumpled it, and canceled their subscription."

In 1962, Gloria had divorced her second husband, symphony director Leopold Stokowsky with whom she had two sons, Leopold and Christopher, and married director Sindey Lumet. Lumet's filmmaking associate Ely Landau obtained the rights to make a film version of *Long Day's Journey Into Night,* with Lumet directing. O'Neill considered this his finest work, and his most personal, and despite the instructions in his will that it not be published for twenty-five years after his death, Carlotta sold it for publication soon after his passing. Perhaps in a strange case of coincidence, Gloria's husband was part of the feeding frenzy Carlotta created over the work.

In the mid-1960s, Oona assisted Truman Capote with several rounds of edits of his non-fiction novel *In Cold Blood.* Written as reportage, the book covers the story and trial of Richard Hickock and Perry Smith for the 1959 murders of the Clutter family of Holcomb, Kansas. The book was an instant success and it is still one of the best-selling true crime books in history.

Oona's mother Agnes eventually settled back in Point Pleasant, New Jersey. She published several books including *Part of a Long Story*, a memoir of her romance with Eugene. Her physical and mental health declined in her later years, and Oona was called to come to the US, her first visit in fifteen years, to attend to her affairs in 1967. During her visit, she spent time with her nieces and nephews, Shane's children with his wife Cathy. The following year, on November 25, 1968, Agnes died. She was 77.

By the 1970s, McCarthyism and the Red Scare was an embarrassing episode in American history, and the hearts and minds of Hollywood recalled Charlie Chaplin, one of the creators of Hollywood as they knew it, now living in exile in Switzerland. The movie world looked around and saw it had treated some of its founding artists abominably, and if they wanted to reclaim Charlie as an American legend, they'd better act now, before it was too late.

He was to be honored at a ceremony at the Academy Awards, but it took Oona's persuasion to convince him to come back to America for the first time in twenty years to receive the award.

A gala began upon their arrival in New York City, a celebration at the Lincoln Center. The entire trip from New York to California would be covered by a beautiful and talented young photographer, actress, and model named Candice Bergen, who had scored the prime assignment of covering the Chaplins' visit. She would photograph the couple for the April 21 issue of *Life* magazine, beginning at the airport in New York, continuing through Gloria Vanderbilt's welcome party at her East Sixty-Seventh Street townhouse, and on to Carol Matthau's celebration at her home in Pacific Palisades, California. Bergen took candid shots of Oona and Charlie behind the scenes at the Academy Awards, as Oona reassured

Charlie it would all be okay, that everyone there loved him. Once her assignment was over, Candice Bergen reported being moved by their relationship, saying they were "conspicuous in their simplicity" and that she had been "struck by the obvious depth of their feelings for each other."

By this time Gloria was married to her fourth husband, writer and editor Wyatt Cooper, a fine man by all accounts and with whom she seemed to have finally found true love. Together they had two sons, Carter Cooper, who tragically died in a fall from Gloria's Eastside apartment, and Anderson Cooper, popular CNN broadcast journalist. Carol's true love had turned out to be a beloved star of stage and screen, *The Odd Couple*'s curmudgeonly Oscar Madison, Walter Matthau.

Charlie was honored with a record twelve-minute standing ovation at the Academy Awards ceremony, and he insisted Oona join him on stage. He pointed to her as if to say, *This is all because of her. This woman. The best thing that ever happened to me. I wouldn't be here without her.*

1975 brought another prodigious honor to Charlie, and to Oona, when HM Queen Elizabeth offered him a knighthood. The Welsh Guards band played the theme from *Limelight* as a royal guard pushed his wheelchair up a ramp covered in red carpet while Oona walked beside him. They found themselves inside the grand ballroom of Buckingham Palace, only a few miles from where Charlie had once lived in a south London workhouse. Now, he sat in a place of honor in front of the queen.

He was unable to stand for the ceremony, and the queen lowered her scepter to his shoulders as he remained seated. Oona's eyes filled with tears as her husband—her world—the rest of the world's beloved, iconic Tramp, was conferred the title of Knight Commander of the British Empire.

With the eyes of the world on them, Lady Oona stood by her Knight.

ᘓᘔᘓ

Also in 1975, Truman made the choice to publish part of a long-awaited story called "Answered Prayers." "La Cote Basque, 1965" was printed in *Esquire* magazine. In it, he famously exposed nearly all of his "swans," the beautiful high-society women whose friendships and confidences he collected and prized. Why he chose to do this is a mystery still, but from the day of its publication, Truman Capote's life went swiftly downhill. While he told the deepest secrets of friends like "Babe" Paley, Lee Radziwill, and Slim Keith, his friends from the earlier days, Carol Marcus and Gloria Vanderbilt came off rather better in the story. Just one of all his "swans" came away from the book completely unscathed:

Only Oona

ᘓᘔᘓ

On June 24, 1977 Oona received a telegram bearing the tragic news that her brother Shane had died the previous day. His sensitive nature never recovered from the abandonment of his childhood, and as he grew into an adult, he struggled with addiction. His death was a tragic end to a life that had held much promise. Sadly, Oona learned Shane had jumped from a fourth-floor window and was taken to Coney Island Hospital, where he died the next day. He left behind a wife and four grown children. He was 57.

Charlie and Oona were married for thirty-four years, until his death on Christmas morning, 1977. Oona's statement two days later read:

> *All the presents were under the tree. Charlie gave so much happiness and, although he had been ill for a long time, it is so sad that he should have passed away on Christmas Day.*

Sir Charlie Chaplin was 88 years old.

⳹⳼

Lady Oona O'Neill Chaplin was only fifty-three years old when she became a widow. Despite her attempts to forge on, she found it difficult recover and go on to a new life after the death of her beloved Charlie. She caused a stir in 1979 when she dated actor Ryan O'Neal, who happened to be the star of the only other movie besides his own that Charlie allowed the children to watch: Stanley Kubrick's *Barry Lyndon*. Gloria was quoted as saying to society columnist Liz Smith, "Ryan wanted to marry Oona just to make her an O'Neal again."

Oona also had a close relationship with musician David Bowie, who had a home nearby in

Switzerland. She encouraged his participation in the 1980 Broadway play *The Elephant Man*, for which he won acclaim. She also dated Walter Bernstein, an acclaimed screenwriter and film producer who, like Charlie, had been blacklisted in the McCarthy era. At his encouragement, she bought a Manhattan penthouse, but she traveled back and forth across the Atlantic to the Manoir in Vervey, Switzerland, with great frequency, unable to feel comfortable anywhere for too long. She turned down all offers to publish her memoirs, including a blank-check offer by Jacqueline Kennedy Onassis in her role as editor at Doubleday.

Oona's relationships with her closest friends continued. Carol visited often, bringing her new husband Walter Matthau and their son, Charlie. Carol was intermittently estranged from her two older children, Aram and Lucy, but Aram wrote the book *Trio*, about his mother and her two friends. Carol also wrote several books, including the memoir *Among the Porcupines*, in which she gave her own colorful account of her life. Oona's relationship with Gloria had a mysterious ending. Although the reason is not specified in biographies of either woman, it may be that this break came after Gloria encouraged Oona to see her own psychotherapist, a childhood friend Dr. Christ L. Zoist, whom she said had helped her immensely after the tragic death of her son Carter Cooper (brother of journalist Anderson Cooper). Like her brother Shane and step-brother Eugene Jr., Oona had begun to succumb to the fabled "O'Neill Curse," relying more and more on alcohol to help her get through her days without her beloved Charlie. Dr. Zoist took advantage of Oona's emotional fragility, declining mental health, and increasing dependence on alcohol, and used her name as security on a loan. The same man also swindled Gloria out of millions made through her famous eponymous fashion line. Around this time, according to Oona's daughter Jane, a rift occurred between Oona and Gloria that was never mended.

Even as she descended ever further into grief, Oona fulfilled her desire to be a patron and donor to the arts. Her generous donations to the MacDowell Colony helped many artists produce work which would become world-renowned. She allowed the MacDowell Colony board to use her New York City Penthouse for meetings, but never attended, staying instead in the darkness of her bedroom.

An intensely private person, Oona stipulated that her diaries and letters be destroyed upon her death, but some of these materials may have been preserved in the family vaults in Paris. Her children remain highly protective of her legacy.

On September 27, 1991, Lady Oona Ella O'Neill Chaplin died in Switzerland of pancreatic cancer.

She was 66 years old.

☙❧

*B*ios

Eugene O'Neill was a Pulitzer and Nobel Prize-winning playwright. He was married three times and had three children, two of whom came from his second marriage to Agnes Boulton. He largely ignored his children, allowing his second wife Carlotta to form a wedge between them, and he berated and ultimately disowned his children when they displeased him. His older son Eugene Jr. was a brilliant classicist, but he suffered from alcoholism and committed suicide at forty. Shane, his son with Agnes Boulton, also suffered from substance abuse and committed suicide in 1977. Oona also suffered from alcoholism and in her later years fell to its grips after her husband Charlie Chaplin passed. Eugene O'Neill suffered from alcoholism, and he was wrongly diagnosed and treated for Parkinson's Disease. He died, as he'd been born, in a hotel room in Manhattan. The cause of death was pneumonia brought on by aspiration on November 27, 1953. He was sixty-five.

Agnes Boulton was a writer, the second wife of playwright Eugene O'Neill, and Oona O'Neill's mother. She also had a daughter, Barbara, from a previous marriage or relationship. Agnes left Barbara with her parents when she moved to New York City to live in Greenwich Village, supporting herself by writing stories for the pulp magazine *Breezy Stories*. She married Eugene O'Neill in 1918 and largely set aside her own career in order to support his. However, after having two children, he left Agnes to marry actress Carlotta Monterey soon after achieving notoriety as a playwright. After an acrimonious divorce, Agnes sent her children to boarding school and again focused on her own pursuits, but when her daughter Oona came of age, she became interested in forwarding the girl's future by means of her good looks, charm, and wit, either by marriage or by a career in movies. Agnes published several books, including *Part of a Long Story: Portrait of a Young Man In Love.* She died in West Point Pleasant, New Jersey, November 25, 1968. She was 75.

Shane O'Neill was the second son of Eugene O'Neill, the only son with wife Agnes Boulton, and Oona's older brother. He was a sensitive and intelligent boy who never recovered from his father's abandonment and inexplicable disapproval. Like his father and grandparents, he suffered from substance abuse and struggled to find peace his entire life. He died by suicide on June 23, 1977, after jumping from the fourth floor window of his girlfriend's apartment the previous night. While it is widely reported that he jumped, there is some question among the family of whether he jumped or fell due to ongoing problems with his hip. The tragedy of losing her brother came only months before Oona also lost her husband Charlie in December. Shane left behind a wife and four children. He was 57.

Carlotta Monterey (Hazel Neilson Taasinge) was an actress, the third wife of Eugene O'Neill, and stepmother to his children. She was married three times before her marriage to Eugene. She had one child of her own, a daughter who she left in the care of her mother. During their marriage, O'Neill believed a trust fund she received was left to her by a generous aunt. However, it was revealed after many years that the fund was from an old lover whom she had later enlisted to act as Eugene's financial advisor. She insisted on separation from his children, and also acted as a wall between Eugene and his friends, making him increasingly isolated over the years. O'Neill's will stipulated that his final work, the auto-biographical *A Long Day's Journey into Night,* was to be held from publication until twenty-five years after his death. However, Carlotta had seen to it that she was left full control of his estate and that his children had been excluded from his will. She authorized the publication of the play immediately after his death. In her later years, she edited and rewrote years of her diaries, many of which have been used as his-torical sources on the lives of Eugene O'Neill and his children and associates. However, changes and dis-crepancies were noted in Authur and Barbara Gelb's comprehensive 2016 O'Neill biography *By Women*

Possessed. Carlotta Monterey died in a nursing home on November 18, 1970.

Jerome David "J.D." Salinger was a writer who attained worldwide literary fame with his novel *The Catcher in The Rye*, a story which became known as the voice of a disillusioned generation. The character of Sally Hayes was said to have been inspired by Oona O'Neill, the first girl he truly loved and hoped to marry, and the one Salinger biographer David Shields said "formatted him forever." J.D. Salinger moved to Cornish, New Hampshire, and lived out his years in relative reclusively. He was married three times and had two children. He died on January 27, 2010, at the age of 91.

Carol Grace Marcus Saroyan Matthau had two children with Pulitzer Prize-winner William Saroyan. Their son Aram Saroyan is a renowned author and poet, and he wrote the book *Trio* about his mother's friendship with Gloria Vanderbilt and Oona O'Neill Chaplin, and their daughter Lucy Saroyan, was an actress and stage craft engineer before she passed away in 2001. Carol divorced Saroyan in 1949, and they remarried in 1953. After a string of affairs with prominent men, she married stage actor Walter Matthau who went on to film stardom in the movie version of *The Odd Couple*. They had one son together, Charles "Charlie" Matthau, an actor and director, and they had been married for forty-one years when Walter died in 2000. On September 21, 2003, three months after the passing of her daughter, and less than a year after the release of *A Daring Young Man*, a biography of William Saroyan that utilized the man's own diaries, Carol Grace Marcus Saroyan Matthau died of a brain aneurysm. She was 78 years old.

Elinor Marcus Pruder was a designer, socialite, and half-sister to Carol Marcus Saroyan Matthau. She worked in advertising before becoming a sought-after interior designer. Upon her first marriage, she gained the title Baroness de la Bouillerie and lived in Switzerland and France, having two children. She then married Walter Gruber, a journalist with *Newsweek Magazine*, and had two more children. Her third husband was distinguished civil engineer Elgin Pruder to whom she was married for twenty-five years until his death in 2009. She was known for her charity work and large circle of friends. Elinor died in 2020 at the age of 94.

Gloria Vanderbilt was an artist, designer, actress, author, and heiress. Famous from childhood due to the custody battle between her mother, the elder Gloria Vanderbilt, and her aunt Gertrude Vanderbilt Whitney, she married four times, the first time at age seventeen, and had many, many well-publicized affairs. She also suffered true heartbreak in the loss of her fourth husband, author and screenwriter Wyatt Cooper, at the age of fifty during open-heart surgery, and later the tragic, possibly accidental, suicide of their older son Carter Vanderbilt Cooper. She was the mother of two sons from her marriage to conductor Leopold Stokowski, whom many said she chose because he was even older than Oona's husband, and her youngest son is journalist and author Anderson Cooper. She licensed her name to a clothing factory and became the face of Vanderbilt jeans, the iconic 1970s-80s fashion jeans line with the white swan logo. She and Oona were lifelong friends. However, according to one of Oona's daughters, they had a falling out in later years from which their relationship never recovered. Gloria died of stomach cancer on June 17, 2019.

Truman Capote was a novelist, playwright, and screenwriter most famous for his novella *Breakfast at Tiffany's.* He first made a name in the literary world with his 1948 novel *Other Voices, Other Rooms.* His true crime novel *In Cold Blood* was a sensation in 1966. As a teen, he befriended a young Carol Marcus through Carol's sister Elinor whom he knew from school, and through Carol met Oona O'Neill and Gloria Vanderbilt. For the several years before the girls each got married, they were all friends. He had many private relationships, but his partnership with Jack Dunphy is said to have lasted from 1948 to 1984. His childhood friend was author Harper Lee who wrote the beloved classic *To Kill a Mockingbird.* His story "La Côte Basque, 1965," featured fictionalized accounts of sordid details of the lives of many of his society friends, and upon its publication in *Esquire,* he was shunned by his collection of glamorous friends, women he referred to as his "swans." He fell into depression and alcoholism. In August 1984,

Truman's health was failing and he flew across the country to Los Angeles, California, where he went to the home of a friend who had stood by him through the scandal: Joanne Carson (ex-wife of comedian and *Tonight Show* host Johnny Carson, a fictionalized version of whom Capote had also depicted in a very poor light). Truman died there only days later, and Carol Marcus Saroyan Matthau held a memorial service for him. He was 59.

Ryan O'Neal is an actor and former amateur boxer. He has starred in productions on television and on the big screen, including NBC's *Empire*, the primetime soap opera *Peyton Place*, Stanley Kubrick's *Barry Lyndon*, and Peter Bogdanovich's *Paper Moon*, among many others, but he is perhaps most well-known for his role of "Oliver" in Arthur Hiller's *Love Story* (1970). According to one of Oona and Charlie's children, their father received a copy of *Barry Lyndon* after meeting Kubrick in London and hitting it off with the director, and he was so impressed with it that it became the only film the children were allowed to watch in the home besides Charlie's own. Oona and Ryan had a short-lived relationship after Charlie passed away. Gloria Vanderbilt apparently didn't approve of the age difference between Oona and Ryan, wondering what they would have to talk about, and is quoted as shrugging the relationship off as Mr. O'Neal only wanting to "make Oona an O'Neal again."

David Bowie was an iconic musical artist from England. He met Oona after Charlie's death, when Charlie and Oona' son Eugene, an engineer at Monster Studios in the Montreux, Switzerland studio where he was recording, informed him of his parentage and invited him over to his house for dinner. David became a great friend of Oona's, sparking romance rumors in the time shortly after Charlie's death. However, Oona was never able to forget Charlie and fully move on. Bowie invited Oona to attend his Broadway premier of *The Elephant Man*, which he said she had encouraged him to take on despite his misgivings at the time, while he in turn encouraged her to take a part in an art film, which she did, giving a fine performance although the film was not released widely. During this time, Oona was tragically descending into the depth of alcoholism. According to Jane Chaplin, David Bowie was a great family friend and they spent many fun times together at the Manoir. Bowie was married twice, and had been married to the model Iman for twenty-four years when he died of liver cancer on January 10, 2016. He was 69.

Michael Jackson believed he was spiritually connected to Charlie Chaplin, and he was inspired by him throughout his career, basing many of his famous dance moves and costumes on images of The Tramp. He visited Oona at the Manoir in Vervey, Switzerland in 1988 during his *Bad* tour, after Sophia Loren, star of Charlie's final film *The Countess from Hong Kong*, requested a visit on his behalf. Jackson's favorite song was "Smile," composed by Charlie Chaplin (lyrics by John Turner and Geoffrey Parsons), and he intended to release his version of the song as the last single from his 1995 album *HIStory: Past, Present, and Future, Book 1.* The song was never released as a single, and the few copies of the single version that made it into the market are now considered one of the rarest of Michael Jackson's recordings.

Candice Bergen is an American model, actress, and photographer. At the time of Charlie Chaplin's first visit back to the U.S. after his exile, she was given the assignment to cover the family's entire visit for *Life* magazine. These are the only official photographs of Charlie and Oona's visit, and in her coverage she stated that they were "conspicuous in their simplicity." She observed the couple's deep love, and she has since said that their relationship stood as an example of devotion. Candice Bergen became a world-famous actress, known for the title role in the CBS sitcom *Murphy Brown* and ABC drama *Boston Legal* on television. In film, she starred in *Starting Over* and *Gandhi.* She has won five Primetime Emmy Awards, two Golden Globe Awards, a BAFTA Award for Best Actress, and was nominated for the Academy Award for Best Supporting Actress.

Selected Bibliography

n.d. Historical Newspapers from 1700s-2000s - Newspapers.com. http://newspapers.com.

n.d. Charlie Chaplin Archive: Home. http://www. charliechaplinarchive.org.

n.d. Independent Order of Odd Fellows – The Sovereign Grand Lodge. Accessed July 19, 2022. https://odd-fellows.org/.

n.d. "Theater Talk." On Youtube. https://www.youtube.com/watch?v=BxV5SpkBGPY&t=622s.

Ackroyd, Peter. n.d. *Charlie Chaplin*. N.p.: Knopf Doubleday.

Adams, Samuel H. n.d. *The Harvey Girls*. N.p.: Dell.

Bergen, Candice. 1972. "Hello Charlie," article and photographs. In *Life Magazine*.

Boulton, Agnes. 2011. *Part of a Long Story: "Eugene O'Neill as a Young Man in Love."* Edited by W. D. King. N.p.: McFarland, Incorporated, Publishers.

Capote, Truman. 1988. *Answered Prayers: The Unfinished Novel*. N.p.: Plume.

Chaplin, Charlie. 1964. *My Autobiography*. N.p.: Simon and Schuster.

Chaplin, Jane. n.d. personal interviews.

Chaplin, Patrice. 1995. *Hidden star: Oona O'Neill Chaplin : a memoir*. N.p.: Richard Cohen.

Egan, Leona R. 1994. *Provincetown as a Stage: Provincetown, the Provincetown Players, and the Discovery of Eugene O'Neill*. N.p.: Parnassus Imprints.

Epstein, Jerry. 1988. *Remembering Charlie: The Story of a Friendship*. N.p.: Bloomsbury.

French, Lawrence. 1970. "Orson Welles as a special guest on The David Frost Show, May 12, 1970." Wellesnet. https://www.wellesnet.com/orson-welles-as-a-special-guest-on-the-david-frost-show-may-12-1970/.

Gabler, Neal. 1996. *Walter Winchell: Gossip, Power and the Culture of Celebrity*. N.p.: Papermac.

Gelb, Arthur, and Barbara Gelb. 2016. *By Women Possessed: A Life of Eugene O'Neill*. N.p.: Penguin Publishing Group.

Kozol, Jonathan. 2015. *The Theft of Memory: Losing My Father, One Day at a Time*. N.p.: Crown.

Leggett, John. 2002. *A daring young man: a biography of William Saroyan*. N.p.: Knopf.

The Louis Sheaffer Collection of Eugene O'Neill Collection, Connecticut College. n.d.

Lynn, Kenneth S. 2003. *Charlie Chaplin and His Times.* N.p.: Cooper Square Press.

Matthau, Carol. 1992. *Among the Porcupines: A Memoir.* N.p.: Turtle Bay Books.

Murphy, Brenda. 2018. *Becoming Carlotta.* N.p.: Bricktop Hill Books.

Nebraska State Journal. 1894. "Amusements." January 26, 1894. https://cather.unl.edu/writings/ journalism/j00031.

"New Chaplin in Limelight," magazine article. 1964. In *Life Magazine.*

O'Toole, Finton. 2017. "Our Worst Great Playwright." *nybooks,* (MAY). https://www.nybooks.com/ articles/2017/05/25/eugene-oneill-our-worst-great-playwright/?lp_txn_id=1366234.

Plimpton, George. 1998. *Truman Capote: In which Various Friends, Enemies, Acquaintances, and Detractors Recall His Turbulent Career.* N.p.: Anchor Books.

Poling-Kempes, Lesley. 1994. *The Harvey Girls: Women Who Opened the West.* N.p.: Hachette Books.

Salerno, Shane, and David Shields. 2013. *Salinger.* N.p.: Simon & Schuster.

Saroyan, Aram. 1985. *Trio: Oona Chaplin, Carol Matthau, Gloria Vanderbilt : portrait of an intimate friendship*. N.p.: Linden Press/Simon & Schuster.

Scheaffer, Louis. 2002. *O'Neill: Son and Playwright*. N.p.: Cooper Square Press.

Scovell, Jane. 1998. *Oona: Living in the Shadows: a Biography of Oona O'Neill Chaplin*. N.p.: Warner Books.

Scovell, Jane. n.d. personal interviews.

Slawenski, Kenneth. 2012. *J. D. Salinger: A Life*. N.p.: Random House Publishing Group.

Thomas, D. C. A Formidable Shadow: The O'Neill Connection. Lulu.com, 2014.

Vanderbilt, Gloria. 1986. *Once Upon a Time: A True Story*. N.p.: Random House Publishing Group.

Vanderbilt, Gloria. 1987. *Black Knight, White Knight*. N.p.: Knopf.

Vanderbilt, Gloria. 2004. *It Seemed Important at the Time: A Romance Memoir*. N.p.: Simon & Schuster.

Waters, Joy B. 1992. *Eugene O'Neill and Family—the Bermuda Interlude*. N.p.: J.B. Waters.

Acknowledgments

Thank you to Jane Chaplin, Oona's sixth child and now someone I consider a dear friend, for letting me ask you questions about your mother, even when it was hard. I hope you see in these pages the image of your lovely mom.

Thank you to Jane Scovell, author of Oona's definitive and fascinating biography, whose unexpected phone call in response to my awkward emails nearly made me faint—twice! Your knowledge and generosity helped me believe I could write a novel of Oona's life.

Thank you to Arielle Haughee, editor extraordinaire, who loved this manuscript when it was a mess and who made my heart soar when she said, "I want it!" You are so incredibly talented at what you do, and your insight was everything.

Dan Champagne, thank you for putting together my amazing author website. Your talents know no bounds.

Benjamin Panciera, curator, Sheaffer Collection on Eugene O'Neill, Connecticut College, many thanks for the valuable information and assistance regarding documents housed in the archives.

To my children Sophie, Joseph, Isabelle, and your amazing spouses Billy and Madison, you are all wonderful and don't you ever forget it.

James, thank you for your constant support and encouragement. You help me to be brave.

Book Club Discussion

1. What surprised you most about the early life of Oona O'Neill? Was she more or less privileged than you would have thought?

2. Do you think societal changes about appropriate ages for marriage (for men and for women) influences the way we view or judge figures who lived several generations ago? Is it fair/useful to view them through the lens of modern ideals?

3. Who was your favorite 'character' in this novel? Great care was taken to cast each in as realistic a light as possible. Would you be friends with any of them yourself?

4. Do you think Oona made the right choice regarding J.D. Salinger? Could she have been happy with someone whose temperament was eerily like that of her own father?

5. If Agnes had not decided to send Oona to Manhattan to finish school, how might Oona's life have been different? What are some of the threads of her story that depended on that one choice?

6. How about discussing the obvious: Oona's child-
    hood pain at being abandoned and emotionally
    abused by her father played some role in her
    choice to marry a much older man. What was
    it about Charlie that may have filled an empty
    place in her heart?

7. In the afterward, we see that Oona's life spiraled
    downward after the death of her beloved Charlie.
    How does this speak to the idea that her mar-
    riage and life with Charlie saved her from "the
    O'Neill Curse" of depression, self-medication,
    and addiction? Was she ever 'cured'?

8. How do you feel about the idea of a 'family curse'?
    What is really at the core of generational issues
    passed from parent to child?

9. Oona was a voracious reader, and in fact was said
    to have helped her friend Truman Capote with an
    editorial reading of his book *In Cold Blood*. What
    might be some reasons she did not choose to
    take up a career in the literary world, in the same
    way Jackie Kennedy Onassis did, for instance?

10. What elements of Oona's upbringing and life
    would not be acceptable today? Would Eugene
    O'Neill have been vilified for his treatment of
    his children? How has the image of the 'tortured
    genius' changed in light of society's further
    understanding of mental illness?